For Ruth —

THE LIGHTHOUSE

With my best
wishes

Elaine

Also by Elaine Kozak

Root Causes

THE LIGHTHOUSE

ELAINE KOZAK

The Lighthouse
Copyright © 2020 by Elaine Kozak

All rights reserved. No part of this publication may be reproduced, distributed, or transmitted in any form or by any means, including photocopying, recording, or other electronic or mechanical methods, without the prior written permission of the author, except in the case of brief quotations embodied in critical reviews and certain other non-commercial uses permitted by copyright law.

Tellwell Talent
www.tellwell.ca

ISBN
978-0-2288-1055-1 (Hardcover)
978-0-2288-1054-4 (Paperback)
978-0-2288-1056-8 (eBook)

In memory of my mother, Josephine Kozak

And for my siblings
Sid, Livia and Donna

Chapter 1

Leah Larsen dropped her backpack on a table in the café and nodded at the other customers as she went to place her order. She wouldn't have done either in New York but since coming to this small lakeside town in the Adirondacks nine months previously she had come to know, if only by sight, most of its inhabitants. Even though she could have recited its contents she studied the chalkboard menu, itching—as she always did—to correct the four spelling errors. She craved a latte but ordered a plain black coffee. With small economies like this she could afford to live here for another few months. But then what?

A racoon-eyed, sooty-haired woman with Yakuza-like tattoos snaking up her neck took her order.

"Thanks, Flory," Leah said, accepting a brimming mug.

She returned to her table. *Maybe I could get a job here.* Flory would probably need help after the thaw, when the cabin dwellers and tourists flocked back to the town. If she did, the first thing she'd do is rewrite the chalkboard.

She sat down and pulled a laptop out of her pack. Her visits to the coffee shop were in part to counter a worrying preference for solitude, but mainly to access the Internet. Today, her research was completed quickly. In no rush to head back out into the cold she topped up her half-empty cup with milk from the condiments table and tasted the lukewarm liquid. *Poor man's latte.* If Flory noticed, she didn't say anything.

Back at her table she studied her computer screen, wondering what else to do. She didn't have an email account and avoided social media. She was about to access the *New York Times* website when she remembered that she hadn't checked on her parents in a long time.

Calling up Google she typed in "gabriel findlay larsen musician." Family and friends knew her father as Fin, but the Internet didn't. There was little new in the results since her last search. She leaned forward and scrolled through the lines of images of her father as a young man intermixed with more current ones. The deep-set eyes and raptor-like features remained the same but the luxuriant dark hair was threaded with gray, and he now wore glasses.

Her father was rarely photographed alone. She recognized some of his companions: other musicians and singers, a famous film director, a Canadian prime minister. One picture was of him and his wife. By no conventional standard was Leah's mother a beauty, but her high cheekbones and slightly Asiatic stargazer eyes were memorable. In this picture, Fin was sharing a laugh with someone out of the frame while her mother looked abstractedly in the other direction, like she was reflecting on the mysteries of the universe. As she probably was.

Leah moved the cursor to the query box and typed in "alexandra tarnovsky physicist." The images had caught her attention first, which was why she didn't immediately notice the lead item of the search results. It was an obituary—her mother was dead.

Chapter 2

"You okay, honey?" Flory said.

A storm raged in Leah's ears. She shook her head. Flory sat down and placed her hand on Leah's arm. "What's up?"

Leah gestured to the computer. "My mother." The tears started.

Flory glanced at the screen, closed the lid and picked up the laptop and backpack.

"Come on, honey."

She led Leah past the cubbyhole kitchen to a back room and set the computer and pack down.

"You stay here until you feel better," she said and returned to the front.

Leah sat down at a desk messed over with bills and letters and dirty cups and buried her face in her hands. After several minutes she straightened up, wiped her eyes and inhaled sharply.

It was time to go home.

"Go ahead, I've got a plan. Daughter's in Montreal," Flory said, waving away Leah's offer to pay to use her phone.

Her father's housekeeper answered at his Vancouver home and said that he was at Azar, the family ranch near Taos, New Mexico.

"No, no message," Leah said and hung up, trembling.

What was I thinking? What would I have said if he had been there? Their first conversation after almost ten years needed thought, preparation.

She returned the phone to Flory with thanks and left the café. She enquired at the gas station convenience store that served as the bus depot about routes and schedules and fares, then headed to the small bank to empty her account. She fingered through the bills the teller handed her and stuffed them in her pocket. Not much, but at least enough to get to New Mexico.

Boarding the bus to New York the next morning, Leah braced herself for a long, uncomfortable ride, but it was only half full and the time passed quickly. The trip from New York to Denver was a different story. People thronged down the bus aisles, all elbows and oversize bags, and claimed their seats, quibbling over perceived encroachments in the overhead bins and on the floors. The air thickened with the fug of bodies and breaths and wet winter clothes. Leah huddled in her window seat against the onslaught, suffocating after the space and silence of the Adirondack cabin. At one stop, she got off to use the washroom and buy food and returned to find the woman next to her had taken her seat.

"Thought you was gone," the woman said.

"But I left my book on the seat."

"Thought you forgot it."

"I've had that seat since New York."

The woman gave her a dismissive shrug and turned her face to the window.

When Leah tried to recline her new seat, the man behind her dug his knees into her back to block it. No position offered comfort. As the miles ticked by, her head lolled like a bowling ball on a flower stalk and her joints burned as though spiked with hot nails.

The Lighthouse

She arrived in Denver shortly before midnight to find that the next bus to Taos was to leave in the morning. In the women's restroom she washed up as best she could and made a nest in one of the dank corners with a discarded newspaper. She screwed wads of toilet tissue into her ears to block out the bathroom noises and covered her face with a scarf against the light and the smells. The traffic in and out of the facility lessened as the night wore on and she fell into a fitful sleep.

On the bus to Taos the next day she reflected on the long journey she was about to complete. Its ending was far from certain. She had decided against telling her father that she was coming, afraid he would tell her not to bother. She watched with indifference as the blue and white magnificence of the Rockies gave over to the dun mesas of New Mexico, her mind crafting alternative scripts for the difficult reunion ahead.

In Taos, she wound her way through the streets to the plaza hoping that the Lighthouse, the resort owned by her Aunt Ris and Uncle Lucas, still ran a shuttle between the ranch and the town from there. She found the small sign marking the stop and mingled with the others waiting for a ride, boarding the van last when it arrived. The driver eyed her dubiously. She stared him down and took a seat. She had only to identify herself to sort him out, but it wasn't something she was ready to do. Not in her current state, anyway.

The trip took just over ten minutes. She let the other riders exit first so she could approach the Lighthouse alone. The resort was the last structure her grandfather Niels had designed. She had been seven when he started, and he had explained each step in the process as his hand-drawn sketches evolved into detailed drawings and finally blueprints for construction.

She remembered the fuss at the Lighthouse's opening; its remote setting, intriguing mandate and notable architecture attracting a mix of admiration, curiosity and skepticism. Critics remarked that the resort's elegant geometry appeared alien, like an outpost on a distant planet and that—thousands of miles as it was from the ocean—calling it the Lighthouse was no doubt a kind of irony. One could torture a metaphor out of the name, as the resort's main purpose was to offer physical and spiritual rejuvenation to the troubled and the weary, those who, say, risked floundering on the rocks of their lives. The reality was simpler. In designing it, her grandfather had conceived a paean to light in the form of a pavilion, one wall of which comprised a massive stained-glass window in the shape of a tree. He had called the window the Tree of Light and the name for the resort had followed.

Leah went up to the building and pressed her palm against the wall. For a brief moment she felt her grandfather's presence, like a muscle rippling under the grainy warmth of the structure's adobe skin. She dropped her hand and turned away. She would visit the Tree of Light sometime, but not today. The afternoon was slipping by and she still had a ways to go.

The Lighthouse sat at the northernmost point of Azar. Las Sombras, her father's house, was at the southern end, more than three miles away. She trudged down the resort driveway to the road that wound through the ranch. Half a mile along she came within sight of a complex of white colonial-style buildings where her Aunt Ris and Uncle Lucas lived. She considered stopping there to warm up and get a drink but decided to carry on. After all this time she couldn't appear unexpected at their door—although that was exactly what she intended to do to her father. Her steps faltered. Maybe she *should* have called first. What if he wasn't home? *Too late now.* She carried on.

A truck approaching behind her stopped and the driver lowered the window.

"You lost, girl?"

Leah recognized one of the men who worked at the ranch

stables. Older now, but so was she; he wouldn't know who she was.

"I'm going to Las Sombras," she said.

"I can take you as far as the stables."

"Oh, yes please!"

She walked around the back of the truck and got in on the passenger side. Foam stuffing erupted from a crack in the bench seat. The cab smelled of cigarillos and manure, but the heater was going full blast.

"Thank you *so* much," she said, buckling her seatbelt.

The man nodded acknowledgement and stepped on the gas. They arrived at the stables before she could do anything more than taste the warmth. She got out, her knees sagging as she hit the ground. Grunting with fatigue, she slung her pack onto her back and carried on, one cold, sodden step after the other.

The road to her father's house tracked up a slope and her pace slowed. After climbing for several minutes she entered the courtyard of Las Sombras. Her grandfather had designed and built the sprawling hacienda as well, naming it after the shifting patterns of light and shade created by the surrounding pines. She stopped at the entrance to the house and studied the massive plank door, conscious that her life was about to pivot on what lay behind it.

After a moment, she lifted the heavy knocker and rapped three times. No one answered. She knocked again. Nothing. She was about to leave when she heard scuffling sounds. The lock snicked and the door opened. Her father filled the frame: tall, dark, formidable.

"Jesus H. Christ," Fin said after a long moment of stunned silence.

"Hello, Dad."

He brought his hand to his mouth then opened it out in a question. "What … why…?"

"I found out that Mom had died."

Her throat closed and she swallowed hard to stop a sob. Her pack suddenly felt unbearably heavy. She shrugged it off and set it on the ground. Fin continued to regard her silently, his mouth slack with disbelief. She made a small movement.

"Can I come in? It's awfully cold out here."

He held up a palm. "No! No."

She stepped back. "No?"

"Wait here."

He ducked back into the house and she heard keys clink. He came out zipping up a vest. "I'll take you to Ris's."

"Why?" she said, but he was striding towards the carport and did not answer. She picked up her pack and followed. By the time she reached the late-model Volvo SUV he had started it and was revving the engine. She threw her pack on the backseat and climbed into the front. The vent was blowing hard to clear the windows. Fin turned to her, his nose twitching.

"Christ! You smell."

She could sense it herself, an amalgam of the unwashed bodies and dirty socks, farts and booze breath, soiled diapers and worn clothing of her traveling companions.

"I've been on a bus for three days." She opened her door. "I can walk."

"Don't be ridiculous." Fin put the car in gear and began to reverse out of the carport.

She slammed her door shut. "Why are you taking me to Aunt Ris's? Why can't I stay here? What, do you have a woman here or something? And Mom only dead a couple of months?"

"Don't start!"

Leah fell silent, regretting the jab. Her father's affair while teaching music at a college in Boston had caused the initial rift between them. He had stunned everyone by accepting the year-long posting only weeks after his parents had died, and then going alone. While he was away, Leah had called him one weekend when her mother had fallen ill. A woman had answered.

"Oh!" the woman had said, when Leah asked for her father. "Silly man! He must have taken my phone when he left this morning. They *are* similar."

At fourteen, Leah had been old enough to understand. When her father returned the call she had screamed at him for leaving them, for his infidelity, and for not being there when his wife was sick. It had set the tone for their relationship after he returned home, and for all that followed. She would try to be civil now.

"Yes, all right," she said. "But I still don't understand why I can't stay at Las Sombras."

Fin slowed to avoid a rut. "Because Theo's away and the boys will be home soon."

"Theo?"

"Your cousin. Surely you remember him."

"Not really."

"I guess he wasn't around much when you were growing up."

"And the boys? Who are they?"

Fin shot her a sideways glance. "Theo's son Fox, and Niels, of course."

A monstrous fist closed around Leah's heart and a vast blackness filled her mind. She slapped the dashboard. "Stop, stop!"

Her father pulled the car over to the side of the road and shifted to park.

"What's wrong?"

"You have Niels?"

"Yes."

"But, but…! Why is he with *you*?"

"You abandoned a newborn baby and took off. Who knows where he would have ended up if Alex and I hadn't taken him?"

Leah clasped her hands together until the knuckles whitened. "I didn't *abandon* Niels, I *relinquished* him," she said, her voice shaking. "There's a difference."

Fin shook his head. "Semantics. You'd never said anything before about not wanting to keep the baby. Why did you decide to give him up then?"

"I, ah…" She gulped air. "I don't know what I expected beforehand but when I saw this tiny, helpless little being I was completely overwhelmed. I was sixteen, Dad. I didn't know anything about caring for an infant and I didn't have any money, not even cab fare to get home. And there was nothing for him at home—no clothes, no diapers, nothing."

Fin frowned. "How can that be? Alex should have set you up."

Leah made a helpless gesture with her hand. "Mom, well, you know what she was like. The housekeeper left just after you went to Berlin and it was all we could do to keep the house clean and food on the table. Mom talked about taking me shopping for baby things a couple of times but she never got around to doing it. When she left for the conference in Toronto, neither of us realized Niels was about to be born."

"Still, why didn't you have any money?"

"Don't you remember? When you found out I was pregnant you grounded me and took away my bank and credit cards."

"It wasn't because you were pregnant, although I can't say I was thrilled about that. It was because you were being so damn stubborn about the father."

"I wasn't being stubborn; I didn't know who the father was, or how I got pregnant for that matter. I still don't."

Fin snorted. "Oh, come on."

Leah grimaced in frustration. "There's no point in going through all that again. If I knew, why on earth wouldn't I tell you? Especially now?"

"I stopped trying to understand your behavior a long

time ago. But why didn't you call someone when it started to happen?"

"I tried to call Mom but the phone rang in her study; she had forgotten to take it again. I had no idea how to reach you in Berlin. Ben was in London and Aunt Ris and Uncle Lucas were here at the ranch; what could they have done? Who else was I supposed to call? Mom's colleagues at the university? Your musician friends? Neither of our neighbors really lived in their houses. Any friends I had were back at boarding school. There wasn't anyone. I just went to the hospital."

Fin leaned towards her. "But then why leave? Why run off? Why didn't you just stay at the hospital until one of us got home, explain to the people there what was going on?"

Leah stared into space without speaking for several moments then released a long sigh and dropped her eyes. "There hasn't been a day when I haven't thought about that and regretted leaving." She shook her head. "You don't think very clearly after giving birth. It all seemed so impossible at the time. Part of it was how things were between us at home. I couldn't see raising a child in that toxic atmosphere, being dependent on you, having to ask for everything. I figured Niels would be better off with proper adults as parents, in an environment without conflict." She looked at her father. "But why wasn't he adopted?"

"You can't just leave a baby with a note pinned to him saying he's available for adoption. A process needs to be followed, forms completed. A social worker from the hospital tracked us down and thank God she did. I sure as hell wasn't going to have someone else raise my grandson."

"At least you kept his name."

"You named him after my father. Why would I change that?"

Neither spoke for a while, until Fin finally stirred.

"If you had no money, how did you manage? Where did you go?"

"When I was packing I came across that Piaget watch you gave me one Christmas and pawned it. They gave me enough to buy a bus ticket to Banff and I got a job washing dishes in a restaurant there." She shrugged. "At the end of the summer I hitched a ride to Montreal with one of the servers."

Fin shook his head. "Jesus. But if you regretted leaving Niels, why haven't you come back until now?"

"Because the only thing for me at home would have been your condemnation and contempt."

"But Niels was there!"

"I didn't know that! The last thing I expected was that you and Mom would want to raise him. You had so little time for me when I was growing up and you were even busier then. I wanted him to have a different upbringing, to be raised by people who wanted and loved him. I assumed that's what had happened."

"We loved you, Alex and I!"

"Perhaps, Dad, but there was always something more important than me claiming your attention. I don't know why you and Mom bothered to have a child."

Fin sagged against the steering wheel. "God, Leah, what a complete and utter disaster. Your disappearance was so hard on Alex. I think it was what ultimately made her sick."

Leah eyes widened and her mouth worked. She leaned forward, her body vibrating with anger. "How dare you," she said, her voice shaking. "How *dare* you. If we're going to assign blame for Mom's cancer why don't we start with your goings-on in Boston."

"Please, not that again." A seam of weariness ran through Fin's words. "God knows I've beaten myself up enough about it."

They looked at each other for a long moment. The gulf between them was vast; all that they had lost hung suspended across it like a string of tattered laundry. A digit on the car clock clicked over. Fin swore softly and put the car in gear.

The Lighthouse

"What exactly did you have in mind, coming back?" he said, driving forward.

"Just to see you. With Mom gone, I just wanted to see you all again," Leah said, her voice trailing off. She took a deep breath and tried to corral her scattered emotions. "But I still don't understand why you're taking me to Aunt Ris's. Especially since Niels is with you."

Fin glanced at her. "That's precisely the reason why," he said. "I can't let you see Niels."

Chapter 3

The warbling of his phone jolted Theo Wilde awake.
"Theo?"
He rubbed his eyes. Who else would be answering?
"Hi, Mom," he said.
"Where are you?"
Her question was reasonable as he had planned to spend the night in Santa Fe.
"Here, at my place."
"Oh, good. Could you possibly pick your father up this morning? I have some business at the Lighthouse."
He glanced at the clock by his bed: Eight forty-three. "Yeah, sure. What time?"
"Around ten-thirty. And if you can, look in at the house when you come for the car."
"Why? What's up?"
"It's Leah."
He stifled a yawn. "Who's Leah?"
"Fin's daughter. Your cousin. She's come home."

He crawled into the shower, opened the faucet and tried to ignore the tightening in his groin as the water needled his body. Who'd ever have thought that sex would become such a bother? Take last night. The woman he'd been seeing on his

The Lighthouse

occasional trips to Santa Fe had gone all serious on him. "This thing between us, it's not going anywhere, is it?" she had said. When he replied that he thought they both had understood it wasn't intended to, she showed him the door. Despite it being near midnight he braved the icy February roads and headed back to Taos, stopping at a gas station on the outskirts of Santa Fe for a coffee. Still buzzing when he arrived home, he had popped open a can of beer and gone to his studio to dab at a half-finished canvas before crawling into bed around four.

Fatigue rimmed his eyes like grit. Theo lifted his face to the spray, opened his mouth, chewed the water and spat. He'd often wondered how his father had endured celibacy during his years in religious orders but never had the nerve to ask. He turned off the tap and squeezed water from his hair. It would be nice to be married, he thought. Someone to talk to and do things with. Another beating heart in his bed. Like his brother Ben—but then Ben always got things right. The matter was academic since he'd never met a woman with whom he'd wanted to spend more than a few hours. Except for Fiona, Fox's mom, but seven months living with the crests and troughs of her emotions had been enough. More than anything he would never thrust a strange woman into his son's life, not until he had finished school, anyway. *Which means ten more years of making do,* he thought ruefully.

He stepped out of the shower, grabbed a towel and scrubbed himself dry. Broomstick, Ben had called him when they were kids. Clothes rack. Beanpole. He had spent hours in the gym fleshing out his frame, but still didn't carry an ounce of fat. He swiped the condensation from the mirror and studied his face. A day's worth of stubble: it would do. He dressed, put on a sheepskin jacket and headed out to his Jeep.

Theo's small wood and glass house sat on a ridge that afforded an expansive view of the Sangre de Cristo mountains.

He paused on his front stoop and looked out to them. Snow mantled their shoulders and their clefts were traced out in blue shadows. Before returning to live at the ranch eight years previously, he had wandered the world, and those mountains had initially felt like the walls of a prison. He and they had since reached an understanding: he would glorify them in paint and they would occasionally set him free.

He drew in a deep breath of clean icy air. It scoured his lungs and ignited his brain. Exhaling slowly, he lifted his face. In all his travels he had never found anything to match the candor of the sky here, the purity of the piercing light. Faced with such truth you couldn't lie; not to yourself, anyway. He got in the Jeep, started it and turned the defroster on full blast. When the window cleared he glanced back at his house. He had forgotten to lock up again. He shrugged, put the Jeep in gear and rolled slowly down the slick driveway.

The house Theo lived in was his grandfather Niels' old studio, perched above the grounds of Las Sombras. He tapped his brake as he approached the hacienda then carried on—Fox would already have left for school. He continued descending and turned onto the road that ran through the ranch, following its muddy course towards the stables.

As he drove by the main paddock, a whiskery wolfhound and a fat Jack Russell tracked him on the inside of the fence. He exchanged waves with a young Pueblo Indian replacing a broken post. Andy Coriz's family had been involved in the stables since Theo's grandfather Niels had bought the ranch fifty years previously to help his bachelor brother Tomas breed and train horses. Andy's grandfather Billy helped set it up and his father Chester was now in charge.

Theo continued on through the sagebrush-studded countryside, dull and scrappy under its dusting of snow, the Jeep's tires spitting up slush. As he approached his parents' house he reflected on his mother's news. Leah had been a small child when he was shipped off to boarding school at the age of fourteen and it was, he calculated, twelve years since he had last seen her at the premiere of the requiem Fin had composed for his parents. An image of a scowling adolescent with short, dark, spiky hair came to his mind. She had refused to sit with the rest of the family in the seats reserved for them. *Spoiled brat,* Theo had thought at the time, ignoring his own antics at that age. Ben had taken her to another section and stayed with her through the performance. *Benedict the Good.* When she had disappeared a couple of years later Theo had been on the other side of the world, and to the extent he had thought of her since—and it wasn't much—he'd figured that like most teenage runaways she had been drawn into addiction or prostitution, or was perhaps even dead.

He parked his Jeep next to the Mercedes sedan in the courtyard of his parents' house and went in. A waft of the fresh coffee his mother had said would be waiting greeted him. He shed his jacket in the mudroom and went in search of a cup.

Leah sat over the remains of her breakfast at the far end of the pine table that filled a solarium next to the kitchen. He poured a coffee and walked over.

"Hi. I'm Theo," he said.

"Yes, I know." She straightened up in her seat and regarded him down the length of her nose. "Are you here to make sure I don't abscond?"

"Not really."

He sat down and studied her. If they had passed in the street he wouldn't have known who she was. Her dark hair was long now and fell in waves around her face. Uneven bangs that looked like they had been cut by an inexpert hand using blunt scissors covered her brow. Her eyes were slightly slanted, her cheekbones high, her jaw square, her mouth fine-cut. If he were to draw her it would be with short, crisp lines.

"Do you plan to?" he said.

She shrugged and looked away.

"So where've you been?"

"Here and there."

Whatever. He drank his coffee in the lengthening silence. Leah played with a napkin, folding it into different shapes, her forehead creased by a slight frown.

"What's Niels like?" she said suddenly.

Of course. She's the boy's mother. "He's a nice kid, quiet, thoughtful," he said. "He and my boy are really close; being a year older he's a good foil for Fox, who's full of beans and tends to get wound up."

"So how do you fit in here?"

He gave a short laugh. "Not sure I do. When Fox's mom and I split I didn't know she was expecting. After she had him she was offered a job with a TV station back home in Australia. Guess she decided a baby would hold her back so she dropped him off here, with my parents. He was only a few weeks old. Mom tracked me down in South America to let me know. Fox and I've been here ever since."

Leah drew her knees up and hugged them. "Fox—an unusual name."

"It's a contraction of Forrest Xavier. It suits him; you'll see when you meet him."

"If I ever do."

"You're not really thinking of taking off again, are you? With Niels here?"

"Dad won't let me see him."

Theo's eyebrows shot up. "Why ever not?"

"He said I have to commit to staying and becoming part of Niels' life first."

"Makes sense."

Leah released her legs and rested her elbows on the table. "Yes, it does. The thing is, Niels doesn't know me at all. What will he think when I suddenly appear after all these years? How do I explain why I haven't been around? He might be better off carrying on as he is. And then there's my dad…" She shook her head. "Living with him would never work."

"Shouldn't be too hard to find a place in town."

She grimaced. "I'm almost broke. Getting here took most of my money."

"This family's not exactly short of dough."

She jerked back in her chair and squared her shoulders. "I don't want any charity. Anyhow, I should get dressed."

She rose and carried her dishes to the kitchen. She was, he observed, of average height and just this side of skinny. She wore a limp white T-shirt over washed-out black tights. Her feet were bare. She opened the dishwasher and bent to place the plate and cup inside, presenting a tidy little bottom.

Whoa! Theo jerked his eyes away.

"I expect I'll see you later," she said on her way out of the room.

"Yeah, sure," he said to the dregs in his cup.

Chapter 4

The small jet kissed the runway, decelerated noisily and taxied to an empty spot on the apron. Lucas Wilde, seated in the co-pilot's chair, removed his earphones.

"Thank you for the soft landing, Trevor," he said to the pilot.

The young African American flashed him a smile. "A pleasure, sir."

Lucas pushed himself out of the seat and twisted to exit the cockpit. It was an awkward space for a man of his height and heft to maneuver, and a white-hot pain shot up his right leg. He winced and sucked in a sharp breath. There was no specific locus to the pain. When it struck it was like a long, thin bolt of lightning, agonizing but usually mercifully short. Invariably, the pain was accompanied by memories of being sucked down a chute of churning mud and water and bouncing off cartwheeling tree trunks and jagged boulders. The pain ended as abruptly as it had started. Over time, Lucas had come to embrace it as an affirmation of the life he'd been gifted, a life that by all logic he should have lost. He released the breath he had been holding, steadied himself and moved to the exit. Trevor had preceded him and activated the control to open the door. He descended first with Lucas's small suitcase and cane and held out a hand to help him down the narrow stairs.

On the ground, Lucas accepted the case and cane from Trevor, said goodbye and turned wearily towards the terminal. The private jet, shared with two other businesses in the area, was a blessing. The trip home would have been several hours longer with a commercial airline, the closest major airport a two-hour drive away in Albuquerque. A wicked gust of wind spun dust around his feet and messed with his hair. He shifted his bag into his cane hand and brushed it off his face. At Ris's insistence, he wore his salt and pepper mane long and, although he grumbled, he secretly enjoyed this small concession to vanity.

As he approached the terminal building he caught sight of Theo, struck again by how much he resembled his mother. She had been a volunteer at the workcamp in Bolivia where, as part of his religious work, he had been leading the construction of a school and clinic. Despite his monastic vows, they had fallen in love. While his subsequent brush with death in the storm-swollen torrent had strengthened his belief and inspired his life's work, it had paradoxically also prompted him to seek release from those vows to marry Ris, whom he tracked down after she had returned home, thinking him dead.

"You look tired," Theo said, reaching for his father's suitcase.

"A bit, perhaps," Lucas said, surrendering the bag. "The sessions were long and the group unusually argumentative. A faction within it took exception to some of the ideas in my latest book, particularly the notion of seeking spiritual growth through the commonplace. I'm not sure why they invited me to the retreat."

Theo led the way to the Mercedes and stowed the suitcase in its trunk. "Do you want to drive?" he said, offering the keys. Lucas declined with a wave of his hand and they got into the car.

"So Leah has returned," Lucas said when they were underway.

"Yeah, but who knows for how long. She's trying to decide whether to stay or not."

"But she must stay! Niels needs her. And she needs us. We cannot let her go again." Lucas shook his head. "What a dreadful business that all was. We were quite fond of her, you know. Living just down the street, we saw her often. She was such a precocious little thing, all big eyes and somber thoughts. She and I used to have the most wonderful chats, and Ben was like a big brother to her. We even talked of adopting her once."

The car swerved as Theo glanced at his father in surprise. "What?"

"Steady there," Lucas said. "It was Ris's idea. We had always wanted a girl." He smiled at his son. "We'd rather hoped you would be one."

"Well, sorry I didn't oblige!" Theo stopped at an intersection and waited until a vehicle went by before proceeding. "But adoption? Why?"

"She was often alone, you see. Oh, there was always a nanny, but Fin and Alexandra were mostly caught up in their own worlds. Our doorbell rang one day and there was Leah with a pillow in one hand and a grocery bag with some clothes in the other, announcing that she had come to live with us. She was five or six. We took her back home, of course. She didn't cry but I haven't often seen such despair. That's when Ris suggested adoption."

"What did Fin and Alex have to say about it?"

"In the end we felt we couldn't raise it with them."

"Why don't I know any of this?"

"You weren't much interested in family then. In fact, I think you were already gone." Lucas paused. "It could be that in suggesting we adopt Leah, your mother had been trying to fill that void."

Chapter 5

Theo parked the Mercedes in its original spot, cut the engine and got out to retrieve his father's case from the car. Lucas led the way to the house, leaning on his cane more heavily than usual. Theo made a mental note to mention it to his mother.

Leah was waiting in the entrance when they came through the door.

"Leah, my dear," Lucas said, opening his arms.

She rushed into them. "Uncle Lucas!"

They embraced for a long moment. Lucas set her back and studied her face. "The prodigal returns," he said.

Leah laughed shakily. "I feel more like the fatted calf."

"Can I take your coat, Dad?" Theo said.

"Thank you, son," Lucas said, shrugging off his overcoat. He turned to Leah. "Now, come my dear, and tell me what's been happening to you."

Theo left them and headed home to his studio; it was time to get to work. After a spartan lunch he picked up painting where he had left off in the early morning. When the shadows began to lengthen he put his paints and brushes away and headed down to Las Sombras to prepare dinner.

After Alexandra's funeral, Fin and Niels had come to Azar

for the Christmas holidays. As the new year approached, they were loath to return to their sad, empty house in Vancouver.

"Why don't you stay on?" Theo had said. "Niels can go to school here. He and Fox get along so well; it would be good for them both."

Fin had agreed. Las Sombras was equipped with a complete sound studio and he could work there. Niels entered the local school and he and Fox bunked together in the hacienda. Theo took his meals and spent his spare time with them, returning to his studio to work and sleep. When Fin was away he spent the night. They made an odd household, the four of them, but it seemed to work.

Theo was surveying the contents of the refrigerator when he heard the drum of feet on the walk leading to the hacienda. Fox burst through the door, dropped his school bag and flung his arms around Theo's waist.

"Dad! You're home."

Theo lifted the boy and tossed him up. "Geez, buddy, you're getting big," he said, setting him down. "It seems that every time I turn around you're taller. How old are you again?"

Fox wiggled out of his grasp. "Come on, Dad, you know I'm eight."

Fox had what Theo called his winter face, with the scattering of freckles across his nose faded almost to nothing. He had drawn and painted his son many times but never to his satisfaction; it was like trying to capture quicksilver. "Hey, what's happened to your hair?" he said, scrubbing the red-gold fuzz on Fox's head.

Fox made a face. "Chrystal wasn't there."

"It was a new guy, Dylan. He scalped us," Niels said, entering the room. "I don't know what he was thinking." He rubbed his own buzzcut. "I hate it."

"Why didn't you say something?" Theo said.

"I did, but he said Aunt Ris told him to cut it really short. By then it was too late anyway, he had already cut half of it off."

Theo grinned. "You look like a couple of shorn sheep."

Niels sniffed. "It was bad enough at school. We don't need *you* to laugh at us too."

Theo pulled him into a hug. The boy hesitated then leaned against him. Niels had, he observed, the same gypsy eyes and dark brows as his mother. "It's kind of cute, actually," he said.

"Cute!" Niels snorted and pushed away, but his cheeks flushed with pleasure.

"Anyhow, it'll grow back," Theo said.

Fin entered the kitchen shortly after. When Niels and Fox had left the room he fixed Theo with a hard stare and lowered his voice. "Not a word to Niels about Leah, understand?"

After the boys had eaten and were settled in bed, Theo headed home. Despite the lack of sleep the previous night and the long, busy day, he felt inexplicably restless. After hesitating a moment at the turnoff that would have taken him to his own place, he drove to his parents' house. His mother was the only one still awake, at work in her office.

"Thought I'd stop in, see how you guys were doing," Theo said.

Ris's face brightened when she saw him. "Theo! I'm so glad you've come by." She pushed some papers aside and took off her glasses. "I could use a scotch. Why don't you pour a couple?"

Theo brought glasses and ice and a bottle of the whisky his mother favored to a sitting area in front of the fireplace. Ris carried in a basket of logs and set it down. She walked tall for her sixty-eight years and handled the load without apparent effort. She threw a couple of logs into the fireplace and poked the quiescent coals into life. Dusting off her hands, she accepted the glass he handed her, sank down into an armchair and took a swallow with an appreciative noise.

"What are you working on so late?" he said, sitting down on the sofa next to her.

Ris thrust her fingers through her short cap of silvery hair. "Lighthouse stuff. We've found some financial irregularities."

"Can I help?"

"I don't think so. I need to talk to Ben."

"You mean I wouldn't be able to understand."

"No, I mean there's a legal dimension to it."

"Umm." He took a sip of his drink. "Where's Dad?"

"In bed already. A touch of jet lag, at least I hope that's all it is."

"He did seem quite tired."

Ris nodded, her eyes troubled. "I do wish he wouldn't travel so much." She threw back the rest of her scotch and held out her glass. "A bit more?"

Theo reached for the bottle and refreshed their drinks. "And Leah? How's she doing?"

"Who knows. I worry about that girl."

"What do you think she'll do?"

"She and Lucas spent most of the day talking but we still have no idea." Ris set down her glass and rubbed her eyes. "The whole thing was all so appalling."

"How's that?"

Ris gazed at the fire for a moment before answering.

"You know, between them Fin and Alex had an IQ equivalent to that of the population of a small town," she said. "But they were incredibly stupid when it came to raising Leah. Imagine, leaving her all by herself when Niels was due. But Fin was pretty useless at this kind of stuff and Alex, well, I doubt she even knew what to do. When Leah was born, Alex couldn't cope at all with the crying and the disrupted sleep, the breast feeding, the diapers. Sara took over—Leah being her first and much-anticipated granddaughter—and between us we found some reliable nannies.

The Lighthouse

"After Dad and Sara died, we didn't see much of Fin and Alex. We were preoccupied with the Lighthouse and they were always so busy. I hadn't realized how bad things had gotten between Fin and Leah. Leah's pregnancy distressed us but we didn't think there was anything we could do. Her disappearance really shook us up, though."

She leaned forward and looked intently at Theo.

"We tried to help then, and I ended up having the most awful argument with Fin. He refused to report her as missing. Can you imagine? I said for God's sake she's still a child, but he was so angry he wouldn't budge. He said that legally she was an adult, and after a taste of living rough she'd be home soon enough." She sat back in her chair. "I think he expected Leah to return at any moment, and I believe, I have to, that he would have acted differently had he known she was gone for good."

The white-hot skeleton of the burning logs imploded in a fan of sparks. Ris moved to tend to it.

Theo set down his glass. "Here, Mom, I can do that."

She crouched down on the hearth. "It's okay. I like to play with fire," she said, smiling at him over her shoulder. The dancing light erased the lines on her face and Theo caught a glimpse of the young woman she once had been. His throat tightened at the poignancy of her lost youth and he coughed to dissipate the emotion.

Ris selected and threw in two more logs and prodded them until they were well settled among the seething coals. She rose, added more whisky to their glasses and sat down again in her chair. They sipped their drinks and continued talking until the fire had consumed itself. When Theo glanced at his watch it was almost midnight.

"I should go," he said, rising. His head spun and he sat back down.

"I don't think you should drive," Ris said, regarding him

closely. "Even though it's just to your place. Why don't you stay here tonight?"

"I'm okay," Theo said, his tongue thick in his mouth. "I'll just lie down for a few minutes, then I'll go." He swung his legs up on the sofa, tucked a cushion under his head. He closed his eyes and began a long, slow slide into a delicious blackness. A cover drifted down over him, a cool hand rested briefly on his cheek.

"Goodnight, son."

He may have responded, he wasn't sure. At the moment before completely losing consciousness, his eyes fluttered open at a thought: Had he really just gotten wasted with his mother?

Chapter 6

"Well, if you must," Caro said in the frostiest variant of the different British accents she used in preference to her original, unglamorous one from England's midlands. Ben Wilde withdrew his arm from the round of his wife's belly and rolled onto his back. The unfocused desire that had inspired the tentative advance shrank into a black hole and died. He lay for a minute while his breathing slowed then swung his legs over the side of the bed, rose and slipped into his plush bathrobe.

"Where are you going?"

Ben glanced back at Caro. The shadow created by the shade of the bedside lamp hid her face. "Make a cup of tea. Maybe read a bit." He waited, giving her a chance to make amends.

"It's just, well, I have that early flight tomorrow."

"Yes, of course," he said and left the room.

He decided against the tea, opting for a glass of bourbon. He headed to his study—the soles of his feet making soft sucking noises on the polished hardwood—dropped some stale ice cubes from the small bar fridge into a wide-mouthed glass and added a good inch of the liquor.

After re-reading the same paragraph in a legal brief for the fifth time he got up from his desk and went down the hall to the media room. He turned the television on, pushed a couple of cushions against the arm of the sectional sofa and lay down, stretching out his legs. It accommodated his six-foot-five-inch frame, but only just. A late-night talk show was playing, the banter inane but comforting. He turned the volume down and wriggled his back into a more comfortable position against the pillows. The bourbon had reached the point of dilution he liked and he held the liquid in his mouth for a several moments before swallowing. He took another long pull and set the glass down. A fine wool throw in a paisley pattern was draped over the back of the sofa. He shook it out and draped it over his legs. The alcohol trickled through his system, melting the knots in his muscles. He closed his eyes and drifted away.

The sound of heel clicks on tile, a clasp snapping shut and keys dropped on a glass tabletop woke him: Caro in the kitchen getting ready to leave. Would she come to say goodbye? More heel clicks, some scraping, a door opening and closing, then silence. *I guess not.* He sat up, stretching. The television still burbled, a weathergirl in a too-tight skirt and too-high heels pointing to a cloud vortex in the middle of the Pacific Ocean. He turned it off, picked up the bourbon glass and padded in the direction of the kitchen.

In the great hall he paused, as he often did, to marvel at his grandfather Niels' design that, even on a gray Vancouver morning, snagged what little light there was and drew it down into the large open space. He continued on through the dining room with its long Indian laurel-wood table. The house had never seemed big to him when he was growing up, with people coming and going, the table regularly crowded with family and friends. Few people visited now, and it felt like a tomb: cavernous, echoing.

He wasn't often given to whimsy, but he wondered sometimes if the house missed all that life and energy, if he wasn't breaching a kind of trust in living there. His parents had offered it to him in anticipation of his having children. It was why he and Caro had married after all, in a quick civil ceremony before he returned home from London after completing an advanced degree in law. Caro had stayed behind to finish her own legal studies. Sometime before she joined him three months later, the baby was lost.

He fiddled with the espresso machine and made a cup of coffee. There had been no other children in the ten years they had been married. At first it was to let Caro complete her articles and the bar exams, then it was to allow her to build her practice. After growing pressure from Ben and promises of as many nannies as needed to let her return to work quickly, Caro had agreed to try, but nothing happened. The previous year he had accidently swept her handbag off the kitchen counter. Among the scattered items he returned to it was a half-empty strip of birth control pills.

Until then, Ben would have said that his marriage was happy. The evidence of Caro's deceit shook him to the core. Why hadn't she told him she didn't want to have children? At least then he would have known where they stood. Knowing she'd be furious at his intrusion into her privacy, inadvertent though it was, he had not raised the matter. But he realized that he had been mistaking their routines for a shared life, civility for intimacy.

Ben understood that this in itself would not condemn a marriage. Several couples he knew had few common interests and seemed content with a relationship that was the sum of duties and schedules and proscribed roles in public settings. He had not married Caro out of a great passion. He had tasted that once, for an exchange student from Argentina named Sonia when he was twenty-two. Completely besotted, he had followed her back to Buenos Aires only to discover that she was engaged. Her fiancé and his friends had ambushed and beaten him badly. He had returned home chastened, and with an enduring suspicion of strong emotions.

A wild affair, a dust-up—that was more Theo's style. Ben could only imagine the trail of broken hearts that his brother, with his Hollywood looks and bad-boy, motorcycle-riding persona, had left around the world. He had never understood the restlessness that had driven Theo to drop out of art college and squander his portion of the education trusts their grandparents, Niels and Sara, had set up for them on years of travel. All Ben had ever wanted was a home like his parents had created, warm and secure and with children to fill it, and it was why when Caro had told him she was pregnant he hadn't hesitated to marry her. But here they were.

The coffee machine blew and hissed to signal the completion of its task. Ben stirred the cup of scalding liquid and took a sip. How ironic that wayward, careless Theo ended up being the one with a child and a cozy family life.

He swallowed the last of the espresso and trudged upstairs. Caro had left the bed unmade, as she usually did. Always in a hurry to leave, she was. He shook out the sheets and covers and smoothed everything down, tucking the corners in smartly. Caro practiced criminal law and her work was full of unpredictable demands, small dramas, long hours. And when she blew off steam it was with her girlfriends: similar well-off, hard-driven women. Or so she said.

Ben punched and smacked the pillows and set them into place. When all was tidy he showered and thought about the day ahead. An ordinary day, nothing unduly demanding. There was never anything unduly demanding. At school he had been seduced by the complex and subtle dimensions of law, and the studies in London were intended to explore the possibility of an academic life. Marriage and the anticipation of a family to support had put an end to that. Using the legal work associated with his parents' real estate and business holdings as a base, he had built a law practice with his friend, Jay. The practice thrived but, like the big house, his work had become hollow and empty.

His razor blade was dull but he persisted, using bits of tissue to stop the bleeding from a couple of nicks. He tore the cleaner's wrapping from a laundered shirt, pulled trousers and a jacket from their hangers. The red and gray patterned tie he put on inexplicably irritated him and he unknotted it and selected another. Dressed, he sat down on the edge of the bed to lace up his shoes. That done he lay back, closed his eyes and let his thoughts drift.

A few minutes later he rose, went downstairs and collected his briefcase, overcoat and keys. He set the house alarm, shut the door and got into his well-appointed sedan. He drove the familiar route to his office automatically and was mildly surprised to find himself in his parking stall. As he was turning off the car's ignition, his phone rang.

"Hi, Mom," he said and hurried on. "If it's about your email, sorry, things ran late last night. I'll look at it as soon as I get in."

"Yes, do, I need to know what you think," said Ris. "Is there any chance you can come out here in the next few weeks?"

"I'll check my schedule and get back to you. Is something wrong? Are you and Dad okay?"

"It's not us, it's the Lighthouse. I've explained it all in the email. And there's something else, Ben. Remember Leah?"

"Of course I remember Leah. Is there news?"

"Yes, the best kind. She's come home."

Chapter 7

"*Toad* in the *hole, toad* in the *hole,*" Fox sang, punctuating the words with one-legged hops around the kitchen table. The pain in Theo's head pulsed to the beat of Fox's dance. He flipped over a slice of the eggy bread in the frying pan and winced. *It's all this clean living. Can't handle whisky any more.* He was about to ask Fox to please stop when Niels said, "Sit down Fox, you're making me dizzy." Theo shot the boy a grateful look which he acknowledged with a bashful smile.

As he was dishing out the breakfast, an image drifted through his mind, evanescent as smoke. A bridge and sky … a bridge over sky. He stopped to let the idea take shape but it eluded him. After the boys headed down the driveway to wait for the Lighthouse shuttle which drove them and the children of workers who lived on the ranch to town for school, Theo poured out a cup of coffee, sat down at the table and let his mind drift, trying to recapture the image that had swirled around earlier.

It had started to coalesce when he heard a car door slam. He started out of his chair and pitched the rest of his coffee into the sink. He had forgotten that Angie, Fin's housekeeper, worked today. She kept the hacienda in good order, and was entirely trustworthy, but she'd talk your ear off given half a chance. She and Fin understood each other and if she went on too long he would brusquely tell her to go away because he needed to work. Theo didn't think he enjoyed the same privilege and tried to avoid her. He quickly made motions to leave, but Angie nailed him as he was sidling out of the kitchen, and he shifted from foot to foot for five minutes listening to her berate her feckless husband and saucy daughter-in-law. When she finally paused for breath he smiled engagingly, patted her on the shoulder with assurances that everything was sure to work out, and skipped out the door.

Outside, he paused and tried to order his thoughts. The stipend he received for overseeing the stables kept Fox and him housed and fed. To earn more he painted archetypal Southwest landscapes sized and priced to sell easily through the Lighthouse gift shop and a gallery in Taos. Their surprising popularity embarrassed him as he considered them uncomplicated works requiring little thought. He was doubly surprised when one of Santa Fe's top galleries invited him to be part of an exhibition to be held later that spring. His recent trip to that city had been to discuss the matter. It wasn't a solo show, two other painters would be featured, but still meant exposure in an important market.

What he hoped would break him out of the landscape rut and raise his profile, not to mention fatten his slender bank account, was a recent commission from his parents to paint a mural in a new wing planned for the Lighthouse. The construction was scheduled for the following winter, at the same time as an extensive renovation of the existing fifteen-year-old facility. Theo didn't expect that his mural would match the distinction of his grandfather's Tree of Light, but he hoped whatever he created would also be considered by visitors to the Lighthouse to merit a viewing. An idea for it was forming, he could feel it. He tried to goose it along. A bridge? The sky? Had there been a door? Nothing came. *Darn that Angie and all her complaints.* He inhaled and emptied his mind. Best to let it come on its own.

Chapter 8

Leah sat at the end of the pine table in the solarium trying to focus on the screen of her computer. She gave up with a sigh and stared out the window. Her body ached from the anguish and strain of the last week. She shuddered and hugged herself. All those years away she had imagined coming home, sitting down with her parents as an adult, everyone speaking calmly, kindly, the stress associated with her disappearance tempered by the passage of time. How brutal the reality of it: her mother gone, her son present when she had never thought to see or hear of him again, and the enmity between Fin and her still fresh and raw.

She quaked and burned in equal measure at the possibility of seeing Niels. What would she say to him? How could she defend her decision to give him up all those years ago, her absence all this time? She ground the heels of her palms into her eyes. Would Niels be able to understand the desperation that had seized her then, her absolute panic over the responsibility of caring for a newborn child? And to step into his life now, under the daunting scrutiny of her father...

A car drove into the courtyard and a minute later Theo swept into the room. His unbuttoned Drover coat billowed behind him exuding a whiff of horse. He took after the Nordic side of the family: sea-green eyes, ash-blond hair, his face all clean, sculptured lines. He moved with the contained power and lithe grace of a large cat, owning the space around him. What she would give for his assurance, his apparent ease with the world.

"Where are Mom and Dad?" he said.

"They've gone to the Lighthouse."

"Ah, yeah, some kind of problem there." He dropped a manila envelope on the table. "Could you give this to Mom when she gets back? It's the monthly report from the stables."

"Of course."

"How's it going?" he said, sitting down.

"I've had better days."

"Have you decided what to do?"

Leah nodded. "This morning I told my father that I would stay."

"Dad convinced you?"

"I think I've known all along that I would and have just been getting used to the idea."

"Well, that's good. Niels will be happy."

She smiled faintly. "You think?"

"To reconnect with his mom? Sure. But how about his dad? Does he know what's going on? Are you going to bring him into the picture now too?"

Leah looked away without answering.

"Sorry, none of my business. I guess I'm kind of sensitive on the matter, having been in a similar position."

All this poking and prodding. Well, she might as well get used to it.

"I don't know who Niels' father is," she said.

Theo's eyebrows shot up.

"It's not what you're thinking. I wasn't seeing anyone, and I have no idea how I got pregnant. At all."

He frowned. "How can that be?"

"I don't know. It just is."

He studied her for a moment. "It obviously happened somehow. Could you have been drugged?"

She raised one shoulder in a shrug. "That's the most likely explanation but I can't think of who would have done it or where." She paused. "If something traumatic happened, I could be experiencing a kind of memory loss called psychogenic amnesia."

"Doesn't sound very pleasant."

"No."

"Can you do anything about it?"

"I expect it could be probed through psychoanalysis or even hypnosis, but quite apart from not being able to afford therapy, I'm not sure I want to go there."

She fell silent. Theo stood up. "I'd better get to work." He stood and looped his scarf around his neck. "When are you going to see Niels?"

Leah drew in a long breath. "Dad's away tomorrow. He said I can come over when he returns on Saturday."

Chapter 9

"Hey buddy, you need to get a move on," Theo said. He pulled the duvet off Fox's bed and smoothed down the sheets.

Fox held up an articulated plastic figure. "I think it's broken."

"Bring it to the kitchen and I'll have a look after breakfast."

Fox put down the toy and pulled on his pants. Theo replaced the duvet and fluffed up the pillow.

"Where's Niels?"

"I think he's talking to Uncle Fin." Fox glanced around. "Where's my other sock?"

Theo helped him find it and left to set out the boys' breakfast. Niels came in and sat down at the kitchen table.

"Good morning," Theo said.

Niels turned to him, eyes wide with shock, but didn't respond.

"Everything all right?"

"Granddad said my mother is here."

"Ah." Theo put his arm around the boy's shoulders. "You okay?"

"I..." Niels said and blinked.

Fox slid into one of the chairs. "Why are you crying, Niels?"

Niels pulled away from Theo. "I'm not."

"Eat your cereal and leave Niels be," Theo said.

Breakfast passed in silence, Fox giving Niels troubled glances as he ate. Niels managed only a few mouthfuls before pushing his dish away and leaving the table.

"What's wrong with Niels?" Fox said, wiping his mouth with his sleeve.

"Here, use this," Theo said, handing him a paper napkin. "He'll tell you when he's ready."

After the boys left for school, Fin came to the kitchen dressed in his overcoat and carrying a small leather grip. "I'm off," he said.

"Where to?"

"New Orleans. Just overnight."

"So you've told Niels about Leah?"

Fin glanced around as though trying to get his bearings. "I'm not sure how he took it. Maybe I should have waited until I got back. Anyhow, keep an eye on him, would you?"

On Fridays, Angie usually made up a batch of pizza dough. When Theo arrived at the hacienda that afternoon he found a bowl of it swelling softly under a tea towel in a warm corner.

"Pizza tonight!" he said to Fox and Niels when they got home from school. Fox whooped and danced around the kitchen. Niels dodged his flying elbows and carried on to their room.

"Come on, you goofball," Theo said to his son. "Get changed, then you guys can give me a hand getting the oven ready."

After starting the fire in the pueblo-style oven outside, they returned rosy-cheeked to the kitchen and began to prepare the toppings.

"How're you doing?" Theo said quietly to Niels.

Niels raised a shoulder in a manner reminiscent of his mother's shrug. "Okay, I guess."

The Lighthouse

"So you're going to meet your mom tomorrow?"

"That's what Granddad said, but I don't know why I have to wait until tomorrow."

Theo looked at Niels thoughtfully. "I don't know why you have to wait either."

When he telephoned Leah with the invitation to join them for pizza and a movie she didn't answer right away.

"My father won't like it," she finally said. "I think he wants to control our meeting."

"Forget Fin for the moment; do *you* want to come?"

Her deep inhalation whistled down the line. "Yes. Yes, of course."

When he arrived at his parents' house to pick her up, Ris greeted him with a raised eyebrow. "Stirring things up, are we?"

"How's that?"

"Just remember: Leah may be his mother, but Fin's his guardian."

"Well, today I'm *in loco parentis,* and Niels said he doesn't want to wait until tomorrow to meet his mom."

"Think you can handle anything that happens?"

"What can happen?"

Ris shook her head. "Oh, Theo."

"Nervous?" Theo said.

Leah glanced at him. "What do you think?"

After he had called, she had fluttered about her aunt and uncle's guesthouse, unable to keep hold of a single thought, agonizing among the few garments she owned about what to wear. When she had pulled on the sweater she had chosen, her hands were shaking so badly it took several tries to get her arms into their sleeves. She stared at herself in the mirror. *What will Niels make of me?* She tugged out the elastic that held her ponytail in place, thinking it too juvenile, then decided that the resulting effect was too disheveled and bound her hair up again.

Now she sat in the passenger seat of Theo's Jeep, the nails of her clenched fists digging into her palms. Soon, very soon, in mere minutes, she would see her son. In all her imaginings about Niels she had never anticipated this moment. Had he? What would she say? What would *he* say? Were either of them ready?

"It'll be fine," Theo said.

She nodded and clenched her jaw to keep her teeth from chattering.

When they arrived at Las Sombras, the two boys were waiting for them on the porch.

"Hey, where're your jackets?" Theo said, getting out of the Jeep.

Neither boy responded, their eyes fixed on Leah who had remained in the vehicle. She stared back. Which one was Niels? One had dark hair, the other was a strawberry blond. Neither was obviously older than the other. Something that felt like a small sharp-toothed animal ripped at her insides. *My God! I don't even know my own child.* She took a deep breath, opened the door and got out.

The dark-haired boy stirred. "Are you my mother?"

"Yes," she said softly, her eyes burning.

Niels frowned. "How old are you, anyway?"

"Hey, let's go in," Theo said. "It's freezing out here."

The boys turned and entered the house, hovering just inside the door. When Leah didn't move, Theo took her gently by the elbow. "Come on." She let herself be led to the kitchen where Theo pulled out one of the chairs at the table for her. "We were just starting to get dinner ready," he said.

She sat down, her back rigid. Niels and Fox clambered into the other chairs and regarded her in silence. After a few moments she took a deep breath. "You asked how old I was," she said to Niels. "I am twenty-six."

"I thought you'd be an old lady," he said.

Leah eased back into her chair. "I was quite young, just sixteen, when you were born."

Niels nodded, his face solemn. "Where have you been?"

She chose to interpret the question literally. "In New York, mostly."

Niels was perched on the edge of his chair, one leg kicking back and forth under the table. "Why didn't you ever visit?"

Here it is. She stared at the hands she had clenched in her lap, casting about for an answer. After several long moments she raised her eyes to Niels. "Like I said, I was very young when you were born, and I couldn't take care of you by myself. I didn't have my own home, or any money. I thought it would be best if you were brought up by people who could give you a safe place to live, and anything else you needed. I also thought that you should consider these people as your parents, that it would be confusing for everyone if I was around. Then I heard that my mother, your grandmother, died…"

Niels' forehead cleared. "So with Gran gone, you've come back to take care of me!"

Leah leaned back and released a long breath. She glanced at Theo. He nodded encouragingly and she turned to Niels. "Yes, I would very much like to help take care of you."

Fox, who had sat quietly through the exchange, bounced up. "Do you want to see our room?"

"We share it," Niels said.

"Fox, wait," Theo said.

Leah felt as though a tight spring had begun to uncoil within her. She felt a smile forming, a large one. "No, no. It's okay." She rose on jelly legs and accepted the hand Fox offered, holding the other one out to Niels. After a moment he took it and they headed in the direction of the boys' room.

Theo watched them go, hands on hips. *Well done.* Leah had answered without lies, or fulsome expressions of regret, or tears, or discomfiting displays of affection. He resumed the interrupted task of assembling the toppings for the pizzas.

Back in the kitchen, the boys vied with each other to show Leah how to form the crust, sending disks of dough spinning into the air. She laughed at their antics and applauded the results, her cheeks flushed. *Was I that goofy when I was young?* Theo wondered, dropping a glob of dough that had hit the floor into the compost bucket.

When the pies were cooked and eaten and the movie was over, the boys agreed, reluctantly, to go to bed. As they said goodnight, Fox flung his arms around Leah's waist.

"Oh!" she said, startled by the hug. She returned it, laughing. When she turned to Niels he hesitated before allowing her to hold him briefly.

"I guess I should be getting back to your parents' place," she said to Theo when the boys were gone.

"Why don't you stay here? There's lots of room—as I expect you know."

She hesitated. "If it's okay."

"It's *your* family's house. I'll call Mom to let her know." He motioned to a door down the hall. "I'm there, in the blue room. You can choose from the guest rooms in the other wing. Their bathrooms should have toothbrushes and lotions and stuff." He held up a finger. "Wait, I'll get you one of my T-shirts to sleep in."

He went to his room and returned with the garment.

"Thanks," Leah said, accepting it. "For this, and for tonight. It was so … easy, so natural."

"Yeah, I thought it went well."

She hugged the T-shirt to her. "As a start, yes, but I expect there will be a day of reckoning, when Niels is older and understands more."

"But you two will have a relationship then, a basis to deal with whatever happens."

"I hope so." She looked at him, her eyes glistening in the dim light. "But aren't they beautiful, the two of them?"

Chapter 10

When Theo entered the kitchen the following morning he heard noises in the mud and laundry room. Thinking that an animal might have gotten in, or that the boys were up to something, he went to it and flung open the door.

Leah stood, hair loose and arms folded across her stomach, in front of the dryer, the source of the *thump, thump* he had heard. All she had on was his T-shirt. It fell to mid-thigh, showing slender, shapely legs.

"Oh! Sorry!" he said, averting his eyes and stepping back.

"I washed some things; they didn't quite dry overnight."

"No problem. I was just wondering what the noise was." He closed the door. *Whoa!* he thought and returned to the kitchen.

She arrived not long after, dressed and groomed. The boys danced around her, still in their pajamas. Over breakfast, Theo explained that Saturday mornings were busy with music lessons for Niels and art class for Fox in Taos.

"Do you want to come with us? We usually finish with a burger somewhere."

"Yes, why not?" Leah turned to Niels. "What instrument do you play?"

"Cello. I started last year," he said through a mouthful of mush.

"Don't talk with your mouth full," Theo said.

"Is that what your grandfather wanted?" Leah said.

Niels swallowed and wiped his mouth with a napkin. "No. He wanted me to learn piano. I did for three years."

"So you were, what, five when you started?"

Niels shrugged. "It was a small piano."

Leah looked at him intently. "Did you want to?"

"I don't remember. I guess it was okay."

"I started to learn piano when I was five as well. I didn't find it much fun, though. What made you choose the cello?"

"It sounds like someone talking; I like that," Niels said and spooned up more cereal.

"Are you going to stay here now?" Fox said to Leah. His eyes glowed with adoration.

Oh, my... Theo had raised his cup to his mouth but set it down without drinking.

"Maybe not here exactly, but somewhere close," she said.

"Yay!" Fox said, clapping his hands. Soggy flakes flew from his spoon.

"Hey! Now finish up, you two, and get dressed," Theo said. "And don't forget to brush your teeth."

Leah gazed after the boys as they headed to their room. "They look like baby birds with their hair so short."

Theo laughed. "An over-enthusiastic stylist got ahold of them. Listen, why *don't* you stay here? Plenty of room, as you can see, and the boys would like it."

"If it were just the boys..." She shook her head. "But with my father—I can't."

"So where will you live?"

"I have no idea. Before I do anything, I have to find a job."

"What kind of work do you do?"

"I don't exactly have a profession." She gave him a crooked smile. "I never did finish high school. So I'll do just about anything."

"I'm sure something can be found for you at the Lighthouse."

Leah waved the thought away irritably. "I don't want someone to fabricate a job for me."

"Hang on, who said it would be fabricated? This family has a lot of going on; there's always room for good people. When I came here for Fox I was in the same position you're in. I had no base, no job. Mom needed someone to oversee the stables and I was glad to be useful. There was no shame in it."

"No. No, of course not. I think… I think it's really more a matter of maintaining some distance." Her arm sketched a ring. "I don't want to get completely swallowed up by family."

"Yeah, it can get suffocating. You need your own space. Too bad there wasn't another…" He straightened up and snapped his fingers. "There's a trailer we keep for summer help if they need a place to live, but it's empty right now."

Leah leaned forward. "That might work."

He eased back in his chair. "Maybe, maybe not. It's near the stables, and I'm not sure what kind of shape it's in."

"That doesn't matter, I could fix it up."

"I suppose it's worth a look." He stood up and started clearing the table. "If we leave soon, we can check it out on our way to town."

The trailer lay within a stand of pines behind the long, windowless back of the building containing the stables, tack room and office to which it was connected for power, water and sewage. The four of them clambered out of the Jeep and stood looking around. The surrounding grounds were rough and strewn with cones and dry needles. Grime was embedded into the seams of the trailer windows, and its silver panels were dull with dirt.

"Gee, I don't know," Theo said.

The stable dogs gamboled up barking and sniffed them all methodically.

"Is this the security patrol?" Leah said, laughing.

"Yeah, there's not much goes on around here that they miss," Theo said. "The wolfhound's name is Linc—after the president—and the little guy's called Jammer."

Linc leaned against her and she stroked his shaggy head. "Aren't you a big boy?" she said.

"Anyhow, let's have a look." Theo turned the handle on the trailer door and pushed it open. Dust motes floated in the air inside. The floor was tracked with footprints etched in desiccated mud, and the table and counters were speckled with mouse droppings. The bedroom was at the far end, and held a stained mattress upturned on a coil bedframe. Theo stood against the bathroom door to discourage Leah from looking inside.

"This is great!" she said, peering into the tiny closet.

"It's disgusting."

She closed the closet door and flashed him a smile. "You obviously have never been apartment hunting in New York."

The boys had found some empty beer bottles in one of the kitchen cupboards and were mimicking drunks glugging from them.

"Gross, guys. Totally gross." Theo moved forward, waving them all toward the door. "Anyhow, we need to get going if we don't want to be late."

When they were on their way, he said to Leah, "The trailer's in pretty rough shape."

"It will clean up fine. Any idea what the rent would be?"

He snorted. "Rent! Good grief. I don't think we even charged the summer help any rent."

"That would help a lot."

He glanced at her. "You're serious, huh?"

"Yes. It's close, but separate. I can get started on it as soon as we get back." Her brow furrowed. "Or do I need to speak to someone first?"

"The person you need to speak to is me. And you don't have

to clean it, I'll get Vince and his guys to do it." When Leah started to protest, he said, "It's his job; he's responsible for maintenance of all the ranch buildings. But you're sure it'll work?"

"It's perfect."

"Well, okay." He grinned at her. "But I'm going to have to tell Chester and Andy to watch their language."

When they returned to Las Sombras that afternoon and tumbled, laughing, out of the Jeep, Fin appeared at the entrance.

"Hello, Granddad," Niels said as he passed him on the way into the house.

Fin rested his hand briefly on his grandson's shoulder and nodded distractedly in response to Fox's greeting as he followed behind. When the boys were gone he turned, hands on his hips, and regarded Leah with steely eyes.

"I thought we'd agreed that you'd wait until I got home before seeing Niels."

Leah's chin rose. "You mentioned that, but I didn't specifically agree. I've committed to stay; I don't know why it matters when I first saw him."

"Look, the boy's been through a lot in the last year. I can't let you get him all upset and confused."

Leah opened out her hands. "That's the last thing I want to do."

Theo stepped forward as though to shield her. "It's not her fault, Fin. It was my idea. Niels wanted to see her and didn't understand why he had to wait. There was no harm done."

"No harm done? And how would you know that?"

"No one got upset; we had a good time."

"Stay out of this, Theo. It's not your concern." Fin turned to his daughter. "And from now on, we're going to do this my way."

Her eyes blazed. "And what way, exactly, is that? Are you

going to give us a script with what to say, what to do, every morning?"

Fin gritted his teeth. "Christ, you're impossible! Maybe you should have just stayed away."

"You can't mean that!" Theo said.

Fin made a dismissive gesture and went back into the hacienda. Theo turned to Leah. She stood deflated, her defiance gone.

"He's just pissed off that he didn't get his way," he said.

"Yes, I get that but…" She grimaced. "He always wrong-foots me, gets my back up. It's how it was at home, like no time has passed at all. It's one of the reasons I left in the first place. I couldn't imagine bringing Niels up with him there. The trouble is, he's awfully good at telling me what *not* to do, not so much what he expects." She sighed heavily and turned to leave.

"You're going?"

"Not exactly welcome, am I?"

"Man, you're just as stubborn as he is." Theo pulled his keys out of his pocket. "Here, I'll drive you."

She shook her head. "Thanks, but the walk will do me good."

"Look, it'll work out; you both just need some time."

"Maybe." She nodded in farewell and left.

Chapter 11

"A trailer? Don't be ridiculous," Fin said. "You'll live at Las Sombras with us."

Leah took a deep breath. *Calm. Just stay calm.*

The family was gathered for Sunday dinner at the home of her Aunt Ris and Uncle Lucas. Leah hadn't seen her father or Niels since leaving the hacienda the previous afternoon. On the long walk from Las Sombras to her aunt and uncle's house she had resolved to do whatever it took, put up with whatever her father dished out and demanded of her, to make it work. With negotiation where possible, of course.

"It's close by, I can visit often," she said.

"It'll be like my set-up," Theo said. "Leah can come for meals and maybe stay when you have to travel."

Leah gave him a grateful glance.

"But it's a piece of junk," Fin said.

"It's in okay shape, just needs a good cleaning. Vince'll look after that," Theo said.

Fin scowled at his nephew. Niels had stopped eating and was following the exchange with a slight frown.

"Perhaps we could talk about it later," Leah said.

"Yes, that might be best," Lucas said and gave her a reassuring smile.

Fin started on some other gripe but Leah tuned him out.

She glanced at her son; he had resumed eating. She gorged on the sight of him, filled with awe at being in his presence and the possibility of a life with him now. She had no sense yet of how he viewed her. He was a self-contained child, guarded and watchful. If he had been brought up like her he would have spent much time alone. She had had her grandfather Niels and Nana Sara; if her son let her she would give him the same attention and affection she'd received from them. She turned at a burst of laughter at the other end of the table where Fox was in animated discussion with Ris. The boy was the opposite of her son, exuberant and warm, hugging everyone in greeting when they had arrived for dinner. Niels had followed suit hesitantly and awkwardly, but he was learning. Living with Fox was good.

"A word before you go, Fin?" Ris said as people were preparing to leave after dinner.

Her brother turned, coat over his arm. "I suppose."

She turned to Lucas. "Could we use your study?"

"By all means."

"You come too."

Lucas followed them into his study and closed the door. They sat down and Fin regarded Ris with an eyebrow raised in enquiry. In the brief silence before she spoke, Lucas studied his brother-in-law. At the age of five, Ris had lost her mother to a car that had run a red light. She had been glad when, after several years alone, her father had married Sara, the scion of a hotelier family who had hired him to design one of their properties, and happier still when Fin was born. "He was such a marvel as a child we couldn't help but spoil him," she had said once to Lucas. She spoke now with the authority of an older sister.

"What's going on, Fin? Why are you being so hard on Leah?"

Fin frowned. "Hard how?"

"Oh, come on. One couldn't breathe for the atmosphere

at dinner and Theo said you really gave her a rough time yesterday."

Fin chopped the air with his hand. "I wish he'd stay out of it. It's not his or anyone else's concern."

"Of course it's our concern. We're all living together here. What happens between you two affects the whole family." Ris turned to her husband. "Don't you agree, Luke?"

"It's not us so much, Fin. It's the effect on Niels," Lucas said. "Discord between you and his mother could be quite disturbing."

Fin looked away and chewed on his anger for a moment. "She's never taken responsibility for her pregnancy, you know. Won't say how, won't say who. That for me is an essential condition for some kind of understanding between us. And now that she's back after all those years she thinks she can just step in as though nothing ever happened."

"I don't think for a moment that's how Leah views her return," Lucas said. "She understands the price she's paid for the choice she made to leave and is fully aware of the extraordinary chance she's been given to know her son and be part of his life."

"And how wonderful for Niels to have her back," Ris said.

Fin leaned forward. "You don't understand what we went through, especially Alex. You have no idea. That last year, do you know how many times she mentioned Leah? 'If only she'd come home,' she'd say. 'If only I could see her again.' Once, she said that she only hoped Leah was still alive—" His voice caught and he leaned back and raised his hand to his mouth.

They sat in silence for several moments.

"You could have looked for her. There are ways to do it, people you can hire," Ris said quietly. "You could have done that anytime. Why did you never look for her?"

"Because she obviously didn't want to be found," Fin said, but his voice lacked conviction.

Ris rested her hand on her brother's. "I'm sorry, Fin dear,

but the reality is that we all failed Leah, and terribly. She was a child thrust into an adult situation then left alone to deal with it. None of us was there when she needed help the most. But she's an adult now and should be treated like one. Despite everything, we—and you especially—owe her a chance and all the support she needs to assume the responsibilities of being a parent."

"And try to rejoice in your child's return," Lucas said. "All those years Theo stayed away and even though we knew he was okay…" He shook his head. "We are so grateful he eventually came back to us."

Chapter 12

Leah got off the Lighthouse shuttle at the Taos plaza and stopped to get her bearings. Under her arm she had a leather portfolio lent to her by Lucas to carry copies of the résumé she had prepared using the equipment in his office. The résumé was meagre: no formal education and nine years working in bookstores. She hadn't felt her stint as a dishwasher worth mentioning.

She gathered her jacket around her, conscious of the shabbiness of her attire. A new wardrobe would have to wait until she found a job. The option of working at the Lighthouse was always there—Ris had mentioned it again—but it would be awkward. As a member of the family she was unlikely to be given chambermaid or kitchen helper duties. A position would be found, perhaps carved from others' duties, possibly prompting resentment. No, she thought, shaking her head, better to find something, anything, in Taos.

Yet a job in town was not without challenges—how to get to it, especially once she moved to the trailer, for a start. Then there was the question of hours: evening or weekend work would make it difficult to spend time with Niels. After the painful family dinner the night before, Fin had unexpectedly knocked on the door of her aunt and uncle's guesthouse where she was staying.

"I just came to say goodnight," he had said gruffly. "And, ah, to say that you can come over to Las Sombras anytime to see Niels. And if that trailer business doesn't work out, you know you're welcome to come live there."

She had stammered her thanks and, after he had left, stared open-mouthed at the door, stunned by the change in his tone and manner.

Now she set off in the direction of the town library; she figured she might as well start with jobs involving books. Taos had changed little in the ten-odd years she had been gone. Gentrified a bit, more galleries and boutiques, specialty food stores, coffee houses. She gazed around her as she walked, drawn to the low, gentle, soft-edged buildings with their earthen colors, rough timber posts and simple, bright window trims, so different from the towers of New York and the uptight brick structures of the Adirondack town she had just left. She remembered once asking her grandfather Niels why he moved back and forth between the West Coast of Canada and the ranch here near Taos, why he didn't just choose one of his houses to live in and stay there. He had replied that the restless blue-gray seascapes of the Pacific inspired in him a sense of lightness and drift, while the timeless earth and stone of the Southwest grounded him, and that between them his life maintained a kind of balance. She hadn't fully understood him then but did now. *Will I ever achieve that kind of equilibrium?*

At the library she asked to speak to whomever was in charge.

"Is she expecting you?" the older woman at the front desk said.

Leah's cheeks burned. *How stupid.* She realized that she should have made an appointment. She had little experience job-hunting. The cashier job at the McGill bookstore had been a matter of being in the right place at the right time during the fall rush and then Ingrid, her boss there, had taken Leah along when she relocated to the Columbia University bookstore in New York.

The Lighthouse

"I'm sorry, no," she said.

"I'll see if she's available," the woman said and left. She returned shortly. "She's on the phone but can see you in a few minutes."

The head librarian was a round, cheery woman in her forties. She nodded throughout Leah's little spiel then shook her head. "We're pretty small here and I don't need anyone right now. And usually we like staff to have some kind of training. But you can try the bookstores, Hot Print and Cactus Books." She offered directions. "Although I'm not sure about Cactus Books. Cassie, she's the owner, she's not been doing too good recently."

Leah thanked her and left. Outside, she debated whether to make cold calls on the stores or go home and call ahead. *Well, you're here now.* She pressed on. She decided to try Hot Print, the more promising one, first. On the way, she crossed the street on which Cactus Books was located. The store was at the end of the block. She hesitated then headed towards it.

The Cactus Books window was dingy and the interior dull and dimly lit. Books slumped on shelves and stood in piles on the floor and the shelves were thick with dust. Leah paused in the entrance and looked around for the front counter. There wasn't one.

I don't think so. As she turned to leave she heard voices.

"There's no price on this book," said an unseen man.

"Okay, how about ten dollars?" said another after a pause.

"But maybe it doesn't cost that much."

"Look, just give me five dollars then. The book's hardcover; it can't cost less than that."

Leah peered around the side of the shelf towards the back where an ornately carved oak desk served as a counter. The customer, an older man in a ski jacket, was holding out a twenty-dollar bill. A younger man with a boyish face and floppy spice-brown hair was working the till. He wore a white dress shirt with the sleeves rolled up and tails loose over skinny black jeans. Silver knuckle-duster rings flashed when he threw his hands up in frustration. "Sorry, can't get this thing to work. Why don't you just take the book."

The customer stood perplexed for a moment before sliding the bill back into his wallet. "Funny way to do business," he said.

The younger man opened and shut desk drawers. "Looks like we don't have any bags either."

The older man palmed the book. "Well … thanks anyway," he said and headed out the door.

When the customer was gone, the young man put his hands on his hips and looked blankly around. "Fuck!" he said. He caught sight of Leah. "Oh, man, sorry! I didn't know you were here."

She went to the desk. "You seem to have a problem."

He motioned to the cash register. "I can't for the life of me figure out how to use this damn thing." Seeing her puzzled look, he continued, "I just bought the place. Three days ago. The girl who was supposed to work today didn't show up."

Leah peered over the desk. The register was an older model she was familiar with. "Here, let me have a look," she said. She walked around to the other side and quickly ran her fingers down the keys. "Do you mind if I try some? I can cancel the entries after."

"No, hey, go ahead."

She pushed a few buttons and nodded. "It's actually fairly straightforward." She took him through the different departments and functions, showed him how to complete a sale.

"Oh, wow," he said, laughing. "I've written code but I couldn't decipher something this simple?" He looked at her. "Say, any chance you could stay and help? If you're not doing anything? I'd really appreciate it." He opened out his hands in appeal. "I'd make it worth your while—just name your price."

Leah laughed. "You not going to make much money if you make offers like that and give books away." She thought quickly: she could try Hot Print later. "Yes, I can stay. And maybe I could help put things in order." She gestured to the rest of the room.

The guy's face lit up. "Could you? That'd be great. The woman I bought it from left things in quite a mess. She wasn't well, and the other girls who work here are just kids." He leaned towards her. "You wouldn't by chance know anything about books, would you?"

"As it happens, I do," she said and described her experience.

"Terrific!" His face fell. "But you're probably not free, huh? What're you doing now? Whatever it is, I'm prepared to pay you more."

Leah blinked. "You're offering me a job, like, full-time?"

"Well, yeah. Save me having to advertise. Look, I've got plans for this place, big plans, and if I had someone who knew what they were doing I could get started on them right away."

Leah stared at the guy in astonishment. He knew nothing about her but on the strength of a ten-minute acquaintance was offering her a job. She knew nothing about him either, nor was she sure what kind of big plans an old bookstore might inspire, but he seemed decent enough.

"I, ah, yes, actually I could. I just moved here and I'm looking for work."

"Fan-fucking-tastic!" The guy thrust out his hand. "By the way, I'm Ethan."

Leah introduced herself and they settled on a wage and some terms and shook on the deal.

"Now how about if I start by cleaning up?" she said.

One morning the following week, Theo was about to leave the Lighthouse after using the gym when he saw Leah enter the Tree of Light pavilion. He turned and followed her in.

"Hey," he said, sitting down next to her.

She smiled and put her finger to her lips. "We have to be quiet," she whispered, nodding in the direction of three other people who were wandering around the room.

The pavilion often served as a venue for gatherings and events at the Lighthouse, but its main function was as a room of repose and talking was discouraged. The fame of the Tree of Light brought many people to the resort to see it and a sign requesting silence and a box inviting donations to the charities supported by the Lighthouse Foundation greeted them.

While waiting for the current visitors to depart, Theo studied the window. It rose to the full height of the twenty-five-foot ceiling. The lower section was a column of patterned glass in various shades of brown, gray and green depicting the tree's trunk. Beyond that it exploded into a massive crown of branches and leaves formed by innumerable pieces of glass in an array of golds, greens, reds and browns. The wall into which the window was set curved, allowing it to capture the sun's rays as it tracked across the sky. The mid-morning light shining through the window splattered bits of luminous color across the floor.

"I get an amazing sense of peace here," Theo said when the visitors had gone. "I should come more often."

Leah nodded. "You know, I watched Granddad design this. He had to do it to scale, of course, and there were all these tiny bits of colored paper—he didn't use a computer then. I helped cut some of them out—he said it was easier for my small hands to do—and I was with him when he saw it completed for the first time. He, ah ... he wept then. I think he knew it was the last thing he would ever create." Leah trailed a finger under her eyes. "It's thirteen years now since he and Nana died, but I still miss them terribly."

"Sounds like you were quite close."

She nodded. "I spent much of my free time with them before I went to boarding school, and then weekends and holidays after. In the last years I think I was actually of some help to them." She sniffed. "Anyhow, thanks so much for the car. It's made all the difference getting around."

The fleet of vehicles available to the stables and the ranch office included a small electric car which was rarely used, Vince and the cowboys preferring the pickups and all-terrain vehicles. Theo had had it reassigned to Leah.

She studied him for a moment. "You've been so kind."

He smiled. "I've been called a lot of things; *kind* is nice."

"No, really. I don't think I could manage here without all your help."

"You're welcome." He looked at her closely. Something was different: she'd had her hair properly cut. "By the way, how's the job going?"

"It's early days, of course, but fine, I think. Speaking of which, do you have the time? I start at ten."

He checked his watch. "It's nine twenty-five." She stared fixedly at his hand and he tipped the face of the watch to allow her to see better. "Plenty of time."

She gripped his wrist, her fingers light and cool on his skin, and lifted it to examine his vintage Movado piece with its tiny gold dot at the twelve position on a blank black face. Raising her eyes to his, she said, "This is Granddad's watch, isn't it?"

"Yeah. It's what I chose after he died when Mom asked me if there was anything of his I wanted. It had fascinated me when I was a little kid, how there were no numbers but I could still tell the time. He explained the power of representation to me, the meaning a symbol can convey, the importance of context. He introduced me to art."

She nodded and looked at the watch a moment longer before releasing his wrist. After she left he gazed at the glass tree, its leaves shimmering from the subtle shifts of the sun as though a breeze were passing through them, and wondered why he had let its creator fade from his life.

Chapter 13

"Amen!" Lucas started at the vehement punctuation of the grace he had offered to begin their dinner. He often spoke a few words of thanks before family meals, for the fact of their being together, their good fortune, and the abundant food, but did not frame them religiously. Emily, the woman who had spoken, was the local Methodist church minister. Old friends, they tussled often over matters spiritual, and she never missed an opportunity to call him on the secularization of his faith.

"Touché," he said softly. She tipped him a wink. Addressing the rest of the table, he invited everyone to eat.

Before starting himself, Lucas sat for a moment, delighting in the company: his beloved Ris at the other end of the table; then Marni, Emily's stout, braided partner; Theo; Fox; and Emily next to him on one side of the table; and Fin; Caro; Niels; Ben and Fin's assistant Hailey, visiting from Vancouver, on the other. An empty chair between Emily and Fox awaited Leah's return from work, expected in time for the main course. The boys dispatched the terrine that Marni had contributed to the meal quickly and turned back to the game they were playing on the tablets held in their laps—a concession Ris permitted during long, adult meals. Everyone else ate leisurely and chatted, except for Caro who ignored the food and refilled her glass of wine.

Lucas studied his daughter-in-law. The shadows under Ben's eyes and his vague air of displacement, so unlike his usual alert and incisive self, made Lucas wonder if all was well in his son's marriage. On the surface their match made sense—two smart, successful professionals would have much in common. But what lay beneath? To Lucas, their rapport seemed superficial, their endearments perfunctory. When he and Ben had spoken privately earlier in the day he had delicately probed the matter but Ben had ignored the subtext and changed the subject.

Lucas sighed and picked up his fork. The peculiar irony of his life was that he regularly helped strangers deal with their troubles, but never his children. For some reason—embarrassment or pride or some fierce self-sufficiency—Ben and Theo had never sought his counsel and on principle he would not offer it without being asked. And where he most desperately wanted to intervene was on the matter of the rift that existed between his sons. He glanced at them, each quietly ignoring the other as they ate their food. Not that they ever argued; their interactions were, if anything, painfully polite. Lucas would have welcomed open hostility rather than the indifference they demonstrated towards each other. Its genesis may have predated Theo's departure at fourteen for boarding school—as children the difference in their temperament and character was already well established—but his younger son's effective absence from the family from such an early age and for so long had no doubt only deepened it. He prodded the gelatinous square on his plate. That he could not find a way to bring Ben and Theo together was, he thought, his singular failure as a parent.

Ben closed his eyes and let the familiar voices wash over him—his father's euphonious baritone at one end of the table, parsing some biblical reference with Emily; his mother's lilting alto at the other, relating a travel anecdote to Fin and Marni. He felt close to tears and shook his head to clear it. This emotional frangibility was new, and bothersome. The smallest thing—a single, withered apple clinging to the leaf-shorn limb of a tree, an old man tenderly tucking a blanket around his wife in a wheelchair, a three-legged terrier trotting after its owner—would close his throat and he would have to stop to compose himself.

He had welcomed this trip to Taos to discuss the problem at the Lighthouse, hoping that a visit with his family would help restore his balance. Ben had sensed his father's concern when they spoke earlier but not responded to it. What would he say? That his work was tedious and lacked meaning? That his friends were all busy with their young families and no longer had time for him? That he feared his marriage was falling apart? That when he tried to visualize his future all he saw was a large white blank?

As a matter of course, and not expecting her to accept, he had invited Caro to accompany him. When she did, he realized how much he would have preferred that she hadn't. Hearing her laugh, he opened his eyes and glanced down the table. It was one of her less attractive qualities, an incongruous little-girl titter ending in a snort. She had learned to control the snort but it still sneaked out if her guard was down, like now, when she had had too much to drink. He had quietly chided her when she had poured out a generous martini before dinner.

"It's the only way I can endure your tedious family," she had said.

"Why on earth did you come then?"

She had shrugged, and when he turned away he had realized that Theo, who had been setting the dining table at the end of the large room, might have heard their exchange. Which may account for the tiny frown that drew Theo's brows together as Caro gushed and preened across the table from him.

Ben sighed. She obviously didn't have a problem with this member of his family, but then women tended to go all goofy and giggly over Theo. He hadn't appreciated how striking his brother's looks were until Theo had entered middle school two years after Ben. Many at the all-boys institution had worn their hair long and in his tween years, before his features had hardened into those of a man, Theo's androgynous, sylph-like beauty had created a stir. Quite the little diva, he had been. Dora, the older boys had called him, playing on his name. No confusing his gender now. And darned if he didn't look even better for the small lines that were beginning to form around his mouth and eyes.

"I hope he doesn't end up being defined by his looks," Ris had said of her younger son. Theo no doubt traded on them when it came to women—what man wouldn't? But beyond that he never seemed to bother with his appearance: un-styled shoulder-length hair, a plain gray pullover, faded jeans, worn boots. Ben smoothed down the front of his fine-knit Italian sweater; he could never get away with dressing like that. Or with wearing a necklace, he thought, eying the jade ouroboros medallion suspended by a black cord at the base of Theo's throat. But then it could be a kind of reverse chic, like when musicians showed up at award shows looking like they'd just fallen out of bed. Theo's way of saying, *See, I don't have to bother.*

Caro laughed again. Theo's forehead smoothed out and his mouth settled into a polite smile. Ben shook his head. *Forget it, lady. You are so not his type.* Although he couldn't say what that was, exactly; all he knew about his brother's love life was his reputation.

"Check," said Niels, sitting on Ben's right.

He had missed the boy these last few months. Living near Fin's house, he had spent a lot of time with Niels, particularly in the last year of Alex's life. When Ben had returned from London to find Leah gone and Niels with Fin and Alex he had offered to adopt the baby if they didn't want the responsibility of raising him. They declined, unsurprisingly, but it had still caused his and Caro's first big argument. In her absence, and not yet used to thinking in terms of *we*, he had made the proposal without consulting her.

Fox, seated opposite, groaned. Next to him, Theo turned his attention, gratefully perhaps, to the screen of the tablet his son held, considered a moment and pointed out a move.

"Thanks for waiting," Leah said, entering the room.

Another reason Ben had come to Taos was to see Leah. He still bore a sense of responsibility for her disappearance all those years ago—if he hadn't delayed his return from London to marry Caro he would have been there to help when Niels was born, and Leah would not have left. She had been at work when he and Caro had arrived earlier in the day. His eyebrows rose when she sat down across from him. The quirky-looking duckling he remembered had turned into a swan.

"Hello, Button," he said, grinning hugely.

Leah leaned forward and smiled back. "Hello, Bear."

"Craig? But he's been running the Lighthouse almost since it started!" said Ben.

"That's what makes this so sad. Your father is *so* upset. You know he sees the staff almost as family," Ris said.

They were in her office reviewing the results of the audit that had been done to investigate unexplained losses at the Lighthouse.

"But why did he do it?"

"His wife has cancer—we knew that—and he's used the money, so he says, to finance treatments, some of them non-traditional. That's what got Lucas. He asked Craig why he hadn't told us he needed the money rather than taking it. We would have been more than happy to help."

"How much did he take in all?"

"Over six hundred thousand dollars."

"How did he do it?"

Ris sighed. "It gets worse. Craig's been having an affair with Jenny in accounting. She was in on it with him, made up the fake purchase orders, cut the checks. No doubt for some piece of the proceeds. It's sordid and pathetic at the same time. When we confronted Craig with the findings he just sort of disintegrated and blubbered it all out."

"So what now? Are you and Dad going to press charges?"

"No. Craig and Jenny have both been summarily dismissed but Lucas doesn't want to go any further."

"That's nuts!"

"Well, you know your father. He says we can afford it and Craig has enough troubles as it is. He also proposes we cover the rest of Craig's wife's hospital bills—she is, I think, very near the end. But no references or anything more beyond that."

They discussed the financial and legal dimensions of the embezzlement for a while longer.

"You'll need to bolster the financial controls—the place has been run pretty loosely to this point," Ben said.

"Yes. The auditors have made some specific recommendations in that regard."

"And you should also strengthen the board. The expertise on it is more weighted to the programs and services side of the resort. We could use a banker or accountant on it."

Ris nodded in agreement. "And, of course, we also need to get a new CEO. Jonas, the head of operations, is acting, but it's a stretch for him. It'll take a few months at least to find someone capable who fits, and who we can trust. This couldn't come at a worse time as Craig had just started organizing the renovation and expansion. We've already stopped taking bookings after the New Year." She paused. "You wouldn't happen to know someone who might fit the bill; someone from among your clients' companies perhaps?"

"Not offhand but let me think about it." Ben glanced at his watch. "I guess we should get ready to leave. Trevor wants to fly out at three."

On returning to Vancouver, Ben forgot about the matter of finding a new CEO for the Lighthouse. He remembered, guiltily, only after he accidently pulled the file of material his mother had given him from his briefcase while looking for another. He thought it unlikely anyone suitable would be found in Vancouver but blocked off fifteen minutes in his schedule for the next day to make a few phone calls.

That night he slept fitfully. Something seemed to be nibbling on the edge of his consciousness, trying to get his attention. Around five in the next morning he sat bolt upright, prompting a grumble and an indignant tug of the covers from Caro.

"Sorry," he whispered and slipped out of bed. He went down to the kitchen, made himself a coffee and sat watching the dawn break. When his cup was empty he picked up his phone and dialed his parents' number.

"Sorry for the early call," he said when his mother answered.

"Not at all. Lucas and I are having breakfast."

"About this business with Craig and finding someone to take over…"

"Oh, yes? Have you thought of someone?"

"Sort of." He cleared his throat. "How about me, Mom? I could do it. At least until you find someone else."

He struggled to work through his distraction that day. When his mother had asked how he planned to deal with his practice he had responded confidently that he'd figure something out. By the day's end he had a plan. He knocked on his partner Jay's door.

"You got a minute?" he said.

Jay listened with his usual calm attention while Ben summarized the problem his parents were facing. "They're in a tight spot and I'd really like to give them a hand getting the resort's operations and finances back to normal, and moving the renovations and expansion forward," he said in conclusion.

"How do you see it working?" Jay said.

"I thought we'd keep Chris on after he's done his articles—he's mature and competent—and we can get another graduate to fill in behind him. It's so easy to keep in touch now, I could deal with him and any issues online or by phone, and I'd come back once or twice a month. Mom said the plane would be at my disposal."

It was after he left the office, buoyant and confident at Jay's support, that he realized he hadn't discussed the matter with Caro. On the way home he picked up some of her favorite foods and wine.

"Oh, sorry, I've already had dinner," Caro said when she arrived home. "Jim and I needed to do a final review of the strategy for the trial tomorrow."

"How about some wine? There's something I need to discuss with you."

Ben poured out a couple of glasses and they went to the living room. He tried to remember the last time they had sat together there.

"What's up?" Caro said.

He outlined the situation and his plan to take over running the Lighthouse.

"What about your practice? Can you leave it for that long a time?"

Ben slowly released his breath. He had been holding it in anticipation of an outburst over his not having consulted her prior to making the decision. He explained the proposed arrangements to cover for him while he was gone.

"I've got a month or so to set things up."

"So you'll be living there, then?"

"I'll come and go a bit—Mom and Dad are giving me full use of their plane—but yes, I'll be based in Taos for whatever time it takes to find someone else. Several months, I expect." He intended to stay until the completion of the renovations and construction the following year but didn't say so.

Caro nodded. "Okay."

"You wouldn't mind?"

"Not if it's what you want."

They left it there. He was relieved that she hadn't made a fuss, but he couldn't help wishing she had expressed some reservations or regret. That night she allowed him to make love to her with something approaching enthusiasm and he wondered momentarily if going off to New Mexico was the right thing to do given the uncertain state of their marriage. *A break could be just what we need*, he thought as he was drifting off to sleep. *Get perspective on things, help us start over.*

Chapter 14

"How're you doing?" Theo said.

Fox glanced up at him, his face tight with anxiety. The elevator dinged to signal their arrival. They exited into a plush cream and gold hallway lit by discrete wall sconces.

"We want number 3204. It's the one at the end," Theo said, turning right. At the door, he squeezed Fox's hand and rang the bell.

A man with broad shoulders and sun-bleached hair opened the door and studied them for a moment. "Better come in," he said in a marked Australian accent.

Fiona rushed forward in a flurry of color. "Forrest! Darling!" She dropped to her knees and wrapped herself around her son.

"Let's move on in," the man said, waving them forward.

Fiona rose and drew Fox into a bright open room. Her husband closed the door and thrust his hand at Theo. "Matt," he said.

Theo introduced himself, shook Matt's hand and followed him down to the sitting area.

"Will my mom come back like Leah did?" Fox had asked that morning on the flight to Miami.

Theo had shuddered at the thought. "I don't think so. She's married now and Australia is her home."

"Beer?" Matt said.

"Sure, why not?"

Theo sat down on the sofa: an ultra-modern biscuit-colored leather affair. Through a wall of windows he could see Biscayne Bay where watercraft of various kinds dotted the water. The door to a shallow balcony was open and the hot, humid outside air sparred with the air conditioning.

Fiona led Fox to a low table piled with parcels wrapped in colorful paper. She wore lime-green leggings and a silky print top with a parrot pattern that floated around her as she flitted about the room. *Still gorgeous*, Theo thought.

He had fallen hard for Fiona all those years ago. They had met the fall he returned to San Francisco after years of traveling to finish his last year at art school. She was studying journalism at Berkeley. She had burned bright and hot, and he had been swept away by her beauty and by the reckless way she had seemed to devour experience. Her auburn hair had been waist-long then, now it was short and fashionably tousled. She was tanned as well; inevitable, he figured, living under the Australian sun. He remembered her natural skin, pearly and translucent, and how he used to track the tracery of her veins with his finger. Even after all this time, and despite what had happened, she still gave him a buzz.

She caught his glance and came over to him. "Theo! But I never said hello!" She leaned over and pecked his cheek. "It was lovely of you to bring Forrest here." She stepped back and batted at him playfully. "Why do you live so far away from anywhere? We have only the four days and it was just impossible to find any reasonable flights to come see you."

You fly halfway around the world to attend the wedding of some friend but can't add another day or two to see your son? he thought, but said nothing. No point in spoiling the visit.

Fiona fluttered back to where Fox was unwrapping the gifts. Matt brought Theo the beer and sat down in an armchair next to the sofa. It was a thick amber ale, heavy in the heat. Theo took a sip and set the bottle down on a glass coffee table.

"Did you have a good flight?" he said.

"Yeah, was all right."

"Pretty long haul."

"Nah, not so bad. Stopped in Cape Town. Business."

"Oh! But it's too small!" Fiona said, holding up a sweater against Fox's chest.

In the eight years since Fiona had left Fox with Ris at the ranch she had only seen her son twice, the last time when he was six. The sweater was about the size that would have fit him then.

"They have a habit of growing," Theo said.

A fuzzy white teddy bear and a green plastic sand pail and shovel that Fox unwrapped were also suited to a younger child. A large red dump truck inspired more interest, but the big hit was a bright yellow boomerang.

"Look at this, Dad," Fox said, waving the boomerang in the air.

Matt put down his bottle and rose. "Show you how to throw it."

"Not in here!" Fiona said.

"No worries. Just the moves."

While Matt was demonstrating how to handle the boomerang, Fiona came and sat down beside Theo.

"How are you doing?" he said.

"I'm okay." She gave him a tight smile. "Still need meds, of course."

A couple of months after moving in with Fiona, Theo had realized that the distraction of living together was affecting their studies and they both risked failing their courses. When he moved back to his own place she responded by overdosing on sleeping pills. The doctors treating her had diagnosed bipolar disorder.

"Otherwise?"

"Fine. I've got a great job at an all-news network." She glanced at her husband. "And Matt's really good to me. And for me." She turned back to Theo. "Forrest seems well?"

"Yes. You shouldn't have gotten him so many presents, though."

"They're for all the Christmases and birthdays I missed."

"A card or a letter at the time would do."

Fiona dropped her eyes and smoothed out the wrinkles in her top. "I do try to remember."

"Do your mom and dad know about him yet?"

He had met her parents once: no-nonsense Presbyterians from a small town in the Australian outback, twitchy at the decadence of San Francisco—the scantily clad women, hand-holding men, wanton consumption. On her first visit to see Fox when he was three he had asked her if they might want to see him sometime as well.

"They don't know about him," she had said.

"They don't? Why the hell not?"

"I can't tell them. They wouldn't understand. They expected better of me."

Now she shifted away. "No."

Theo shook his head. "Do you think it's fair to them? To him?"

Her eyes hardened. "This is my concern; mine alone. You'll not say or do anything, you understand?"

He shrugged. "Whatever."

The doorbell pealed and Fiona leapt up. "Ah, the goodies."

A server wheeled in a cart and set trays, plates, cutlery and glasses on a round table at the end of the room.

"Matt love, the food's here," Fiona said.

He finished the boomerang demonstration with some final words and led Fox to the table. They all sat down before an array of finger food and tiny cakes. Fiona cracked a can of cola open and poured it into a glass. "Here," she said, setting it in front of Fox. He glanced at Theo—sugary soft drinks were forbidden.

'It's okay this time," Theo said.

"Can't drink that piss," Matt said, rising.

"Language, Matt love," Fiona said.

"Yeah, sorry." Matt looked at Theo. "Beer?"

"No, I'm good, thanks."

Matt headed to the small bar. On the way, his cellphone rang. He fished it out of his hip pocket and listened for a few moments. Turning to them, he said, "Business," and disappeared through a door beside the bar.

Fiona smiled brightly at Fox. "Go ahead, take whatever you like."

He ate carefully while she peppered him with questions, swallowing his food and wiping his mouth each time before replying.

"Nice manners," Fiona said, glancing at Theo.

"I try."

Fox was talking about his new scooter when a cellphone resting beside Fiona's plate rang. She glanced at its screen. "Sorry, darling. I have to take this." She rose and walked to the window. After listening for several minutes, she said, "This evening?" The voice at the other end of the call buzzed like an insect. "But it's not entirely convenient." The voice buzzed some more. "I see." She glanced at Fox. "Yes, all right."

She ended the call and came back to where they were sitting. "Forrest darling, I'm afraid I have to go somewhere right away."

"Seriously?" Theo said.

Fiona bit her lip. "It's important. I'm sorry."

"I guess it's time to go, Fox," Theo said, rising.

Fox set the cake he was eating back on the platter, wiped his fingers and got off his chair. Fiona pulled him into a hug.

"It was so nice to see you." Releasing him, she turned to Theo. "Thanks, again."

He touched Fox's shoulder. "Why don't you wait for me at the door?"

Fox glanced at him, then at Fiona, and left.

"We came all this way," Theo said.

Fiona ran her fingers under his lapel and gave him an uncertain smile. "It's work, darling. There's a development in one of the stories the station's following in Washington and I have to interview someone there."

He pushed her hand away. "I'm not sure we're ever going to do this again, Fiona."

"Yes, well." They stood in silence for a moment. "I really must go," she said and drifted off in the direction of what Theo assumed was the bedroom. He joined Fox at the door.

"What do we do with the presents?" Fox said.

"Take what you like."

Fox ran down, grabbed the boomerang and came back.

"Let's go home," Theo said.

As they descended in the elevator, Theo thought about Fiona. Her bipolar diagnosis after the overdose had made sense: some days it had been all she could do to get out of bed, then she'd pull a string of all-nighters catching up on her schoolwork. Feeling responsible, he had moved back to her place but the suicide attempt had jolted him out of his infatuation with her. As time passed he had felt increasingly trapped but did nothing, afraid of how she would react if he left. A few months later he was nursing a beer in a quiet corner at an end-of-term party for Fiona's class when he heard a couple of women snickering nearby about Fiona's dress, a full-length robe with voluminous sleeves.

"Hail the druid," said one.

"Yeah, always the drama queen. You know, I was

stunned—stunned!—to hear she completed the program. Like, did she ever get anything in on time? She was hanging on by her teeth."

A laugh. "Well, I'm not surprised."

"Yeah? Why?"

"I figure she's been getting it off with the department head."

"*What?*"

"I saw them in the stairwell once. He was all over her."

The next day Theo packed up his belongings while Fiona slept off a hangover. When she was finally up and drinking a coffee he sat down at the table across from her.

"So, sleeping with your professor, Fiona?" he said. "I didn't think that happened anymore. Aren't there rules against it?"

Her eyes flew open and she stammered a denial.

"You don't lie well," he said.

She stared at him, hot spots of color blooming in her cheeks. "It cost my parents a great deal to send me here. I could not fail."

He nodded in apparent understanding and rose from the table. "Take care of yourself," he said and walked out of her life.

There were times in the early days caring for Fox when Theo wondered whether he was in fact the baby's father. As Fox grew, he thought he saw some family resemblance: Lucas's brow, Ris's shapely head, his own narrow palms and slender fingers. The elevator doors slid open on the ground floor. Theo put his hand on Fox's shoulder and guided him through. No matter how the boy came to be, he was his son now.

On the return flight, Theo took control of the family jet to help accumulate the flying hours he needed to maintain his license. They had just reached altitude when the yellow boomerang spun past his ear and clattered against the cockpit windows.

"You'd better get back there," Trevor said, taking over.

Theo removed his earphones, unbuckled his seatbelt and squeezed out of his chair. He picked up the boomerang and went back to where Fox was sitting. "Listen, Fox, you can't play with that in here. You could damage something, even cause an accident."

Fox scowled at him. "I don't care."

"You threw it in there on purpose, huh? Are you upset about visiting your mom?"

Fox folded his arms and turned his face away. Theo sat down in the seat next to him and tried to put his arm around the boy's shoulders. "You want to talk about it?"

Fox squirmed out of his hug. "No!"

Theo dropped his arm. "Okay." He glanced at the cockpit, sighed, and buckled his seatbelt. It was going to be a long flight.

Chapter 15

Leah dropped the bag of her belongings in the trailer's bedroom and returned to the small open space with its built-in banquette table, playhouse kitchen and tiny sitting area. Her eyes glowed. She turned to Theo who was unpacking a box of kitchenware.

"It looks and smells almost new. Vince did a terrific job, much better than I could have," she said.

He placed the last of the dishes in the cupboard. "Yeah, maybe, but it's still awfully small."

"There's plenty of room," she said. She flung out her arms for emphasis and hit his shoulder. "Oh, sorry!"

"See what I mean? Not even enough room to swing a cat."

"It's perfectly adequate for me."

A knock sounded on the door. Theo reached out and opened it. Chester and Andy stood below the narrow steps, the stable hands lined up behind them.

"Just wanted to say welcome," Chester said.

Andy thrusted a bouquet of daffodils at Leah. "Here."

She descended the steps and accepted them with thanks, ignoring the wisps of straw that clung to the cellophane wrapping. The hands pulled off their hats and stepped forward in turn to shake her hand.

"Do you ride?" a youth with curly black hair and dancing blue eyes said.

"No. I'm afraid I never learned."

"I could teach you," he said, flashing a toothy grin.

Leah laughed. "We'll see. You never know."

The youth winked, slapped on his hat and stepped back.

"You behave, now," Theo said, shaking his finger.

During the introductions, Linc and Jammer had nosed their way to the front. "Oh, wait!" Leah said. "I have some treats."

She went back into the trailer, set the flowers down in the small sink and dug some dog biscuits out of a box. Returning outside, she held one out to each of them.

"Sit!" Chester said.

Both dogs promptly dropped their bottoms to the ground. Jammer snatched the offered treat and ran off to eat it. Linc lipped his gently from her hand and stayed.

"You sure are a big boy," Leah said and gave him another.

"That's enough; don't want to spoil them," Chester said. He motioned to the wolfhound. "Come on, dog. Let's go."

Linc gave him a languid glance then turned to Leah and slid into a down position. The stable folk left, Chester grumbling about useless dogs, the others laughing. Leah squatted down and scratched the wolfhound behind the ears. He grunted and twisted his head so she could reach under his chin.

"Looks like you've made a friend," Theo said.

"A few, I think," she said, rising.

"Don't worry, they won't bother you."

She dusted her hands. "I'm not worried. It will be nice having someone nearby. And being this close to Las Sombras I can come and help with meals every day now. If that's all right."

"Of course it's all right! The boys will be happy. Niels anyway, Fox is in a real state."

"What's up?"

Theo put his hands on his hips and gazed unseeing into the

distance for a moment. "It's the visit with his mom," he finally said. "It was only the third time he's ever seen her and then it was only like an hour or so. I don't blame him for being upset, but it's a couple of days now and he won't snap out of it."

"Can I help?"

"I dunno. Maybe. *I* can't seem to calm him. He's cranky as hell, fights with Niels over nothing and then they both start crying." He shook his head. "Good thing Fin's gone away; they were getting on his nerves."

"Shall I come and stay while Dad's gone?"

He shook his head. "No, I'd better be there. But it might help if you came for dinner."

That night, Fox snarled at Leah when she tried to talk to him. When Theo reprimanded him he ran off to his room in tears.

"Christ!" Theo said. "I don't know what the hell to do."

"Maybe he needs to see a counselor?" Leah said.

"Yeah, maybe," he said, but he was afraid of what a professional would say: that Fox was emotionally unstable like his mother.

At breakfast the next morning, everyone tiptoed around the boy, careful not to disrupt preparations for school. Dinner that evening started the same way. Uncertain of Fox's mood, the others hesitated to speak. As the silence lengthened, Leah glanced around the table.

"Tell me, Niels: today, what do you take from it?" she said.

Niels paused in the act of shoving a loaded fork into his mouth. "What do you mean?"

"Think of something that happened today, something you saw or heard or did that was noteworthy, something to remember."

"I'm not sure I want to remember today. Jeremy fell and got

hurt. One minute he was on the bars and then he was on the ground and there was blood everywhere."

"Maybe what you can take from that is how quickly things can change," Leah said. She turned to Fox. "How about you?"

"Mrs. Stoddart farted during class and everybody laughed."

"That wasn't very nice," Theo said.

"I know, but someone started and then everybody did. We couldn't help it."

"So what do you take from that?" Leah said.

"Well, I didn't think old people farted, especially ladies."

"Everyone does, no matter what their age, and fourteen times a day on average," Leah said. "It's completely natural."

"Fourteen times! Oh, no," Fox said, covering his eyes in mock disgust.

"Where did they get this information? Who counts their farts?" said Niels.

They laughed through the rest of the meal and the boys left the table trading fart jokes.

"Thanks for that," Theo said to Leah as they cleaned up.

"For what?"

"Getting Fox to laugh. I think he's finally getting back to normal."

Having Niels and Fox reflect on what they had taken from the day became a regular feature of their dinners. The boys started a game of their own, making Leah spell and explain the big words she often used: *quixotic, penultimate, concomitant, vilify*. They'd then make up sentences using the words, each more outrageous than the last. When Fin returned he raised a quizzical eyebrow at the exchanges.

"The business about taking something from the day, where did that come from?" he said.

Niels gave Leah a bashful glance. "It was my, ah, mom who started it."

The Lighthouse

She smiled encouragingly at him. Their interactions were still awkward. She hoped that for Niels it was lack of practice rather than some deeper difficulty in accepting her. He would study her surreptitiously from time to time, blushing and turning away when caught out. Although she was invariably warm and friendly towards him she kept her distance. She would leave it to her son to define the terms of their relationship.

Fin turned to her. "An interesting concept. Did you read about it somewhere?"

"No, I, ah…" She too was still uncomfortable speaking to her parent despite the new spirit of détente between them. "In the beginning, after I had left, it was sometimes the only way I could derive meaning from my life, stay tethered to it, you know…" She flushed—too much, too revealing, too soon.

Something like sympathy flashed through Fin's eyes. Leah looked away.

"What does tethered mean?" Fox said.

Chapter 16

"You're going to Vancouver?" Leah said at dinner one evening.

"Yeah," Theo said. "Trevor's flying someone out to Alaska and I'm hitching a ride to deliver some pieces to a gallery there that carries my stuff. On his way back he'll night over in Vancouver and take me down to California the next morning before returning home."

"Is there any chance I could go as well? To Vancouver and back, I mean. Not California." She glanced at Fin. "If you don't mind taking care of the boys for a couple of days, of course."

"What's happening in Vancouver?" Fin said.

"Oh, nothing really," Leah said. "It's been so long I thought it would be nice just to see it again. And maybe visit Ben."

Fin shrugged. "Fine with me. Do you want to stay at the house?"

"More convenient if you stay with me at Mom and Dad's place, Leah," Theo said. "Just let me call Trevor to confirm there's a seat on the plane."

They flew out early the following Tuesday, landed in Vancouver mid-morning and went directly to Theo's parents' penthouse in the West End to drop off their luggage. On arriving, Leah left her backpack in the bedroom Theo had indicated for her use and wandered around the space. Her grandparents had lived in it before their deaths and, although it had been redecorated since, the open space and expansive view of English Bay was the same.

"I expect to turn and see Granddad in his chair," she said to Theo with a choked laugh.

They parted on the sidewalk in front of the building, agreeing to meet back at the apartment in the late afternoon before joining Ben and Caro for dinner. Theo had several wrapped canvases to deliver to the gallery and hailed a cab. Leah declined his offer of a ride, saying she wanted to stretch her legs. When his cab was out of sight she set off in the direction of the downtown core. She arrived at the office tower that was her destination, wavering in her purpose. She sat down on the edge of a planter to rest and revisit the logic behind the meeting she was about to have, filled with both anticipation and dread of its outcome. After a few minutes she rose, squared her shoulders and entered the building.

The office she wanted, the human resources department for the utility company that occupied half of the building, was on the fourth floor. Entering, she asked the receptionist for Rebecca Grisham. "She's expecting me," she added.

Rebecca Grisham arrived in the reception area a few minutes later wearing a professionally courteous smile. A stylish haircut and careful makeup flattered her plain features and a tailored navy suit gave her an air of authority. When Leah rose to greet her she stopped, momentarily perplexed, and slowly lowered the hand she had extended. Her face darkened.

"What are *you* doing here?"

"You wouldn't speak to me on the phone so I've come to see you," Leah said.

"Even if I wanted to see you—which I don't—I can't; I'm meeting someone else."

"That person, Linda Smith, is me."

Rebecca leaned towards Leah. "There is no way I'm going to meet with you. You need to leave, right now," she said between her teeth.

"What *you* need to do is find us a private place to talk," Leah said quietly.

Rebecca started to turn. "If you don't go, I'll call security."

"And tell them what? I'm being perfectly civil while you're throwing a hissy fit." Leah gestured to the woman at the reception who was eyeing them curiously. "As your receptionist will verify if asked."

Rebecca scowled at the woman, who turned purposefully to her computer. "Okay, but I'll only give you five minutes. There's a meeting room down the hall." She turned and strode away, Leah following.

In the meeting room they sat down on opposite sides of the table and regarded each other in silence. After several moments, Rebecca began to chew the cuticle of her thumb. An old habit, Leah remembered, her nails constantly gnawed raw.

"We only knew each other for a few weeks that summer, Rebecca," she said. "Still, I was a bit hurt when you didn't respond to my texts or emails after we went back to school."

Rebecca shrugged.

"I've finally figured out why." Leah paused. "Did you know that I had a child the following spring?"

Rebecca caught her breath. Her fingers began to tremble and she knotted them together. "No, I didn't," she said, speaking to her hands.

"I did, and for the longest time I couldn't figure out who the father was. Until very recently, in fact. I believe now that it was your brother Brad."

Rebecca exhaled sharply. "Yeah, well, that's just too bad. He's gone now."

"Yes, I know. I spoke to your mother."

Rebecca leaned over the table, her eyes flashing. "You leave my parents alone! It's three years since the accident and they're still struggling with Brad's death." She slumped back in her chair. "They wouldn't know anything, anyway."

"Know anything about what?"

Rebecca's face flushed a violent red. She looked off to the side, breathing heavily.

Leah studied her for a moment. "You know, with Brad gone your parents may welcome the news of a grandson."

Rebecca glanced at her and smiled unpleasantly. "If it *is* their grandson. There were three of them, you know."

Leah drew back in her chair. "What do you mean? Three of whom?"

Rebecca sniffed and picked at the torn skin around her thumb.

"I think…" Leah's throat tightened and she swallowed hard to clear it. "You need to tell me what happened."

"No, I don't."

Leah gripped the arms of her chair. "Rebecca, if you have any kind of decency you'll tell me. I swear, I won't leave here until you do."

Rebecca glanced at Leah from under her brows. "It wasn't my fault."

"*Rebecca!*"

Rebecca considered for a minute, then shrugged. "It's not like you can do anything about it now." She shifted in her chair. "That long weekend before school started—both our parents were away so you stayed at my place, remember? Brad and a couple of his friends came over. We sort of partied with them. I was surprised because Brad usually didn't give me the time of day. But it was you, of course, they were interested in." Her voice turned bitter at the remembered slight. "They made us rum and Coke and put something in your drink." She held up her hand. "I found that out later. You were a real goody-goody at first but eventually you drank it.

"Anyway, at one point Brad told me to leave. I asked him why and he said to never mind. I kind of realized they were up to no good, but honestly I really didn't have a clue about exactly what was going on. I mean, I just didn't know much about that kind of stuff yet. And by that time I was a bit drunk." She stopped and blinked rapidly. "Later, Brad told me to, ah, clean you up and take you home. You were totally stoned; I had a heck of a time getting you in and out of the bathtub and then into your clothes."

To this point, Leah had listened to her with a certain detachment, as though she was observing them both from a distance. Now a coldness crept into her face and she began to tremble. "What did they put in my drink?" she said.

Rebecca shrugged. "I don't know, some kind of pill."

"Rohypnol, probably."

"Yeah, maybe."

"I remember nothing of this. How much did I take?"

Rebecca squirmed. "Besides what they put in your drink, Brad made you take another one after, and then he gave me a couple more to give you when I took you home."

"And you just left me like that?" Leah said, her voice shaking.

Rebecca made a helpless gesture. "Look, I feel bad about the whole thing but there wasn't anything I could do. You didn't know Brad; my brother was a class-A jerk, a big bully. He'd hurt me when I didn't do what he wanted: twist my arm, pinch my face, yank my hair." She shook her head. "I can't say I'm sorry he's dead. But my parents didn't know any of that. To them he was the perfect son."

She glanced at her watch. "I've really got to go now."

Leah leaned forward and grabbed her arm. "Wait. You can't just leave me like this. Not now. I need to know who the other two were."

Rebecca pulled back. "Oh, no, no, no. I'm not going there."

The Lighthouse

"Why? You said Brad may not have been my son's father. So, tell me who the other guys were."

Rebecca shook her head. "What would you do then, go to the police? Good luck. It's what, ten years ago? Apart from your kid, you've no proof that anything happened and if you do try to do something I'll swear you're making it up. After all this time, no one will listen to you. And don't you dare bother my parents, it would kill them. They'd never believe Brad would do such a thing anyway. Just drop it and get on with your life."

She rose. Stricken, Leah didn't move. Voices could be heard approaching down the hall.

"You've really got to leave now, Leah. I think someone else needs this room." She went to where Leah was sitting, pulled her up and led her out of the room to the reception area. At the door, Rebecca pushed her out and said softly, "I don't know what you thought you'd gain from doing this. You'd have been better off leaving well enough alone."

Leah stumbled down the hall looking for a washroom, her stomach in revolt. Inside, she slammed into a stall, dropped to her knees and vomited violently into the toilet bowl. Someone entered as she was retching, hesitated, and beat a retreat. Spent, she sat down on the seat and began to shake uncontrollably. *It's shock.* She hugged herself. *You're in shock.* She rose and felt her way to a sink. After rinsing her mouth she held her hands under scalding water until the shaking stopped. Leaning forward, she stared into the mirror. Black eyes in a bloodless face stared back.

"Niels must never, ever know," the face said.

Chapter 17

The penthouse was dark and quiet when Theo returned that evening. Checking his watch, he realized that he had only enough time to freshen up before heading out to dinner. He wasn't looking forward to the outing. Ben had chosen the restaurant: a new, hip offering by a celebrity chef. The meal would probably be a bunch of overwrought pretension and was certain to put an unwelcome dent in his wallet. Besides which he wasn't sure he could endure an evening of his sister-in-law's acerbic asides and knowing glances, and the Bear and Button routine between Ben and Leah. However close they may have been in the past, the names were ridiculous now.

Leah's shoes were in the entrance but she was nowhere around. He knocked on the door of her room and entered when he thought he heard a reply. The room was unlit and the window blinds had been closed against the evening light. He could just make out a shape on the bed.

"Hey Leah, we should probably get going soon. Ben booked a table for seven and it's about a twenty-minute walk from here."

"I can't go," Leah said, her voice muffled.

He moved to the bed, touched her shoulder. "What's wrong?"

She pulled away. "I don't feel well."

"Sorry to hear that. Ah, listen, there's a pharmacy not far from here. Do you need anything?"

"No. Thanks."

"Well, okay then." He hesitated a moment then left the room, closing the door behind him. With some relief he scrolled through his contact list to find Ben's number to let him know dinner was off—he sure as hell wasn't going alone. It wasn't there. Not surprising, he thought, they didn't ever call each other, did they? He searched the Internet for Ben's company's contact information and dialed the number.

"Oh, Theo, good," Ben said. "I've been trying to reach Leah but she isn't answering her phone."

"Yeah, she's not feeling well. That's why I'm calling—we're not going to be able to make dinner tonight."

"Just as well. Something's come up and I can't either."

When they hung up, Theo stood in the hall, uncertain what to do with his unexpectedly free evening. It was too late to call any of the few friends he had in the city, except maybe…

He thumbed through the contacts list on his phone again and found her name: Stacey. He occasionally hooked up with her when he came to town and thought she might not mind a last-minute invitation. As he keyed in her number he glanced in the direction of Leah's room. *Maybe not.* He shut off his phone and headed to a pub in the neighborhood instead.

The main room was crowded and loud so he sat down at the bar and ordered a beer and a burger. When he had finished both, the bartender removed his empty plate and glass and brought him another beer. A hockey game was playing on the flat-screen television attached to the far wall. He wasn't a fan, but as he drank his beer his eyes kept getting drawn to the small figures whizzing back and forth across the screen. Two women sat at the bar under the television and as he looked towards it their glances occasionally crossed. After the third time, the women came around to him, one sliding onto the adjacent stool, the other leaning against the counter.

"Hello," they said in unison. They were attractive in a forgettable way. Both had long, smooth hair, one dark, one a dirty blonde. The blonde wore a form-fitting black sweater with an artfully arranged leopard-print scarf, the brunette a white shirt blouse opened to the third button and a necklace made of large gold links. Their makeup followed the same template, down to the smudge of dark eye shadow at the outer corner of their lids and slash of sparkly blusher high on their cheekbones. They accepted Theo's offer of a glass of wine and chatted with him—the usual stuff: where are you from, what do you do. Theo finished his beer and signaled for the bill. The two women exchanged glances.

"Since you're all alone in town tonight, you wouldn't, um, want to make an evening of it, would you?" the blonde said.

He paused in the act of drawing a couple of bills out of his wallet. "An evening?" he said.

They looked at each other and giggled. "You know," the brunette said.

He dropped the money on the little tray that held his bill and pushed it toward the bartender. The man's eyes flicked to the two women and he glanced back at Theo with raised eyebrows and a smile before palming the tray.

"So, you're working girls?" Theo said.

The women's eyes widened comically and they shook their heads.

"But this isn't the first time you've done this," he said.

"Does it matter?" the blonde said.

"No, I guess not."

Theo studied them for a moment with a slight smile. He had done a threesome once, years ago. The first couple of hours had been fun but afterward he had been desperate to sleep and the women wouldn't let him. *Would I even have the energy now?*

Apart from that there was something else, a sense that something wasn't quite right with these two. He envisioned stolen wallets, runaway credit card charges, drained bank accounts.

"I don't think so, ladies," he said, rising.

Their lips puckered in disappointment, but by the time he had slung on his jacket they were already scanning the room for another mark.

They were scheduled to leave Vancouver at seven o'clock the next morning. Theo woke at five and wandered, yawning and scratching, to the kitchen to make coffee. Leah was already awake, curled up on the sofa watching dawn wash over the bay. Her face was drawn and her eyes bruised and hollow.

"Still feeling rough?" he said, handing her a coffee.

She nodded and clutched the cup in her hands as though chilled. On the plane, she fell asleep shortly after they took off, not waking when the jet touched down at a county airport near Palo Alto to let Theo get off.

"Make sure she gets home okay," he said to Trevor and left the plane.

Chapter 18

"Hey, you old son of a bitch," Mick said. His carroty hair stood on end and his sweatpants drooped under a nascent paunch, exposing a whorled belly button. He slapped Theo hard on the back and waved him into the house: a Victorian classic in the Mission district of San Francisco. It was Mick's family home, left to him after his father died and his mother moved to Palm Springs with her second husband. Theo had lived there when they were both students at the Art Institute.

Mick motioned in the direction of the staircase. "You can stay in your old room."

As Theo climbed he caught sight of a pale figure slipping from the bathroom to one of the other bedrooms.

"Oh, yeah, you may run into Sylvie," Mick called after him.

Theo dropped his bag on the bed and glanced at the painting hanging over it—one of his. When he had gifted the piece to his friend, Mick had consigned it to this room. "To keep a bit of you here," he had said. Theo considered the obscure placement for a moment before going back downstairs. Mick was in the kitchen popping open a beer.

"Want one?" Mick said, waving the can. Foam oozed out and ran down his hand. "Shit." He transferred the beer to his other hand and wiped the wet one on his sweats.

"A bit early for me," Theo said.

Mick's face twisted into a sneer. "*A bit early for me.*"

Theo frowned. "Hey, what's up, man? Everything okay?"

Mick waved his hand apologetically. "Sorry. Listen, it's good to see you. Really."

Theo made himself some coffee and they sat down on old rattan armchairs in the glassed-in veranda. He studied his old friend with concern. Stale booze mixed with old sweat wafted off of him and his unshaven face was puffy and gray. "When did you last sleep?" he said.

Mick drew a hand down his face. "I got a couple of hours last night. Been busy."

As if to underline the point, Sylvie slipped into the room. "I go now, *chérie*."

Mick took her hand and kissed the palm. "Remember the party tomorrow."

"*Oui,* I will come."

After she had left, Mick shook his finger at Theo. "She's mine; you can't have her."

Theo held up his hands. "Hey, Mick, I am not in the least bit interested in having her."

While they got caught up on their news, Mick's eyes blinked until it was all he could do to keep them open.

"Why don't you get some sleep?" Theo said. "I need to make a few calls, check my emails."

Mick nodded, rose. "Oh, and Wes said he'd be here in time for dinner."

Wes drove up later that day in a pickup truck advertising his family's estate winery in the Carmel Valley. He hadn't changed much in the twenty-odd years since he had shown Theo the ropes at the boarding school in Oregon: still tall, stocky and bespectacled. Even then his life path was clear: graduation with honors; a degree in viticulture and enology; then work at and eventual responsibility for the family business. They had kept in touch after Wes graduated, and when Theo moved to San Francisco for his art studies he often came to visit from Sacramento where he was studying at UC Davis.

"How're things going?" Theo said.

"Fine, fine," Wes said. "We planted another seven acres on some leased land. More Italian varieties. My Nebbiolo took a double gold at a competition recently."

"Oh, hey, congratulations man! I've really got to get back to your place one of these days."

While at college they had spent many weekends at the vineyard, pitching tents by the large pond, stuffing themselves with Wes's mother's food, knocking back his father's wine. In return, they helped out where they could: suckering, pruning, pulling leaves, picking grapes. Mick had an unexpected genius for mechanics and was usually found fiddling with one of the many and varied pieces of machinery and equipment found there.

"That'd be nice." Wes ducked his head and smiled shyly. "And, ah, Carey's expecting."

Theo beamed at the other man. "That's great, but be prepared: it'll tie you down real good."

"Yeah," Wes said. "I'd often hoped we three would hit the road again sometime; you know, for old time's sake. Not going to happen now."

Wes's father had both credited and blamed Theo and Mick for leading his conservative son astray. In the summer after their third year of study, when Wes had announced that he was heading to France to work a vintage for the internship component of his degree, Theo and Mick had looked at each other and said, "We're coming with you." It started four years of wandering, shifting from one hemisphere to the other to work the harvest in different wine-growing regions. "Let him get all that stuff out of his system so he won't get restless when he comes home for good," Wes's father had said. They earned some of their keep along the way, with the vineyard work and any odd jobs they could find. The rest Theo had financed from his education trust.

"Wow," Theo said, raising his eyebrows.

They were viewing an exhibition of Mick's most recent work, a series called Frozen. It comprised eleven solid ice-cube-like plexiglass blocks encasing life-size terracotta figures in different postures.

"A new direction, huh?" he continued.

Mick's art after graduating had capitalized on his mechanical bent. One, an installation called Clean! Clean! passed willing participants in rubber pods through a corridor of whirling bands of fabric that mimicked a car wash, while another called Suck it! enclosed them in a cylinder where they were prodded by suction cups that popped out randomly.

Mick pushed himself away from the pillar against which he had been leaning. "Not really."

"Right," Theo said, remembering the subsequent series that had gotten his friend into trouble. The pieces had been based on human forms and incorporated sinister and disturbing elements. One—a lifelike female torso recumbent in a mesh cage whose anatomically correct genitals included a feeder at which live rats busily ate—had received especially harsh criticism.

"It must have been quite a job putting these together," Theo said.

"Well, it's what I do," Mick said. "So, what do you think? Do you like them?"

Theo studied the Frozen pieces. All of the figures in the clear blocks were naked except for the odd item of clothing or accessory which complemented their actions or small dramas. A running woman had on track shoes; a slouched, paunchy man wore a necktie and held a briefcase; a frail-looking female peering over her shoulder dragged a small wheeled suitcase. A part of each figure's anatomy extended outside its block. All but two of them were reasonably decorous. Of these, one—a salute to Mick's infamous rat-gnawed torso—was a woman on her back with wide-open bent legs and a hand delicately hiding her sex. Theo thought the woman's face resembled Sylvie's but avoided looking too closely. The other figure was a middle-aged man, eyes closed, arms braced against the inside wall of the block, pelvis trust out. A penis of implausible length projected beyond the plastic.

"You know it's not about *liking*, Mick," he said.

He didn't want to say so, but Mick's work bothered him; not because of its appearance or content but because he knew he could never muster the audacity or the resources—the latter no doubt supplied by Mick's indulgent mother—required to produce works of such magnitude. He thought of his safe landscapes, tossed off with a minimum of thought: as art they weren't in the same league. The new Lighthouse mural would, he hoped, give him the chance to up his game.

"Each is arresting in its own right, and all together they're very impressive." Theo turned to Wes. "What do you think?"

"Umm," Wes said. It was all he ever offered by way of comment on Mick's work.

Mick thrust his hands into his pockets and grimaced. "Yeah, well. The critics' reviews have been quite mixed. Bella Beecham called it pedestrian, and Stillman out-and-out panned it. Called it derivative, of what or who I'm not sure."

"Ah," Theo said. That explained Mick's black mood.

"Not quite the comeback I had hoped for. And not one sale at the opening."

"They're big pieces, and it's only institutions or collectors with deep pockets who have that kind of dough. The gallery will work that crowd, you'll see."

"Maybe." Mick scuffed the toe of his boot against the grainy wood of the gallery's plank floor. "To get noticed here you always gotta come up with something new, something radical,

The Lighthouse

and if it hits the wrong chord..." He shrugged and flashed Theo an indecipherable look. "Sometimes I think I'd like to give it all up to go live in the middle of nowhere and paint pretty pictures. Like you."

Theo drew in a breath to remonstrate but let it go.

Wes stirred. "Listen, it's getting late. Don't we have to pick up a bunch of stuff for tonight?"

Chapter 19

Leah's gorge rose at the sight of the slice of roast beef sweating blood on her plate. She pushed it away slightly and rested her eyes on Niels who was sawing at his own serving with relish. She had worked a few hours that afternoon and arrived at her aunt and uncle's place for Sunday dinner on the heels of Fin and the boys. When she got out of her little car her son ran up to her and, for the first time of his own initiative, took her hand and held it for the few moments it took to walk to the house. The small act of acknowledgement and acceptance amidst the emotional turmoil of the previous week had nearly brought her to her knees.

"Everything okay?" Ris said. Not much escaped her aunt's sharp eyes.

"Just not very hungry," she said. "Late lunch."

The truth was that she hadn't been able to eat much since returning from Vancouver. Nor had she been able to sleep well, the sickening imaginings of her rape amplified in the dark silence of the night. Tonight, after the boys had left the table, she would tell them—her father, uncle and aunt. Theo hadn't yet returned from California. She wished he were there—he had become her fender against the hard edges of family life—but she didn't want to wait another week to speak.

She rose to help clear the table and dish out dessert. The boys gobbled theirs up and asked to be excused.

"Off with you, then," Ris said with a wave of her hand and they left to play with the electric train in the basement.

As they drank their coffee, Fin talked about an invitation to act as a judge in a music competition that he was considering. Leah let the discussion run its course. In the brief silence that followed its conclusion she cleared her throat and spoke.

"There is something I need to tell you."

Three sets of eyes turned to her. Suddenly daunted, she froze.

Lucas studied her closely. "What is it?"

She held his gaze for a moment and, reassured, continued.

"Last week, when I was in Vancouver, I found out how I became pregnant."

She repeated in stark unflinching words what Rebecca had told her. The three faces before her morphed into masks of horror as she spoke but a kind of release came with the words, like the painful lancing of a festering boil.

"And I know it's going to be hard, but after tonight I never want to speak of it again."

"But Leah my dear, we must speak of it," Lucas said. "How will you deal with it otherwise?"

She shook her head. "Please, I'd prefer it this way. It will be easier than having to chew on it over and over again." She rose. "And now, if you don't mind, I think I'll go home."

"Where is everyone?" Theo said. He had just arrived home from San Francisco and, after dropping off his bag, hurried over to his parents' house hoping to catch the end of the Sunday dinner. The dining room was empty and his mother was in the kitchen cleaning up.

"The boys are playing with the train. Lucas and Fin are in the living room. Leah has gone."

He started towards the living room. "I'll just go say hello."

Ris stopped him. "No, wait. They're talking."

His father was seated next to and speaking quietly to Fin who was hunched over, his face buried in his hands. Theo turned back to Ris. Her face was drawn and her eyes distracted.

"What's going on?" he said.

"It's Leah's news. Fin is very upset. We all are, of course, but he is taking it especially hard."

"What news?"

She studied him for a moment. "You don't know? I thought you would know."

He shook his head. "No, what is it? What's wrong?"

"If you don't know, I think it's something Leah should tell you herself."

"Come on, Mom!"

She sighed heavily. "Theo, the best right now would be for you to take the boys home. Go and get them. And don't say anything."

"How can I if I don't know what's going on?"

Ris raised a placatory hand. "Have you eaten?"

He shook his head.

"I'll make up a plate for you." She made a shooing gesture. "Go and get them."

After a raucous reunion he herded the boys to the kitchen and got them dressed to leave. When they had gone out to his Jeep, he turned to his mother. "You need to tell me what this is all about."

Ris shook her head and handed him the package of food. "It's for Leah to tell."

He drove to Las Sombras on automatic pilot, his mind divided between the chattering boys and wondering what was wrong with Leah. Could she be leaving again? Unlikely, she seemed to be settling in so well and that would make Fin angry, not upset as he had seemed. He remembered that she hadn't felt well that last night in Vancouver. He had assumed it was some female thing so hadn't probed. Could she be seriously ill? *I should have phoned, made sure she got home okay, asked how she was.*

While he was getting Niels and Fox ready for bed he heard Fin come in and go to his studio but let him be. After settling the boys for the night and eating the food his mother had given him he drove to Leah's. When he knocked on her door, Linc levered himself to his feet from where he had been sleeping under the trailer and thrust his nose into Theo's hand. He stroked the dog distractedly.

"Who is it?"

"It's me, Leah."

She opened the door and peered out. "You got back all right?"

"Yeah, fine. Listen, Leah, what's going on? Why's everyone upset? Are you okay?"

She stood backlit, one hand on the doorframe. After a moment, she said, "Not tonight Theo; I'm not up to it tonight."

He didn't move, reluctant to let it go.

"Please."

"Okay," he finally said and backed away.

Leah's goodnight was barely audible. Irked and concerned in equal measure, he stared at the closed door for several moments before getting into his Jeep and driving home.

The next morning he woke late, his body still in another time zone. Swearing, he pulled on some sweats, brushed his teeth and headed down to Las Sombras. On the way to the house he passed Fin heading to his car, small suitcase in hand.

"Off somewhere?"

"Yes, Montreal." Fin's shoulders sagged and his face was gray with fatigue. "Have to go."

They nodded goodbyes and Theo continued on in. The

boys had already left for school. Angie was talking at Leah. He cut her off in mid-sentence.

"I need to speak to Leah, Angie. Can you give us a minute?"

Angie shrugged, picked up a cleaning bucket and left the room.

Leah grimaced. "I can't do it now, Theo. I have to go to work."

"Come on, just a few minutes. Tell me what's going on."

She shook out a cardigan and pulled it on, avoiding his eyes. "This evening would be better."

"Fine." He turned, grabbed a cup from the cupboard and poured out some coffee.

"I *will* tell you," she said to his back. "It's just… It's too much to get into now."

He didn't respond and after a moment she left.

His foul mood carried through the morning. After showering and tidying up he tried to work but couldn't focus. The world seemed to be turning one way while he was going the other. Although he welcomed the chance to get away, see new sights and stretch his mind, re-entry into his quotidian life after days of constant company, noise, and stimulation seemed to take longer with each trip. And there was something about this last visit with Mick. A low-toned dissonance had clouded many of their exchanges. They had always horsed around but now Mick seemed to offer a stroke with one hand and a smack with the other. One of many small ways he had put Theo down was by dismissing his work as *decorative* when an old classmate enquired after it at the party. The fact that there was some truth in the comment made it grate even more.

Even Wes had noticed. "Mick's just upset about the reception that new art of his is getting," he said to Theo.

"Yeah, but why does he have to take it out on me?"

"Maybe Mick thinks that in your own quiet way you've done more than he has."

Theo was not convinced; Mick's comments echoed some of his own doubts. Their goodbyes had been offhand and without the usual promises to try to get together more often.

Then there was Ashya, a smoldering brunette he had met at the party and gone home with. Friday night had been fun but when he had returned on Saturday she had seized on the fact he lived on a ranch and it was all *giddy-up* and *ride'em cowboy*. He sighed; he was getting *so* tired of the game.

And finally, Leah. Something was wrong and he had turned his back on her this morning. He shouldn't have.

He threw down his brush and headed to the stables. After catching up with Chester and Andy he saddled up one of the stallions and headed for the scrubby foothills on the ranch that folded up into the conifer forests of the mountains, letting the horse follow its nose. The rocking rhythm, the quiet, the burn of the cool resin-scented air in his nose cleared his head and by the time he returned to meet the boys coming home from school he was almost back to normal.

That night, Leah arrived at Las Sombras with an overnight bag to stay during Fin's absence. Dinner was lively but Leah focused mostly on Niels and Fox, avoiding Theo, it seemed. He figured he deserved it and left her be. As he was getting ready to go home after the boys had gone to bed she suggested that he stay and have a cup of tea.

He smiled, relieved. "Sure, but after the day I've had I could use something stronger."

"Why not?"

He poked around Fin's well-stocked liquor cabinet, took out a twenty-year-old single malt and two glasses, and followed Leah to a small alcove at the far corner of the living room.

"Did you want some water or ice?" he said, handing Leah her drink.

"No, it's okay like this," she said, accepting it.

He sat down and nosed the glass: salt, smoke, leaves, burnt sugar. He took a slug and his eyes watered. "Whoa!" He picked up the bottle and examined the label. *Cask strength* it said. "You sure you don't want something to dilute it?"

Leah tasted her drink. "No, it's fine."

Well, if she can handle it, so can I. He took a second, smaller sip, rolled it on his tongue. They sat savoring the liquor for a few moments then Leah drew in a deep breath. "This is very difficult, Theo."

He nodded encouragement.

"You remember when I first got here—hard to believe it's only three months ago... Anyway, the boys had those really short haircuts?"

"Yeah?"

"They've grown out now."

Theo frowned. *All this fuss about haircuts?*

"So?"

"Have you noticed the way Niels' hair grows in the front? Up straight from his forehead? Like a cowlick?"

"What about it?"

"I knew a guy whose hair grew like that. The resemblance came to me out of the blue, early in the morning a couple of weeks ago. I was in that state between being asleep and awake, and *pop*..." She flicked her fingers to describe the motion. "There it was." She glanced out into the room, confirmed they were alone, then turned back to Theo. "I think he was Niels' father."

"Whoa!" Theo absorbed the information for few moments. "So, who is he?"

"The brother of a girl I used to know."

Theo took another sip of scotch. *An interesting development. But why is everyone so upset?* "So what are you going to do?"

Leah set her glass down on the table. "That's why I went to Vancouver—to see what I could find out."

"Ah. Why didn't you say something?"

Leah looked away. "I wasn't ready to then."

"So what happened?"

"I found out that Brad—that was his name—had died in a boating accident so I tried to contact his sister. She wouldn't take my phone calls so l went to Vancouver to meet her in person."

His mind flashed back to that day. "And you found something out," he said slowly. "That's why you weren't feeling well that evening."

Leah nodded. "It was all pretty upsetting."

She relayed what Rebecca had told her.

"I could have died," she said, shaking her head. "And it worked. I had no idea, no memory at all of what had transpired." She leaned her head against the back of the chair and released a deep sigh. "And for all that, because there were three of them, I still don't know who Niels' father is."

Listening to her, Theo had grown still. At her last words he set his glass down with a clatter on the coffee table. "Three," he said in a strangulated voice. "Again."

Leah lifted her head and gave him a puzzled look. "What?"

He blinked; he hadn't meant to speak aloud. His face felt numb, his breaths came tight and shallow. He buried his face in his hands.

"Theo? Are you okay?"

He felt the heels of their palms grinding into his shoulders; the smell of sweaty, dirty fingers over his nose; the salty, sour taste of the fingers when he bit them. The prickling of his skin from the sudden cold when they yanked down his pants, and then the pain and unspeakable indignity of the rest. It had been a long time, a very long time, since he had thought about it.

He heard Leah move, felt her sit down next to him. "What is it?"

He shook his head.

Her fingers pulled his hands down and she looked at him intently. "Tell me, Theo."

"I, ah…" He swallowed. "It was in middle school. There were three of them as well, seniors. I was only thirteen, still small. I couldn't fight them off."

She drew back. "Oh, Theo!"

He grabbed his glass and drained it, welcoming the burn.

Leah shifted beside him, radiating concern. "What did you do? Did someone help you?"

He rolled the glass between his palms. "I didn't tell anyone. The guys, they said that if I reported them they'd say they found me with the English teacher. He was an effeminate guy and everyone assumed he was gay. Anyhow, I figured no one would believe me if I said it was them. And I didn't want that teacher to be blamed for something he didn't do, and, more than anything, I didn't want anyone else to know."

"But three guys … you must have been hurt. Didn't anyone notice?"

"I hid until dark." He had crawled behind a dumpster outside the equipment shed on the school grounds where it had happened and sat, shivering, on cold wet leaves until night fell. "Mom and Dad were out that evening and Ben was, I dunno, somewhere. I got to my room without anyone seeing me. The next day I got rid of my clothes and the other stuff."

He drew in a long slow breath. "You're the only person I've ever told about it."

"You've never told your parents?"

He shook his head. "It would only have upset them." He glanced at her. "I'd like it to stay that way."

Leah gave him a troubled look. "All right. But how awful. You were barely older than Niels. How did you ever deal with it?"

He tipped more whisky into his glass and held the bottle out to Leah. She shook her head. He took a sip and leaned back.

"That's when everything went sideways. I started skipping classes, then stopped going altogether."

He set his glass back down; the drink was making him light-headed.

"I told my parents that I was tired of being picked on all the time and wanted to change schools. I shifted to the school in our neighborhood but the kids I took up with there were, well, troublemakers. I started messing around, you know, staying out late, sometimes stealing booze from the cupboard. Occasionally someone got some dope. We'd go looking for trouble. Smashed things up—garbage cans, plants, windows. Spray-painted graffiti on buildings and fences." His mouth twisted. "Mine was very nice graffiti, but still. When we got busted for shoplifting, Mom and Dad threw up their hands and sent me off to that Jesuit school in Oregon. I was very relieved."

He fell silent and they sat for several minutes lost in their own thoughts. Finally, he rubbed his eyes and said, "Haven't thought about it for a long time; it's been buried pretty deep."

"We're quite the pair, aren't we, with our incidental children and now this," Leah said. She rose and returned to her chair. "But never being able to forget must be awful. At least I can't remember what happened to me."

Theo smiled wanly. "At least I didn't get pregnant. But you, what will you do now? Will you go to the police?"

She warded off the thought with her hand. "No. It probably would be easy to find out who Brad's friends were at the time but, as Rebecca pointed out, I have no proof of anything and it would be my word against theirs. But more than anything, Niels must never know what happened."

"But what those guys did to you—it can mess you up for a long time."

Leah gazed off into the distance then turned back to him. "After the horror, after the appalling images I can't help but imagine, it's a relief of sorts to know what happened, what I've been torturing myself over all this time. Part of the guilt I've borne was the notion that I had somehow invited this fate. And maybe I did." Her cheeks reddened. "I had a bit of a crush on Brad and, who knows, maybe he was aware of it. Maybe that's what he figured gave him license to do what he did."

Theo shook his head. "Nothing gives any guy license to do that."

"I know." She lifted a shoulder in a shrug. "In the end, what happened happened. I may never get over it, but I'm adjusting to the fact. And I am very, very grateful that I don't remember any of it. Then there is Niels—that something so beautiful and good could come from such an ugly act. Would I prefer that it not have happened at the cost of not having him in the world?" She gave him a weary smile. "I accept the perverted logic by which the universe has brought him into being. And I think that I'm ready, finally, to move on."

Chapter 20

"So, I arrive and you all leave," said Ben.

His mother laughed and put a hand on his cheek. "Yes, funny how it's turned out."

It was the first week of July and his parents were on their way to Counter Point, their summer retreat on Vancouver Island: a rocky little peninsula on the ocean dotted with groves of fir, arbutus and Garry oaks. He had driven them to the airport and Trevor was loading their luggage into the belly of the small jet. His father had already said goodbye and was settled in the plane's cockpit running through the system checks preparatory to take-off.

"Could you connect with Caro when you get there? See how she's doing?"

"Yes, of course," said Ris. Had he imagined a slight hesitation? "But it will only be a phone call."

Fox ran up to them. "Gran! Gran! Look at my new fishing rod," he said, waving a slender pole.

"Hey, careful, Fox. Don't poke anyone in the eye," Theo said, following behind.

He wore a cowboy hat with a flat crown against the hard noon sun. Ben raised a disdainful eyebrow. *You'd think he just stepped out of a Western.* When he was fifteen, Ben had strutted into the stables at the ranch one day sporting a Stetson. The stable hands had fallen over laughing at how it had looked over his long corkscrew locks. "Little Bo Peep," they had called him. After, he had cropped his hair close to his head to control the eruption of curls and he never put on a cowboy hat again.

Ris said a last goodbye to Ben and he went over to help Leah and Theo transfer the luggage from the baggage cart to the plane. When it was all stowed away, Leah wrapped her arms around Fox and Niels. "I'm going to miss you two something awful."

"Why can't you come?" Fox said.

"I have work here; I can't leave my job."

"But we can Skype, can't we?" Niels said.

"Of course, every day when you have access to a computer."

The boys finally released Leah and climbed into the plane. She fingered a tear from the corner of her eye and turned to Theo. "This canoe outing, is it safe? With bears and white water and things like that?"

"They both swim like otters and know how to handle themselves in the wilderness. I'll make sure nothing happens to them," Theo said. "How about you? Are you going to be okay? Will you move into Las Sombras?"

She shook her head. "I'd just rattle around in it with all of you gone and I'm quite happy in my trailer."

"It might get pretty lonely out there behind the stables."

"I'll be working much of the time."

"Well, okay. But if there's a problem, or you need anything, talk to Chester. I've asked him and Andy to keep an eye on you."

"Don't worry, I'll take care of Leah," Ben said, putting his arm around her. "Won't I, Button?"

Theo rolled his eyes.

"What?"

"Nothing."

Leah laughed and shifted away. "I'll be fine," she said.

The Lighthouse

Theo sketched a salute. "See you at the end of the summer." He mounted the steps into the plane and the door closed behind him.

"I guess it's just you and me, kid," Ben said.

They pushed the luggage carts back to the terminal and continued on to where his parents' Mercedes and Theo's Jeep were parked. Leah stopped to watch the small jet taxi down the runway and take off.

"Time to go," Ben said when it disappeared into the sky.

Leah nodded—sadly, he thought. He'd make sure she didn't get too lonely. They got into the vehicles left in their care and headed off on their respective ways.

Ben placed the file he had been reading in his outbox and rubbed his eyes. His stomach rumbled and he glanced at his wristwatch: Seven fifty-two p.m. Time to stop. His pushed his chair away from the desk and pulled his jacket off the hanger dangling from the hook on the door. Glancing back at his inbox, he hoped there wasn't anything among its contents that needed immediate attention.

He questioned, and not for the first time, his impulsive offer to take over the management of the Lighthouse. It had been sheer hubris to assume he knew enough to do the job. Serving on the board had, it turned out, given him only a superficial understanding of the operations. Directing the various components—client services, marketing and sales, housekeeping, food and beverage, retail, grounds, maintenance, systems, wellness and recreational programs, special events ... not to mention the proposed renovation and expansion—was proving to be much more complex than running a law firm with its singular focus and homogeneous staff. His first weeks had been devoted to getting an overview of all the operations. He spent time with all the section heads, sat in their staff meetings, had them walk him through their respective operations. And he read a seemingly endless stream of correspondence, reports, analyses, financials.

On the whole, the employees he met were friendly and helpful, but he discovered a thread of resentment running through a small group over the sacking of Craig and Jenny. Not wanting to damage their reputations more than necessary, his parents had been circumspect in giving their reasons for letting them go. It was, Ben thought, excessive consideration given the transgressors' breach of trust, but his father lived by the principle that one should always err on the side of kindness. The resentment manifested through silly little incidents: invoices—which now all came to him for signature—being held past their due dates requiring penalties to be paid, scheduling confusion requiring that he choose one party to meet with over the other, vital information withheld so that he would be upstaged or corrected in meetings.

The mischief didn't end there. He had expected to live in his parents' guest cottage, but his mother had said that because their housekeeper would be absent over the summer he should stay instead in a suite at the Lighthouse that was kept on permanent reserve for the family's use. There, on different occasions, he found unaccountable irregularities, like no soap in the bathroom, sour milk in the fridge, the air thick with cloying floral air freshener. He ignored these incidences, hoping they would eventually run their course, until he returned after one particularly long, hot, tiring day to find the heat turned on and the suite suffocating. The resort was fully booked and he had no choice but to suffer through the discomfort, furious at the effrontery and violation of his privacy.

The perpetrator turned out to be the executive assistant he had inherited from Craig. When challenged she responded with such defiance that he wondered if Craig had been having it on with her as well. Dismissing her sent out another ripple through the close-knit organization, an unpleasant bit of business which had only been concluded the previous day. This morning he had asked Cindy, the daughter of one of the Pueblo ranch workers, to step into the position. His parents had given her a job and a future when she was recovering from drug addiction and he was confident of her loyalty. She had started out working in the laundry and now managed guest services. A pert-faced, raven-haired, five-foot-nothing dynamo who wore only red, she knew everyone at the Lighthouse and most of what went on. She'd asked for a few days to train someone to take over her responsibilities, leaving him to bumble along on his own until her arrival.

Back at his law firm things were working reasonably well around his absence, but he inevitably had to field two or three calls a day, some of which involved substantive conversations. Shifting back and forth between the two worlds was disorienting and there were times when he had to get out and walk around the grounds to clear his head. Not having someone to talk to made it harder. In the beginning he had called Caro every day. As time passed he began to suspect that she was screening his calls. He had made a trip to Vancouver the previous week, but one of his days there was consumed by an unavoidable discussion with Jay and on the other Caro was away at a company retreat. He cancelled plans to go back later in July after Caro announced she'd be visiting her family in England at that time.

The loneliness was a surprise. He had expected to be too engaged, too stimulated to mind being on his own. He had welcomed the break from what his and Caro's life together had become, thought that the time away would bring perspective to their relationship, scour away the tarnish that had formed. Yet he missed her. Despite everything—her coolness, her frequent indifference—she had been there. He was not, he realized, cut out to be alone.

Ethan pivoted, his arms outspread as he surveyed the bright, fresh, orderly interior of the bookstore. That morning it had reopened after being closed for a week of frantic decoration with fresh paint, modern bookshelves, displays of artwork, crafts and other gift items, and a new chic front counter. "Fan-fucking-tastic!" he said.

Leah set out towers of nested paper cups for the refreshments they were offering to customers to celebrate the event, and wearily pushed hair out of her eyes. The previous night had been late, the morning early with the final preparations. "Yes."

He turned to her. "You've done wonders, you know."

She smiled her thanks. "It was hardly all me."

She had started the bookstore job with little sense of Ethan as a person and even less as a boss, but he had proven to be more capable and focused than their initial encounter suggested, carefully shaping his plans for the business before making changes. She had done what she could to clean and bring better order to the old store but the refurbishment was desperately needed.

"You have a much better sense of style than I do," she continued. "People will come here just to see the place."

"And buy, I hope! But the substance of the place is all your doing, and the name, the Anachronism, that was your idea and I love it. I could kiss you."

He pulled her into a tight hug. The bell attached to the door tinkled and Ben walked in just as he smacked her full on the lips.

"Oh!" Ben said, stopping short. "Am I interrupting something?"

Leah pulled out of the embrace laughing. "No, not at all." She made introductions and the two men shook hands. "We've just finished some renos and are celebrating the store's re-opening."

"Actually, I was at the bank and thought I'd see if you had time for a coffee." He hesitated. "But I guess not."

"Hey, you're our first customer, have one here," Ethan said, indicating the table.

"Let me pour you a cup," Leah said. "I could use one too."

"If I'm your first customer I should buy something, don't you think?"

They drank their coffee and Leah suggested some books Ben might find of interest. He selected two. As Leah rang them in, Ethan slipped the books in a bag and handed them to Ben.

"I'm having kind of a launch party on Saturday. Why don't you come along with Leah?" he said to Ben.

Ben glanced at her. "Wouldn't want to intrude."

"Not intruding at all, Ben," she said. "Do come."

"I still feel a bit awkward about coming tonight," Ben said. "I mean, I barely know Ethan."

Leah buckled her seatbelt and smiled at him. "He wouldn't have invited you if he hadn't meant it."

"He seems like a decent guy, although I'm not sure about that business when I walked in on you two. You could have him up on harassment."

"He *is* rather expressive, but it's not an issue."

"Doesn't look like the type to be in the secondhand book business."

"And what type would that be?"

Ben did a three-point turn and drove away from her trailer. "Oh, I don't know. Rimless glasses, bowtie, argyle cardigan?"

"Ethan made a fortune creating video games and is now indulging his first love, which is, yes, books. And Anachronism is just part of it. He's using it as a base for an online store for books that are rare or out of print. He's already acquired over three thousand volumes and has first dibs on an estate library in Atlanta. Now that the bookstore is finished and staffed, my focus will shift to that side of the business." She smiled and shook her head. "I can't believe how lucky I was to have met him when I did."

Ben glanced at her. "Hummm, do I detect some romantic interest?"

Leah laughed. "Hardly. You'll meet his partner Jeff tonight."

"Glad I went," Ben said on the way home that night. "I was starting to feel a bit isolated."

Leah glanced at him. "Sorry, I should have done something, but the bookstore renos have been all-consuming these past few weeks."

"I didn't mean to put it on you. But since we're all by ourselves out here, why don't we try to get together more often?"

They began to meet for a quick meal at the Lighthouse on busy days or more leisurely evenings in Taos when they had the time. Ben had forgotten the sheer pleasure of light conversation with an attractive woman—dinners with Caro were either hurried, distracted affairs or filled with shop talk. As time passed he spoke to his wife less and less, and one Friday evening as he was wrapping up for the week he realized that it had been several days since he had thought about her at all.

Chapter 21

Theo was having a good summer. The canoe trip had gone well. He and the boys had been joined on the outing by one of their Counter Point neighbors and his ten-year-old son. A visiting Danish professor who taught at the university with the neighbor had also come along, lightening the load for the two men and adding to the entertainment with his extensive repertoire of bad jokes and humorous stories.

After the trip they settled into life at Counter Point. The compound included the Big House, another of his grandfather Niels' creations featuring cedar beams, soaring ceilings and massive windows, set on a bluff overlooking the Salish Sea with a cottage lower down on the shore of a protected cove. Lucas and Ris preferred the coziness of the cottage and lived a quiet, stripped-down life there, only coming to the Big House for Sunday dinners and meals when visitors were present. Others were left to fend for themselves in the Big House, and this is where Theo and the boys stayed.

A shed on the property served as a studio for Theo. Typically he did little work during the summer, preferring to spend his time with Fox. This year he had even more reason to take a break—all his paintings featured at the Santa Fe exhibition had sold. Yet he found himself slipping away to the shed whenever he was free. The concept for the Lighthouse mural burgeoned within him. The bridge over the sky now led to a massive wooden door set in a wall made of large worn stone blocks that opened to a night sky dripping with stars. The bridge was peopled with figures that he was slowly deciphering. He laid out a grid to section off the mural and worked out the details in numerous sketches. The mural would be a trompe l'oeil, so perspective and shading would have to be carefully done to create the optical illusion of depth. Still, he harbored misgivings about this new direction in his work. He neither understood what was driving it nor where it would take him, and he was unsure how his parents would react. When they commissioned the mural they had no doubt expected him to produce a landscape in his usual style. What he had in mind would be a major surprise. A pleasant one, he hoped.

The boys spoke to Leah through Skype daily. After dinner one night, Theo said a quick hello to her and left her chatting with the boys to finish cleaning the kitchen. They were still at it when he was done, and he told them to say goodbye and go to bed. After leafing through the local newspaper over a glass of wine, he headed to his own room. On the way he heard noises in the boys' bedroom and opened the door. The beds were stacked bunks and Fox was hanging over the edge of the top one.

"What's going on here? Why aren't you asleep?" he said.

"We're just talking," Niels said.

"Yeah? What's so important that it's keeping you awake this late?"

The boys snorted and twittered.

"Come on, out with it."

"We think you and Niels' mom should get married," said Fox.

"You do, do you?" He placed his hands on his hips. "Now, get into your bed properly before you fall down, and both of you go to sleep."

He stepped back and closed the door. *Marry Leah*? What a thought.

The owner of the Vancouver gallery that carried Theo's work had recommended him to teach a week-long landscape painting workshop offered by the college in a small city in the Kootenay Mountains during the second week of August. He traveled to the assignment in the fourteen-year-old Ford SUV they kept at Counter Point, longing for his old motorcycle which he had left in South America when he rushed home to care for Fox and never replaced. The whistle of the wind through an ill-fitting window and the rattle of the exhaust soon faded and he gave himself over to the rare pleasure of a long, solitary drive.

The base of operations, and where the participants and he were staying, was a chain motor hotel in the city. The course organizer, a short, balding man in his fifties named Stan, was registering participants when Theo arrived. There were sixteen in all, a mix of men and women of different ages. At the reception following, Theo moved among the registrants, introducing himself and trying to get a sense of their expectations for the workshop.

As Theo went from one person to another, a bronze-toned blonde whom he judged to be in her late twenties appeared to move away whenever he approached. When he finally reached her he learned that her name was Serena and she worked as a receptionist in Calgary. He asked her what she wanted to get out of the week.

"Oh, I don't know," she said. "It was Daddy's idea."

Great. He gave her a tight smile. "Well, I hope you'll enjoy it anyway."

She tilted her head and arched a brow. "Things are looking up already." People started to drift away and she moved towards him expectantly.

Whoa. Theo took a step back. Stan bustled towards them.

"Don't go anywhere," Stan said. "We need to review arrangements for the week. How about we get a bite and I take you through them?"

"Yeah, sure." Theo gave Serena a half-shrug in apology. She made a little moue of disappointment and turned away.

Over the meal, Stan explained that the group would be taken by bus to a different location each morning where they would spend the day painting. The settings included the forest, a farm, a mountain meadow, a beach on a glacial lake and the old town square. The locations all had basic conveniences and the restaurant would provide box lunches and beverages. Theo's job was to start off each session by exploring approaches to the subject, circulate and offer comments and advice on participants' work as it progressed, and then finish with a discussion of issues or themes that arose during the day. The workshop would conclude with an exhibition at the hotel on the Saturday afternoon to which the public was invited.

The first two days went well. All of the participants had some ability and previous training. A small number showed exceptional talent, including Jerome—a wheelchair-bound African American from Boise who had an edgy sense of color—and, to Theo's surprise, Serena. *Daddy's no fool*, he thought.

On the second evening, Theo returned to his room after a walk around the town and opened the door to find the light on. He thought nothing of it and proceeded down the short hallway to the room, pulling off his sweater as he walked.

"Well, hello, honey," a voice said.

He freed his head of the pullover and gaped in astonishment. Serena reclined on his bed, leafing through the book he had left on the side table. She was wearing a gold locket studded with what looked like a diamond, a pair of lacy white briefs and nothing else. Her tan, he noticed, was uninterrupted.

He tossed the sweater onto a chair. "What are you doing here? How did you get in?"

She closed the book and placed it back on the table, got up and came to him. "The nice boy at the front desk gave me the card." She bunched the front of his shirt in her fist and pulled him down to her. "Should be obvious what I'm doing here."

"I'm not sure it's appropriate…"

He could feel her smile against his lips. "Honey," she said, "this isn't high school."

Theo caught himself singing in the shower the next morning and laughed at it. Serena had left earlier after giving him a fine good-morning. Nonetheless, on his way to breakfast he stopped at the front desk and asked to have the lock on his room reprogrammed.

"Someone gave a keycard for my room to another person last night," he said.

"That would never happen!" the desk clerk—a middle-aged woman in a snug gray suit, whose nametag identified her as "Evelyn"—said.

"Well, it did. It was a young guy, apparently."

Evelyn's eyes narrowed. "That would have been Chip. I'll speak to him."

"Thanks. And the lock?"

"Yes." She glanced around him at the line that had formed. "Will later this morning be soon enough?"

He nodded and slid his card across the counter.

After his sleep-deprived night, the constant interaction with his flock—as he thought of them—and the long drive to and from the mountain meadow where they had set up for the day, Theo was beat when they finally arrived back at the hotel. He stopped at the desk to pick up his new keycard, addressing the request to the young man whose nametag identified him as Chip.

"Why did you give my card out?" he said.

Chip's ears reddened. "She said she was your girlfriend. She wanted to surprise you."

Theo took the card and pocketed it. "She's not my girlfriend. Please don't do that again."

In his room, he ordered a bowl of pasta for dinner and ate reclined on his bed watching television. At some point he fell asleep, waking to a rolling movement. Serena was sitting on the edge of the bed.

"How the *hell* did you get in here?" he said, pushing himself up.

"I had to find an obliging chambermaid. Told her I left my card inside." She slapped him lightly on the arm. "Bad boy, changing your lock."

"Look, I prefer to invite visitors."

She pulled her mouth into a pout. "But we had such a good time last night."

"That was last night. I'm tired tonight."

"But you've just had a nap."

"It doesn't matter." He tried to get up but she blocked him. "Move, please," he said.

Serena stood and pulled out a small gold metal box from her handbag. She cocked her head and shook the box. "Look what I have."

Theo rose from the bed. "What's that?"

"Thought we could have some fun."

"I don't do that shit, and I don't want it in here."

"Ah, honey. Don't be such a bore."

"Come on, Serena. Time to go." He grabbed her arm with one hand and her bag with the other and steered her towards the door.

"I don't think so," she said. She curled her free arm around his neck, pulled his face down and ran her tongue over his mouth.

Anger is a potent aphrodisiac. He dropped the bag and they tore at each other's clothes. He wasn't gentle but neither was she—biting and scratching and growling.

In the morning, he woke with a start and looked anxiously around. She wasn't there. He lay back with an exhalation of relief and rubbed his face. Her smell was still on him. He vaulted out of bed and went to the bathroom. The shower spray was hot and hard and he gasped when it needled his back. His fingers found ridges of broken skin. He beat his fist against the tiles, cursing his lapse of judgement. He should have pushed Serena out, thrown the deadbolt, called for security if she wouldn't go away. He turned and thrust his head under the biting stream, churning through the sordid details of the previous night, loathing himself.

When he was dressed he went down to the front desk. Evelyn was on duty again.

"Someone got into my room again last night," he said. "This time it was the chambermaid who let her in."

Evelyn swallowed a snicker and tried to arrange her face into serious lines. The desk staff were no doubt having a good laugh over the whole thing. "I'm sorry to hear that, sir," she said, her lips twitching. "I'll speak to the cleaning staff."

"I'd like you to do more than that," he said. "I'd like you to find me another room."

"Well, I don't know, I'll have to check."

"Please do." He didn't move.

Evelyn raised her eyebrows. "You mean right now?"

"Yes."

She motioned to people wanting to check out. "It's kind of busy."

"Then try to do it quickly."

She narrowed her eyes. "If you insist."

He knew he was being a jerk but he wasn't going to back down now. "I do."

Her mouth drew into a hard line but she got busy at the terminal and in a few seconds had found a vacant room.

"Is it ready now?" Theo said.

"Yes, but…"

He held out his hand for the keycard. After a moment she handed it over. "I'm going to have to charge you for the extra half-day," she said.

He wasn't the one paying, but he regarded her levelly. "Really?"

She held his gaze for a moment then looked away. "I think we can make an exception."

"Good," he said and left.

Shortly after, he stood by the bus waiting for the workshop participants to load. *Three more days.* He groaned inwardly. Jerome was the first to arrive.

"Don't want to make the other folks wait while he fusses with the rig," he said, referring to the lift the driver used to load him into the vehicle.

Theo gave them a hand. "Hey," he said when Jerome was in place, "do you have any plans for the evening?"

"Just the usual: have some chow, watch TV, go to bed."

"Don't imagine you've seen much of the town then."

Jerome shook his head. "Not really. Don't know the place."

"How about we go out tonight?" Theo said. "Have a look around. Get some dinner. Do you like Thai? I hear there's a decent place at the edge of town."

Jerome's face split in a wide smile. He held out his hand and gave Theo's a big shake. "That's mighty nice of you, and it'll be my treat."

That morning the group set up on the narrow beach of a

long glacial lake. The water was emerald green, the mountains rearing up on the far side ominous. A vague mist hovered over the water, tempering the light. Beautiful, Theo thought. After his preliminary comments to the group about different ways to approach the scene and particular techniques they might want to try, he set up his own easel to do a sketch before making his rounds. Delaying them, actually. He wasn't sure what he'd say to Serena. When she got on the bus she had responded to his terse greeting with raised eyebrows and a smirk. The thought of being anywhere close to her nauseated him.

When he couldn't put if off any longer he wandered among the painters, offering comments. He knew them well enough now to chat easily, and there were a few whom he especially enjoyed. When it was Serena's turn he came up and looked silently at her canvas. She glanced up, gave him another of her sly smiles. She had chosen as her subject a tree that had fallen into the water, creating a reflection. Her handling of it was masterful: the muted light, the textures and tonalities of the woods and the lake, the subtle differences between the parts of the tree above and below the water. The painting breathed. *Why doesn't she channel all that misguided energy into her art?* He made a couple of suggestions, small things really.

"Have you thought of painting seriously?" he said. "Your work is certainly strong enough."

She leaned back and looked up at him. "Oh, Daddy said he'd set up a gallery for me. I don't mind painting now and again, but it's not, like, something I want to *have* to do."

After returning from dinner with Jerome, Theo headed for his new room one floor up and on the opposite end of the building from where his previous one had been. As he walked he read the front page of a newspaper he had picked up. When he paused to insert the keycard in the door he felt the air stir near him.

"So this is where you've got to," Serena said.

The hair rose on Theo's neck. He turned slowly. "What are you doing here? Your room is downstairs."

"Why, waiting for you, of course."

She tried to put her arms around his neck. He blocked them. "I don't think so, Serena."

Her lips curled in a pout. "But I'm lonely."

Her eyes were bright, the pupils big and black. *No doubt thanks to the little gold box.* "Serena, I don't want to be with you tonight," he said. "I'm tired and I'd like some time alone. Now be a good girl and go back to your room."

She waggled her shoulders and stepped towards him. "But I'm *not* a good girl."

He held up his palm to ward her off. "*No!* I don't want you."

"But I want you," she said, punctuating each word with a light poke at his chest. "And I *always* get what I want."

Theo stepped back. "Come on, Serena."

Her eyes glittered dangerously. "You know, I could scream. I could say that you're trying to drag me into your room."

A chill slithered down Theo's back. "Now, why would you do that?" he said, his voice even.

She twisted away, looked at him over her shoulder. "So you'll reconsider."

"Serena, no one would believe you. Everyone at the front desk knows that you've been tricking staff to get into my room. Now go away."

In a swift movement he opened the door to his room and slipped inside. He closed it quickly, threw the deadbolt and slid the chain into its grove. Leaning against the door, he exhaled slowly. There was a sound of movement outside, a light scratching.

"You'll be sor-ry," Serena chanted softly.

Jesus! That woman is fucking dangerous. He stood for several minutes unsure of what to do. "This is nuts," he said, shaking himself. Inside the room he spotted the packed suitcase he had tossed on the bed that morning. "But, still."

He picked up the bag, went to the door and pressed his ear against it. There was no sound so he opened it slowly. The corridor was empty. He offered up a quick thanks, slipped down the hall to the fire exit and ran down the stairs, the clacking of his heels on the metal steps echoing up the well. Outside, he ducked into the old Ford SUV and drove to a motel he remembered seeing at the edge of town. The neon sign had dark gaps, like missing teeth. A room was available and he took it.

Despite the thin walls, through which he shared the sound of his neighbors' television, flushing toilets and, during a commercial, brisk coupling, he woke rested. He picked up a take-out breakfast from MacDonald's and ate it as he drove back to the hotel.

By the time he had parked and gone in, the workshop participants were assembling in the lobby. They were painting in the old town that day. He tensed, anticipating his encounter with Serena. She wasn't there, nor did she show up by the scheduled time. When she still hadn't arrived after ten minutes everyone looked at Theo expectantly.

"I'll call her," he said, heading to the house phone. She didn't answer, and after eight rings he hung up. *Shit! What's she done now?* He went to the counter and waited, shifting from foot to foot, until Evelyn was free. When she finally turned to him with a flat smile he asked if someone could check on Serena.

"There's just Jim and me," Evelyn said, "and we can't leave right now." She pointed to the people behind him waiting to check out.

"Is there someone in the office who could go? Or whoever is responsible for security?" *Such as it is*, he thought grimly.

Evelyn gave him an exasperated look but went to the back room and returned with a man in a short-sleeved shirt and loosely knotted tie.

"We just can't barge into a guest's room," the man said.

"She should be here, and she's not answering her phone. I just want to make sure she's okay."

Evelyn and the man conferred briefly for a few moments, then the man nodded and turned to Theo. "Best Evelyn goes. I'll cover for her on the desk."

Theo returned to the group, who were chattering softly among themselves. They quietened at his approach and turned like so many sunflowers towards him.

"They're checking on Serena," he said.

As one, the people nodded and returned to their conversations. He waited, his stomach grinding, remembering the whispery voice through the door. *You'll be sorry,* she had said. Had she done something stupid just to spite him? He remembered Fiona, the overdose, the frantic trip to emergency. How the hell had he gotten into this position again? Why hadn't he seen right away that she was trouble, thrown her out the first night he found her in his room?

Evelyn returned after a few minutes. "She's got a headache. Says she's going to stay in today."

Relieved, he thanked Evelyn with a wide smile. She blinked and smiled shyly in return. He moved toward the group. "Serena won't be joining us today. Let's get going," he said.

The day seemed endless. As it was their last evening, a group dinner was planned. Serena didn't show up for it and neither Theo nor any of the others bothered to find and include her. He returned to the motel for the night, ignored the rumbles and thumping on either side, and fell into a dreamless sleep.

Stan had worked the local radio station and tourist office and there was a surprisingly large turnout at the Saturday afternoon art exhibition. Theo made one last round among the participants, offering encouragement and saying goodbye, hoping to leave as soon as he had spoken to them all. He considered skipping out without speaking to Serena, wary of what she might say or do, but in the end headed to the part of the display where her paintings hung. She was with two men, both wearing sports jackets over polo shirts. The older one had a shaved head with the shadow of a tonsure and the build of a wrestler. The younger was slim and dark with long-fringed, hazel eyes. Serena stood between them looking vacantly off into the distance.

"I'm leaving shortly, Serena. I just wanted to say goodbye and wish you luck," he said.

Something flickered in her eyes when she turned to acknowledge him, but she only nodded.

"You the teacher?" the older man said. He grabbed Theo's hand and pumped it. "Ned Gibb, Serena's dad." He gestured at the paintings. "I think my daughter's pretty darn good."

"Yes," Theo said. "Yes, she is. She could make a career out of her painting."

"That's what I say." He gestured to the younger man. "This here is Dean, Serena's fiancé."

Theo blinked, and after a brief moment shook the hand that had been extended to him. He glanced at Serena's left hand. She smiled faintly and twisted her wrist so that he could see the chunk of ice on her finger. Dean eyed him coolly.

"Well…" he said, taking a step back. "I should be on my way. All the best." He turned and stepped smartly towards the exit, feeling the sharp hazel eyes boring into his back. He got into the old SUV, revved the engine and blew out of the parking lot like a man who had just dodged a bullet.

Chapter 22

Ben pushed the sheets of paper away and pinched the bridge of his nose. The columns of figures had been hard going, in large part, he suspected, because he needed reading glasses.

"It's time to get someone," he said to Cindy. "We're ready, I think."

She nodded. "Tell me what you're looking for and I'll draft something."

He rattled off several points that described the scope of the job and necessary qualifications. "Oh, and they need to have at least five years in a senior position, ideally as chief or deputy financial officer. I don't have time to train anyone."

Cindy took it all down in a personal form of shorthand. She was proving to be a godsend: energetic, industrious, quick to learn. The ad for the financial officer position was posted in the dog days of August and drew only nine responses. He and Cindy eliminated four for lack of the necessary credentials. He asked her to meet briefly with the remaining five to determine their motivation in seeking the job, confirm key facts and requirements and, most importantly, get a sense of whether the person would fit in at the Lighthouse. Among her other attributes Cindy was a shrewd judge of character, quickly cutting through pretense, insincerity and other flaws.

"If none of them are okay, we'll just run it again in September," he said. "I'm not going to hire someone who doesn't suit just for the sake of it."

Of the five, Cindy figured three had oversold their qualifications. She recommended he talk to the remaining two: Gregory Pitt and Beth Wallace. As she pushed Pitt's curriculum vitae and her notes on their meeting across the desk to Ben, she remarked that the man might be difficult to work with. When Ben asked why, she shrugged and said, "It might just be me." She slid another set of clipped sheets toward him and tapped them with her index finger. "I think this Beth woman is the one you want." Her Pueblo eyes crinkled in a smile. "Even though she's part Navaho."

She arranged for the two candidates to come in the following morning. Gregory Pitt was first and demonstrated that he was indeed highly qualified for the position, although Ben had a difficult time paying attention, distracted by Pitt's habit of punctuating his words with lizard-like flicks of his tongue out the sides of his mouth. When Cindy interrupted their meeting to say that there was an urgent call from Jay he dismissed the man with apologies and gratefully picked up the telephone receiver.

Ben's gratitude dissolved on hearing that one of the firm's main clients had been served an injunction by a community group hoping to prevent a planned development from proceeding just as the contractor was about to break ground at the site. He was obliged to cancel his meeting with Beth Wallace to participate in a conference call with the client. The plan of action included Ben flying back to Vancouver the next day. The flight was scheduled for mid-morning, leaving time to meet with Beth Wallace beforehand.

When Cindy announced Beth Wallace the next morning, Ben pushed aside some documents related to the injunction and picked up her CV. He hadn't reviewed it yet. "Give me a minute before you bring her in," he said. "Oh, and if you don't mind, maybe make some tea?"

"What kind?"

"Anything will be fine."

Beth Wallace had an MBA from Stanford. *Well, that's a good start.* He got up and, still reading, headed to reception to get her. He first noticed her legs: long, tanned, one knee crossed over the other, a trim ankle leading to a slender foot in a pale pump. She turned from studying one of Theo's painting—an autumn landscape in ochre, dark green and slate gray—and rose, smiling at his approach. She was tall, close to six feet. Her face was long, her nose aquiline, her eyes a deep, rich amber. The ceiling lights sparked bronze notes in her long dark hair. She was full-bodied but trim. He choked out a greeting and clasped her extended hand, remembering, just before it became awkward, to let it go.

Somehow, he got them to his office and her seated in the chair facing his desk. Cindy brought in the tea, snapping him out of the trance into which he had fallen. As she set the tray down on his small meeting table she raised her eyebrows and dipped her head in Beth Wallace's direction.

"Yes, thanks," he said, and she left wearing a satisfied smile. "It seems Cindy's given us a choice of tea," he said to Beth Wallace. "Mint, plain Ceylon, or tea au lait."

"Tea au lait? That sounds interesting." Her voice was low and honeyed and woven through with laughter.

He mixed two cups of strong black tea with sweet condensed milk. "Tea is big in our family—my father's Welsh. There's one for each circumstance, every mood: bright and aromatic for conversation, green and light for reading, black and smoky for music, sweet and milky when you need a lift."

Stop chattering like a monkey, he said to himself as he handed Beth her drink. When she lifted her left hand to accept it he noticed the narrow gold band on her ring finger. A small, dying moth of regret fluttered through his soul. He carried his own beverage to his side of the desk, sat down and took a deep breath.

"So, you're interested in working at the Lighthouse?"

"Yes, it's a unique place and I'm drawn to its purpose."

"Are you from around here?"

"My mother lived near Farmington before she left to study in California. She married there and stayed, and that's where I grew up."

"So you've come home?"

"In a way."

He tried to focus on what was written on her application. "A business degree, then, ah, eight years with the same company, then nothing for five years?" He glanced up at her.

"I have a young child."

He nodded and was about to speak when Cindy stuck her head through the door. "Very sorry to bother you, but your wife is on the phone."

He frowned. "I'll call her back."

"Yeah, I told her that, but she said she's going into court and won't be reachable all day and she needs to speak to you before you leave."

He sighed. "Okay, put her through." He turned to Beth. "My apologies."

He picked up the receiver and went outside the office, closing the door behind him. Caro rarely called; why now of all times?

"Yes?" he said curtly.

"Hello to you, too," she said. "Just wanted to let you know that I have to fly to Prince George late this afternoon and won't be home when you arrive."

"So between last night and this morning you were able to find an excuse to leave town?" Cindy glanced up from her desk; he turned his back to her and looked out the window to the parking lot.

When she replied, Caro spoke in her version of the Queen's cut-glass accent. "Don't be ridiculous. I will be home tomorrow night."

"Sorry," he said. "Have a good trip. I'll see you then."

He went back into his office, momentarily startled to see Beth Wallace sitting there. She had finished her tea au lait and he offered her another.

"It was delicious but no, thanks."

He sat down and took a large draft from his own cup. "Let me tell you about the situation here," he said. He reviewed how the Lighthouse had been previously run, how it had come off the rails and what he thought would be necessary to fix things and get them going in the right direction. He outlined the scope of work for the position that she had applied to fill. "So that's what we need. You've done this kind of stuff before?"

Beth nodded. "All of it and more. The company I worked for was a start-up when I joined and over the years I was involved in one way or another in pretty well everything related to finance and administration."

"And progressed up the ranks?"

Beth smiled. "High-tech companies are too dynamic to maintain ranks. Change was a constant so one flowed with it, did what was necessary, wherever that happened to be."

"The reason you left?"

"The company was bought out and for personal reasons it was a good time to move on."

"Did you have a title upon leaving?" He held up his palms. "I know, high-tech companies operate under different rules, but what would the position you occupied have corresponded to in a more traditional organization?"

She was about to answer when Cindy knocked on the door and stuck her head in. "I'm very sorry again to interrupt, but Trevor says he's ready to go and he'd like to get out as soon as possible because he needs to pick someone up in Portland this afternoon. I've called the car for you; it will be waiting in the front."

He nodded at her. "Right." Turning to Beth, he said, "Look, if you don't mind walking with me we can wrap up on the way out."

He quickly gathered up the papers he needed and shoved them into a briefcase then picked it and a small duffel bag up. On his way out, Cindy handed him a small pack.

"I had Chef prepare some sandwiches for you and Trevor, and there's some hot coffee."

He thanked her and started juggling what he was carrying to make room for the container of food.

"Why don't I take it?" Beth said, reaching for the pack. Their hands touched and something hot and sharp pricked his heart.

As they swept down the hallway in the direction of the lobby, everyone they met greeted Ben, obliging him to reply. When they reached the car he opened the back door, said hello to the driver and threw his overnight bag and briefcase on the seat. Beth handed him the food pack and he added it to the others and closed the door.

"We didn't actually have a chance to talk, did we?" he said to Beth. "Why don't I give you a call in the next couple of days and we can cover anything remaining."

"That'll be fine," she said and gave him a magnificent smile.

He had a sudden urge to kiss her goodbye but caught himself in time. "Well, then, I guess I should go," he said.

She nodded and stepped back. "Have a safe trip."

After he got in the car he gave her a small wave and, as they drove away, watched in the side mirror as she grew smaller, her hand raised in farewell. They turned a corner and she was gone. He sat back in his seat and stared, wide-eyed, ahead.

There is no way I can hire her.

Chapter 23

Lucas leaned back in his chair and gazed out the window. Summer had raged on into September and the bright late-morning sun burnished the water lapping against the shore of the cove. He loved the ocean, its fluid colors and shifting moods, the seduction of its far horizon—he could look at it for hours. But not today. He sighed and turned back to the papers on his desk.

A knot of pressure pushed up under his ribs. His morning tea and toast were not sitting well. A belch brought no relief. He tried to focus on the pages before him: the draft of an article on living spiritually in the face of growing intolerance, discord and nativism. Why had he ever agreed to write it? He needed neither the fee nor the profile the article offered.

He picked up the red pen he used for corrections. He could have been lifting a lead pipe for the effort it required. As he leaned forward the knot of pressure exploded in his chest. Cold sweat beaded his forehead and he gasped for breath. Another jolt of pain lifted him out of his chair. He turned towards the French doors that separated his little office from the cottage sitting room.

"Ris..." he said, the word emerging as a string of sibilance. His head spun and he sank to the floor.

She was at his side within seconds.

"Heart," he breathed.

She left swiftly and he heard her speaking on the phone. One would have to know her well to catch the panic shadowing her cool, controlled words. She was back at his side a minute later.

"Here," she said, slipping a finger between his lips. "Under your tongue. It's crushed aspirin." A sour astringency flooded his mouth. Ris sat down beside him and drew his head onto her lap. "The ambulance will be here soon."

He closed his eyes, comforted by her warmth and touch. He collected his being into a small ball of light and nestled it under his unruly organ. There were worse ways to die.

Lucas's eyes opened and drifted over the bed, the monitor screen, the intravenous lines plugged into his arm.

"Luke, darling, are you awake?"

He turned his head towards Ris, seated at the side of the bed. She leaned forward and clasped his hand.

He smiled weakly. "It appears that you are not rid of me yet."

Her eyes filled with tears. "It's no joke!"

"A close call, nonetheless?"

"It could have been worse. The doctor says you'll be fine in time. You can come home in a day or two."

He nodded. His eyelids fluttered. "I'm sorry, my love, but it seems that I must sleep."

Ris straightened up. "It's probably from the sedative they gave you for the angioplasty. I should go home, anyway. In the rush to leave I didn't take my phone. I have yet to call the boys and let them know."

His fingers tightened around hers. "Please, don't."

"No? Why not? I'm sure they'd want to know."

"They don't need to if I am going to recover. I really don't want the burden of their concern."

Ris studied him for a moment. "It seems odd not telling them."

He smiled weakly. "It's not like we haven't kept secrets from them before."

"Well, okay," she said. "But from now on a few things are going to have to change."

Chapter 24

Mona stubbed her cigarette out in the ashtray and leaned back in her chair. She studied Theo for a few moments, her pale face impassive. "If I understand correctly, then, you don't want to see me anymore."

Theo heaved a silent sigh. Taos was a small town; it was very likely he *would* see her again. Which was why he was trying to do this gently. "What we had was great," he said, "but I think it's run its course."

He hadn't set out that night intending to end their relationship, if sleeping together once in a while qualified as one. They had met at a party four years previously, shortly after her marriage had broken up. The split in assets had left her with a freight company to run. Between that and raising her son and daughter she had neither time nor desire for a serious relationship, and it had suited them both to meet in this hotel from time to time, usually when her children were visiting their father. He hadn't seen her since spring and had welcomed her text suggesting they get together.

On his way into town he had stopped at Las Sombras where Leah was looking after the boys in Fin's absence. She was negotiating with Niels and Fox over possible additions to Angie's tomato sauce for their spaghetti dinner and they were falling over laughing at the outrageous proposals being made. Theo defended Fox's suggestion that raisins be added, citing a recipe that also included sardines, fennel and pine nuts. "Yuk," said Fox. "Bleh," said Niels. Leah had added that it sounded way too complicated to make.

"It's actually delicious and straightforward, and I'd make it for you if I weren't going out."

"Yeah, but you gotta go see your girlfriend," Fox said, drawing out the last word and making a face.

He left them rooting through the freezer for frozen meatballs and was halfway to town when it struck him that he'd rather be at home cooking up Sicilian pasta and laughing with Leah and the boys. But he carried on.

Mona was already in the restaurant, at one of the outside tables despite the September chill. Their meals were perfunctory, a veneer of civility on what was basically an arrangement for sex. They made desultory conversation about the weather, the food, the town, people they knew, occasionally their work. Mona knew little about art and nodded at regular intervals when he spoke on the subject, her eyes darting around the room. He similarly tuned her out when she spoke about her business. She was nattering on about a waylaid shipment and a driver who drank when he suddenly recalled Fox's derisive comment about his *girlfriend*. He had never let any of these relationships intrude on his life with his son and assumed that Fox didn't understand what he was doing when he slipped away for an evening. How did Fox know about tonight? Was he guessing or had he overheard something? Or maybe he had played with his phone and found her message? He still thought of Fox as a small child but he was almost nine now. What had he known about the world of men and women, of sex and games, at that age? And with media virtually uncensored these days, not to mention what anyone who could spell could find on the Internet, it was likely Fox knew more than he had. Mona's text had been particularly racy. If Fox had read it, what would he think? Theo's face burned and he groaned. It was then he told her he wanted to end things between them.

"Is there someone else?" she said.

Theo blinked. "You didn't think we had an exclusive arrangement, did you? I doubt you've ever turned down a chance to have a good time when the opportunity arose."

Mona's eyes flickered and she sniffed. She shook a cigarette out of the pack sitting next to her plate and raised it to her lips. Theo dutifully reached over, picked up her lighter and clicked it. She leaned towards it, drawing a wing of platinum blond hair off her face with red-tipped fingers. A cluster of stones in a heavy gold setting winked in the light of the small flame. Her vaguely cinematic, *noir* style and tough, slightly brittle persona was what had attracted him before and despite himself he felt a worm of desire turn in his belly.

Mona drew back and blew out a plume of smoke. He started to lift a hand to wave the smoke away but caught himself. *It'll be over soon.* She tapped a cylinder of ash into the remains on her plate and smiled at him.

"I've paid for the room. How about it? You know, for old time's sake?"

He was tempted; he hadn't had sex since Serena. Relieved to have escaped her craziness, he had put her out of his mind. The memory of those few days flooded back, sobering him. He rose, pulled out his wallet and tucked some bills under his plate.

"It's a nice thought," he said, "but I should get home."

The boys had already gone to bed when he returned to Las Sombras, but they were still awake.

"Dad! You're back!" Fox said, bouncing up. He kibitzed with them for a few minutes then firmly turned off the light and closed the door. *I've got to talk to Fox about this stuff, but what to say?*

He went to the kitchen, opened a bottle of Sauvignon blanc

he found in the refrigerator and filled a glass. Leah was in the dining room working on some papers spread out on the large table. He dropped his jacket on the back of a chair across from her and sat down.

"Want some wine?"

She shook her head.

He drank deeply. The wine was cool and tart and cleansed his mouth.

"You're home early," she said.

"Yeah. How'd the spaghetti turn out?"

She smiled ruefully. "I think I overcooked the pasta, but the guys didn't seem to mind."

Theo took another sip of his drink. "So how long is Fin gone this time?"

"Until Wednesday."

"He's away a lot these days."

"Yes, well, he's finally getting back into the swing of things. Ben said he hardly did anything in the last year before my mother died. No commissions or recordings or performances. I think it's good that he's getting busy again."

"You're at Las Sombras much of the time now. Why don't you move in permanently?"

She shook her head. "I like having my little bolt hole. And Linc misses me when I'm gone."

He reached over and drew some of the pages on the table towards him. "So, what are you working on?"

Leah leapt up and slammed a palm on top of the pages. His mouth fell open in surprise. "What?"

"You can't read this."

He hung on to the sheets of paper. "Why not?"

Her face reddened. "It's personal. Private."

"Really?" He tugged the pages closer.

She bent farther over the table, trying to keep her hand down on the pages. "Let go!"

Her stretch gave him a full view of the rounded tops of her breasts. Before averting his eyes he observed with surprise that the bra she wore under her worn college T-shirt was black and lacy. He quickly looked up. Her eyes blazed, her nostrils flared. The air between them crackled. He thought she might strike him; he held on to the papers to find out if she would. She glared at him for a long moment then lifted her hand and fell back into her chair, breathing hard.

"I would appreciate it very much if you would return those to me, unread."

He turned the pages towards him, spreading them out with his fingers. He knew what he was doing was wrong but her reaction intrigued him. The pages had neat, even margins and were filled with text—not what would come off your printer, but crisp and stylized. *Three* was printed at the top of the page. He looked up at her.

"If I'm not mistaken, this is the proof for a book," he said.

She folded her arms and looked away.

He pulled more of the pages towards him, shuffled through them, found the title page. *Three*, it repeated, *by L.A. Larsen*. He looked at her again. "You've written a book. I didn't know you were a writer."

She sniffed. "I daresay there are a few things you don't know about me."

"But this is wonderful. Why are you so upset?"

She scowled at him. "Because it's private."

He motioned to the pages with his hand. "But it's apparently about to be published. How can it be private?"

She drew in a deep breath and looked away. After a long moment, she said, "I wrote it last year. Last winter, a publisher said she was interested. It seemed like a good idea then. But now, back here..." She shook her head. "I don't want anyone to read it, not anyone I know, anyway."

"Why? What's it about?"

She pushed herself away from the table and stood up. "I think I'll have some wine after all."

"Bring the bottle," he said.

In the kitchen, Leah stopped in the act of opening the refrigerator door and leaned against it, flushed with indignation at Theo's egregious violation of her privacy and some other disturbing emotion she didn't want to identify. Previously, when Theo had gone out for the evening he had not returned until morning and she had thought she was safe spreading out her work. *Three* was part of the life that had ended when she returned to the ranch and she needed it to remain there. She did not want to share or explain it.

Why hadn't he stopped when she had asked him to? It was so unlike him to insist, to intrude. Their relationship had not gone beyond the daily interactions involved in taking care of the boys. With no shared history there was nothing to reminisce about as there was with Ben. She welcomed the distance they maintained; it meant she could avoid talking about her past. Except, she suddenly remembered, that night when they had talked about the abuse they each had suffered. She slowly straightened up, opened the door and took the wine out of the refrigerator. Theo had shared a secret then, and it was deeper and darker than her book. She would trust him with hers.

She returned to the dining room, filled both their glasses and sat down. Theo sipped his wine and regarded her—oddly, she thought. She filled her mouth with the cool liquid, swallowed, and began.

"There's this young guy, in his twenties. He's an autistic savant, socially and emotionally challenged but with an encyclopedic knowledge of streets and roads. His mother leaves him in a gazebo in a small park near their home in the morning when she goes to work and collects him at the end of the day.

Parks him with bottle of water and a sandwich and one or two of his collection of atlases and maps.

"There's a prostitute who lives in a seedy apartment at the edge of the park—this is in the Bronx, by the way. She's an illegal immigrant from Russia, existing in the gray zone these people inhabit, trying to survive. She lives for the day when she has enough money to go home and see her son, who she left with her mother. She notices the young man, how he sits in the same place day after day, gets curious, invites him to her apartment for tea. Talks to him, more like at him, as he is a blank emotionally. Sometimes in English, sometimes in Russian. She has no one else, just her clients, her johns. She recognizes him as another lost soul. The relationship evolves." Leah blushed. "For various and complicated reasons she gifts him sex. She gives him a key, points out three o'clock on his watch, tells him that's when he should come, before the others."

She swirled her wine and took another drink. "She becomes ill but can't afford treatment. As she gets sicker—it's an aggressive cancer—she realizes she will never go home or see her son again."

Leah stopped and stared at the table. After several long moments she glanced up and grimaced. "It gets a bit gross at this point. He continues to visit her at three o'clock, even as she declines, even after she dies, until he arrives one day to find her gone and strange people milling about the apartment. They figure he's just curious, shoo him away. He goes back to sitting throughout the day in the gazebo in the park. Just like before except that around three in the afternoon he feels bothered, restless. He knows something's missing but doesn't understand what." She fell silent and fiddled with her wine glass.

"A bit heavy, no?"

She nodded. "I can't imagine why anyone would want to read it, let alone publish it."

"The publisher obviously sees something in it."

"I guess so. It's a pretty small house, hopefully the book won't get too much exposure. I'd stop it if it wasn't so far along."

Theo shook his head. "I don't get you. Any writer, any artist, would be thrilled to have their work get this kind of attention."

She frowned, searching uncharacteristically for words. "The book was borne of a bad time, of some corrosive emotions. It came to me fully formed. I didn't see it while I was writing it, but now, with the benefit of several months and a lot of distance, well … I feel exposed. It is fraught with references to my life."

Theo raised his eyebrows. "Really?"

She blushed again. "Not the prostitute part, if that's what you're thinking. Nor the necrophilia. Metaphorical references, I mean. I don't like what the book says about me, what it reveals." She paused. "Don't you feel that way sometimes about your painting?"

"I paint landscapes."

She gave him a faint smile. "And you don't think that's revealing?"

He studied her thoughtfully for a moment. "Maybe I need to think about that sometime." He drank some wine. "Are you working on another book?"

Leah hesitated. *Might as well.* "Yes, a biography of my mother. As a way of honoring her, of working through … you know." She gestured with her hand.

"Have you told Fin?"

She shook her head. "I won't until I know what he's likely to say." She leaned forward and looked at him intently. "And I don't want him to know about *Three*, either, so please don't mention it to him. Or to any other of the family for that matter, not even Ben. I especially don't want the boys to know about this book or, God forbid, read it. Not now, not ever."

Chapter 25

"Here, try this," Beth Wallace said, setting a neon-turquoise gel capsule and a cup of hot, sweet, milky tea in front of Ben. "Cindy said you had a headache."

Ben had overheard Cindy, and what she actually had said was, "Watch out! Boss has a sore head and he's as cranky as a bear with his nuts caught in a trap." Even if he hadn't found it funny he wouldn't have rebuked Cindy for this apparent disrespect—she would just have laughed at him. His smile of thanks prompted a sharp pain to short circuit between his temples. Swallowing the capsule with a sip of the tea repeated it. By rights he should have canceled the meeting, but he needed a final review with his managers before the Lighthouse board of directors met the following day. He sighed, slouched in his chair and closed his eyes, hoping the turquoise pill would bring some relief.

He could hear Beth's low greeting to another person in the room, then the scrape of a chair being pulled out farther down the table and the swish of paper sliding across the tabletop. Whatever may have caused the throbbing in his head, it wasn't Beth. It had been, paradoxically, Caro who made him change his mind about not hiring her. She had been unusually accommodating on his last home visit: freeing her evenings to be with him, listening with apparent interest to his news, rising to his pent-up passion. He wondered if he was exuding some kind of pheromone that signaled his powerful attraction to someone else; she had claimed once that women had a heightened awareness about threats to their security. As the days passed the thunderclap of his encounter with Beth faded, and it began to look like he and Caro were recovering the lost footing of their marriage. Being attracted to someone other than your spouse was inevitable, he told himself. Beth was not the first woman he had looked at, although he had to admit that none had ever jolted him as she had. The bottom line was that the Lighthouse needed someone desperately, Beth Wallace was the right choice for the job and he should be mature and adult and get on with it.

It had taken little time for Beth to grasp the situation at the Lighthouse, and not much more to start fixing things. Where Ben had painstakingly gone through columns of numbers and pages of reports she seemed to inhale them, getting their gist at a glance, quickly finding the weaknesses in their procedures, the points of vulnerability in their controls, the operational problems to be addressed.

"See, I told you," Cindy had said, jabbing Ben at the top of his thigh bone.

Ben had rubbed the sore spot where her elbow had connected. "Yes, it was a good call."

He was happy to give her the credit for Beth's arrival. The rapport that had quickly formed between the two women was a bonus. He had wondered what it would be like seeing Beth every day, worried things would be awkward, that she would distract him, that he might inadvertently expose how strongly she still attracted him. But she was a consummate professional: conservatively dressed; sedate; friendly in a neutral, detached manner. He responded in kind, but his head would lift whenever he heard her melodic voice and throaty laugh and, when he thought no one was watching, he treated himself to the sight of her retreating back—the long, elegant legs and luxurious hips shifting subtly under the fine wool of her skirt. They never spoke of personal things, never engaged in the easy banter of their first encounter. Above all he avoided looking into her eyes, afraid of what his own might reveal.

The magic turquoise pill eased his headache. He opened his eyes and straightened up.

"Feeling better?" Beth said.

Was he imagining things or was she looking at him with something more than professional courtesy? *Irrelevant and immaterial*, he told himself. He nodded, picked up the cup of tea and gulped it down. The last of his managers entered the room and sat at the table.

"Okay," he said, putting the empty cup to the side. "Let's get started."

"Do you think we're doing the right thing?" Lucas said.

Ris looked up from pulling a casserole out of the oven. "Yes," she said firmly. "We have to remember what's important."

He nodded slowly, unconvinced.

A vehicle grumbled into the forecourt of their house and a door slammed. Theo swung into the room, dropped his hat and keys on the counter and said hello.

"Thanks for coming," Lucas said. "I hope it wasn't an inconvenience."

"No problem; Leah's got the boys' dinner covered."

While Theo was setting the table, another vehicle drove in and a moment later Ben entered.

"Glad you could make it on such short notice," Lucas said.

Ben nodded, distracted. "But I can't stay long. Even with your delay in returning I'm still up to my neck in the final preparations for the board meeting." His mouth twisted in a brief smile. "I'm the one on the hot seat now."

"Dinner's ready," Ris called and they headed to the table.

"Hey, Ben," Theo said.

Ben nodded briefly in response and sat down in his chair. Lucas eased into his own and sighed as he shook out his napkin. His older son's curtness may have stemmed from his preoccupation with the meeting the following day, but he feared it was also a result of their decision to have Theo fill the spot Ben had vacated on the Lighthouse board.

"But he's never been involved before," Ben had protested. "What's he going to be able to contribute? Besides, if the audit indicated anything it's that we need more, not less, competent oversight."

"The new lawyer and Gail from the bank will add that," Lucas said. "Your brother will bring an interesting perspective."

As a rule, they didn't talk business during meals so they all ate quickly, making only light conversation. When the after-dinner coffee had been poured, Ris exchanged a glance with her husband.

"Lucas and I have decided not to proceed with the construction of the new wing," she said.

"But we're constantly turning people away," Ben said. "How are we going to respond to demand without increasing our capacity? Not to mention the time and expense that's gone into its planning and design."

"Yes, we've taken that all into consideration, but we had a good think about things this past summer, about where we are in our lives and what we still want to do. We concluded that, for a variety of reasons, expanding the Lighthouse is not the direction we want to go in right now."

"The renovations as well?" Ben said.

Ris shook her head. "No. After fifteen years they're really needed." She paused. "I hope you're not too disappointed, Ben. I know this was a big part of what you had expected to do here."

"No…" Ben said. "In fact, it takes some of the pressure off. The renovations will be demanding enough."

Lucas glanced at his younger son. "How about you, Theo?"

Theo's shoulders sagged and he made a helpless gesture. "What can I say? Of course I'm disappointed. The mural would have been a great commission."

"Quite some news, huh?" Ben said as he and Theo walked to their vehicles later that evening. He glanced at his brother. "You seem a bit upset about not being able to do the mural."

Theo grimaced. "Yeah, it would have raised my profile and the money would have been nice. Thought I'd finally be able to replace this old Jeep of mine."

Ben stopped. "I thought … I didn't know you were short of money."

Theo had gone a couple of steps ahead. He paused and looked back. "Yeah, well, not all of us can afford a big new Beemer every year."

"It's not every year," Ben said hotly. "The car is leased. I get a new one when the lease expires."

"Never mind." Theo turned and continued on.

Ben caught up to him in two long strides. He had never given thought to the disparity in their circumstances, or Theo's financial well-being. He realized he didn't know much about that side of his brother's life—had assumed, and occasionally with some resentment, that by living at the ranch Theo enjoyed the benefit of their parents' wealth. Maybe that wasn't the case. He wondered how much of a living Theo actually made from his painting. It struck him that the reason Theo dressed the way he did was because it was all he could afford.

"Look, if you need some money I'm sure Mom and Dad would help. Or I could," he said.

Theo regarded him levelly for a moment then drew the keys for his aged vehicle from his pocket. "I've got to get going. I want to see the boys before they go to sleep."

Chapter 26

"I thought the board meeting went well. Such a relief that things are finally back in order," Ris said.

Ben pushed the bits of red onion he had just chopped for their Sunday dinner salad into a bowl and picked up a tomato.

"Yes, thank goodness."

"I think you've put together a good set of people. Cindy certainly seems to be coming into her own, and I was very impressed by that Ms. Wallace of yours."

Ben pierced the tomato with the point of his knife. "If only she *were* my Ms. Wallace," he said—under his breath, he thought.

His mother glanced up quickly and curiously from stirring a small saucepan of hollandaise sauce. He had forgotten how sharp her hearing was. "What's this?" she said.

He felt the tips of his ears redden. "Oh, nothing," he muttered.

She studied him for a moment, her spoon suspended in the air, drops of pale-yellow sauce slowly forming and falling from its bowl. "She *is* quite lovely."

The heat spread to his face. "Yes, she is, but unfortunately we're both married," he said. He dispatched the tomato in a few swift strokes, swept it into the bowl and grabbed another.

His mother looked back at her pot, made an annoyed sound and stirred vigorously. After a moment she said over her shoulder, "Not everyone is happily married."

Ben looked up in surprise. Did she know he wasn't entirely happy in his marriage? Would she not be sorry to see it end? She was always civil to Caro but the two women maintained a discrete distance. Was she suggesting he could do better? Might she actually be counseling him to violate his marriage vows? Before he could ask what she meant, she said, "You never know," and turned back to the sauce.

A few days later Cindy came into Ben's office carrying his overcoat. "Time to go," she said.

He looked up. "Where?"

"The Halloween party."

He glanced at his watch: Six-eighteen. "Can't someone else do it? I've got some work to finish before I leave tomorrow and I haven't had dinner yet."

"It won't take long and there's lots of food there. And you promised." She gave the coat a shake. "Come on, the judging is about to start."

He stood with a sigh, accepted the coat and put it on. "So who else did you inveigle into taking on this task?"

"In-what?"

"Who are the other judges?"

"Rod from special events and two guests: a Marissa someone or other and Mrs. Burton."

"Shouldn't there be an odd number? What if we can't agree and someone is needed to break a tie?"

"Don't be silly. It's kids' Halloween costumes."

The courtyard behind the hotel was strung with lights for the party: an annual event for resort and ranch staff, their families and any guests who wanted to attend. Tables laden with snacks and drinks lined one side. Various games were underway here and there.

"Good heavens, do kids still like apple bobbing?" Ben said as he followed Cindy past a raucous group splashing about in a trough.

"Guess so." Cindy took his arm and wove them through the crowd to a raised dais. She left him to greet the other judges, returning a few minutes later with a hot dog and a cup of coffee. Ben gulped them down while Rod took them through the planned procedure. The kids in costumes would walk past them twice and then form one long line. From the thirty-odd children they would choose three who would be awarded first, second and third place rosettes.

"Aren't those the ribbons we give out at the horse events?" Ben said to Cindy.

"Shush!" Cindy said. "It's all we had on hand."

Turning to Rod he said, "What are the criteria for selection?"

"Oh heavens, the cutest ones, I guess."

"And how will the other kids feel if they don't get chosen?" Clarissa—a lissome twenty-something blonde—said.

Mrs. Burton—a brisk, British woman—huffed. "Children need to learn that there are winners and losers."

"Oh, they all will have gotten some kind of prize tonight," Rod said.

"Why don't we get started, then?" Ben said.

The children were rounded up and paraded in front of the dais. A couple of teenage boys with masks worked their way into the line, teasing and tickling the younger children, disrupting the flow. The costumes were a blur of skeletons and princesses, devils and superheroes. *How on earth are we supposed to choose someone?* Ben thought, but Mrs. Burton had no difficulty, and when the kids finally settled into the long line she declared the winners to the other judges. Rod and Clarissa agreed with her suggestions. Ben didn't have a problem with the first two: a tween girl in a bodysuit sewn with mirror disks that winked and flashed with every movement and a younger boy in a snake costume, complete with scales and a long red tongue which he flicked out at anyone near him. The third chosen by Mrs. Burton was a little girl wearing a gauzy dress and rhinestone tiara and carrying a wand that blinked when she waved it.

Ben's choice was a very young boy with golden-brown hair and almond eyes who was dressed as a cowboy riding a horse. The horse was a child's life preserver attached to a pair of suspenders that hung over the boy's shoulders, to which was affixed a cardboard head featuring long curling lashes and a laughing mouth, and a mane fashioned from a mop. A small pair of jeans ending in a pair of stuffed socks had been hung over the life preserver, completing the appearance of the boy astride the horse. He regarded the proceedings with a wide toothy smile that dimpled his cheeks. While waiting among the other children for the judge's decision he twisted about, making his bogus legs fly from side to side.

Mrs. Burton sniffed. "Really, a cowboy. Hardly original."

Ben resisted pointing out that the store-bought fairy costume was hardly original either. "The idea, perhaps not," he said. "But the execution is. Quite clever how it's made to look like he's riding the horse."

"Well, I still vote for the little girl." Mrs. Burton turned to Rod and Clarissa. "What about you two?"

Rod shrugged, not meeting anyone's eye. "The little girl *is* quite cute," Clarissa said.

Mrs. Burton turned to Ben. "It's decided then."

She stepped to the microphone and proceeded to announce the winners. They came up to claim their ribbons in turn amid clapping and cheers. When Rod handed Mrs. Burton the ribbon for the little fairy, Ben noticed that there were a couple left in the box. He plucked one out.

"I think we can give the little cowboy a prize as well."

Mrs. Burton's struggles to pin the oversized rosette to the fairy's small chest had brought the child to tears and she hurriedly handed her off to her mother. She turned in time to hear what Ben had said.

"We said *three* prizes. We should not change the rules now."

"Oh, I don't think we have to be that strict." He went to the microphone. "Excuse me, we are also awarding an honorable mention. To the little cowboy." He gestured to the boy. People had started to leave. Some turned back at Ben's announcement and there was a smattering of applause. The little boy smiled at Ben but did not come forward. Ben jumped off the dais and carried the ribbon to him. Kneeling down, he pinned it on the boy's chest.

"This is for you. A prize for your costume. An honorable mention."

The boy bent his head to examine the rosette. He smoothed it down with his small hand and looked at Ben. "Thank you," he said.

"What's your name?"

"Nathaniel."

"I am very impressed by your horse. Does he have a name too?"

The boy nodded, his face serious. "Yes, it's Tonto."

"Tonto! Well, yes, although he wasn't exactly a horse, was he?"

Nathaniel started to reply, then he glanced over Ben's shoulder and smiled. "Mama! Look. I got a on-er-bull mention." He tapped the ribbon on his chest.

"That's wonderful, Nathan."

Ben's blood rose at the sound of the woman's voice. He got up slowly and turned around. "Hello, Beth."

"How nice of you to give Nathan a prize."

"I was quite taken by his horse."

"We had fun making it—didn't we, Nathan?"

The boy nodded. "But it is starting to hurt." He ran a finger under the suspender.

"Let's take it off then." Beth wiggled the life preserver up over Nathan's head. Cheers rose from a corner of the courtyard.

"Looks like they've strung up the piñata," Ben said.

Nathan turned to his mother. "Can I go?"

"Yes, but not for too long. We should go home soon."

The boy ran over to where a couple of children were swinging plastic baseball bats at an enormous donkey-shaped piñata. Ben and Beth stood awkwardly for a moment.

"I hope you didn't give Nathan the prize on my behalf," Beth said.

"No, not at all. I didn't know he was your son. Ah, is your husband here?"

Beth tucked the suspenders into the middle of the plastic preserver. "No. No, he's not here."

Ben exhaled with relief. He wasn't sure he was ready to meet the man in Beth's life. A cry from the piñata corner heralded the shower of candy and toys from the ruptured form. Kids squealed and scrambled around the ground. There were many and the pickings were cleaned up quickly. Nathan came running back to them, clutching a small plastic airplane and a handful of hard candies in wrappers. "Look what I have," he said.

"Why don't you carry the airplane and I'll keep the candies for you," Beth said. She pocketed them and turned to Ben. "We must be going. It's quite late and we have a ways to walk to the car."

"Yes, of course."

Nathan lifted up his arms to Beth. "Carry me."

"Nathan, I'm sorry, I can't carry you that far."

"But I'm tired."

"Really, honey. Even if I could, my arms are already full with Tonto. We'll walk slowly."

"Can I help?" Ben said.

Beth glanced at him. "It's quite far. The main lot was full by the time we got here."

"Not a problem." He bent over, picked Nathan up and swung him onto his shoulders, circling the boy's small ankles with his fingers.

"Oh, boy!" Nathan said. "I like it up here."

They walked slowly—skirting the perimeter of the lot busy with exiting cars—to the far corner where Beth's vehicle was parked. Nathan bounced on Ben's shoulders and made airplane noises as he waved the little plastic toy in the air. Ben and Beth spoke of inconsequential matters: the sickle moon, the party, a meeting with the renovation contractors. When they arrived at Beth's small SUV she unlocked the doors and threw Tonto into the cargo area. She opened the back door on the passenger side where a child's car seat was strapped in.

"Time to come down, cowboy," she said. "Say thank you and goodnight to Mr. Wilde."

Ben lifted the boy off his shoulders and held him for a moment, enjoying his warmth, the feel of the small limbs, the little-boy smell. Nathan wrapped his arms around his neck.

"Thank you," he said and gave Ben a smacking kiss on the check.

"Oh!" Beth said. "I'm sorry, it's how we say goodnight."

"Not at all." Ben lowered the boy into his car seat and straightened up. "It's a very nice way to say goodnight."

Beth tucked the boy in, snapping the restraining belts into place. She closed the door and they walked around the vehicle to the driver's door. "I'll say thanks and goodnight as well," she said, turning to him.

Ben leaned forward and tapped his cheek.

"Oh!" Beth raised a hand to her mouth. They both laughed and stood for a moment, enjoying it. "I really should go," she said. She got in and turned on the ignition. He stepped back, and with a final wave she eased the car forward. He stood for a long moment, watching her brake lights fade into the night. Was that regret he had heard in her voice? Or was it just a projection of his own?

Chapter 27

The cancellation of the mural project hit Theo like a body blow. His proposed work, which he had tentatively titled *Aperture*, had evolved over the months like a complex life form and he mourned its stillbirth. Disbelief kept him up much of the night after he learned the news. He tried to think of other ways to execute the work but its size and the resources and time that would be necessary to create it made it prohibitive to attempt without a commission.

By morning his grief had turned to anger: *How could they? Do they not realize how important that project was for me?* It had made him uncharacteristically sharp with his mother when they spoke after the Lighthouse board meeting the next day.

"We didn't realize how much you had been counting on doing the mural," she said.

Ha! he thought and remained silent.

"We'll give you something as compensation for its cancellation."

"That's not necessary," he said.

"Ben said you're short of money."

His fingers curled into fists. *Where the hell did Ben get off...* "I am not, and he is way out of line saying so. Besides, it's not about the money."

"Still..."

"You and Dad did what you had to do. Look, I have to go, the boys will be home soon."

It continued at the family dinner a couple of days later. Glances were exchanged, and when his family spoke to him it was with a certain delicacy. When the others were leaving after the meal, his parents asked him to stay behind.

"You're pouting, Theo," Ris said when they were alone.

He expelled an exasperated sigh. "You kept me behind to tell me that? Anyhow, I am not pouting. I just wish you'd all stop belaboring the mural business. Could we please just let it go?"

"It's obviously upset you," Lucas said.

"What's upset me is how everybody's talking about my finances."

"Yes, of course," Lucas said. "Then I suspect it's probably not the time to tell you that we've increased your salary for looking after the stables."

"I do not need any help," he said through clenched teeth.

"It's a question of fairness," Ris said. "We set the pay fairly low when you first took on the job because we didn't want you to, well, become completely dependent on that money."

"You mean it was a make-work project?"

Lucas made a placatory gesture with his hand. "Son, we wanted to involve you in some ranch activity to, yes, help you along, but also to encourage you to stay and the stables seemed the best place."

"And it took a real burden off my shoulders," Ris said. "But we've realized that in all the time you've been here everyone else has received a raise but you. Also, there's compensation for serving on the Lighthouse board."

"Oh, for Christ's sake!" he said, throwing up his hands. "For once and for all: I don't need your help." He rose. "I'm going home." As he stalked out of the house he wondered at the churlish manner in which he had received what was surely welcome news. *I'm starting to sound like Leah.*

In the days that followed, Theo's disappointment over the mural and anger over his family's intrusions into his financial affairs evolved into a general despondency. It was in this frame of mind that he greeted his thirty-sixth birthday. The balloons floating over the breakfast table irritated him and he accepted the boys' handmade cards with forced enthusiasm. When he tried to work later his thoughts darted around like a school of fish. He gave up, put on his long Drover coat against the weather and headed to the stables to take one of the horses out for a ride.

He had never fussed over birthdays before but this one bothered him. Thirty-five had been neither here nor there but thirty-six was a definite step to forty and all that that implied. And what had he to show for his life this far? He chewed on that for a bit. Fox was the best part of it, but what had he to offer his son? Despite his protestations to his family, he was treading water financially. If it weren't for living in his grandfather's old studio and all the practical support that came with being at the ranch he wouldn't be able to manage. He sighed. Instead of pissing around with Mick and Wes all those years he should have built some kind of foundation for his life. Like Ben had.

As for his art—there was no grand vision, no creative intent driving his work. For the artistic statement the galleries carrying his paintings insisted on he had written some lofty bullshit about the land speaking through him. He had felt something stirring as the concept for *Aperture* evolved, but with that now a non-starter he was adrift again.

And the state of his love life? He hadn't had sex since his last explosive encounter with Serena. Maybe he shouldn't have ended his relationship with Mona; even her charred kisses would be better than nothing.

His parents and Ben attended his birthday dinner that night. He endured the singing, candle blowing and gift opening with grim tolerance. No one lingered after. Leah stopped him as he tried to escape home.

"Are you okay?" she said.

"Just tired."

She hesitated, then presented him with a wrapped parcel tied with a bow. "This is for you."

He hefted what was obviously a book. "Gee, I wonder what it is."

Uncertainty rippled across her face.

"Sorry, Leah. It's very thoughtful of you. Thanks."

"There's, ah, a condition. I would like it back when you've read it."

"What?"

"You'll understand when you see it." She touched his arm. "Goodnight."

At home, he unwrapped Leah's gift to find a mocked-up version of *Three*. He began reading when he went to bed and didn't stop until he had finished it. Even though it was past three he lay awake for a while longer turning the story over in his mind. He slept through his alarm and missed breakfast. When Leah arrived for dinner that evening he returned the book to her, re-wrapped and bow-tied, as she had requested.

Her face fell when she accepted it. "Did you not want to read it?"

"It's dark and very bleak, as you had mentioned, and some parts are quite raw." He smiled. "But I couldn't put it down."

A week later, Theo woke early with an idea for changing one of the elements on *Aperture*. Despite his attempts to forget the work and move on to other projects his mind persisted in offering up more details and refinements. After tossing and turning for an hour he swore, turned on the light and jotted notes and some small drawings on a sketch pad he kept at the side of the bed for this purpose. With little hope of falling asleep again he dressed and headed to Las Sombras.

He entered the hacienda quietly, not wanting to wake the

boys or Leah, who was staying there in Fin's absence. The house was not silent, as he expected. He shed his jacket and went towards the noise which was coming from the boys' bedroom. Recognizing the sound as crying, he quickened his pace. He entered the room to find Leah cradling his sobbing son while Niels tried to pat his hand.

"Dad!" Fox said, pulling away.

Theo sat down on the other bed and drew him into his lap. Fox trembled violently. "Hey, hey," he said, wrapping his arms around the boy. "What's the matter?"

"He had a bad dream," Niels said.

Leah handed over a wad of tissues. He wiped Fox's face, made him blow his nose. "A bad dream? About what?"

The boy hiccupped. "There were all these people and they were after me. They were trying to take me away somewhere."

"What kind of people? Did you know who they were?"

"No, but they were *awful*."

Fox shivered and Theo held him tighter and stroked his head. He looked at Leah sitting on the other bed, her arm around Niels. They were all still in pajamas. "I should have been here," he said.

"I was here, and if Fox's distress had persisted I would have called you."

After a few minutes Fox quietened down. Theo set him on his feet. "Why don't we go and wash your face, and then you can start getting ready for school."

"I don't want to go to school."

"You'll forget the dream soon, you'll see."

"No! I'll never forget it."

"When you get to school and start doing other stuff it will go away."

"I don't want to go to school!" Fox knuckled his eyes and sniveled.

Theo sighed and drew the boy back into his arms. "What're we going to do with you, Fox?"

"Theo?" Leah said.

He glanced up. "Yeah?"

"Did you have any particular plans for today?"

"The usual. Why?"

Leah leaned forward. "How about we go off somewhere today. The four of us."

"But it's a school day."

She turned to Niels. "Do you have anything special on today?"

"No, just classes."

"How about you, little Fox? Any tests or something like that?"

Fox sniffed and shook his head.

Leah looked at Theo. "What do you think?"

"What about you? Don't you have to work today?"

"Ethan's away in Mexico City and I'm not needed in the store. I can catch up with anything else tomorrow."

"What did you have in mind?"

"An outing somewhere. How about Santa Fe? I haven't been there since coming back."

Theo thought for a minute. A distraction may be just what he needed to get out of his funk. "Why not?"

The boys danced around in jubilation, Fox's nightmare forgotten. Leah phoned the bus driver and the school to tell them the boys would be absent that day. After a leisurely breakfast they piled into Theo's Jeep.

"Okay everybody, buckle up and settle down," Theo said as he started the engine. He glanced over his shoulder at the two boys in the back. "And just so you know, we're not going to head off on a trip every time someone has a bad dream." They grinned back at him. He put the Jeep in gear and, to the sound of cheers, turned around and headed down the driveway.

As they traveled Leah and the boys told jokes and played word games. A popular song came on the radio and Theo joined them in singing. Everyone carried the tune but Fox, who warbled badly off key. "Don't quit your day job," Niels said, and they dissolved into laughter.

Theo felt the gloom of the last weeks lift. There would be other murals, other chances. He would get by. "This was a good idea," he said to Leah. She flashed him a brilliant smile. He looked at her for what seemed like an endless moment until a passing vehicle jolted him back to the present. Something shifted within him. *It could always be like this.*

He spoke little during the rest of the drive, his mind churning. *We think you and Leah should get married*, Fox had said last summer. Out of the mouth of babes. They entered the city and he put the matter aside to navigate the crowded streets. After parking the Jeep he walked them around the sites, pointing out items of interest. At noon they selected a restaurant and sat down to lunch.

When they had ordered and received their drinks, Theo drew on his bottle of beer and studied Leah. The logic of marrying her was evident. They got along well enough and Fox adored her. Heck, they were practically living together as it was. As for the rest? He allowed himself a brief moment considering what it would be like. "Whoa," he said, dropping a shutter on his thoughts—it was neither the time nor the place for that. He had spoken louder than he intended and three sets of enquiring eyes turned to him. The heat started at the tips of his ears and crept over his face. "Ah…" he said, smiling gamely. The food arrived and saved him from further explanation. He shook out Fox's napkin and tucked it under his chin, spread his own on his lap. *But is it even legal?* he thought, picking up his fork.

They returned home that evening tired and hungry. Angie had left a pot of stew for dinner. After the boys had eaten and gone to bed, Theo told Leah that he would sleep at the hacienda that night in case Fox had nightmares again. "You're welcome to stay, of course."

She declined, to his relief, saying she could use the evening to catch up on work at her trailer. When she had gone he pulled out his computer, brought up Google and typed in "cousins marriage legal." He learned many things: that marriage between cousins was a common practice in many parts of the world, with over ten percent of current marriages being between cousins; that the prohibition of marriage between cousins was a fairly recent phenomenon in some of the United States, although not in New Mexico nor in any part of Canada; that the social stigma attached to cousin marriages was deemed by those concerned with human rights and freedoms as a form of discrimination; that he and Leah were technically half-cousins because Ris and Fin had different mothers, and many of the states that prohibited first-cousin marriages were more relaxed about half-cousin marriages; and that the ranks of married cousins included notables such as Johann Sebastian Bach, Charles Darwin, Albert Einstein and Mao Zedong. When he was done he carefully erased his search history and closed the lid on his computer.

"Son of a gun," he said.

Over the next couple of weeks the notion of marrying Leah filled the spaces in his mind not otherwise occupied by his daily concerns. It was such an obvious solution he wondered at not having thought of it sooner. The boys were so good for each other, filling large gaps in each other's lives; it would be criminal to separate them. Altogether they already formed a unit. If he didn't close the circle it was just a matter of time before some other guy latched onto her and upset everything.

Like the routines they had established in caring for the boys, she had become familiar to him. Theo studied her now with fresh eyes, conscious of the vaguely predatory nature of his one-sided scrutiny. She was no longer the skittish, half-drowned kitten who had shown up out of the blue earlier in the year. A stable life and the joy of finding her son and achieving peace with her father had softened and rounded her. He was sufficiently self-aware to recognize that his inability to have more than shallow relationships with women probably stemmed from the degrading assault he had experienced. His connection to Leah was of a different order. An unspoken trust had grown between them; she knew and understood his worst scars. And didn't she herself once say they were a pair?

One afternoon, Theo dressed for walking and headed to the stables to look in on a mare who was about to foal. A fretful wind was tossing a few snowflakes around and he lifted his collar to its icy lick. As he approached the stables he noticed that the light was on in Leah's trailer. When her Anachronism work was computer-based she often did it from home. He hesitated a moment, then turned in the direction of the trailer. As he approached, Linc crawled out from under the trailer and came to greet him, swishing his feathery tail. The dog reeked.

"Been rolling in the manure pile, eh?" Theo said, patting him gingerly on the head.

Leah opened the door to his knock. "Theo! Come in." She stepped back and he entered the small space. "You look cold. I've just made some tea."

"Sounds good." He took off his hat and slid onto the bench seat at the small table. Her laptop computer was open across from him, some papers on the side. "I'm not disturbing your work, am I?" he said.

She glanced back from the tiny counter where she was filling cups with tea. "No, I'm almost done for the day."

"That WiFi booster doing the trick?"

"Yes, I get a good strong signal now. Do you want anything in your tea?"

"Clear is fine."

She closed her computer, pushed it and the papers to the back of the table and set their mugs of tea down. "Sorry, I don't have cookies or anything like that to offer."

"Tea is enough." He took a sip of the hot beverage. "You know, it's going to get pretty cold soon. Have you thought of maybe moving to Las Sombras for the winter?"

"Dad mentioned that as well. I'll see how it goes."

They drank in companionable silence for a short time. Theo set down his mug and cleared his throat. "Leah," he said, "I think we should get married. I think it would be really good for the boys."

Her eyes flew open and she stared at him. After a moment she rose, went to door and, with folded arms, silently looked through its small window at the dancing snow and gathering dark. After several minutes she turned and dropped her arms to her sides.

"Theo, my feelings for you are complex, and I'm afraid that exploring them would be all-consuming. I am embarked on this..." She motioned to her computer. "My mother's biography, it's something I have to do. As an act of expiation, of redemption. It will take some time to complete." She paused, her eyes large, dark, troubled. "I'm not ready for this, Theo."

They regarded each other in silence, then Theo picked up his hat and stood. "Okay," he said and left.

After the door closed behind him, Leah sank into her seat and stared at it. *What the...* Nothing had ever passed between them to indicate that this was on Theo's mind. Though they saw each other daily they were rarely alone, and apart from the times they talked about the abuse they had suffered and her book their relations hadn't ventured into the personal.

That her feelings towards Theo were complex was true. She was grateful for his help in settling at the ranch, found his unreserved affection for both his son and hers touching and enjoyed his company as they took care of the boys. And she was hardly indifferent to him, few women would be. But he was a man one could fall for hard and that was the last thing she needed to do. She shook her head firmly. *No, never again.* And the boys? She'd do a lot to keep them together, but *marriage?*

The sky outside her window had darkened. She looked at her watch: time to go to Las Sombras. She shrugged on her jacket and picked up her car keys. *What will I say to Theo now? How will we deal with each other?* She locked the door and stepped through the blowing snow to her car. *Why did he have to go and spoil things?*

"Theo's staying at the stables to help with the foaling," Fin said when she entered the hacienda. "He asked us to bring them something to eat."

They had a quick meal and made up sandwiches for the men. By the time Leah and the boys arrived at the stables with the food the new colt had arrived, and in the excitement that followed she and Theo spoke easily among the others.

The next morning she arrived at Las Sombras to find him wiping blood from Fox's face.

"He stuck pencils up his nose, to be like a walrus," Niels said. "I told him it was stupid."

They said what was needed as they got Fox patched up and both boys fed and off to school. Fin was present while they ate their own breakfasts, and when it came time to say goodbye and head out they did so naturally.

In the days that followed neither of them referred to the startling discussion in her trailer—Theo never raised it and Leah was darned if she would. Their interactions continued as they had before, to the point where Leah wondered if she hadn't dreamt the whole episode. But it hung in the air like the lingering reverberations of a rung bell and she fumed silently at Theo for having stolen her peace.

Chapter 28

As November progressed, Ben turned his attention to the proposed renovations of the Lighthouse. The resort would be shut down for the first four months of the following year to accommodate the most disruptive sections of the work. Only a core group of managers and staff would remain during that time to help dismantle their operational areas and direct the new installations. The rest of the employees would be paid a reduced wage to carry them through the period until the Lighthouse re-opened. They might lose a few, but with an assured job at the end most welcomed the time off.

Ben reflected often on how much more complicated it would have been if construction of the new building had gone ahead as originally planned. As preparations for the renovations advanced he shifted more of the day-to-day responsibility for running the resort to Beth. Their mild flirtation at the end of the Halloween party was never repeated, although he was conscious of a faint charge in the air whenever she was near. *Not that either of us will ever do anything about it.*

One Sunday afternoon he was working in his office when a small face peered around the door. "Well, hello, Nathan," he said.

The boy entered and crawled onto a chair in front of his desk.

"So what are you up to today?"

"I'm drawing."

"Are you? And what are you drawing?"

Nathan swept his small arm through the air. "Airplanes."

In the course of their chat Ben learned that Nathan had eaten macaroni and cheese for lunch, that the cat who lived next door had died and that Nathan had fallen off the swing the day before. He wanted to ask the boy why he wasn't being minded by his father while Beth was at the office but didn't. Maybe the man worked on weekends; he must remember to ask Beth sometime what her husband did for a living.

Nathan had pulled up his pant leg to show Ben the bandage on his scraped knee when Beth burst through the door. "There you are!" She scooped her son out of the chair. "I'm sorry if he was bothering you."

Ben smiled. "Not at all. We were having a nice visit."

After speaking with him about work matters for a few minutes more, Beth took Nathan by the hand and turned to leave. She wore jeans which molded wonderfully to her superb bottom. Ben held the image in his mind for a long moment, then sighed and returned to his interrupted work.

For Christmas Ben went home to Vancouver, leaving the staff to take care of the last guests before the resort closed for the renovations in the new year. He would have preferred to spend the holiday at home but Caro had arranged a week of skiing in Whistler with some friends. The first few days were an orgy of food, drink and revelry. When he woke on the twenty-seventh with a raw throat and burning eyes he was grateful for the excuse to head home early. "Don't feel obliged to come," he said to Caro. "I don't want to spoil your holiday." She told him she would get a lift back to Vancouver when the time came and let him go without protest.

The days alone nursing his cold weren't unpleasant. He

read a couple of thrillers, watched some movies, slept long and deeply. There were daily emails from Cindy and Beth keeping him up to date on Lighthouse activities. On New Year's Eve he received only one email: from Beth. Cindy had been working full out, it said, and she had told her to take some time off. He had a sudden desire to hear Beth's voice and called her office. She was still there and gave him an update on closing the resort.

"Any plans for New Year's Eve?" Ben said.

"No, we like to spend it quietly."

"Well … all the best." He hung up feeling bereft. It struck him as he was mixing a hot toddy that Caro hadn't contacted him once since he had left Whistler. He sipped the lemony drink, wincing when it burned his lip. But then he hadn't called or emailed her, either.

He woke on New Year's Day feeling unaccountably optimistic. It was going to be a good year, he thought. Caro rolled in late in the afternoon. Claiming a headache, she excused herself from dinner. He took the hint and slept in the guest room. The next morning he finished packing for the return to Taos. Fully recovered, Caro bustled about, scrambling together her work things and rattling off instructions into her cellphone.

"When will you be home again?" she said, snapping her briefcase shut.

"Not for a couple of weeks at the earliest. I have to get the renovation properly launched."

His return to the Lighthouse late that afternoon was heralded with a bottle of champagne that Cindy had pilfered from the cellars. "Perrier-Jouët Belle Epoque?" he said, looking at the decorative bottle. "If I'm not mistaken, this wine costs several hundred dollars."

"Who cares?" she said. "Chef won't know, and you're worth it."

He shook his head at her apparent confusion over who was in charge but let it go. The atmosphere was relaxed and celebratory, like they were beginning a holiday. The few staff who had remained to see the renovation through were dressed casually and went about their business in a light-hearted cheery manner.

He settled back happily into his routine. It lasted three days. Just before noon on January sixth Ben received a call from Jay's wife Miriam. He remembered Jay mentioning that they were joining her American family in Aspen for a ski holiday. Voice shaking, Miriam said that Jay had crashed into a tree and was in hospital with a concussion, broken arm and fractured lower-back vertebrae. Ben hung up and buried his face in his hands, distressed for his partner. After several minutes he sighed, picked up the telephone receiver and punched in Trevor's number. The plane was available and Trevor said he could get them airborne in under two hours. Ben called a hurried meeting of the key staff to put them in the picture. He held Beth back at the end.

"You'll have to take care of things until I return," he said.

She nodded. "I'm very sorry about your friend."

Trevor touched them down in Aspen first and Ben went to the hospital to which Jay had been admitted. He found Miriam in the waiting room working on—judging by the number of nested paper cups on the table beside her—her fifth coffee.

"Oh, Ben!" she said, rising to greet him. "I'm so glad you're here."

Jay was in emergency surgery and Ben stayed with Miriam for the time it took to complete. After checking on his partner in the recovery ward he returned to the airport and took off for Vancouver. He had asked the senior law firm staff to await his arrival and over a take-out dinner they discussed the implications of Jay's accident and anticipated absence. He caught up on his emails before calling a cab to take him home and arrived there shortly before ten o'clock.

As he opened the front door he realized that he hadn't let Caro know he was coming. The kitchen and hall lights were on but she was not there. *Must be upstairs,* he thought and wearily headed to the second floor. Halfway up the stairs he heard noises in the bedroom and assumed she was watching television. "Caro, it's me," he called out. The noise ceased, like she had cut the television volume. "Caro?" he said and walked through the door.

He was surprised at the amount of detail he remembered later when he replayed in his mind the scene that had unfolded, because at the time it came to him in a series of disjointed fragments. It was the round-eyed open-mouthed faces he saw first, Caro's and a man's he recognized vaguely, but could not place. Then Caro, holding the sheet up against her chest in a ludicrous display of modesty. Then the man, out of the bed, covering his male parts with a bunched shirt. Then Caro again, her mouth working. Then the man, his back to the door trying to pull on a pair of boxers, having trouble balancing, grabbing the side table for support. He was hirsute—black hair on his shoulders, his back, his arms, his legs. His buttocks in contrast were bald and they gleamed palely, reminding Ben of a baboon he had once seen at a zoo. This made him laugh. Then Caro again, but he now could hear her. "Get out," she was saying. "Get the fuck out!" He complied, not because she demanded it but because the reality of it all suddenly made him want to puke.

Somehow he got to his study and slopped some bourbon into a glass to settle his stomach. He had collapsed in his chair and was shakily sipping his drink when Caro came in, knotting the belt of her dressing gown.

"How embarrassing!" she said. "How could you do that to me?"

"*What?*"

"You weren't supposed to be home for at least another week!"

He stared at her in stupefaction. "Can you hear yourself?" he finally said.

She folded her arms and paced a few steps back and forth across the room. "You'll have to leave, of course."

Her effrontery struck him like a hammer. "You can't be serious."

She waved at the door. "We can hardly both stay here, not after this."

"I grew up in this house; I'm not going anywhere."

"But you're away most of the time anyway. That's the problem."

His mouth fell open. "You're blaming me for this…?" He motioned with his hand. "For screwing around? Who is he, by the way?"

Caro flushed. "Really, this is quite intolerable."

Ben rose slowly. "I agree," he said, his voice hard. "A week should be enough time for you to pack up and get out. Now leave me alone."

Chapter 29

Theo didn't as a rule place much stock in New Year's resolutions, but when the Christmas commotion was finally over and the first of January dawned cold and bright he vowed to restore order to his life after the disappointments and missteps of the previous year. Chief among them was his careless conversation with Leah about marriage. True, he had been thinking about the whole business, but not to the point of actually doing something about it. All he had had in mind that night was to say hello and tell her he wouldn't be at Las Sombras for dinner. And when he blurted out what he did it was more as a point for discussion than a proposal. Like: *here's an interesting idea, what do you think about it?* When it became apparent that she had interpreted it otherwise he was very relieved by her reply. What if she had said yes? What would have happened next? He had no idea.

Yet he was also disappointed. What did it mean that she "was not ready for this"? Not ready to talk about it? Not ready to give him an answer? Not ready for marriage? Not ready for *him*? He hesitated to ask her to clarify, not knowing where the conversation would lead. She didn't raise the matter either. In fact, she behaved as though it had never happened. Which was fine with him, he supposed.

On top of everything else the confused state of affairs raised a question: what exactly was his status? Was he still free? Or was thinking about maybe wanting to marry someone a form of commitment? He was pondering this when a writer from a Phoenix-based arts and culture magazine came to interview him for an article on up-and-coming Southwestern artists. During lunch, the writer—a thirty-something woman with blunt-cut chestnut hair, crimson lips and vampire nails—let him know in every way besides saying so outright that she was available. He considered taking her up on it; she was attractive enough for an evening's dalliance. In the end he just smiled and deflected her volleys. The town was small and he doubted that Leah would be impressed if she ever found out, or that she'd understand that whatever might have happened between him and the writer had nothing at all to do with the two of them.

In the third week of January the phone rang while Theo was in his studio trying to start a new series of landscapes. Painting was proving to be a struggle. *Aperture* still possessed him and his mind would drift away when he needed it to stay focused on making works to sell. The table in his studio was littered with half-finished sketches and more paint had gone dry on his palette than on a canvas. Glad of the interruption he jumped to answer it, regretting doing so as soon as he heard Fiona's voice. She hadn't sent her son a gift or even a card for Christmas and he assumed this was why she was calling. After they exchanged greetings he told her Fox wasn't there.

"That's okay," she said. "It's you I wanted to talk to."

"Where are you, anyway?" he said, fearing that she was in the States and he'd be obliged to haul Fox over to wherever that was for a visit.

"At home, in Sydney," she said, her words clouded by an echo on the line.

"So what's up? Are you planning a trip out here?"

"No. What it is, Theo … oh, I have the most wonderful

news. I had a baby, a little girl. A month ago. We called her Madeleine."

Theo absorbed the news. *At least this child would have Matt.* "That's, ah, great, Fiona. I'll let Fox know he has a sister," he said, anxious to end the call.

"No, wait, the thing is, I'd like him to come here to meet her."

"What?"

"It will be hard for me to travel so far with the baby. I thought they should meet, get to know each other."

"Look Fiona, Fox is in school and I can't just drop everything and bring him out." *Nor can I afford to.*

"You don't have to come. Forrest can come on his own, and during his school holidays."

"On his own? It's halfway around the world!"

"Kids travel on their own all the time. The airlines are quite used to it. They will take care of him."

He pulled the telephone receiver away from his ear and gaped at it in disbelief. Her voice continued on. He put the handset back to his ear.

"Fiona, there is no way in hell that I'd put Fox on a plane by himself," he said, cutting her off. "Quite apart from that he's not going out to stay with you for any amount of time, let alone the summer. Christ, he barely knows you."

"Well maybe it's time he did. I'm his mother. I have rights too, you know."

Her voice had hardened and he could hear her agitated breathing and, as if it were another person on the line, its echo. He rubbed his eyes.

"Fiona, where Fox is concerned you have no legal rights," he said, slowly and deliberately. "Not since you left him with my mother nine years ago."

"We'll just see what my lawyer has to say about that!"

"Knock yourself out," he said and ended the call.

He gave up any attempt to continue painting, pulled on a sweater and his Drover coat and headed to the stables. Chester said that Onyx, a new big black stallion, needed a workout. Theo stroked the horse's neck and spoke to him for a few minutes before saddling him up and heading for the hills. Onyx stepped warily and startled easily in the unfamiliar setting. The distraction of keeping the horse calm and establishing a steady pace kept Theo preoccupied and it wasn't until they'd had a good hard run and settled into a light canter that he could think about Fiona's call.

He had feared this day would come, when Fiona would wake to the fact of her son and want a role in his life. Her demand that Fox be shipped off on his own to stay with her was so outrageous his blood still rose thinking about it, but he wasn't happy with the way their conversation had ended. He leaned over and patted Onyx on the neck.

"All I need now is for her to go all legal on me," he said.

"You must be Leah!"

A burly shaggy-haired man smelling of cigars, cough drops and pleasant man-sweat enveloped her in a hug.

She extricated herself, laughing. "And you are?"

He stepped back and spread his fingers on his chest. "I am Ebes. I come to visit your father."

"Ah," she said. Fin's many friends often came to visit but usually with some warning.

Fox came running up waving a tablet. "We found it, Ebes! Look."

Ebes held up a finger. "I must go now to see this video he speaks about." He took Fox's hand and they headed off laughing to the boys' bedroom.

Leah shrugged off her jacket and looked at the clock. Where was Theo? It was time to get dinner started. Dusting off her hands, she surveyed the kitchen. A raw chicken in a roaster sat on the counter.

"You're home. Good," Fin said, entering the room carrying several bottles of wine.

"Shouldn't that be in the oven already?" Leah said, pointing to the fowl.

"Ebes is going to make chicken paprikash."

"Well, he's off playing with Fox and Niels. Who is he, anyway?"

Fin stashed the wine in the refrigerator. "A saxophone player I met in Europe. We're talking about doing something together."

"Should I maybe fix something else for the boys?"

Fin held up a hand. "No, wait. I'll get him."

Ebes returned and with a clatter of knives and pans began to prepare the chicken.

"You can give him a hand," Fin said generously and wandered off to take a phone call.

Leah fetched and chopped and mixed. When the food was finally on the stove Ebes left to teach the boys a card trick. She looked at the mess he had left, sighed and began to fill the sink.

The door opened and Theo walked in.

"Hey!" she said. "I was starting to worry about you."

"Lost track of time, sorry." He took off his hat and coat and glanced around. "What's happening?"

"Dad has a visitor and he just prepared dinner. I'm cleaning up."

"Here, I'll help." He plunged his hands into the hot soapy water and began scrubbing the pans. "Would you have some time after dinner?" he said over his shoulder.

Leah paused in the act of wiping up spilled sauce on the counter. "Why?" she said warily.

He rinsed a pot and set it on the drain tray. "Fiona called. I'd like to talk to you about it."

She released the breath she had been holding. "Let's see how the evening goes."

The meal took over three hours to cook and eat and was well lubricated by the wine. After, Fin and Ebes retired to Fin's studio with the bottle of Tokaji Ebes had brought. Theo led the exhausted boys to bed while Leah put the leftovers away and loaded the dishwasher. When he returned to the kitchen she was shaking out the tea towels and hanging them to dry.

"What do you think? Do you have a few minutes?" he said.

Leah brushed a lock of hair out of her eyes. "I guess so."

"Do you want something to drink?"

She waved her hand in front of her face and shook her head. "I had more than enough at dinner."

They headed for the alcove in the living room, startled on the way by a saxophone squawk from the studio.

Leah smiled. "Dad's going to be a mess in the morning."

"They both are, I think."

"It's about Fox," Theo said when they sat down. He scrubbed his face with his hands and took a deep breath. "After all these years and seeing him only four times—and then for only a few hours—his mother has suddenly decided that she wants him to fly over to Australia—all by himself, no less—and spend the summer with her."

Leah sat back. "Oh, my."

"She's had another baby, has discovered the joys of motherhood, it seems. I have complete and sole custody of him and can refuse, but she's capable of making a huge fuss if I don't do what she wants."

"Legally, you mean?"

He nodded. "I don't think she'd get very far—Mom and Dad made sure that the custody agreement was ironclad both here and in Canada—but it would be a hassle and unpleasant. And probably costly."

She frowned. "Sorry to hear that, but wouldn't it be more productive to talk to Ben about this?"

"The issues aren't legal in my mind. It's more a question of what moral obligation I have to her, you know, as a mom who wants to reconnect with her child."

Leah drew back. "Oh, Theo, I'm the last person to advise on moral obligations to women who have given up their children."

"No, you're not. Yours is exactly the perspective I need. I want to know what you'd consider fair."

Her forehead furrowed and she looked down.

"Sorry if this bothers you."

She inhaled sharply and shook her head. "No, it's okay. Just give me a minute to think about it."

He rose. "That chicken was awfully spicy. How about I get some water?"

When he left she hunched over, her chin resting on her interlaced fingers, her mind in turmoil. Of all the things for him to ask of her. On no dimension of this issue could she be neutral. "*Think, think!*" she said under her breath. *And try to be fair.*

He came back with glasses tinkling with ice cubes. She straightened up, accepted one and took a sip. After a moment she spoke.

"You know, I think there's a special circle in hell reserved for women who have left children behind. I expect many would want to reconnect with a child if given a chance, but do they have a moral right to? I don't know. I figure I gave up any rights when I left Niels at the hospital. I've been very fortunate in entering his life the way I have and I think Dad was correct to make me commit to become a permanent part of it first. Think how confusing it would have been if we had met and then I had left again and just popped in and out of his life after."

"Much like Fiona's done with Fox."

She nodded. "But it sounds like Fiona now wants in."

"Yeah, much as I'd prefer that she didn't. There's the distance for one thing, and she's so destabilizing. Remember last spring, how long it took Fox to settle down after seeing her? Fiona's so … clueless. She doesn't seem to understand the complexities in her relationship with Fox. Everything's about her. Maybe that will change as she raises her daughter, but right now? And her judgement. She wants him to travel unaccompanied halfway around the world and then to stay for God knows how long among people who are effectively strangers. I mean, he's only nine." He shook his head. "I can't agree to that at all. But still, I want to be fair to Fox. Maybe he should have a chance to get to know his mother."

"Why not start there," Leah said. "Forget what Fiona's proposing. Do what my father did, make her work for what she considers her rights. Define the terms and conditions of her relationship with Fox and make her commit to them. Like, I don't know, she communicate with him by letter or a proper email once a month for a year so they can get to know each other a bit. Then maybe they progress to Skyping. At an appropriate point you can arrange a visit either here or over there but for days, not months, and with you present. When Fox is older and the foundation is laid he can spend time with her alone—if he wants to, of course."

"That all makes sense but…" He made a hopeless gesture. "I doubt she'd agree or even listen long enough to understand what I'm trying to say."

"Send her a letter. Probably good to have it documented anyway. Establish the framework, the terms you'd accept. Shape things so that you remain in control."

"And if things don't work out? If she doesn't agree, or she doesn't comply?"

"You'll have demonstrated goodwill and that should weaken any challenge she might mount."

"Yeah, that's worth a try." He smiled at her. "Thanks, Leah."

The warmth in his eyes brought the blood to her face. "I should go now," she said, rising.

Chapter 30

"Well!" Fin said, his eyebrows dancing. "That's, ah, nice, I guess."

Leah steeled herself. Her father clearly harbored reservations about her intention and ability to write a biography of her mother. "I won't embarrass you, I promise," she said.

"No, of course not."

"Anyhow, I've done as much background research as I can but I need to start talking to people. You, obviously, are the most important one. If you're willing."

"Certainly..." He looked at her intently. "This is no small undertaking you've embarked on. What's prompting you to do it?"

She didn't answer immediately. Some days she wasn't sure herself. "Mom was unusual, and a woman of note. Her contribution to science was major."

Fin's eyebrows shot up again. "You understand her work?"

"To a point. Anyway, her life should be documented."

They began to talk, usually in the quiet time in the evening after the boys were in bed. The first conversations were awkward, Leah's confidence faltering as she posed her questions, Fin hesitant in his responses, his eyes lanced with pain as he spoke of his wife. She had never seen her father exposed in that way before and it was both moving and disquieting.

"This is hard," he said at the end of their third session.

Leah's heart sank. "We don't have to continue if you don't want to."

"No, no, it's good." He made a vague motion with his hand. "It helps."

She organized a trip later in January to conduct the rest of the interviews. Her destinations were the town in Northern Alberta where her mother grew up, the city of Edmonton where she had attended university and Vancouver where she had spent most of the rest of her life.

"You're nuts to be going at this time of year. The winters there are brutal," Theo said when she announced her plans.

"But it's the best time here. Anachronism is in the post-Christmas lull and I can deal with the online work on the road. Besides, it's cheaper to travel now. Vancouver should be fine."

She had declined use of the family jet when it was offered, in part because of her determined independence and in part because hidden within the itinerary was a short visit to New York for the release of *Three*. Her continued secrecy about the book prompted an argument with Theo.

"I still don't understand why you're not telling family about it. They already know that you're writing the book about Alex and would want to be there for the launch," he said. "*I'd* like to be there."

"Well, I don't want them to either know about it or be there."

"But the fact you've written it is public, all anyone has to do is Google your name."

"Yes, but no one is likely to and even if they do they won't necessarily assume it refers to me. I've just used my initials and there are no doubt other L.A. Larsens in the U.S."

"If you feel so strongly about hiding your identity why didn't you publish it under a pseudonym?"

Leah winced. She didn't want to admit to the unexpected pride that made her choose not to.

"And won't there some kind of promotion, like tours and signings and stuff?" Theo continued.

"They're a small house with a limited marketing budget. Most of the promotion will be on the eastern seaboard and through social media and I'll be doing that behind some solid barricades."

"But won't it be in stores out here? Like Anachronism? What does Ethan think about it?"

"He doesn't know about it and it's unlikely to be a bestseller so I doubt it will get much distribution out here."

"Geez, you'd think you were ashamed of the book."

"I'm not ashamed…" She scowled and thought for a moment. "Look, I fully understand what I have accomplished. But the person who wrote that book is different from who I am now. I don't like that person and I don't want anyone I care about to know her."

"Still, I think you're being a bit ridiculous about it all," he said.

Her eyes flashed. "That's surely my concern, isn't it?"

"They're going to be hurt when they find out."

"There is no reason for them to find out. And if you breathe a word to any of them I'll…" She folded her hands across her chest. "Just stay out of it, Theo."

The *Three* launch was a modest affair in an independent bookstore in Brooklyn attended by a small crowd of the publisher's friends and patrons and some minor media. It was followed by promotions and signings in three other bookstores and a handful of interviews. Leah offered distance as the excuse for not having any of her own friends and associates in attendance.

When it was over she boarded the flight to Canada with relief, confident that news of *Three*'s publication wouldn't reach anyone she knew.

From Fin she had learned a bit about her mother's family. Alexandra had come along late in her parents' lives. It was a second marriage for her father and she'd had two half-brothers from his first. Leah vaguely remembered meeting her grandparents when she was very young but had never met her uncles. Joseph, the only one still alive, was her first stop.

As Theo had warned, the weather in Northern Alberta was harsh and she struggled through deep snow and against bitter winds to the rancher at the edge of town where he lived. Her interview with him turned out to be a party with several previously unknown cousins and their spouses and children in attendance. Leah was given the seat of honor next to her uncle—a raw-boned, angular man with a face leathered by years of farming. Joseph's wife, a woman soft and pale as a ball of rising dough, circled around pressing coffee and cake on the others crowded in the living room. Leah shrank under their friendly but relentless gaze and tried to divert the discussion away from the stream of questions about herself to the subject of her mother.

"Alexandra: she was a strange one," her uncle finally said. "Didn't talk hardly at all. We all thought she was funny in the head, you know—retarded. It happens sometimes when the parents are older. Guess she did okay, though. She went away young." He shrugged. "Lost touch after that."

Leah also met with two of her mother's previous teachers. She didn't get much from the first: a woman who was willing enough to talk but kept losing the thread of the conversation. With the other—a man who had served as the vice principal in Alexandra's school—she hit gold. She knocked on his door expecting to meet another octogenarian with memory issues but was greeted by a sprightly man dressed in a sports jacket, white shirt and tie for the occasion.

"Oh yes," he said, leading her to the dining table in his apartment. "I'm not likely to forget Alexandra. I never encountered a student like her before or since."

When they sat down at the table he asked his wife, who was watching a game show in the living room, to make coffee. She glared at him then snapped the recliner in which she was seated upright with a resentful huff and waddled off to the kitchen. His eyes followed her and when she was out of hearing he leaned towards Leah.

"Teaching your mother was the most astonishing and rewarding experience I have had in my entire life."

He explained that before he got involved Alexandra's first-grade teacher did not know what to do with her.

"She wouldn't stay at her desk, or in the classroom, even. She would wander around the school and take books from rooms and from the library without asking. Initially we thought it was a question of discipline, and to my everlasting horror and shame she was punished." Tears sprang to the vice principal's eyes. "Strapped, you know, on the hand. We still did that then. Can you imagine?"

The coffee arrived, weak and instant, and he took a moment to compose himself.

"I finally twigged onto the fact that something else was going on one time when I had to speak to her about some books she had taken from the library, again without permission. I forget the subjects now but they were at a level far beyond what someone her age should be able to read or comprehend. When I asked her if she could understand what was in the books, I'll never forget the look she gave me—it was something like pity. 'Of course,' she said."

After, he explained, they tested her and when the level of her intelligence became apparent he organized a special study program for her. "We were astonished at how much she had already taught herself," he said. "Depending on where she was at on a subject I had teachers from different grades contribute." He shook his head. "Some were almost afraid of her, thought her a bit of a freak. And when we couldn't offer her anything more I arranged for her to move on to the university."

He fell silent. After a few moments he stirred and drew a thick accordion folder that had been sitting at the end of the table closer. "But I kept track of her—newspaper articles, publications, awards. So easy to do with the Internet now. It was a sad day when I learned that she had passed away."

Leah leaned forward eagerly. "May I see what you have and possibly copy it?"

He smiled shyly. "I've already done that for you."

Leah's meetings in Edmonton were equally productive. Through the remembrances of the people with whom she spoke she tracked her mother's evolution from misunderstood outcast child to awkward, reserved, astonishingly brilliant young woman. In Vancouver, where memories of Alexandra were still fresh, more specific details of her character and life emerged. Some colleagues who may have felt diminished by the international stature she had achieved focused on her absent-mindedness, administrative disorder and lack of diplomacy in critiquing other's work. Most accepted her quirks as the collateral of an exceptional mind. One of Alexandra's former graduate students spoke of her with such intimacy and emotion that Leah had gone home and shed hot tears of envy and regret at having forsaken the privilege he had enjoyed.

While in Vancouver she stayed at her father's house, catered to by his bored housekeeper. She slept in one of the guest rooms—her old bedroom harbored too many bad memories— and used her mother's office to organize interviews, write up notes and sketch out preliminary ideas for the book, enjoying the novelty of being able to work for hours uninterrupted by the demands of life at the ranch. Alexandra's papers and books had all been removed for an archive of her work the university was creating but her desk remained untouched. Leah sifted through its contents lightly, breaking down when she found a small framed school portrait of herself at thirteen in the top drawer. It was the only picture of her in the house.

Chapter 31

"My mom's going to come back, isn't she?" Niels said.

"Yeah, sure," Theo said. "You guys just Skyped with her yesterday. Did she say something to suggest she wasn't?"

"No, but she's been gone an awfully long time now."

Theo stretched from the counter where he was preparing the boys' school lunches to tap on the February 17th circled in red marker pen on the wall calendar. "That's when she's coming home. It's only a week away."

"It's no fun around here with her gone," Fox said.

"Thanks a lot!" Theo said.

The boy's cheeks reddened. "You know what I mean."

Theo smeared some mayonnaise on a slice of bread and slapped it down on the bottom half of the sandwich. Yeah, he did. He missed Leah more than he had expected and it wasn't just because of the extra work when she wasn't around. When Fin and Niels had decided to live at the ranch he thought they were all he and Fox needed to round out their solitary lives. Not anymore. The evenings were lonely without her company and comfortable banter, and without her they couldn't seem to get the lively exchanges going at the dinner table. It was as though someone had pulled the melodic line out of a song and left only the drum beats.

A few days before Leah was scheduled to return, Theo received a call from a number he didn't recognize. He had finally shoved *Aperture* back enough in his mind to focus on other work and was inclined to ignore it, but the insistent ringing shattered his concentration. He let loose a few choice words and snatched up his phone.

"Would you happen to know a Serena Gibb?" a woman who identified herself as an officer with the New Mexico State Police said after she had confirmed who he was.

"No, I don't," he said, squinting at the painting he was working on.

"Are you certain, sir? She had your name, address and telephone number on her."

Awareness dawned and he gave the conversation his full attention. "Yes," he said slowly, "I think I may know her. What do you mean, she *had* this information on her?"

"She got herself into a bad car accident early this morning."

His mind took a moment to absorb the news. "Is she dead?"

"No sir, but she's pretty banged up."

"But why are you calling me? She lives in Calgary, in Canada."

"We know that, sir. Car she was driving had Arizona plates, rented in Scottsdale. Looks like she drove from there. We figure she was on her way to see you. Long drive at the best of times and with that freezing rain last night roads would have been tricky."

A pit opened in Theo's stomach. He carefully set down the brush he was still holding and lowered himself into a chair. "I know nothing about that."

"Anyhow, we need to get in touch with her family and there's lots of Gibbs in Calgary. We need to find her folks quick and it would speed things up if you could tell us who they might be."

Theo thought about the tall man, the fiancé with the piercing hazel eyes. Where were they and why was Serena alone? And why on earth was she coming to see him? "Wait, I met her father." He rummaged in his memory. "Ned, his name was. Ned Gibb."

"That'll give us something to work with," the officer said, a smile in her voice. "And she's in St. Vincent in Santa Fe if you want to see her."

No, I do not want to see her, he thought, hanging up the phone. He sat for a couple of minutes staring at nothing, then sighed and stood up. But he would have to go. She was alone, probably scared, and it would be a while before her dad got there.

He put his paints away, changed into clean jeans and a sweater, grabbed his jacket, wallet and keys and headed out. He stopped at Las Sombras to explain the situation to Fin without mentioning that the friend in hospital was a woman. "I don't know when I'll be back. It could be quite late, maybe not even until tomorrow," he said. Fin gave a preoccupied wave of his hand, assured him he'd take care of the boys and turned back to his computer.

At St. Vincent he learned that Serena was in intensive care. "If you're not immediate family I'm not sure you can see her. I'll call up," the woman at the information desk said. She lifted the receiver but a man interrupted her before she could dial. Theo slipped away and headed for the elevators. The senior nurse at the intensive care nursing station, an imposing woman whose name tag identified her as Audrey, said, "You family?" When he said he wasn't she shook her head and moved away. "I've come a long way," he called after her. "Couldn't I at least say hello?"

"She's in no state to say hello to anyone," Audrey said, scribbling something on a sheet attached to a clipboard.

Theo didn't speak for a moment. "It's bad then, is it?"

The nurse clicked her pen closed and looked up. "We're just waiting for the family to arrive to…" She caught herself. "To decide on the course of treatment to follow."

Theo swallowed his shock. "She's not from here. It could be hours, a day even, before her family arrives. Someone should be with her."

The woman studied him with deep-set dark eyes for several moments. "All right then," she said, nodding.

Despite the nurse's warning Theo was unprepared for the sight of the broken body that lay, seemingly held together by casts and tubes and bandages, on the narrow bed. A monitor to which she was connected ran several lines of green-lit codes, the lurching signal for her pulse punctuated by beeps.

"Oh, Serena," he said softly.

He found a chair, brought it to the side of the bed and slowly lowered himself into it.

"My God, Serena, what have you done?"

He found her hand under a fold of sheet, held it lightly with one of his own and sat, willing her to open her swollen eyes. He searched for any kind of awareness. He thought he felt her fingers move slightly.

"Serena!" he said, leaning forward.

He spoke to her quietly, asking what she thought she was doing driving in such bad weather, why she was alone without her fiancé, what her intentions were in coming to see him. After a while he fell silent. Her fingers fluttered occasionally against his, like she was tapping out a code. He wondered if it was intentional or a kind of unconscious reflex. Whenever it happened he squeezed her hand in response and told her he was there.

Audrey or another nurse looked in regularly, taking blood pressure, administering medications through the intravenous drip, studying the monitor. He had to leave twice, once when the doctor stopped by, the other when the nurses had to perform some private procedure. He used the washroom and had a cup of coffee, taking up his post when the medical staff completed whatever it was they were doing, his mind closed to all but the pressure of Serena's hand in his, waiting for the next movement of her fingers.

Time passed. He had just shifted position to ease a stiff back when he heard an almost imperceptible exhalation and felt Serena's fingers relax in his hand. In the fraction of a second it took him to register the change the sensor marking her heartbeat stuttered and become a solid line of sound. He looked disbelieving at the monitor, then down at the body on the bed. He stood to call Audrey but before he could open his mouth another nurse ripped the curtain aside and pushed him out of the way. The brusque movement jerked Serena's hand from his and it dropped, inert, to the bed. He stumbled to the waiting area near the nursing station and stood there dazed.

A few minutes later Audrey came up to him. "She's gone."

"Wasn't she ... didn't you have her on life support?"

"Sometimes that's not enough."

He looked at her for a moment before speaking. "How do you deal with this, day after day?"

She shrugged. "It's part of life. Just too bad she couldn't have hung on. Her family's supposed to be here anytime now."

As if on cue the elevator doors sprang open and Ned Gibb stepped out, stopping to get his bearings before striding towards them. Dean, Serena's fiancé, followed closely behind.

"Where is she? Where's my girl?" Ned said.

"Is this her father?" Audrey said quietly to Theo. He nodded and she stepped forward and rested her hand on Ned Gibb's arm. "I'm very sorry sir, but your daughter has passed," she said quietly.

"Passed?" Ned said.

"No!" Dean said, his voice raw.

Ned glanced at him, realization draining the blood from his face. He turned back to Audrey. "It can't be."

"I'm sorry, sir."

Theo backed away, desperate to remove himself from the circle of anguish that was forming. Dean noticed him for the first time.

"*You!*" he said. "What the hell are *you* doing here?" In a step he was at Theo's side. He grabbed a fistful of Theo's jacket, thrust his face forward. "This is all your doing!" he said, his spit speckling Theo's face. He drew his arm back, clenched his fist and threw a clumsy punch. Theo blocked it easily.

"Stop it! You stop right now," Audrey said. "This is a hospital!"

Ned pulled Dean back, spoke quietly to him. Dean jerked his arm free and turned away, his shoulders shaking.

Theo took out his hankie and wiped his face. Ned came back to him.

"I apologize for Dean. That was uncalled for. You're that art teacher, the one from last summer, right?"

"Yes."

Ned regarded him with narrowed eyes. "If I can ask, what *are* you doing here?"

Theo tucked his hankie in his pocket. "I live near Taos. The police found my name and contact information among Serena's things so they called me. She may have been coming to see me." He paused. "If she was, I didn't know about it and I didn't invite her."

"So why come here?"

"I gave the police your name but I didn't know how long it would take for you to get here, and this being a strange place and all I didn't think she should be alone."

"So you were here…?" Ned put his hand to his mouth.

"Yes." The word caught in Theo's throat.

Ned inhaled a long, ragged breath. "Look son, I don't know

what you were to Serena, and I'm grateful that at the end she wasn't alone. But I think you should go now."

Theo nodded. "I'm very sorry," he said.

Ned's face suddenly crumpled and his body convulsed with a sob. Theo turned and left.

Chapter 32

Caro did not move out. The morning after Ben had found her *in flagrante* she had approached him while he was brewing a coffee, and with stiff lips told him that she had no intention of leaving.

Ben kept his attention on the espresso machine and spoke only when his cup was full and he had stirred in a spoon of sugar. "Really," he said.

"I can understand that you would be upset."

He bit back several sarcastic retorts that had leapt to his tongue.

"Well, don't you have anything to say?" Caro said. Hot spots of color had bloomed in her cheeks. Her hands were clenched tightly together.

Was she actually wringing them? Ben took a leisurely sip of his coffee. "I don't, actually. The whole thing has left me quite speechless."

"Well, what do you propose we do?"

For a start, you can go to hell. "I don't know, what do you think we should do?"

She was steaming, he saw, and working hard to keep the lid on. He gave her credit for that.

"I think we should let some time pass, let our emotions cool down," she said.

You mean let my *emotions cool down.*

"Then," she continued, "we can see what if any difference this, um, event makes to our relationship."

He suddenly felt utterly fatigued by the whole matter. He certainly didn't want to have that discussion now. Maybe she was right—what they needed was time and perspective. This kind of scenario probably played out daily around the world and not all marriages caved in under it. God knows it could have been him. If Beth hadn't been married, had given him any kind of encouragement, he probably wouldn't have thought twice about jumping into bed with her.

"Whatever," he said.

By silent agreement he and Caro established separate living arrangements in the house—she in the master suite, he in one of the guest rooms—and settled into a curious, bifurcated mode of existence.

"Don't bother Jay; it's your turn to carry the place all on your own," Miriam said when she called to inform Ben that they were heading to their condo in Maui for his partner's convalescence.

Ben forbore reminding her that when he had left to manage the Lighthouse he had hired someone to handle the extra work and continued to help run the practice. He ground through long hours catching up on Jay's active files, a part of his mind and most of his heart still at the Lighthouse. He flew back to Taos twice, but only for the day. It was enough to satisfy him that Beth, Cindy, the chief engineer and the contractor undertaking the work had it well in hand and he could effectively direct the work from a distance.

On the last Saturday in February Beth called him on his cellphone.

"Ben, I'm sorry to have to tell you this but I'm leaving the

The Lighthouse

Lighthouse, effective immediately. I've prepared a letter. Can I send it to you?"

He had sat down on the armchair in his study for what he'd expected would be an agreeable conversation and now stood up abruptly. "What? But you can't."

"I'm really very sorry but I have to."

"What's going on, Beth? If something's wrong at the Lighthouse I can fix it."

"No, everything's fine there…"

"Then why? You know how much I count on you."

"I do know, Ben, and I truly hate to leave you in the lurch, but I have no choice."

"Can't you at least give me a reason?"

The long silence that followed ended with a sigh. "It's personal, Ben. I'd rather not say. I should go now."

"Wait, you can't just leave like this. We need to talk. I'll come out to see you."

"Oh, Ben. It won't make any difference."

"It doesn't matter. I'll be there tomorrow."

As Trevor was unlikely to be available on such short notice, Ben booked an early flight for the next morning to Denver and organized matters at work for his absence. At the Denver airport the following day he rented a car and drove to the Lighthouse where he had arranged to meet Beth. She was leaning against her SUV in the parking lot and straightened up when he pulled in.

"Come on, let's go inside," he said, getting out of his car.

"I'd prefer to talk out here if that's okay."

He strode up to her. "It would be a lot more comfortable inside and I sure could use…" He stopped abruptly. She was dressed in jeans and a leather jacket and her lustrous hair was pulled back into an untidy knot. A ragged cut marred the perfection of her mouth and large bug-eye sunglasses weren't enough to cover the wine-red bruise discoloring her cheekbone.

They looked at each other for a long moment.

"Oh, Beth," Ben said softly.

She bowed her head and pressed her lips together hard.

"Who did this to you?" he said.

"My husband found us. He was not happy."

"What do you mean 'found you'?"

She brushed a lock of hair off her face and leaned back wearily against her vehicle. "It's a long story, Ben. I had left him when I came here. He didn't know where I was and I thought I was okay and that with time we could end things civilly."

A cold anger built in his chest. "What kind of a man hits a woman?"

Her lips twitched in a brief smile. "You'd be surprised."

"But you, Beth. You're so smart, so capable. How did you end up with a guy like that?"

"He wasn't like this in the beginning." She grimaced. "Actually, he probably was but didn't show it then."

"But why go back to him? Can't you call the police or something? There are services for women in your situation."

She looked away. After a long silence she sighed and turned back to him. "He says he won't let me go, that he'd find me, find us, anywhere." She paused. "I believe him, and I'm afraid of what he would do next time."

"But how can you live in this way?"

"It's not always this bad. I know how to behave, how to avoid … eruptions."

"But still. Do you at least have family to give you some support?"

She shook her head. "My mother's gone, my dad left us when I was a kid. I probably have some relatives out here but I don't know them. It's why I came to this area, not to find family so much as a place that felt like it could be home."

Ben suddenly looked around. "Where's Nathan?"

"He's with his father." She straightened up. "And I should go. He barely agreed to let me come and meet you. I told him that I needed to get something I'd forgotten here."

An image of the little boy with the almond eyes and toothy smile came to Ben's mind. "Does your husband also hit Nathan?"

She fiddled with her car keys. "Not … much."

"Bastard!" he said through gritted teeth. "I should talk to him."

She shook her head and reached out as though to stop him. "Oh, no, no. That would only make things worse."

He shifted on his feet angrily, impotently. "Goddamn son of a bitch! I can't stand that you have to go through this. There's got to be something that can be done."

"There isn't, Ben, but it means so much that you care."

They looked at each other and he stepped forward and pulled her into his arms. She resisted briefly then leaned into him. He closed his eyes and tried to imprint the feel of her body and her smell, fresh like windswept grass, onto his mind.

"Come away with me, Beth," he said into her hair.

"I would in a heartbeat."

"Then do!"

"I can't, Ben. He has Nathan." She pulled herself reluctantly out of his embrace. "And now I really do have to go."

A profound sense of loss enveloped him. "Where will you be?" he said forlornly. He didn't know what would be worse, never seeing her again or having her close by and not being able to do anything to help.

"We're going back to Las Vegas."

He gently touched the wounded lip and placed his hand on her cheek. "If you ever need me, Beth, if I can help with anything, anything at all, just call. Promise me you'll do that."

She nodded, not looking at him, got into her SUV and slowly drove away.

Chapter 33

Theo turned up the collar of his jacket, regretting the decision to walk to his parents' house for Sunday dinner. He had forgotten how quickly the weather could turn. Not ten minutes after he had set out a biting wind had whipped up, dragging in dark, low-slung clouds and canceling what was left of the warmth and light.

The walk was yet another bid at clarity, a hope that exercise and fresh air would dissipate the fog in his mind. He had chosen it over going to a movie with Leah and the boys and wondered now whether the robotic ninja film would have been a more effective way to free him, if only for a couple of hours, from his muddled thoughts. In truth he was avoiding Leah. Back home from her travels she had noticed and queried his despondency.

"Everything's fine," he had insisted but couldn't meet her eyes saying it and had felt her troubled scrutiny since.

Over two weeks now since Serena's death and he was still caught in the grip of the experience. At any time and without warning he would be thrown back to the moment of her dying and relive the ineffable sensation of life ebbing from her hand. He dreaded nights the most when at the point of suspension between consciousness and sleep he felt the ghosts of her fingers tapping their indecipherable code on his palm, and he would have to get up and move around until exhaustion drove him back to bed.

He felt responsible for her death. If he hadn't engaged with her, if he had sent her packing on the very first night, she would not have made that long deadly drive. He should have realized from how she had tricked her way into his room that something was off-beam. Why had she been coming to see him? He thought of Serena's father and her fiancé with the hazel eyes. They had clearly been devoted to her and it was unlikely she lacked for anything. What was missing from her life that compelled her to seek him out?

A gust of wind lashed his face. He shivered, and not just from the cold. And what if Serena had not crashed? What would have happened if she had reached Taos?

When he arrived his mother smiled a greeting from the kitchen. Ben sat at the pine table in the solarium, a drink in his hands. Things had become even more awkward than usual between them since their exchange about his finances. Theo knew it bothered their parents and decided to make an effort.

"Hey Ben, didn't know you were back," he said, sitting down at the table.

"He got in this afternoon," Ris said.

"So, how're things?"

Ben shook his head and drank from the glass.

His mother placed a small bowl of nuts in front of Ben. "Eat something with that whisky." She turned to Theo. "Come and give me a hand with dinner."

With a glance at his brother he rose and followed his mother to the kitchen. "What's up with him?" he said when they were out of earshot.

"It's Beth Wallace."

"The woman who works at the Lighthouse? What about her?"

"She's left."

"I know she was good but isn't that a bit of an overreaction?"
"Oh, don't be so obtuse."
"Obtuse?"
"Really, Theo."

Awareness dawned. Ben and Beth Wallace? An image of her came to his mind: tall, dark, not unattractive. *Son of a gun.* And his mother not only knew about it but didn't seem to mind.
"But what about Caro?"
"Yes, well," his mother said. "Now, let's get that roast in the oven."

A few days later Theo woke with a sense of purpose he hadn't felt in weeks. After getting the boys off to school he went straight to his studio. He welcomed the change. His work had suffered over the winter, dragged down first by the disappointment over losing the mural commission then by the Serena incident. Typically he would have rebuilt his inventory by now but here it was March and he had only a few paintings in hand. And interest was growing in his work—the article in the Phoenix arts and culture magazine in which he was mentioned had prompted several enquiries.

He was making good progress when his cellphone rang late in the afternoon, breaking his concentration. He was tempted to ignore it, but recognizing Leah's number he set down his brush and palette to answer.

"You have to come," Niels said. "Fox hurt himself."
Theo's mind cleared instantly. "Where?"
"In his leg."
"No, I mean where is he?"
"On the other side of the house behind the wall. And you need to hurry."

Theo tore out the door, leaving it open behind him. He saw movement beyond a crumbling adobe wall and raced in that direction. He vaulted over the wall and almost landed on Leah.

She was hunched over Fox who lay on the ground, sprawled on his back. His right thigh was impaled on two tines of a rusty four-prong pitchfork. His scooter lay overturned nearby.

"Dad!" The word dissolved into a sob. Fox's face was blurry with snot and tears. His mouth formed a rictus of pain.

Theo crouched down next to Leah. She was stripped down to her bra, her black one. Her sweater covered Fox's chest and she was using her T-shirt as a compress around the punctures. It and her hands were sticky with blood. He reared back. "Oh my God!"

Leah blew her bangs out of her eyes and looked up at him. "I need you to be calm and I need you to keep Fox still and quiet," she said, her voice low and even.

Niels came running up, his arms full. "The pillow, quick," Leah said. He dropped the other items and held out a small throw cushion from the sofa.

"I can't let go here," she said. "Theo, help him. Slip it under Fox's bum. We want to elevate his legs to try to reduce the bleeding and get the blood to his heart and his head. But be very careful, we don't want to dislodge the fork."

Theo did as she said. Fox cried out when they moved him and tears pricked Theo's eyes at the pain in his son's voice. He started to rise. "We've got to call an ambulance!"

"It's the first thing we did," Leah said. "Now the blanket—cover his chest but be careful."

Fox squirmed as Theo carefully tucked the blanket around him. Bright red blood seeped up between Leah's fingers on the T-shirt. She pressed down harder.

"Fox sweetheart, you need to be very, very still." She looked up at Theo. "Talk to him."

"Please Fox, do what Leah says." He wiped his son's face with his hankie.

"It hurts, Dad. Really bad."

He rested his hand on Fox's head. "I know, but it's important that you don't move."

Niels had also brought some tea towels. "Leave them folded and put one down on the side of each of my hands," Leah said.

Niels knelt down and fumbled with the towels. "There isn't much room and it's hard with these other things sticking up."

"I know, love. Just fit them in as best you can."

Niels gingerly tucked the towels in place. Leah swiftly grabbed one then the other and pressed them down hard on the T-shirt compress, now saturated with blood. "Okay," she said. Sweat trickled down her face. "Can one of you wipe my forehead?"

Niels fumbled in his pocket and produced a crumpled tissue. "It's used."

"That's okay." She lifted her face and he patted at her forehead. "My eyes too."

"Can I take over?" Theo said.

She shook her head. "Best not to let up the pressure, even for a moment." She turned to her son. "Niels, love, go to the road so you can tell the ambulance people where we are."

He leaped up and ran off. Fox had gone quiet. His face was alarmingly white, his eyes clouded with pain.

"Fox, sweetheart, I need you to stay awake," Leah said. "We have to keep him from going into shock, Theo. Talk to him."

Theo stroked the boy's head. "How did this happen, Fox?"

"We were on our scooters," Fox said, his voice hollow. Tears welled up in his eyes. "I tried to ride on the wall but I fell off."

"Oh, son," Theo said. He was shoulder to shoulder with Leah. She was breathing deep and hard and Theo could feel her heat. Sweat slicked her face again. He raised his arm. "Here, wipe your face on my sleeve."

She bent forward and rubbed her face against his forearm.

"Fox!" she said, looking up. The boy's eyelids fluttered. "You have to stay awake." She glanced at Theo. "Let's sing."

She started panting out the song they had sung on that long-ago drive to Santa Fe.

"Come on, Fox," Theo said, and joined in.

Fox's voice rose and fell with the words, heartbreakingly off-key. A lump swelled in Theo's throat and his own voice faltered.

The thin wail of a siren sounded in the distance. "Oh, thank God!" Leah said. Her arms trembled with the effort of pressing down on the wound.

Theo briefly closed his eyes and breathed out his thanks. "You're exhausted, let me take over," he said.

"No, I'll be okay now."

They resumed the song, the swelling sound of the siren drowning them out. It stopped suddenly and a minute later footsteps thundered across the terrace.

"They're over here," Niels said.

Two uniformed paramedics appeared at the wall. Theo recognized Jimmy, one of Chester's nephews.

"Oh, hey, Theo," Jimmy said. He and his partner took in the scene for a few seconds then conferred briefly. The other man ran back to the ambulance. Jimmy stepped through the break in the wall. "Puncture wound, is it?" he said.

"Yes, and I think it's nicked the femoral artery," Leah said.

"Ah, yeah, could be," Jimmy said. He set his kit bag to the side, crouched down and put his hand on Fox's forehead. "What's your name?" he said softly.

"Forrest Xavier Wilde," Fox whispered.

Jimmy smiled. "Good boy, Forrest. It's going to be okay." He turned to Leah. "I can take over now."

Leah wouldn't let go. She fired a number of questions at Jimmy. He answered patiently, keeping his eyes averted from her chest. The other paramedic reappeared with more equipment.

"I called in. We've got to be quick," he said quietly to Jimmy. He moved to where Theo was kneeling. "If you don't mind, sir," he said.

Theo nodded and moved away. The paramedic dropped down and whipped a tourniquet around the boy's thigh above the punctures. Leah finally sat back on her heels. Niels quickly wrapped his jacket around her. They silently watched Jimmy replace Leah's T-shirt and the tea towels with proper bandages and bind them tightly, and his partner swiftly unpack intravenous bags and prepare Fox's arm for the line. When these were connected he slipped an oxygen mask over the boy's face.

That done, the paramedics rose and separated the two halves of the scoop stretcher.

"Good thing that fork doesn't have a handle," Jimmy said. He put his hand on Fox's arm. "This might hurt a bit. Yell if you want to."

They slipped one half of the stretcher under the side of Fox that wasn't wounded then moved to the other. It took some maneuvering to get the other half of the stretcher under the pitchfork and to put padding under and around Fox to keep him in position. He cried out as they shifted him up and Theo started forward.

"It's okay, we're almost done," Jimmy said.

With Fox secured they quickly packed up their materials.

"If you guys can help carry this stuff we won't have to make the trip back," Jimmy said.

He and his partner lifted the stretcher, stepped carefully around the wall and set off with long strides towards the ambulance. Theo, Leah and Niels followed with the remaining gear. At the ambulance the paramedics slid the stretcher in and loaded their kit.

"You can ride in the back with him," Jimmy said to Theo.

Theo turned to Leah and Niels. "We'll find you," Leah said. He nodded and hauled himself up into the vehicle.

Jimmy's partner drove—wildly, Theo thought—weaving around other vehicles on the road, their path cleared by the siren. After checking Fox's vital signs Jimmy shifted to the front and spoke on the radio for the rest of the trip. In no time, it seemed, they were at the hospital, but instead of going to the emergency entrance the ambulance drove around the side where a helicopter was sitting at the ready, two people at the controls. When it stopped Jimmy and his partner jumped out and opened the back door.

"What's happening?" Theo said.

"Fox needs a special kind of surgery. They can't do it here," Jimmy said.

"What kind of surgery?"

"They'll explain. You're going to a hospital in Santa Fe." He and his partner pulled the stretcher out and carried Fox to the helicopter. When he was in place Jimmy waved Theo to the craft. "You'd better get in."

"Aren't you coming?" Theo said.

Jimmy shook his head. "This is as far as I go." He put his hand on Theo's shoulder. His dark eyes were soft with sympathy. "Good luck to you both."

"How bad is it?" Theo asked over the beating of the aircraft's blades.

The nurse was taking Fox's pulse. She pulled the stethoscope out of her ears and glanced up at him. "That's for the doctor to say." She explained that a surgical team was preparing to receive him as soon as they arrived at the Santa Fe hospital. It took them just under half an hour to get there. When they landed everything happened very quickly. In Emergency, Fox was borne away and as Theo tried to follow one of the nurses stopped him.

"We need some information," she said.

She took him to the admission office and handed him over

to a clerk who began to take him through a long list of questions and several forms. He answered distractedly, glancing away constantly although he knew he wouldn't see Fox. When the question of payment arose he realized that he didn't have his wallet. Using the hospital phone he called Leah's cellphone, hoping she and Niels were still at home. Niels answered. They were in the car and had just left for Santa Fe. Leah had called the Taos hospital and knew about Fox being transferred. And yes, they had thought to bring his wallet. After a few seconds of fumbling noises Niels read out his insurance policy number.

When the forms had all been completed the clerk directed Theo to the surgical waiting room. She pointed to a set of elevators and mentioned the floor. "Someone will help you there."

He recognized the elevators as he approached them. It was the hospital where Serena had died. His step faltered and he stopped. The person behind him bumped his shoulder and muttered either an apology or a curse. A dreadful foreboding seized him. He shook himself and continued on.

The woman at the service desk in the waiting room, whose nametag identified her as Carla, told him that Fox was being prepped for surgery. Theo asked to see the surgeon and she made a call.

"Someone will come out to talk to you," she said when she hung up.

A few minutes later a young Hispanic woman in scrubs came to the desk. "Mr. Wilde?" He nodded. "I'm Dr. Martinez. I will be assisting on your son's surgery."

"How bad is it?"

"It's a delicate procedure and we have to move quickly. He is in good hands: Dr. Gilman is one of the best vascular surgeons around."

Theo had to be content with that, and at Carla's gentle urging looked for a place to wait. The room had a softness to it: shaded lamps, comfortable chairs, plants, tables with games

The Lighthouse

and things to read, a counter with coffee and tea. Two other parties were present: a young African American woman staring blankly at the opposite wall and two young men in their twenties talking quietly. Theo found a chair away from them in a corner and sat down.

According to the big-faced clock sitting high on one wall it wasn't yet six o'clock. He should be home preparing dinner. Was it less than two hours ago that this nightmare had started? He thought of where Fox was now, what they were doing to him. He would be scared. Was someone comforting him? His chest tightened. He jumped up, paced twice around the room. Another party came in: an older woman with a couple in their thirties. They went to the corner he had just vacated. He found another section of empty chairs and sat down. It would be an hour at least before Leah and Niels arrived. He thought of going to find Audrey, the nurse who had been in the intensive care unit with Serena, for contact, reassurance. No, he thought, shaking his head. No, not a good association. He eased himself back into the chair, clenched his fears within a small gray fist of control, and waited.

"Is there any news?"

Theo opened his eyes. Leah slid into the chair beside him, Niels crowding behind her, his face anxious.

"He went into surgery as soon as we arrived."

Leah nodded. "Sorry to take so long to get here. I thought it best to get a place to stay for the night first." She set his gym bag on the floor. "I've brought you some things you might need."

He unzipped the bag. Inside were clothes, his shaving kit and the book that had been on his bed stand. She also had brought his sketchbook with a couple of fine point pens. "Thanks," he said gruffly, moved by her consideration.

"Here are your wallet and cellphone," she said, handing them over. "I couldn't find the charge cord, though."

"It's in the studio."

"Ah, I didn't go in there. We'll get another one. And I couldn't find the key to lock your door."

"It doesn't matter. If someone wants anything from in there that badly they're welcome to it."

"Also, I called your parents. Trevor's flying out to Vancouver tonight and will bring them back in the morning."

He nodded. The morning was unfathomable, the night a vast dark sea they still had to navigate.

Carla from the service desk approached them. "I'm sorry, but you have to be twelve to wait here," she said. "Can I ask how old this young man is?"

Leah began to speak but Niels cut her off. "I'm staying," he said.

"So you're twelve then?" Carla said.

Niels sniffed and looked off to the side.

"Okay," Carla said with a slight smile. She motioned to the beverage table and a bookcase. "Make yourselves at home. I'll bring you any news as soon as I get it."

"Good boy," Leah whispered when Carla had left. She turned to Theo. "Niels feels responsible for what happened to Fox."

"I should have stopped him," Niels said, his voice quavering. "I told him it was a crazy idea but he wouldn't listen."

"I know you try to look out for Fox but it's not your fault when he does something stupid," Theo said.

"I should have stopped him anyway."

Theo squeezed the boy's knee. "You're a good friend to Fox, and without you we couldn't have gotten help for him as quickly as we did." He rose. "Anyone want some tea? It's going to be a long night."

They settled in to wait, speaking little, watching the clock's long red second hand jerk noiselessly from one black notch to the other around the white face. Occasionally they'd rise, one

The Lighthouse

then the other, to ease their backs and stretch their legs. Niels eventually feel asleep, his head in Leah's lap. Theo had not thought he would ever sleep again, but when someone called his name he woke from a doze. The clock said it was eleven seventeen. He lurched up, shook his head to clear it and went to speak to the man.

The surgeon was shorter than Theo, his shoulders rounded by a permanent stoop. Wild gray hair escaped from under his cap and dark stubble shadowed his face. His bloodshot eyes were deeply pouched.

"Mr. Wilde?" he said. When Theo nodded he held out his hand. "I'm Dr. Gilman."

Theo shook it. "How is he? How's my son?"

"It was quite a mess," Dr. Gilman said. "But I think we saved the leg."

"Saved the…?" Theo's hand flew to his mouth. His throat closed and blood thundered in his ears.

The surgeon put his hand on Theo's shoulder and smiled, his eyes kind. "He's young and it should heal okay. What we have to watch out for now is infection. He's on his way to the recovery room. You can see him there."

When the doctor left Theo buried his face in his hands and stood, absorbing the news. To this point his fears had been formless, now he knew what had been at stake. Even though the danger had passed he was gripped by the horror of what might have been. After a long moment he dropped his hands and turned to Leah and Niels across the room. They had watched his exchange with the doctor and stood clinging to each other, their eyes, so much alike, wide with apprehension.

He reached them in a few long strides and gathered them into his arms.

"It's okay," he said. "I think Fox is going to be all right."

Chapter 34

Ben fidgeted within the tight circle of family gathered around Fox's hospital bed. *What am I doing here? I barely know the boy.* Returning to Taos had been seriously inconvenient—he had to get one of the junior lawyers to fill in for him at a critical hearing—but when his father told him that he was expected to accompany them back it was in a tone that brooked no argument.

He stood and paced, grateful that his mother had secured a private room for Fox; conducting this vigil in an open ward would have been intolerable. He sat down again in the standard-issue plastic chair designed for someone much smaller than he and stretched out his legs. *Another couple of hours to kill.* He groaned. Even then it would only be to return to Taos with Leah. Trevor wouldn't be able to fly him home until the next day.

The boy lay still, drugged and feverish. No one spoke—Niels read, Leah worked on her computer, Lucas and Ris sat silently and gazed at their grandson. The small intimacy of his parents' interlaced fingers constricted Ben's heart. He silently railed against the cruel fate that had torn Beth away from him just at the moment when he discovered that his feelings for her were reciprocated and they might have had a future together. He should have overcome his high-toned scruples and acted on them before. If he had they would be facing her husband together. Instead, he thought bitterly, he had tried to preserve his ash pit of a marriage and Beth was now lost to him forever.

A nurse entered, did whatever nurses do and left. A few minutes later Theo came in. When they had arrived he had gone to the hotel for a few hours of sleep. His hair was still damp from a shower, his face pale and etched with exhaustion.

"Did you have something to eat?" Ris said.

Theo nodded, pulled a chair to the edge of the bed and sat down.

"Whatever possessed Fox to ride on that wall?" she continued.

"Who knows?" Theo said.

Niels looked up from his book. "He's always doing crazy things. You don't know the half of it."

Ris shook her head. "The apple hasn't fallen far from the tree, has it, Theo? I remember taking you to emergency once when you were around Fox's age. You were so violently ill we thought you were dying. Remember?"

Theo shrugged. "Sort of."

"It was nicotine poisoning; you'd smoked the cigar Ted Stowe had left on the patio."

Theo tipped back his chair and rested his foot on the metal base of the bed. "For what it's worth I've never wanted to smoke since."

"That's good, I guess. And there was the time out here at the stables. You were even younger then. I wouldn't let you get up on a horse and while I was busy talking to Billy Coriz you went ahead and grabbed old Bella's tail and hauled yourself up her back leg. Good thing it was her; any of the others would have kicked you clear across the corral." She shook her head. "I'll never forget the look on that poor horse's face."

Theo glanced at his mother. "I am truly sorry for all the grief I've ever caused you and Dad."

"No, I didn't mean to…" Ris bit her lip and tears filled her eyes.

The afternoon ticked down. Leah and Niels left to collect their things from the hotel for the drive back to Taos. Lucas and Ris went with them to check into their own room and rest. Theo remained, passing the time by drawing in a small notebook: tiny, perfect sketches of the water jug on the nightstand, the intravenous bag on its pole, the blanket folds, his own boot—complete with scuffs and creases—braced against the side of the bed. Now and again he glanced at his son, occasionally leaning over to adjust the pillow or smooth the cover. For a brief moment they were strangers to Ben, and he a spectator of their being. He closed his eyes and slowly opened them again.

"Why don't you take a break before I leave," he said.

Theo shook his head. "I'm fine."

"Go on, have something to drink, stretch your legs. It'll be a while before Mom and Dad are back."

Theo considered for a moment then nodded and rose. "Thanks, Ben."

A few minutes later Fox stirred and opened his eyes. "Dad?" he said, his voice hoarse.

Ben moved to the chair Theo had vacated. "He's not here right now."

Fox licked his cracked lips and swallowed. "I'm thirsty."

Ben found a glass with a straw and filled it with water from the jug. "Here," he said, holding the straw to the boy's mouth.

Fox drew on it. "Thank you," he whispered when he was done.

Ben set the glass back on the stand. "How are you feeling?"

Fox gazed at him with clouded eyes for a moment. "It hurts."

"I know, but it will get better."

Fox nodded. His eyes slowly closed and he slept, his head canted to the side, his mouth slightly open. His cheeks were

The Lighthouse

sunken and sweat matted his hair. His chest rose and fell lightly under the covers. *So small, so fragile*, Ben thought. Leah had said that the injury had been serious and Fox was now fighting infection. He leaned forward and tucked the blanket in where it had become loose. As he gazed at his nephew a small knuckle of sympathy nudged his conscience. All those old resentments of his brother's looks, of his talent, of his child—they seemed so shabby now.

When Ben had returned home after seeing Beth he had told Caro in unvarnished words that he wanted a divorce. She had not agreed, saying that they both needed to think carefully about such a move.

"I don't have to," he had said and stomped away.

When he was back from the trip to see Fox at the hospital she button-holed him over his morning coffee.

"If you still want a divorce I'm prepared to proceed," she said.

Hallelujah. "Fine," he said. "I've asked Phil Chen to represent me. Who do you plan to use."

She mentioned a lawyer he didn't know. "And we should start talking to agents," she said.

"What for?"

"The house. We'll have to sell it, of course, and it will be easier to settle if it's done ahead of time."

He took a mouthful of coffee and swallowed it. "Can't be done."

She folded her arms over her chest. "I know it's your family home and all, but that's the way it is."

"No, what I mean is: I don't own the house. My parents do. I'm just renting it from them." He didn't actually pay any rent, only direct costs, but as a newly minted lawyer he had insisted on preparing a tenancy agreement when his parents had offered him the house. His mother had humored him and signed it.

Caro's face drained of color and her eyes bulged. "But … but…" she said, her mouth flapping. "I've always thought this house belonged to us. You never said anything!"

He took another sip and set his cup into its saucer. "You never asked. Like, for example, how a young guy who had just started working could afford a house like this. Like whether there were mortgage payments you could contribute to. All these years you've lived here at no cost, none at all. I've paid for everything: utilities and insurance and maintenance. Even the cleaning service. Did you truly never wonder how I did it?"

"Your parents are rich. I thought they gave the house to you."

"Yes, my parents have many assets, but they don't just give them away." He stood up, carried his cup to the sink and headed to his bedroom to get dressed.

"You'll not get away with this," she hissed at his retreating back.

He had merely shaken his head then but sitting at his desk later that morning he felt a twinge of sympathy for his wife. What a jolt the news must have been. The house was worth a lot and Caro had probably expected to leave their marriage with half of its value. He shook his head. What was he thinking? Now Caro would try to extract as much money from him as possible, and given the devious, scheming mind that served her so well in her work he didn't underestimate her ability to do so.

He shifted in his seat trying to relieve an ache in his tailbone. The chair was a new one that his executive assistant had insisted he needed, ergonomic and all that, but it was too small for him and he wasn't sure how to recover his old chair—if it was still around—without offending her. He sighed, picked up the telephone receiver and, in defiance of Miriam's stricture against phone calls, dialed the number of her and Jay's condo on Maui. Jay picked up on the second ring, catching Ben off-guard.

"I wasn't expecting you to answer," he said.

"Yeah, well, Miriam's been trying to keep me out of trouble."

Ben felt a rush of affection at the sound of his friend's raspy voice and wry tone.

"How are you doing, anyway?"

Jay hesitated before responding. "Doc here says I have a chance of walking again, but it's going to take a lot of work."

"Good news, then."

"I guess so."

Neither spoke for a moment. "Did you get my emails about Bodner?" Ben said.

"Yeah."

"I don't like the sound of the business he wants help with, so if it's okay with you I'm going to blow him off."

"Doesn't matter to me."

"Any idea, any sense at all, when you'll be coming back?"

The silence strung out long and empty. Finally, Jay gave a sigh that filled the length of the telephone connection. "Might as well tell you now. I was going to give it another couple of weeks but I don't think I'm going to change my mind. I'm not coming back, Ben."

Ben's mind went blank. He leaned back in his chair, closed his eyes and rubbed them. "I see," he finally said.

"Sorry to do this to you, but all I want to do right now is get back on my feet. If I can."

"Well, I guess it's good to know sooner rather than later."

"You can buy me out, or maybe some of the young bucks in the shop will. There's always someone out there who's looking for a good practice."

"Can't say I find the idea of getting used to someone new all that appealing."

"Yeah, I know, and again, I'm really sorry, Ben."

Ben remained silent, digesting the news.

"Look, why don't I let you think about it and we can talk again soon?" Jay said.

"No, wait," Ben said. His mind was clearing. He was filled with a feeling that he couldn't identify. It wasn't sadness, or disappointment. "Maybe it's time to end the whole thing, Jay," he said slowly. "Dissolve the partnership altogether. We've had a good run and maybe it's time we both moved on."

They spent the next half hour talking about next steps: who they'd talk to, what they'd have to do. Ben made notes on the actions and paperwork needed to proceed. They ended by laughing at an old joke and their goodbyes were easy and warm. *I'll sure miss him,* Ben thought, hanging up, but the sadness didn't last. He leaned back in his chair, prompting it to groan.

He had told Jay he didn't yet know what he'd do once the practice was sold but that wasn't quite true. On the flight out to Taos with his parents after Fox's accident he had raised the issue of getting a new CEO for the Lighthouse. "Let's talk about it another time," his mother had replied—understandably, given the circumstances. If the sale of the practice was concluded within a reasonable period of time he could continue on at the Lighthouse, maybe even move out to Taos for good. He straightened up and drew a piece of correspondence from his in-basket.

"Yes," he said out loud, "I'm definitely ready for a change."

Chapter 35

"Isn't there a biblical saying about a serpent's tooth and an ungrateful child?" Theo said.

"There is a saying but it's actually a *thankless* child, and it's from King Lear," Leah said.

"How do you know this stuff?"

"I may be wrong."

She looked at Theo with concern. He sat, chin in hand, staring at a cup of cold tea clouded with iridescent film. He hadn't changed from the sweats he had worn at breakfast that morning and his jaw had disappeared under several days of stubble.

"What's up, Theo?"

He sighed and leaned back in his chair. "I yelled at Fox this afternoon."

"What about?"

"Something stupid with his homework. We've only been back a few days but I'm at my wit's end. I'm not sure I can handle it until he's able to go back to school." He shook his head. "After all that time in the hospital sitting all day, then going back to that hotel room every night—I thought it would be so much better when we got home. But I didn't realize how much the hospital staff did until I had to do it myself. Bathing and dressing and bathroom—he can't manage any of it himself. And he's nine, with all the energy of that age, and it's hard being immobile. So I've got to keep him occupied, cheer him up when he gets frustrated, and I'm always on call for drinks and snacks.

"It's like when he was a baby, the constant care, but now I'm dealing with a kid with an attitude and a hell of a vocabulary. He told me I should be more *empathetic* towards someone in his *predicament* rather than *castigating* him." He gave Leah a ghost of a smile. "You've got a lot to answer for."

She returned his smile and sat down at the table.

"I could take some time off work, give you a break."

"It's enough you help in the evenings."

"Anyway, just let me know. Should I go see him now?"

"Niels is with him; they're playing some game."

They were silent for a moment. Leah raised a finger. "I have an idea: how about hiring a tutor? For both of them. It would keep Fox occupied and up to date on his schoolwork. Niels can stay home and help keep Fox company. I think he'd enjoy that."

Theo considered for a moment. "It's a thought. Where would I find a tutor?"

"The school can probably recommend one."

"Probably be expensive."

"I'll pay half of course, for Niels."

Theo grimaced and waved his hand to dismiss her offer, but she ignored him and made enquiries the next morning. The school suggested a substitute teacher they used named Guy who was in the area doing research at the Taos Pueblo on an obscure topic in psycholinguistics for his doctoral thesis. She arranged for him to begin the following Monday.

"So, Guy, what do you think? Will this space work?" said Theo, taking the tutor to the dining room.

"Oh yeah, it's perfect. Lots of room and we can pull Fox's wheelchair right up close."

Fin entered the room. "Is this where you're going to set up?" he said.

Guy was slight and sandy-haired, and when Theo introduced him to Fin his pale-lashed eyes blinked rapidly behind his black-framed geek glasses. "Are you *the* Gabriel Larsen?" he said, clasping his hands together. "I am a *huge* fan. Your *Concerto for a Cloudless Sky*? My absolute favorite."

Oh, great, Theo thought, but when Fin had graciously accepted the accolade and continued on to the kitchen Guy grew serious again and talked about how he proposed to organize the boys' studies.

Fox and Niels had happily agreed to be taught at home, viewing it as a kind of holiday. They and Guy hit it off quickly and the boys easily fell in with his arrangements. In addition to taking them through their lessons, Guy looked after Fox's other needs and pitched in with lunch preparations. Theo hovered until mid-afternoon on Guy's first day to make sure the setup was working. When it became clear that he wasn't needed he headed to his studio, both relieved and dejected by his son's happy chatter and laughter.

Since Fox's accident he had only been home briefly to pick up clothing or other items, and the place was chilly and damp from disuse. A fire would have fixed that quickly but there was no wood in the box. He thought of going to the shed to collect some, decided it wasn't worth the effort and turned on the electric heater. In his studio, the unfinished canvases he had been working on sat on their easels like eyeless faces. The palette he had dropped when Niels had called him about Fox's injury was encrusted with dried paint. He pitched it and the paintbrush he had been using into the waste bin.

He looked around the room distractedly. *Maybe tomorrow.* He left and closed the door behind him. *I should check in at the stables,* he thought vaguely but couldn't muster the effort to go. *Maybe later.* A profound fatigue enveloped him like a wet cloak and he sat down and rested his head on the back of the sofa. His eyes closed, and after a moment he leaned to the side, stretched out and fell asleep.

The buzzing of his phone woke him. He sat up and looked around. The sky was darkening. When he answered his mouth felt like it was lined with felt.

"We're about to start dinner," Leah said.

"Look, can you manage without me?"

"Yes, of course. You do sound tired. Dad has friends visiting and the boys will be eating off trays in their room anyway. I'll get Fox ready for the night and stay over in case he needs anything."

He thanked her and ended the call. Rather than refreshing him, the afternoon sleep left him listless and woolly-headed.

"I need food," he said to the silence. "And light."

He flipped several switches and headed to the kitchen. He heated a can of soup, ate it, cleaned up. The effort drained him and he sank back down onto the sofa, turned on the television and flipped through the channels.

At midnight he went to bed and lay for a long time staring at the dim outlines of the objects in his bedroom before drifting off. An acute sense of menace woke him and he sat up breathing heavily, his hand on his pounding heart. The digits of his clock showed that it was eight minutes to four. Gripped by an undefined sense of urgency he pulled on a pair of jeans and hurried to Las Sombras. The hacienda was dark and quiet. He made his way soundlessly to the boys' bedroom, entered and stood for several minutes looking at his sleeping son.

The feeling of foreboding slowly faded. He considered going to his bedroom down the hall to sleep but his body still vibrated from the surge in adrenalin that had woken him. He returned to his house trailed by a pale shadow formed by the moon's cold light and made a cup of tea.

As he drank it he was struck by the realization that sometime

The Lighthouse

in the last few weeks he had lost hold of Fox. He hadn't been able to prevent his son's injury and he had been helpless when infection burned through the boy's body after the surgery. Strangers had saved his life and Guy, another stranger, was proving to be much better than he at helping Fox cope with his convalescence.

He stared into the amber liquid in his cup. And Fox was becoming more and more his own person. Their paths would begin to diverge soon. He remembered himself, not much older than Fox was now, the secrets he had kept from his parents, the distance between them he had allowed to form. Fox too would have experiences Theo would never know, joys and woes he would never share, dangers he would not be there to counter. Others would come to mean as much to him as Theo, probably even more.

He thought of wild and willful Serena. Her father and fiancé combined weren't enough to keep her off a destructive path. *Nothing lasts. Right from the beginning, all we face is separation and sadness, death and decay.* He felt stupid for having taken so long to grasp this obvious reality. *Everyone must know this. How do they live with the knowledge? Why does anyone even bother?* The distress of it gutted him. He remained immobile for a long time, bloodless with unfocused grief. The sun rose and began to arc through the sky. At some point he lay down on the sofa and slept.

The ringing phone jolted him awake. "What?" he said thickly into the receiver.

"Theo?"

"Who else would it be?"

Leah paused. "Just wanted to know if you are coming for dinner."

"No."

"Are you okay?"

He exhaled sharply. "I'm fine. I just want to be left alone."

He hit the off button without saying goodbye and sat massaging his temples. He knew he had behaved badly but didn't care. The evening followed the pattern of the previous night but this time, when he was poking through his cupboards for some food, he found a case of beer. He opened a bottle and drained it in three long gulps. It was warm but he opened another anyway, putting the rest in the refrigerator to chill. He sucked at the bottle as he made his way to the sofa and switched on the television in the hope that the distraction would keep his morbid thoughts at bay.

Over the course of the evening he drank all the beer, eventually falling into a twitchy sleep. A couple of hours later he woke, staggered to the bathroom and vomited. After rinsing his mouth he swallowed some painkillers, struggling to keep them down. Night pressed against the windows. He lay down on his bed but rose minutes after, still queasy. He sank onto the sofa again and turned the television back on.

Time passed. The sun rose and he finally slept. It was setting when the telephone woke him. He glanced at it but did not answer. Lassitude pinned him to his seat. If it hadn't been for having to use the washroom he might not have gotten up. He thought he should eat but had no appetite. He felt little else either. The sofa seemed to offer an oasis within this deadness and he stayed on it, mindlessly watching the television's flickering images. One of the stations was running a marathon of a popular crime series. He turned the television's volume up and tried to concentrate on the action.

Over the next day he slept and woke intermittently, rising occasionally to relieve himself or for water and food—a tin of beans, stale crackers, some microwave popcorn he overcooked and then threw out when the smell nauseated him—but otherwise remaining marooned on the sofa like a castaway. Thoughts crawled through his mind like slugs. He observed his shrunken world as though through a telescope backwards. When the phone rang in the late afternoon he didn't even hear it.

A knock woke him. The television was still on and for a moment he assumed that's where it had come from and turned his face away from the noise. The knock sounded again, insistent. He opened an eye but before he could answer, the door opened and Leah entered. She surveyed the room for a few moments then sat down across from where he was sprawled on the sofa.

"Sorry to barge in. I called but you didn't answer your phone."

He squinted up at her. "I didn't hear it."

Leah reached for the control and turned off the television. "You haven't been at the hacienda since Monday and we're getting a bit worried."

"Oh?" His mind began to clear, his thoughts loosening like a crumpled ball of paper. He looked around. "What's today?"

Leah regarded him with concern. "It's Friday. What's going on, Theo?"

"I haven't been sleeping well."

His movements had released a stench of sweat and sour breath and he stood abruptly, hoping Leah was far enough away to not notice. "I need to take a shower," he said and hurried to his bedroom. He brushed his teeth first, scouring his tongue with the bristles, then shaved and showered until the water ran cold. When he emerged clean and dressed Leah was filling a cup with coffee.

"You're still here?" he said. "Don't you have to go to work?"

"I called and told them I'd be late." She handed him the coffee. "I would have made some toast but you don't have any bread."

"That's okay, I'm not hungry." He took a cautious sip from the steaming cup.

She gazed at him, her brow furrowed with concern. "Something's obviously very wrong, Theo. What is it?"

He focused on his coffee, trying to formulate a coherent response. When he spoke it was as though from the bottom of a barrel. "I'm really messed up, Leah."

Chapter 36

It was Leah's idea that he talk to his father. When she moved to telephone Lucas to arrange it, indignation drove him to reply that he was quite capable of contacting his own dad. She smiled at this show of spirit and to his relief finally departed. Lucas answered on the second ring and told Theo to come right over.

"Sorry to bother you, Dad," he said, hesitating at the entrance to Lucas's study: a spacious room lined with overflowing bookcases. French doors opening to a small courtyard studded here and there with potted succulents admitted the rosy mid-morning light. "I know you're really busy."

"Not at all," Lucas said, motioning for him to enter. "Come in, come in. I'll ask Estrella to bring some coffee."

Theo held up a palm. "Only if you'd like some."

"Later perhaps, then. Let's sit." They moved to a long sofa and armchair upholstered in glove-soft oxblood leather set around a low dark-wood table. Theo chose the sofa knowing his father found it easier to rise from an armchair.

"It's good to see you," Lucas said.

Theo nodded. "Yes. Where's Mom?"

"Tessa, her photographer friend, has an exhibition opening in Denver tonight and Ris has gone to it." He looked at Theo expectantly.

This was a stupid idea, Theo thought. "*I'm really messed up*" sounds pretty pathetic.

His father broke the lengthening silence. "And how is Fox coming along? He seemed much improved when we saw him last Sunday."

"I think so."

They fell silent again. His father regarded him with eyes full of kindness. "There was something you wished to talk to me about?" he said, his voice gentle.

Theo held his father's gaze for a moment, struggling to bring some order to his scattered thoughts, then startled himself by saying, "There was this woman—" He raised a hand to his mouth in shock.

His father's expression of benign interest did not change. After a moment he said, "Go on."

Unsure of where he was heading, Theo hesitantly described meeting Serena at the painting workshop and how she had attached herself to him. "She was a bit crazy," he said.

His father smiled. "A woman wouldn't have to be crazy to want to attach herself to you."

Theo waved away the comment with his hand. "Anyhow, we had … a brief relationship." His face flushed. There probably wasn't much his father didn't know about sex but he still couldn't say the word. "She got silly about it—like, stalking me. On top of it all I found out at the end of the workshop that she was engaged to another guy. He and Serena's dad came to take her home. I was awfully glad to get out of there. But that wasn't the end of it."

Theo paused for a moment and looked out at the courtyard. An Easter cactus had bloomed, its spiky pink flowers tipping the spiny stems. His father waited without speaking. *Why was he talking about Serena?* Theo wondered. *Wasn't it the crisis with Fox that had brought him down?* But he continued, recounting Serena's night drive from Arizona and the call from the police.

The Lighthouse

"I didn't want to go to the hospital but I figured it would take a while to get in touch with her family and she'd be alone until then."

He described being with her when she died. "I was holding her hand; I can still feel what it was like, how it went from being alive to ... nothing." His voice cracked and he swallowed. "It was awful."

His father's eyes softened. "It is a profound experience to attend someone's death. A privilege even."

"A privilege!" Theo shook his head. "It sure didn't feel that way. You have this bundle of flesh and feeling, of thinking and doing and being that's a person, now here, now suddenly gone."

"So this has been troubling you?"

"Yes. I guess so." He pinched a fold in the fabric of his jeans. "No, actually there's more." He drew in a deep breath and looked directly at his father. "She was such bad news that I don't know what would have happened if she hadn't had the accident, if she had arrived here. I can't help being relieved she didn't make it. I mean, I'm not glad she died, but it prevented what would have been an ugly situation." Tears pricked his eyes. "I feel like a real shit for that."

"Ah," Lucas said.

"Then just a few weeks later Fox gets hurt. Like a kind of cosmic payback for me being glad that Serena didn't arrive and complicate my life. To teach me a lesson, you know? And it brought home to me how arbitrary the whole business of living and breathing is, how we're no more than rocks skipping on water until there's no momentum left and we just sink."

He made a vague motion with his hand. "It's all seems so pointless; I mean, what's life about anyway? It's just pain and loss and then we die. There are no happy endings, are there? While I was taking care of Fox I didn't dwell on it, but now...? The last few days—I don't know where they went. I had, I dunno, some kind of a breakdown. I was completely out of it and now I can't seem to clear my head, to find my footing. It's like I don't know which way is up, and I'm just so tired…"

His father placed a hand on his shoulder. "Why don't you rest, then?"

"I've been trying to; I'm not sure I can."

"I mean here."

Theo looked at the buttery leather surface of the sofa. "Here?"

"Yes, why not?"

"But my boots…"

"Don't worry about your boots."

Theo hesitantly swung his legs up and stretched out. His father reached over and adjusted the cushion under Theo's head, then rested his hand gently on his crown, like a blessing. A point of warmth formed behind his eyes and flowed down his body, melting his limbs. His heartbeat slowed. He drew a long, slow breath and drifted off to sleep.

Theo woke and blinked, uncertain for a moment of where he was. The light flowing through the French doors had thickened and seemed saturated with gold dust. The stutter of computer keys peppered the silence. He sat up slowly.

"Ah, you're awake."

The motion of turning in the direction of his father's voice seemed to be broken into a series of discrete frames. Lucas sat at his desk, his body haloed by a faint glimmer.

"What time is it?" Theo said.

"Just after two."

"After two!"

His father smiled. "Estrella has been dancing around, waiting for you to wake. She has made a lunch for us."

Theo scrubbed his face. "Wonderful, I'm starving. But I have to visit the washroom first."

When he returned to the study Estrella was setting down a

laden tray on the coffee table. Her dark eyes glittered and her teeth flashed in greeting, white in her dusky face. She placed a couple of thick-cut roast beef sandwiches on a plate and handed them to Theo. He accepted it, smiling his thanks. When he took a bite of the sandwich a riot of flavors—nutty bread, sweet butter, earthy meat, pungent mustard—exploded in his mouth. It watered painfully. He and his father ate in an appreciative silence.

When they were done Lucas poured out cups of tea and handed one to Theo. As he sipped it he regarded his father curiously.

"Dad ... did you do something to me to make me sleep?"

"Why do you ask?"

"When I woke up everything was hyper-real. It's fading now, but my senses were super-heightened. Things seemed to glimmer, to vibrate even."

His father smiled faintly. "You always were a sensitive boy."

"What did you do exactly?"

Lucas studied Theo, his face impassive, for a long moment before replying. "One of the consequences of that experience I went through—when I was swept away down that torrent in Bolivia—was an amplified ability to channel energy for healing. It took me a few years to realize it, a few more to accept that it was a gift and even longer to figure out what to do with it. It must be carefully directed and I don't do that lightly. I use it from time to time in counseling; it seems to be particularly effective in helping people who are tied up in moral, emotional or spiritual knots that can't be loosened with reason, with words. As you were."

Theo absorbed this revelation. It didn't surprise him, somehow. His father had always exuded a quiet power. "Why didn't you ever say anything about it?"

His father shrugged. "It was not something I wished to have widely known. Anyway, how do you feel now?"

"How do I feel?" Theo drew in a deep breath and considered. "Cleansed, somehow. Refreshed." He smiled. "Like I've been rebooted."

"Good. In the next few days think gently on the matters you spoke about. Let your thoughts follow their own course. See where you end up. We can talk again then if you like."

Theo nodded. "Tell me, have you ever done this—what do you call it? Touch therapy? Have you ever done it to me before? Like when I was younger? If you did, I don't remember."

His father shook his head. "I wanted to once, when you started skipping school and vandalizing buildings and stealing things. I thought it might help but you wouldn't let either Ris or me near you."

Theo stiffened.

"And when we sent you to the boarding school in Oregon you seemed to be so happy, so willing to leave us. That was the hardest to accept. Your mother was inconsolable. She wept for a week." He regarded his son curiously. "What had we done to estrange you so much from us?"

Theo swallowed hard. He had not seen this coming. In all the years he had lived at the ranch they had never spoken about that time. "It wasn't you and Mom…" he said.

"If not us, what, then?"

"Nothing."

His father straightened in his chair, his eyes alert. "It doesn't sound like it was nothing. Surely, after all this time you can speak of it."

Theo dropped his eyes and shook his head.

Lucas slowly set his cup and saucer down on the table. "Did something happen to you?"

"I really don't want to talk about it."

"Were you hurt somehow? Did someone do something to you?"

"Please, Dad."

Lucas's eyes hardened. "Did something happen of a sexual nature?"

Theo's face flushed and his heart began to thud.

"Was this at school? One of the teachers?"

"Not a teacher."

"A student, then?"

Theo sagged against the back of the sofa. It seemed pointless to deny anything now. "Seniors," he said.

Lucas drew back in shock. "More than one?"

"Three."

"My God! How many times?"

Theo looked out the window. The sense of well-being he had felt on waking had vanished. "Just the once but I was afraid it would happen again and that's why I stopped going to school."

"Where was your brother?" Lucas said, his face ragged with distress. "How could he have let this happen?"

"Oh, Dad, Ben didn't babysit me. This wasn't his fault."

"But why did you never say anything?"

"Because of this—because I knew how much it would upset you."

"But it should have been reported! Those fellows should have been held to account."

"That would have just made the whole thing worse. You and Mom would have made a big fuss. I would have had to talk to people about it, to face those guys. It was so … humiliating. I just couldn't bear for anyone else to know."

"So instead you exiled yourself from us?"

Theo drew in a breath and released it in a long sigh. "I was only thirteen then; I didn't know how to deal with it. At the new school the kids who befriended me liked horsing around. Going along with them was thrilling. It felt good to smash things, to deface them. At the beginning, anyway. I wanted to stop after a while but I didn't know how to break with those guys and that's why I was glad to go away to the boarding school. It seemed the only way out." He paused. "Look, Dad, please don't tell Mom about this."

His father opened out his hands. "How can I not tell Ris?"

"It was so long ago ... can't we just forget about it?"

"Oh, son," his father said bleakly. "How can we forget all those years when you were lost to us?"

They regarded each other through a painful silence.

"I'm sorry I've been such a disappointment to you and Mom," Theo said quietly.

His father's eyebrows shot up. "You think you are a disappointment to us?" He rose abruptly. "I need something stronger than tea."

Lucas went to a small liquor cabinet built into the bookcase and opened the door. He placed his hands on the base and pressed his forehead against the upper shelf. What pain his son must have endured, what wounds he must still bear. And he had no inkling. *It's just Theo acting out,* he and Ris had assured themselves. *He will grow out of it, he just needs more structure and discipline.* He shook his head to clear it and selected a bottle. *So much for my much-vaunted sensitivity, my supposed skill at healing.* He poured brandy into a glass. *My own son was horribly abused and I had no clue. And now he seems to be harboring some sense of failure.*

He turned and held out the bottle to Theo. "Would you like one?"

"Ah, no thanks."

He returned to his armchair with the drink. "In what respect do you think you're a disappointment to us?"

Theo grimaced and made a helpless gesture with his hand. "I haven't exactly made much of my life, have I? Wandered around, inadvertently had a kid. Thirty-six now and still barely able to support myself. Fox and I wouldn't be able to manage without your help."

"You earn whatever you get from us."

"Yeah, well, maybe."

"Uncertain finances are the lot of many artists though, aren't they?"

"Am I really an artist? All I produce are mediocre paintings."

"Hmm," Lucas said. Theo's well-executed works were hardly mediocre but he had often thought them cool and non-committal. There was nothing either in his chosen subjects or their representation that spoke to the abuse he had suffered. *Or perhaps the real meaning lies in their lack of emotion.*

He regarded his gifted, finely wrought son with new eyes. He and Ris had thought that Theo's unregimented ways and lack of emotional attachments reflected a carefree, even careless nature. Could they actually mask deep turmoil and self-doubt? Fox's accident and the death of the woman, Serena, may have been a catalyst for the release of long-buried anguish. *How to help, to restore his harmony and confidence?* Was this the time to share his own past? *Yes. Some good may come of it.*

"We are much alike, you and I," he said.

Theo drew back in surprise. "I'm like you? I thought it was Ben who was like you."

"He resembles me physically, yes. But you are more like me in nature." Lucas paused. "I have never told you about what prompted me to join holy orders."

"I always assumed you had a calling."

"Umm..." Lucas hesitated briefly. "Very few people know what I'm about to tell you, only Ris, and in the past her father and Sara. I ask that it remain between us, at least until I am gone."

Theo's forehead creased in bewilderment. "Ah, yeah, sure."

"As you know, my parents divorced when I was young. I was not happy when Father left to work abroad, or with my mother's new husband, and fell into a pattern of what's now called attention-getting behavior. I sought trouble out, and if there was none on offer I created it." His eyes twinkled. "My friends used to say, 'Wilde by name, wild by nature.' Your exploits pale in comparison to some of the things I got up to."

"Like what?" Theo said, his eyes wide.

"Stories for another time, perhaps. After university I worked for a civil engineering firm. The pay packet financed quite a high life for a young man. Weekends passed in a blur of drink and partying. Holidays were raucous excursions to Mediterranean beach towns."

He set his glass on the table, leaned back in his chair and looked off into the distance. He conjured up the young man he had been then—lacking in direction, emotionally stunted, a moral vacuum. After a minute he shook his head to free it of the image and continued.

"At a party one evening I objected when one of the other fellows flirted with the girl I had brought. We began fighting and knocked a small table over. The candles on it ignited the window drapes. They were made of some synthetic material, and in no time the room was engulfed in flames."

He grimaced, remembering how in his panic his mind had tried to identify the chemicals causing the acrid smell from the burning curtains.

"We got everyone out of the flat and raced up the stairs banging on doors. Someone responded from all but one on the fourth floor. We assumed no one was home and went outside to watch the firemen try to bring the blaze under control. Arrogant, ignorant fools that we were, we congratulated ourselves that, whatever we had done, no one had been hurt."

His chest tightened with pain. "There were in fact three children in that flat, left alone while their parents went to the pub. The oldest, a boy, was only seven. There was another boy, four, and a three-year-old girl.

"The fire was deemed an accident, our quick actions in emptying the other flats lauded as heroic. The parents of the three children were blamed for their deaths because they left them alone." He shook his head. "Those poor people. I tried to shrug it off but the photos of the children in the newspaper stayed with me. My sense of responsibility for their deaths knocked me sideways. I had to drink myself into a stupor every night to sleep. My work suffered and after a few weeks of showing up late and hungover I was fired."

He tossed back the rest of his brandy and rose. "I'm having a refill. Are you sure you don't want any?"

Theo stirred. "Maybe a small one."

Lucas prepared both drinks, returned to his chair and handed a glass to Theo.

"The days that followed were very dark indeed. I was stuck, my resources were rapidly dwindling and I couldn't even think about finding other work. I wandered around in this hopeless state for weeks. One day, after walking for several hours, I sat down on a bench in a small park. A bell began to toll and as I listened to it, it came to me that I must somehow dedicate the rest of my life to those children."

Lucas remembered the moment as though it were yesterday: the washed-out winter sky, the bare trees gauzy with mist and then the long tones—crystalline, plangent, inexpressibly beautiful—rolling through the air.

"I felt a surge of hope and purpose. When the idea of joining the Franciscan order came to me shortly after it immediately seemed to fit—the self-abnegation, the discipline, the opportunity to do good. And it did fit, for a while. It gave me a community, a family even, that I had been missing. The rhythms and routines were soothing, the spiritual exercises fed a hunger I had long felt but not identified.

"I chose the Franciscans because they do good works out in the secular world. My assignments usually drew on my engineering background. The project to build the school and hospital in that Bolivian village where I met your mother was one of these."

Lucas smiled, remembering. "When I learned that the carpenter joining the project was named Ris Larsen, I expected a big, brawny Swede and I was even less impressed when the young woman who showed up was sick in my truck on the drive to the village. But as time passed I realized she was the person with whom I was intended to spend my life. When it became apparent that she wasn't indifferent to me I asked her to leave."

"You asked her to leave! But why, if you wanted to be together?"

Lucas smiled faintly. "I had taken vows and saw giving up Ris as the ultimate sacrifice I had to make as penance for my role in those children's death."

"So what changed?"

Lucas set down his glass. "You know the story of the rainstorm at the village. It happened the day before Ris was to go."

"That's when you made that plank bridge to help the people cross over the washout, right?"

"Yes, Ris and I were at opposite ends holding a rope people could hang on to when they walked on the narrow plank. Then the bank on my side started to dissolve and the plank fell away. I realized I had no retreat and was about to follow it."

He fell silent, reliving the moment yet again and the feeling that had overwhelmed him then, like his heart had burst.

"I looked at Ris for what I thought was the last time and let go of the rope."

Theo leaned forward. "Why on earth did you do that? Why didn't you hang on?"

"Because I would have dragged her down with me," he said softly.

Neither spoke for a long while.

"But you were rescued," Theo eventually said.

Lucas shook himself. "Yes, but I've never told the whole story. The torrent tossed me about like a cork. I went under several times and was almost done for when I slammed up against a tree that had fallen across the flow and had the presence of mind to grab on to a branch. That's where my leg was smashed."

He tapped his right leg, the one that limped and ached.

"I managed to pull myself along the trunk to solid ground and dragged myself forward on my elbows until I could not move anymore. I was sure it was over then. I remember thinking that I should have just let myself go in the water, it would have been quicker and less painful. I curled up and waited to die.

"I woke in the hut of the man who had found and saved me. He and a neighbor with an old truck drove me to a town with basic medical facilities. The roads were horribly rutted and the trip took over three hours. The only thing between me and the metal floor of the truck box was some sacking filled with rushes. I don't know how I survived, the pain was so unbearable.

"At the little hospital they patched me up as best they could, but then my wounds became infected. I really should have died then—there were no antibiotics and I burned for days with fever. But I survived."

He remembered the moment of waking, bathed in cold sweat in the middle of the night. There was a window in his room through which he could see the sky and his mind, voided by days of delirium, had filled with the pure, quiet light of the moon.

"Eventually I was taken to a larger center where I convalesced until I was able to travel home. I had a great deal of time to think then, and much to think about. The ordeal had left me with a clarity of vision and a sense of the divine that I had never attained through the previous years of prayer and meditation. At the heart of it was the conviction that the trials I had been put through were a form of expiation for the death of those three children, a settling of accounts. Three times I should have died, three times against all odds I came back from the brink. One time for each child.

Lucas paused and looked at his drink thoughtfully before taking a sip. "I also knew then that I was meant to live out in the world. I tracked Ris down; she thought I had died." He smiled. "You know the story of our reunion. There was a process for me to be released from my vows but we were happy to wait. The time it took was a small price for the gift of being able to spend our lives together."

"Why haven't you ever said anything about this before?" Theo said.

Lucas smiled faintly. "It is deeply private, and a tale that requires a context."

"Does Ben know?"

Lucas shook his head. "I will find the right moment to tell him."

They sat comfortably in silence for several minutes. The late afternoon light slanted through the French doors, heavy and honey-hued.

Theo stirred. "I should go," he said. "It's time to think about making dinner."

Lucas walked him to the door.

"This day was quite…" Theo paused, his eyes eloquent with feeling. "Thank you, Dad."

Lucas nodded. "I hope you will come by often to talk."

"I will." Theo smiled faintly. "So, you think there might be hope for me?"

"Oh, Theo." Lucas placed his hand on his son's shoulder. "One thing I am sorry about is that among all the women you have known you haven't found a mate. The right person can bring such richness and harmony to one's life."

Theo gave him a thoughtful look. "Well, maybe I should do something about that," he said.

Chapter 37

The sale of Ben's practice proceeded quickly, as though destined to happen. Two of the younger lawyers in the company leapt at the chance to take over, joined by a friend who was languishing in one of the mega-firms in town. Within a month the paperwork had been completed and the organizational changes set in motion.

Ben had always held his parents' legal matters separate and private, and it required little effort to remove the related files from the premises. On his last day he stood in his empty office amid the boxes that held them. The new partners' tastes ran more to urban industrial styles and movers had just taken the last of his heavy cherrywood furniture away for disposal by an auction house. Listening to the talk about the proposed redecoration of the space made him feel old. Was it only ten years since he and Jay had been that keen, that bright? There were voices in the hall leading to the office, two of the legal assistants talking about the placement of their desks within the room. The new partners intended to exercise a strict egalitarianism, each keeping a small private office and providing this choice location with its expansive city views to the junior staff. *We'll see how long that lasts.* He took the cue, and with a last glance around loaded the file boxes, his laptop and his briefcase on a dolly and headed out the door.

There being little to keep him in Vancouver now he packed for a long stay and headed to Taos to resume running the Lighthouse full-time. When he arrived his parents hosted a special family dinner in welcome.

"You have made many changes in a short time," his father said. "It must be taking some adjustment."

"Umm…" Ben said. He would not admit to the uncertainty that had niggled at him since the sale of his practice and relocation to New Mexico. "What concerns me most is that Caro may interpret my leaving Vancouver as somehow ceding the house to her." He explained briefly about her confusion over the ownership of their home.

"But that's nonsense," Ris said. "Lucas and I are not part of your marriage, and if I recall correctly she isn't a signatory to that rental agreement you insisted we sign."

"That is unlikely to stop her. Her skill at argument is legendary."

"You have a tenancy agreement with your parents?" Leah said.

Ben nodded.

"Then why don't you terminate it if you no longer reside there? Or have your parents evict you."

Ben burst out laughing. "It just might work," he said.

"A coat of paint throughout, I think," Ris said as she and Ben walked down the hall of the Vancouver house. In the living room she flipped the edge of the rug over with the toe of her shoe. "And maybe it's time to re-do the floors as well. They haven't been refinished since we moved in forty years ago."

Ben had sent Caro a copy of the letter terminating his tenancy and she had replied swiftly, calling it an obvious ploy to get her to leave. He reiterated simply that his parents wished to have possession of the house for their own use in two months' time. She countered that the use must be demonstrable otherwise she would challenge it as spurious and vindictive and a form of harassment. To avoid the issue his parents decided to undertake some needed renovations to the building that would require emptying the place, and Ben and Ris had gone to Vancouver to determine what work should be done.

In the dining room Ris traced her fingers along the polished wood of the long table. "So many good times here," she said. She turned and pointed to the doors of a cabinet built in under a line of windows. "Remember when Theo crawled in there and then couldn't get out?" She shook her head. "The things that boy got up to."

"Yes," Ben said. "Maybe that's why we figured that the bad business at school was just part of his mischief. At least that's what *I* thought."

His parents had quietly told him about the sexual assault Theo had suffered and asked if he had known anything about it. Shock had prevented him from replying immediately. Later he told them how much Theo, with his extraordinary looks, had stood out in the all-boys school, and how the other boys had constantly teased him, calling him *Dora* and *Girlie*. He said it didn't mean anything at the time because the boys were always teasing each other. He didn't tell them that he had resented the attention Theo had received, seeing it as yet another way in which his brother had eclipsed him.

Ris touched him lightly on the arm. "Now you, you were always my steady boy," she said with a smile.

Chapter 38

"You should have signed it last week!" Cindy said. "Now I don't know whether we're going to get them in time."

"I would have if I had known it was there." Ben lifted a pile of papers from a file box on the corner of his desk and dropped them back down with a thud. "It was stuck in the middle of all this stuff. If you need something dealt with quickly you should put it in a folder with a red priority sticker and leave it right in the middle of my desk."

"It wasn't a priority when I put it in there a week ago; it's beyond being a priority now. You need to clear your inbox more often."

"And you need to triage the stuff that goes into my inbox better."

Cindy's face reddened. She was on the verge of tears.

Ben picked up the papers in the inbox and handed them to her. "Here," he said in a conciliatory voice. "Go through these, separate them into what needs attention today and this week and what I can ignore indefinitely."

"But that's *your* job! I have other things to do."

"Cindy, someday you will go too far."

She snatched up the papers and sniffed. "I'll pretend I didn't hear that," she said and flounced out the door.

The Lighthouse

Ben rubbed his eyes and sighed. The Lighthouse was set to reopen in five days with more than half of the rooms already booked and everyone was worn to a frazzle. He regretted the exchange with Cindy—she had been putting in twelve-hour days as the deadline approached—but she was getting downright overbearing in her dealings with everyone. He picked up the glasses he had recently bought at the pharmacy and put them on. Despite having laser surgery to correct his shortsightedness when he was younger he had begun to have difficulty reading. *And not even forty*, he thought in disgust. He peered at the document before him but the lenses weren't quite strong enough. He cursed softly and angled the reading lamp to throw more light on the print.

He finished reading the report, scribbled some comments on the top of the first page and tossed it into his outbox. The windows were beginning to darken but he still had a pile of papers to go through. He rolled his shoulders to work out the cramp. Another hour then he'd call it a day. He thought longingly of the bottle of gin that waited in his suite. He was starting to look forward to his evening martini a bit too much. *It'll all get sorted when this damn place is operating again*, he assured himself.

A few minutes later the private line on his phone rang. He didn't recognize the number but snatched it up to stop the ringing and growled a hello.

"Ben?"

He sat bolt upright, his heart identifying the speaker a half-second before his mind did. "Beth?" he breathed.

"Yes, it's me."

"Where are you?"

"Here, Las Vegas."

"It's so good to hear your voice."

"Me too."

"How are you? Is everything okay? Are you coming back here?"

"Ben, I can't talk long and I have something to ask you. When I saw you last, at the Lighthouse...?"

"Yes?"

"You said, I hope you remember, you told me that if I ever needed anything I should call you."

"Of course I remember. What is it? What can I do?"

"It's a big favor."

"I'll do anything."

"You should maybe hear what it is before you agree."

"It doesn't matter. Just ask."

"Could Nathan possibly come and stay with you?"

"Nathan? Why?"

"It's a long story. My husband..."

Ben tensed. "Is he hurting Nathan?"

"No, it's not that." Beth sighed wearily. "He's always run little schemes and one of his latest has backfired and put him on the wrong side of some very unpleasant people. They, ah, torched our house a couple of days ago."

He leaned forward as though trying to shorten the distance between them. "Are you okay?"

"I am, but we have to get out of here. I don't know what's going to happen and I don't want Nathan to be part of it."

"But what about you? Why don't you come with him?"

She didn't reply for several moments. "I can't leave my husband now, not this way. I have to see him through this." She rushed on. "It's a lot to ask, I know, but I couldn't think of anyone else. Nathan likes you, you see. And I know with you he'll be safe."

Ben's mind reeled and he didn't answer right away.

"It *is* a lot to ask. Too much," Beth said, her voice heavy with resignation.

"No, no, I'm happy to do it," he said, his mind racing through the logistics. "Will you bring him here?"

"That's the other thing. I can't come that far. Could you by chance meet me part-way, say at Flagstaff?"

"When?"

"As soon as you can. I don't know how long we have here before they find us again."

He did some rough calculations. "Look, we're set to open very soon…"

"Yes, I remember, and I'm sorry. You must be overwhelmed."

"No, it's okay. It's just that I don't think I can arrange it for tomorrow. But the day after? Will you be okay until then?"

"I think so, yes." Her relief was audible. They confirmed telephone numbers to work out the meeting arrangements and hung up. Ben rubbed his eyes. *What did I just agree to? Can I pull this off?* He picked up his pen and turned to the document he had been working on with a new urgency. He would do whatever it took to see Beth again.

Trevor and the plane were not available all week and when Ben checked commercial flights it turned out that it would be quicker to drive to Flagstaff than fly. He explained the situation to his parents, who to his relief accepted the news of Nathan's arrival as though taking in a small unknown child was nothing out of the ordinary.

"Could one of you possibly come with me?" he said. "It's seven hours each way, and what with being this close to opening I can't take the time to stay overnight somewhere."

"Oh, son," Lucas said raising his eyebrows. "I don't think either of us is up to such a long trip. Why don't you ask your brother?"

His brother wouldn't have been Ben's first choice as a companion on the trip but he could hardly refuse to ask him after his father suggested it. Theo agreed and Ben picked him up at five o'clock the next morning.

"Leah packed some food," Theo said, dropping a gym bag

on the back seat. "And I brought some coffee. Hope you take it black."

"Later," Ben said. He pulled out onto the road and accelerated. A coyote stepped out in front of them and froze in the beam of the light. "Shit!" he said, swerving to avoid it. A shot of adrenalin jolted him, clearing his sleep-fogged mind. "I think I'd better have that coffee now," he said.

He accepted a thermal mug and glanced at his brother. "I expect you think I'm crazy for doing this," he said stiffly.

"No. When a friend needs help you gotta give it." Theo eased his seat back and tipped his hat over his eyes. "Wake me when you want to change."

They drove in silence, Theo dozing, as far as Gallup. After they had gassed up, had a break and eaten a sandwich, Theo took the wheel. When they were back on the highway he turned to Ben.

"Did Dad ever put his hand on your head?"

Ben gave him a quizzical glance. "I expect he did when I was younger. Why do you ask?"

"It's nothing. Never mind."

Ben puzzled over the odd question briefly before falling into a dreamless sleep. He woke to a light touch on his arm.

"We're entering Flagstaff," Theo said.

"Already?" Ben said, sitting up. He yawned mightily. "Sorry, didn't mean to sleep that long."

"Expect you needed it. Now how do you want to do this?"

Ben glanced at his watch. "Let's go directly to the truck stop where I'm meeting Beth. We can pick up some gas there and food for the way back."

The gas station was busy with large rigs pulling in and out. Beth's small beige sedan was parked on the far side of the lot in the shade of a grove of trees and it took them a moment to find her.

"That's her car," Ben said, peering through the windscreen. "The license plate matches."

They pulled up and Ben got out. The door of the sedan opened and Beth emerged.

"I'll go fill up," Theo said.

Ben nodded and walked towards her.

"You've come," she said.

He opened his arms in response, and she came into them like a storm-tossed boat finding a safe harbor. *If we could just stay like this forever,* he thought. Soon, too soon, she stepped back and looked at him. Her cheeks were hollow, he noticed, her body thinner.

"So what's happening, Beth? What are your plans?"

She brushed a strand of hair off her face. "We need to get away, somewhere far. Hopefully the guys after my husband will decide that scaring the hell out of him was enough."

"Where will you go?"

"North, I think. We know a place in Idaho where we can lie low for a while."

Theo returned from gassing up and parked nearby. A small cry issued from Beth's car.

"I'm coming, sweetheart," she called, turning towards it.

Ben followed behind. Nathan was strapped into a child seat in the back of the car. Beth released the buckles, lifted him out and set him on the ground.

Ben held out his hand. "Hello, Nathan." The boy hesitantly shook it. "Does he know what's going on?"

Beth brushed the back of her hand against her forehead. "As much as he's able to. It's all been quite upsetting: the fire, fleeing in the middle of the night, hiding out. I'm sorry, but I can't say how he is going to be." She glanced at her son then back at Ben. "I hope he won't be too difficult."

She reached into the car and disconnected the child seat from its restraints. "He'll need this," she said, handing it to Ben.

"You'll have to show me how to set it up."

Theo appeared at Ben's side. "I know how to do that." He took the seat and held a hand out to Nathan. "Why don't you come and help me." The boy stuck a finger in his mouth and pressed against Beth.

"There's something in the car for you," Theo said. "It has fuzzy ears and a long tail. Let's go look."

The boy giggled and glanced at his mother. She touched him lightly on the shoulder. "Go on," she said. He stepped forward and took Theo's hand.

"And you'll never guess what color it is," Theo said, leading him away.

Beth watched them go with tear-filled eyes. After a moment she opened the trunk of her car and took out some carrier bags. "We lost pretty well everything. I got him some new clothes and a few toys. I hope it'll be enough."

Ben accepted the bags. "We'll manage." He looked at her. "I guess this is it."

She nodded. "I should get going. It's a friend's car and I need to get it back."

"Can I reach you at the number you gave me?"

"No, the phone is also my friend's. I'll have to return it as well."

"Get in touch as soon as you can."

"I'm not sure when that will be."

He set down the bags and placed his hands on her shoulders. "Are you going to be okay? I mean, with these guys after your husband, are you in danger as well?"

"I…" She looked around distractedly. "I don't know, I've completely lost perspective. My main concern has been making Nathan safe."

"Leave your husband to sort out his own mess and come with us, Beth."

She grimaced. "I can't. It's the deal I made with him. It was the only way he would agree to let me hide Nathan."

"But he's not here. You've come this far, why go back?"

Her eyes pleaded for understanding. "He needs me and my money. He said that if I helped him get away, once he was safe and settled he'd let me go too, for good." She paused. "It's the only way I can see ever being free of him."

"And if he changes his mind?"

"Then I'll let certain people know where he is," she said.

Theo drove for the seemingly endless trip back while Ben comforted Nathan, who became querulous when he realized Beth was not coming with them. They arrived at the ranch late in the evening, bone-weary.

"Where are you guys going to stay?" Theo said.

Ben looked down at Nathan, curled up like a small animal on his lap. "I don't know, didn't think to set anything up. I'd rather not take him to the Lighthouse."

"Why don't you stay at Las Sombras tonight? I doubt Fin would mind. You can use my room."

At the hacienda Nathan fell asleep quickly when he was tucked into bed. He woke in the night needing the bathroom and mewled a bit in the dark strangeness. When the warm little body finally went limp with sleep against him, Ben stared at the ceiling and wondered what he had gotten himself into.

At breakfast the next morning Nathan peered over the edge of the table at the others, his almond eyes bright with curiosity. He observed Niels and Fox closely, dipping toast pieces in his boiled egg like they did, echoing their preference for cherry rather than strawberry jam.

"Why don't you find some toys for Nathan to play with?" Leah said to her son.

"Okay," Niels said. He stood and held out a hand. Nathan flashed his dimples, slid off his chair and grasped it.

"I have no idea what to do with him right now," Ben said when the boys had left. "There's probably daycare available somewhere but I haven't had a chance to arrange anything and right now I really need to get to work. We open in a couple of days."

"Ask Mom, she might be willing to keep him. Estrella would help," Theo said.

Angie had arrived and was tidying the kitchen. "I can look after him here." She glanced at Fin. "If it's okay with you, boss."

Fin shrugged.

"Really?" Ben said. His face fell. "But there's also evenings. I don't think it's a good idea to have Nathan stay at the Lighthouse."

"Well, just stay here then," Fin said. "With all of us, we can keep an eye on him."

"I wouldn't want to impose."

Fin waved his hand. "A couple of extra people aren't going to make much difference. As long as you don't disturb my work."

They talked logistics then everyone headed off to start their day. Outside, Ben turned to Leah. "It's awfully good of your dad to take Nathan in. Are you sure he doesn't mind?"

She smiled. "Trust me, if he did he'd say so, and it's really Angie taking care of him."

"And I wouldn't worry about Angie," Theo said. "She'll love having someone to talk at."

Chapter 39

A few days later Fin stopped Leah as they got up from the table after dinner. "Can I see you for a minute?"
"Yes, of course."

She rarely entered her father's studio and looked around curiously after following him inside. A bank of sound equipment and a large screen filled one wall. A sleek leather sofa set sat adjacent to it. A baby grand piano stood in a corner and other instruments were ranged around the room. A conventional desk and a podium offered places for Fin to work.

Fin indicated a chair across from the desk. "Sit," he said and took the one behind it.

Leah sat, disconcerted by the formality of the arrangement. Had something happened? Had she done something wrong? Her father regarded her with a neutral expression that gave no indication of what was to come.

"I received an interesting call on the house phone this morning," he said. "A woman from Santa Fe wanted to invite you to speak to her club about your recent book. I assumed she was referring to Alex's biography and said that it hadn't yet been published. She insisted she was holding a copy in her hand. I suggested that perhaps she had the wrong Larsen, but she said if you were Leah, you were the right one."

Leah drew back in her chair.

"After promising to pass on the message I checked out Amazon and there it was."

"I, ah…" Leah said. Her face flushed beet-red. They regarded each other for several moments.

"Why haven't you said anything?"

"Because I did not want anyone to know," Leah said through her teeth.

"Why ever not?"

"Because I don't want anyone to read it."

"But that doesn't make any sense at all."

"If you ever read it you'll understand why."

"I did read it." Fin studied his daughter for a long moment. "Where did all that come from?"

"Where do your ideas for compositions come from?"

He shrugged. "Many places. But whatever inspired your work must have been extraordinarily bleak."

She blinked back tears, not yet ready for his understanding.

"Nonetheless, it is quite an achievement. I'm proud of you."

"Please don't mention it to any of the others."

Fin raised his eyebrows. "Too late, I'm afraid. I've already sent everyone digital copies."

"She means after the boys leave," Theo said to his mother, seated next to him at dinner the following Sunday. Leah's book was the first topic of conversation and she had cut it off, asking that they speak of it later.

"Oh, I see." Ris nodded. "I understand, I think."

They duly talked of other things, and when Niels, Fox and Nathan had left the table to play with the electric train they all turned towards Leah.

Ben started. "Why didn't you tell anyone?"

Leah clenched her jaw. "Because I did not want anyone to read it."

"Why put all the effort into writing a book if you didn't want anyone to read it?" Ris said.

"I mean people I know."

"Still, why?" Ben said. "The reviews say that it's quite accomplished for a first novel."

"Some of them also say it's disturbing and depraved," Leah said. "Since you *have* read it, I'm sure you see why. And that's why Niels and Fox must never know about it."

"Yes, not now, certainly," Ris said. "Although I doubt they'd understand those parts." She looked at Theo. "Would you have understood what was going on at that age?"

Theo touched his fingers to his chest. "Why ask me?"

He had said it jokingly but a look of anguish crossed his mother's face. After his father had told her about the rape she had come to his studio and clung to him, weeping into his shoulder.

"What you must have gone through—it is so awful I can't bear to think about it," she had said through her tears. "Why did you never tell us? Why didn't you let us help? We wouldn't have done anything you didn't want us to."

He had stroked her head in comfort. "I know that now. It was all just so overwhelming and confusing then."

"All that time, all those years you were away. And more than anything you let us think the worst of you."

Now she said, "I didn't mean…"

"It's okay, Mom."

Lucas studied Leah with troubled eyes. "You say a great deal in that book."

Leah glanced at him then bit her lip and looked down at her cup. "The story shaped itself, I simply wrote it."

They continued to enquire about the book's characters and its plot but she deflected their questions with short responses.

After a few minutes Lucas rose. "I think I will call it a night," he said, putting an end to the interrogation.

Everyone but Leah followed. As the clatter of cups and saucers and the voices of the others trailed off into the kitchen, Theo sat down beside her. She glared at him.

"I suppose you think it's all pretty funny."

"You're obviously upset; why would I find that funny?"

She picked up her napkin and plucked at it. "Sorry."

"What's bothering you? Why are you blowing everyone off? They can't help but be interested in what you've done, and you know they only wish you well."

She inhaled sharply and waited a moment before responding. "The thing about writing, it's what I think I'm meant to do but I don't like how it exposes me. I don't like having people poke around in my head. It's got me stuck with my mother's biography. I need to put myself in the story to bring it to life. I don't know if I can."

"What are you afraid of?" Theo said.

She looked at him, her eyes troubled. "After I left home the only way I could deal with it all was by folding myself up into a tight little package. It's how I survived."

They sat in silence for a moment, Leah pleating her napkin. Theo placed his hand over hers, stilling her agitated fingers.

"But that's all over, Leah. You're back home now."

Late one afternoon the following week Theo was returning from a ride in the hills above the stables. He had taken Spider, an old quarter horse the stable hands tended to ignore, out for some exercise. A chill wind had come up, blowing in low-hanging clouds and blotting out the sun. He was about a mile from the stables when he saw a small hooded figure moving swiftly through the scrub off to one side. *Who the hell is that?* he wondered. People from the Lighthouse or the stable hands rarely came out to this part of the ranch, preferring the hills with the well-marked trails farther north. Someone must have gotten seriously lost.

The Lighthouse

He turned Spider in the person's direction. "Hey!" he called as he cantered forward.

Leah stopped and turned as he pulled alongside her. "Oh, Theo, it's you."

"Leah! What are you doing out here?"

"I've been out walking."

"Walking! You shouldn't be out here by yourself."

"Why not?"

"Nothing's marked here, it's totally wild. You could get lost. And there are wild animals, bears and cats."

Leah looked back in the direction she had come. "I've never had a problem before."

"You come here often?"

She shivered and hugged herself. "Look, I've got to get going. It was nice when I set out but now I'm freezing."

Theo slid off his horse. "Here, I'll give you a ride."

Leah glanced at the horse. "Can he carry two people?"

Theo patted the horse's neck. "What do you say, Spider? Can you handle both of us?" The horse flattened his ears and rolled his eyes. "Should be okay. He's a solid old beast and it's not far."

"Well, okay then."

He lifted her onto the saddle and slung himself up to sit pillion behind it. Spider shifted under their weight and he gave the horse a few moments to adjust. Leah peered down then glanced back at him, brushing aside a lock of hair that had blown into her eyes.

"It seems awfully precarious," she said.

"Grab the horn."

"This thing?"

"Yeah, and I'll hang on to you."

He slipped an arm around her and held the reins with his free hand. They set off slowly, Spider picking his way down the rocky terrain. The wind blew Leah's hood off and she slid sideways on the saddle. He tightened his grip, drawing her against him. He caught the scent of neroli in her hair, and as they rose and fell with the horse's gait his arm bumped up against the swell of her breasts. Suddenly he was glad of the cantle separating them.

They reached Leah's trailer a few minutes later. Theo loosened his arm, took a deep breath and slid off the horse. He reached up for Leah and lifted her down. When she touched the ground he didn't let her go.

"Leah, I think it's time we talked," he said.

She had rested her hands on his shoulders for balance and held them there while she studied his face. "Maybe it is," she said.

There was a noise and they sprang apart. Linc thrust his head under Leah's arm. "There you are," she said, patting him.

Theo bent to stoke the dog. "Phew! I think he's been rolling in the manure pile again. I'll tell Chester to get him washed." He straightened up. "How about tonight?"

"I guess that would be all right," she said after considering for a moment. "Maybe after the boys have gone to sleep."

"I don't mean there. How about at my place?"

"Can you get the boys ready for bed?" Leah said after dinner. "I have to go home—Ethan's in Singapore and he's Skyping me at eight."

Theo glanced towards the living room where Ben was talking to Fin. "I thought we were getting together tonight."

She slipped on her jacket and pulled a car key from her pocket. "I'll come over to your place when I'm done."

Theo settled Niels and Fox for the night and went home. He set an Internet station featuring light jazz to play, plumped up cushions, flicked the switch on two lamps. *It's too bright*, he thought, and turned one of them off. He stood for a moment hands on hips observing the effect. *Why am I so nervous? It's only Leah.*

She arrived a few minutes later. He poured her a glass of wine and they sat down in the living room across from each other and chatted about Fox's return to school, Ethan's trip to Southeast Asia in search of old colonial book collections and Nathan's adjustment to life at the ranch. It struck Theo that Leah might not have understood what he meant when he had said they should talk, that she may even have forgotten their electrifying conversation in her trailer. He cleared this throat.

"Have you given any more thought to what I said last fall about us getting married?"

She dropped her eyes and didn't immediately reply. Looking up at him, she said, "In truth not that much. It seemed like such an extraordinary notion, coming as it did out of the blue."

"Why extraordinary?"

"To start, why me? Surely, you haven't lacked for opportunity to marry before."

"To this point I haven't met anyone I've wanted to spend my life with."

"And you think I'm that person?"

He raised a shoulder in a shrug. "Yeah."

She studied him for a moment. "Tell me, am I someone you would have pursued if we had met in other circumstances? At, say, a party?"

He considered her. Would he have taken special notice of her if they had just met? With her enigmatic eyes and mildly exotic looks she would have stood out but he probably wouldn't have done anything about it. He'd have gone after the party girls, the easy ones who'd give you a good time. A woman with Leah's cool self-possession would have been too much work.

"Yeah, sure," he said. "And how about you? Am I someone you'd have been interested in?"

"Probably not."

His eyebrows shot up. "No? Why not?"

"Because I've found that men with your kind of looks tend to be vain and self-absorbed." She smiled. "And other women would have been all over you."

"You think I'm vain and self-absorbed?"

"No, surprisingly. But I expect I'm right about other women."

"Yeah, well," he said. A slow piece of music started to play. He set down his glass. "If I'd met you at a party I would have asked you to dance." He stood up and extended his hand. "What do you say?"

Leah hesitated, then shrugged. "Why not?" She rose and took his hand and they went to the small open space between the sofa and the table.

They assumed their positions but she held herself away from him and they moved stiffly.

"You remind me of some of the new mares that come into the stable, pulling back against the reins when you try to lead them," Theo said. He realized he was talking about the ones that were brought in to be serviced and shut up.

She glanced up at him. "You're comparing me to a horse?"

"Only in the nicest way possible."

Her shoulders shook with laughter and he took the opportunity to draw her closer. They danced through two more pieces before sitting down again. Theo rested his arm on the back of the sofa and Leah settled easily against it. They listened to the music and drank their wine, speaking desultorily of different things. A song came on, the singer a woman with a low, caressing voice. Theo closed his eyes, lulled by the languorous music, the wine seeping through his veins, the warmth of Leah against him. She slipped her hand under his sweater and placed it on his chest, and the surprise of it shot adrenalin through his body.

"Your heart is racing," Leah said softly.

"Yes, it is," he said and turned towards her.

The next morning they stumbled, late, into the kitchen at Las Sombras and hurried through breakfast and school-lunch-making with heavy-lidded eyes. When Ben had taken Nathan off to daycare and the boys had left for school they sank into chairs at the table with cups of coffee and regarded each other with wonder. Theo reached out and hooked his finger around one of Leah's.

"Hey," he said.

She gave him a sleepy smile. "Hey."

The back door opened and Angie stamped into the vestibule. Theo and Leah sprang apart, gulped down the rest of their coffee and rose to leave. They exchanged greetings with Angie and grabbed their jackets, shrugging them on as they left. Outside, they stopped to button and zip up. A gust of wind swirled around them, salting them with dust. Leah brushed her hand across her face and blinked as though suddenly awakened. She looked at Theo, her eyes troubled.

"Last night was a mistake," she said. "I don't think it's going to work."

He made a calming gesture. "Let's just wait and see," he said.

Chapter 40

In early June Ben flew to Vancouver to move his possessions from the house before the renovations started. He had timed the trip for a weekend when Caro was away.

The sorting took longer than he had expected. Late Sunday afternoon he left a note listing the items—furniture, rugs, crystal, china—he was leaving for her. He found her reply when he returned to continue the next morning. At the bottom of his note she had scribbled *Aren't you generous.*

She will regret writing that. He put the piece of paper in his pocket to give to his divorce lawyer. Before he left that day he wrote another note commenting on how much longer it was taking him to box up everything than he had expected. He suggested that given her many commitments she tackle her own packing sooner rather than later. Her reply was terse: *Piss off.* He saved that one too. His note after he finished on Tuesday afternoon was short. *Done,* it said. When he returned the next morning to await the moving van that would transport his things to the storage locker he had rented he found her response: *Can we meet for a drink tomorrow? I'm tied up today. The Fairmont lounge at 6:30?* He considered the request for a few moments then shrugged. *See you there,* he wrote.

"So I guess I'm officially homeless now," Ben said.

His parents had also come to Vancouver and he was staying at their penthouse. The comment had been made lightly but it gave voice to the sense of uprootedness that had dogged him throughout the day. When the door had slammed on the van bearing his worldly possessions away to storage that morning he felt like he had cut the moorings of his life and set himself adrift on some unknown sea. It wasn't a condition that suited his nature. Among everything he had envied in Theo was his ability to live like a vagabond. All those years spent wandering all over the globe with only what fit into his backpack. The places Theo had seen, the adventures he must have had. Ben's mother had called him *steady*, but was that the epitaph he'd want written on his headstone?

"But you have a home," his mother said.

"I'm not sure living with one's uncle qualifies, especially at my age."

"A home is a home wherever it is, especially when there's a child to care for," said Ris. "Have you any sense how long it will be before Beth returns for Nathan?"

He shook his head. Three postcards had arrived for Nathan from points in Utah and Idaho but nothing in the last couple of weeks. None of them gave any indication of how he could contact Beth. "Soon, I hope."

"You have had many upheavals in your life all at once," Lucas said. "Your practice, your marriage, your home—now this woman and her child."

"Yes, but isn't that how it is sometimes?" Ben said. "It's like the different parts of your life are all propped against each other, and when you shift one the rest are dislodged."

Ris glanced at her husband and he gave her a small nod. "Ben, given the state of flux your life is in, your father and I wanted to raise something for you to think about as you consider your next steps. Our business affairs are all being managed okay but they still require active oversight and we're beginning to tire of the work. You've done so well with the legal aspects we were wondering if you might want to take on more." She held up her palm. "No rush for a decision, of course, but do think about it."

Ben considered for several moments before answering. The offer didn't surprise him. Given his parents' age the question of succession was inevitable. With the knowledge of their business concerns that his legal work had afforded he was the logical person to take over. It would provide him with an attractive mix of security and flexibility and answer the question of what he was going to do with the rest of his life. Even a day earlier he would have welcomed the opportunity, but the act of removing his possessions and severing the ties to his home base had disconnected something inside him and it was rattling around his mind like a loose bolt.

"I really appreciate your confidence in me…" he said and stopped, unsure of where to go from there.

"Ah," his father said with a slight smile. "The idea does not, as we used to say, turn your crank?"

"No, no, it's not that. It's just…" Ben struggled to clear his thoughts. "I'm a bit discombobulated. All the changes you mentioned earlier, I'm not sorry to have made them but I haven't figured out where they're taking me, and there is still the question of Beth." He sighed and shook his head. "Of course it's of interest, but I'm not ready to commit just now. Maybe when things are more settled. Sorry that I can't answer more definitively."

Ris rested her hand lightly on his. "We didn't mean to confound matters even further for you. It can wait."

Lucas regarded him thoughtfully. "Ben, if you had no concerns and commitments and could do whatever you wanted, what would that be?"

"I'd go back to school," he said without hesitation.

"Really? To study what?"

He sat back in his chair. "When I was at the London School of Economics I had a mind to go further and do my doctorate. I was particularly interested in legal theory and comparative law. There was a certain excitement starting to build, a sense that legal research, which in the past had been cramped and limited, was about to open up and break out of its constraints. It could have led to an academic career; I would have liked that. But then…" He gestured with his hand. "I got married and decided I needed to be practical about things."

"Oh, Ben, we didn't know," Ris said. "And here we've tied you up in our own affairs when you would have been happier doing something else."

He shook his head. "Starting the firm, building the practice, that was good too."

"But now that you have the chance to reset your path you must do this, if it is still what you want," Lucas said.

"Well, maybe, if it's not too late," Ben said. "But I can't do anything until Beth comes back."

The next day, his last in Vancouver before returning to Taos with his parents, Ben finalized the arrangements for the renovations. He also stopped in at his old firm to say hello to the staff. Their greetings were friendly but brisk, and he didn't stay long.

At the end of the day he went to the Fairmont lounge to meet Caro. He arrived before her, was led to a table and ordered a beer. When Caro approached several minutes later he stood but didn't react to a slight movement on her part that invited an embrace.

The server came immediately and greeted Caro by name. "The usual," she said. She was carrying a boxy briefcase and they spent a moment finding a place to put it. The waiter returned and set a brimming martini glass down on the table with a flourish. While Caro drank it they talked about her current cases. The server appeared again and, in response to a nod from Caro, left and returned shortly after with another drink.

The conversation stalled. Ben waited—he wasn't the one who had asked to meet. Caro swirled an olive pick around her glass then looked up and held his gaze for a moment.

"Ben," she said, "this has been a huge mistake, don't you think?"

"What, exactly?"

"Your moving out, the business of a divorce. All of it."

"Well, your little fling with Paul was certainly a mistake."

"Oh, I know," she said impatiently. "But these things happen. Anyway, it's all over."

He wondered idly who had ended it, whether Caro had seen the error of her ways or the affair had not survived the indignity of Paul being caught with his pants down.

She took a deep breath. "I think we should give it another chance. Go to counseling, maybe. I'd be willing to do that. I think our marriage deserves that much."

He looked at her without speaking for several moments. "The thing is, Caro, our marriage ended some time ago, maybe even a long time ago. The divorce just acknowledges the fact."

"But we can try again. Perhaps I *have* been too taken up with work, trying to get ahead and all that. Perhaps I did lose sight of *us*. I'm sorry for that and I'll change. Really, I will." She placed her hand over her heart for emphasis.

This was a major concession for Caro and Ben knew what it cost her. He sympathized, briefly. "I don't think we can go back, Caro."

"No? Aren't you willing to at least give it a try?" Her voice tracked a line between pleading and irritation.

He shook his head.

"Why not?"

"Caro, there's someone else," he said gently.

The Lighthouse

She reared back and her face worked, then hardened into a mask. "So that's the way it is."

"I'm afraid so."

Her nostrils quivered with the effort of controlling her breathing. "Busy Ben. Who would have guessed? And there you were, playing the injured party."

"For the record, it happened after we had separated."

"Ah, yes, always treading the moral high ground."

"I should go."

Her hand shook as she raised the glass to drink. She set it down.

"You know why I married you, Ben?"

"Because you had to?" He started to pull out his wallet.

"You were my ticket out of that bloody country. Even after all this time, how you get on still depends on the way you speak and who you know. I couldn't have gotten very far there, not into the top firms, the good jobs."

Her accent had coarsened, he noticed.

"But there you were, and I had you figured out right away. Rich and privileged like the others, but so earnest, such a good boy. I was pretty sure you'd see me right."

He glanced at her. "What do you mean?"

She leered at him. "It wasn't hard to get pregnant; it was always any time, any place with you."

He paused in the act of opening his billfold. "Can't say I'm surprised you did it deliberately but it's the oldest ploy in the world, Caro. I'd have thought you'd have more imagination."

"Ah, but that's not the whole of it. You see, I didn't *lose* the baby, I got rid of it. I wasn't going to have this whole new world open up and be stuck home warming bottles and changing nappies."

He stared at her appalled. A knot formed in his chest, so tight he couldn't squeeze a breath through. He'd have been the first person to defend a woman's right to rule her own body, but to knowingly commence a pregnancy with the sole intent of terminating it was grotesque. A devastating sense of loss shook him—of the child, *his* child; of the abandoned studies; of the years he had given this woman. He struggled to contain the play of emotions on his face; he would not give her the satisfaction of witnessing his anguish. He wanted to hit her to clean that vile smirk off her face. He might have if they had been alone, and the thought that she would have brought him to that point disturbed him the most.

He pulled a couple of bills from his wallet and rose. Mustering all the control he could command to keep his hand steady he dropped them on the table.

"Glen and his crew will be at the house to start work on the second of July. Make sure you're out by then," he said as evenly as he could, then turned and walked away.

Chapter 41

Theo slipped his arm around Leah's waist and nuzzled her neck. Something quivered in the pit of her belly and she inhaled sharply.

"I thought we'd agreed there'd be no touching in public," she said, shifting out of his embrace.

"There's no one here."

"There might be at any time. The boys are in the living room and Dad will be home soon."

Leah had thought that with sober second thought on the morning after that first night together they had tacitly agreed not to repeat it. Circumstances helped. Their day-to-day lives afforded them little opportunity to be alone and among family they automatically fell into their established roles and routines. Then a few days later she had opened her door to a knock to find Theo leading a glossy black stallion.

"Do you want to go for a ride?" he said.

Her breath had caught, and despite the look of condescension the horse had leveled at her she had allowed Theo to lift her up into the saddle and ridden off with him. After, they seized on any opportunity to be together, usually in the hills but twice in Theo's studio, one morning when Fin was away and Angie was at the dentist and a glorious afternoon when Ben had taken all three boys to a movie.

On that occasion she had sat up in Theo's bed and drawn the sheet across her breasts.

"We need to stop this, Theo."

He drew his fingers down her back. "Why?"

She arched away. "Because it's getting way too complicated and I can't afford the distraction. I don't have time, not just for this…" She motioned to the bed. "But for thinking about and waiting for it. I absolutely have to finish the book about my mother and there's so much to do. I can't concentrate and I need all the spare time I have to write."

He studied her for a long moment before replying, his eyes unusually pensive. "How about a little timeout then," he said. "I'm kind of behind on things myself."

She nodded and slipped out of bed. "And nothing ever in front of anybody; no one must know about us."

"Aargh, but you're a hard lass," Theo said now. He lifted the lid off a pot on the stove. "Chili for dinner I see."

"I turned the oven on. I thought you could make some cornbread."

"You did, did you?"

"You would do it much more quickly than I."

"That's true." He opened cupboards and pulled out ingredients. "By the way, I ran into Chester's nephew Jimmy in town today. The paramedic, remember? Funny, he asked me if you had had medical training. Said it seemed like you had, given what you did and the questions you asked."

Leah went still.

Theo glanced at her. "I said no, but how did you know what to do anyway? Jimmy said you probably saved Fox's life."

She busied herself at the sink. "I lived with someone who was studying medicine."

"Oh? So, what, you read her textbooks?"

She hesitated. *He might as well know.* "It was a he," she said.

"He'd repeat what he had learned in the course of a day to me as a way of fixing it in his mind."

Theo turned and stared at her. "You lived with a guy? For how long?"

"Could you please keep your voice down? Anyhow, it was five years."

His jaw dropped. "You were with a guy for five years?" he hissed. "I can't believe it!"

She glanced at him over her shoulder. "Yes, that may seem odd to someone who's had who knows how many liaisons."

"When was this? What happened?"

"It's a long story."

"I've got lots of time."

"Well, I don't feel like going into it right now."

"Where is he?"

"I don't know." She paused. "Actually I probably do, but it's irrelevant."

"But five years!"

A car rolled into the driveway. Leah glanced out the window.

"That's Dad. Now please let it go, Theo."

Throughout dinner Theo kept stealing glances at Leah. She studiously ignored him. Her revelation about living with a man had turned his notion of her completely on its head. From the state she was in when she had turned up at the ranch he'd assumed that she had lived a marginal existence all those years she was gone. Apparently not. It was like the business with her book. *What other secrets is she keeping?*

And five years together meant the relationship must have been pretty serious. He tried to envisage *that* Leah, part of a couple, sharing a home. And a medical student to boot, probably a doctor now. His mind buzzed with questions: What did he look like? How had they been together? Why had it ended?

When had it ended? Had it ended? He couldn't help doing the math and calculated that in that time she would have had more sex than he had had in his entire life. Which would explain a few things. An unfamiliar emotion churned in his chest. It took him a moment to recognize what it was: Jealousy.

Later that week Theo paused as he was leaving the Lighthouse gym. Since learning of Caro's revelation when Ben had returned from Vancouver he had wanted to say something to his brother, but despite sharing meals regularly the awkwardness between them persisted. He turned resolutely in the direction of Ben's office.

"Come!" Ben said in answer to his knock.

"Hey, Ben," Theo said, opening the door. "I've just been working out. Nice to have the gym available again."

Ben signed a letter and pushed it to the side. "Yes. I should check it out one of these days."

"Anyhow, thought I'd say hello. How's it going?"

Ben scrubbed the back of his head with his hand. "Fine, I think." He indicated a chair in front of his desk. "Have a seat."

Theo dropped his bag next to the chair and sat down. "Any chance you have time for a coffee?"

"Actually, I just made some tea." Ben rose and went to a side table bearing a tray with tea makings. He smiled wryly. "Have to make my own these days. Cindy's told me she has better things to do." He poured out two cups. "How do you take yours?"

"Clear is fine."

Ben handed a cup to Theo and sat down with his own. They sipped in silence for a moment.

"Ben, I ... ah, just wanted to say how sorry I am about that recent business with Caro," Theo said. "It really sucks."

"Thanks." Ben grimaced. "I'm hoping she made it up just to spite me. For that matter I wouldn't put it past her to have made up the whole business about being pregnant." He shifted in his seat. "And I've never said how sorry I am about what happened to you with those guys from school."

Theo drew back in his chair. "I didn't know you knew."

"Mom and Dad told me. They were trying to understand how something like that could have been allowed to happen." He shook his head. "I honestly had no idea. Why didn't you tell me they were bothering you? I would have sorted them out."

"Yeah, well, everybody seemed to pick on me then. I never understood why."

Ben raised his eyebrows. "Really?"

Theo shook his head. "I hated that place." He set his empty cup down on the desk. "You know, Ben, there are a whole bunch of things we don't know about each other. I'm sorry about that; I wish we'd been closer."

"Well, you went away when you were so young."

"There was that. But even before." Theo smiled faintly. "You were a hard act to follow, Ben. You did everything so well, and you accomplished so much. I always had to scramble to keep up and I could never do anything right. I think that's what made me push back so much."

Ben's mouth fell open.

"What?" Theo said.

"I had no idea." Ben gave a dry laugh. "And *I* always thought that things came to you so easily, that you'd been given so much. Your talent..." He made a vague motion in Theo's direction. "Everything."

"Son of a gun," Theo said.

They regarded each other in silence for a moment.

Theo stood up. "I should let you get on with your work." He took his cup to the side table. At the door he stopped and turned back. "Look, Ben, let's fix all that," he said.

Ben nodded. "Yes, let's."

Chapter 42

"Please don't stay on my account," Leah said. Theo had just told her that he and Fox wouldn't be going to Counter Point for the summer as they usually did until all four of them could go out when Leah took her vacation leave in August. "In fact, I'd prefer that you both were out there to keep Niels company."

"Niels is going? I thought he'd be staying here with you."

"Dad is taking him to Canada with him when he goes to start rehearsals for the new opera."

"Why?"

Leah released an exasperated sigh. "Ludmilla Bogdanovich, a well-known cellist Dad knows, is going to be in Vancouver and he wants her to give Niels some lessons and assess his talent."

"But that's good, isn't it?"

"I suppose. The thing is, Dad's going to be away much of the time. Niels will be left with the housekeeper until he heads to music camp later in July. If you and Fox are at Counter Point he could spend some time there."

"Do you have to go right now?" Ben said when Theo told him that he and Fox would in fact be going to the coast with their parents. "It's going to be awfully lonely for Nathan without anyone here. Couldn't you at least stay until Beth arrives?

I got a card from her a couple of weeks ago saying she expects to be here soon."

"Sure, we can wait a bit," Theo said. "I could use the extra time in my studio."

"But what about Niels?" Leah said when he told her of the change of plan.

Theo threw up his hands. "Look, it shouldn't be long. Isn't that cellist supposed to be seeing Niels soon anyway? He'll be fine until we get there."

"Well, okay," she said. "But just so you know, I'm not going to come around every day. I had intended to get a lot of writing done while you all were away."

Fox was not happy about staying behind. After Niels left he sulked and ignored Nathan who trailed behind him forlornly, not understanding.

"Come on, be nice," Theo said.

"He's just a baby," Fox said, curling his lip.

"That wasn't a problem when you played with him before. Come on, you're hurting his feelings."

The few days Theo had expected to wait for Beth's return stretched to two weeks, then three. True to her word, Leah stayed away. With only each other for company, Theo and Ben began testing their newfound understanding. They spoke initially as casual acquaintances might, on neutral subjects like day-to-day matters, food and wine, books and music, travel and current events. Their conversations progressed to shared memories and their extended family and then, tentatively, they began to speak about themselves.

Theo set up the last blank canvas on its easel and rubbed his forearm across his brow. The dense, flat heat of late July crowded into his studio. He peeled off his T-shirt, wiped his chest and underarms and tossed the crumpled top into a corner. After studying the canvas for a minute he quickly sketched out the lines of a composition. He poked among the tubes of paint on a table and selected the combination of colors he proposed to use.

"No, I don't know where Beth is," Ben had said over dinner the previous night. "It's weeks now since I received that last card and the postmark was smudged so I don't even know where it came from."

"Did she say where they were going?"

"She mentioned Idaho, and it was supposed to be only until that bad business in Las Vegas was behind them. But it's over three months since they left there. I'd have thought things would be resolved by now."

"Do you regret taking Nathan?"

Ben had given a decisive shake of his head. "No. I do believe he's better off here than with them."

"Is it possible she won't return at all?"

Ben had paused and thought before answering. "From what I know of Beth, and I've come to realize it's not a lot, I'm pretty sure she'd never abandon Nathan. That's why her long silence is so worrying. I can't help but wonder if something has gone terribly wrong."

Theo wondered the same thing. He and Ben had grown close in the previous weeks and he shared his brother's growing apprehension. He set down the palette and scrolled through the choices of music on his computer, found a blues playlist. A guitar squealed over the punch of a drum. He turned up the volume, squeezed a few more blobs of paint on the palette and considered the four blank canvases arranged in a semi-circle around him.

Women! Don't they end up just driving you crazy. Take Leah. When he had initially thought of marrying her he figured it would basically mean continuing the way they were but with some side benefits. He wasn't prepared for the tumult of feelings that had followed going to bed with her. So he was initially okay with her idea that they cool things while she worked on her book, even welcomed it as a kind of a breather to try to make sense of it all. He'd have a hard time putting into words what was going on between them, he only knew that he wanted it to continue. But Leah seemed to be avoiding him, rebuffing all his attempts to spend time with her. Nicely, but still. Was writing the book real or an excuse? And if it was real, was she talking weeks or months, or even years? On top of it all there was the doctor guy she'd lived with for so long. Could this new distance between them be because of him? He sighed and leaned towards one canvas to study the faint lines that marked out the subject. Hopefully it would all get sorted when they went to Counter Point in August. Although she'd no doubt insist they maintain the no-physical-contact policy there.

"I didn't know painting was such a noisy business."

He jumped back. "Geez, you startled me!"

"Sorry," Leah said.

He reduced the volume of the music.

"I hope you don't mind. Your door was open," she said.

"No," he said warily as though afraid she might flee.

She motioned at the easels. "Why do you have so many going at the same time?"

He set down the palette. "It's efficient. I can do the same operations on them—preparing the canvas, sketching out the compositions, blocking out the base colors—all at once. Saves the time you'd normally spend shifting from one job to the other."

"It's certainly a different approach to the creative process."

"Creative process? I churn out crowd-pleasing Southwest scenes to make money."

Leah gave him an odd look. "Theo, you insult yourself and the people who buy your work by suggesting that what they like has no value. As far as being able to execute a painting quickly, surely that's a measure of your skill. And you actually make a living from your art—"

"Hardly a living."

"Still, you seem to sell what you produce. Not all painters do."

He put his hands on his hips and cocked an eyebrow. "So, you've come here to lecture me on the merit of my work?"

"No." She stepped forward and slipped her arms around his waist. "I've come because I miss you, Theo."

"Ethan's timing sure sucks. Is the split serious or has he just gone off in a snit?" Theo said as they walked down to Las Sombras to prepare dinner later that afternoon.

"He says it's over. He's met someone else, and because he's feeling so guilty about it he's given Jeff until the end of August to find another place. He doesn't want to be around here during that time."

"But he promised you this time off."

"Yes, I know, but he said he really needed me to be there for him and that he'd make it up to me when he got back." Leah glanced up at him. "It's no reason you and Fox shouldn't go."

"I don't want to go without you! Maybe it's just as well. There's no sign of Beth and I don't want to leave Ben and Nathan alone either."

Theo informed their parents of the change of plans. Two days later, Fin called to say that he and Niels were flying in that afternoon and needed a ride home. When the plane landed Niels was the first to emerge. His broad smile was matched by Fox's grin.

"Hey, troglodyte," Fox said, punching the other boy lightly on the arm.

Niels returned the punch. "Hello, asymptote."

Theo noticed a difference in the boy, something in his face or his stance. "Have you grown?" he said.

Niels shrugged. "Probably." He looked around. "Where's my mom?"

"At work. Her boss took off and left her in charge of the whole operation. I sent her a text." He ruffled the boy's hair. "She's going to be awfully glad to see you, that's for sure."

Fin approached them loaded with bags and grumbling. "You could have at least taken your backpack," he said, handing the item to his grandson.

"Sorry, Granddad."

They carried the luggage to the Jeep and got in.

"Why didn't you bring the Volvo?" Fin said as he buckled his seat belt.

"It's not my car."

"About time you replaced this old heap, don't you think?"

"It runs just fine." When Theo turned on the ignition the engine leapt to life as though validating his confidence. "You're sure in a good mood. Everything okay?"

Fin jerked his thumb in the direction of the boys in the back seat. "When he heard Leah wasn't coming to the coast he insisted I bring him here. Wouldn't give me any peace. I had to reschedule a meeting in LA."

"Niels is playing with the boys in their bedroom," Theo said to Leah when she burst through the kitchen door later that afternoon. "But watch out for your dad," he called after her as she headed down the hall. "He's not a happy camper."

Fin's mood had not improved by dinner.

"How did Niels' session with Ludmilla Bogdanovich go?" Leah said.

Fin scowled at the boy. "Not well; in fact, quite poorly. You would have thought he didn't know one end of the instrument from the other."

"She made me nervous," Niels said placidly and took a bite of his burger.

Leah glanced at her son, her eyes dancing. "Another time, perhaps?"

"Huh!" said Fin.

Fin returned to the matter over breakfast with her and Theo the next morning. "He messed up deliberately, I'm sure of it. It was embarrassing. I had told Ludmilla that I thought he showed an uncommon mastery of the cello for someone of his age and with only a couple of years of study."

"What did she say?" Leah said.

Fin smiled grimly. "Oh, she was diplomatic: He no doubt had good potential but was perhaps not quite ready for advanced instruction."

"He may not have thought he was ready yet either," Leah said. "At least to commit to the intensive study you had in mind."

"If he's going to make anything of himself as a cellist he needs to commit soon."

"Maybe he's not sure it's what he wants to do with his life."

Fin waved his hand dismissively. "He's too young to make decisions about what he wants to do with his life."

"And you're ready to do it for him?"

Fin glared at her for a moment. "All I'm trying to do is keep it open as an option. The boy has talent, possibly even exceptional talent. He can always decide later not to make a career of playing the cello. What's more difficult—a lot more difficult—is to suddenly decide when he's older that it's really what he wants to do and try to make up the training. He's at the optimal age for learning. It'll be a heck of a lot harder a few years from now."

"But can't he just continue with his studies here?"

Fin pushed his crumb-covered plate away and leaned back in his chair. "He's taken all he can from the woman teaching him in Taos. There may be someone in Santa Fe or Albuquerque who can offer more but it would mean going there at least once a week. His options would be much better in a larger center."

Was Fin seriously thinking of taking Niels back to Vancouver? Theo thought. He glanced at Leah. Had she known this? Was it what she had been brooding about these past weeks? Why had she not spoken about it to him? Understanding slowly dawned. If Niels left what would happen to her? He turned back to Fin. Would he really split them all up?

"You too—if you're planning to be a writer you really should get some kind of an education," Fin said, stabbing a finger at his daughter.

"I'm not *planning* to be a writer, I am one."

"Nonetheless, you should think about going to university. Or do you still have to finish high school?"

Leah clasped her hands and raised her chin. "One of the advantages of working for a university is the opportunity to audit classes. Over the nine years I worked at McGill and then Columbia, I audited three or four classes a semester. In the morning before work, over lunch or in the evening. So in that time I attended lectures in…" She paused for a second, calculating. "Probably seventy to eighty courses. In all disciplines, even physics, biology and commerce. First year, mostly, but for the ones that interested me—history, philosophy, literature—I talked myself into senior classes. So spending several years at a university to get a piece of paper would be redundant, to say the least."

Theo stared at Leah as she spoke. *Add to that the cozy lessons in medicine.* He realized his mouth was hanging open and snapped it shut.

Fin slowly smiled. "Well that's all right then." He glanced at his watch and rose. "I've got to be at the airfield for ten-thirty. Can one of you take me there?"

Theo tore his eyes away from Leah. "Ah, yeah, I'll give you a lift."

"Good. I'll go and pack."

"Your dad wouldn't split Niels and Fox up, would he?" Theo said after Fin had left the room.

Leah glanced at him, still flushed from the exchange with her father. "Dad can be pretty stubborn, ruthless even, when he thinks he's right. As I have reason to know. And he *is* Niels' legal guardian."

"But he can't ignore other parts of Niels' life."

Leah shrugged.

Theo paused. "You're seriously smart, Leah, aren't you?" he said. "Not surprising I guess, given your parents."

"I am nowhere as smart as my mother. She was off the chart."

"Still, maybe Fin's right about your doing further studies. Maybe you need to be somewhere that offers more options as well." His heart sank saying it but there was no denying that life here at the ranch might be limiting for her as well as Niels.

"Theo, I am where I want to be and doing what I want to do," she said levelly. She stood and began gathering the dishes that littered the table. "And now I have to get to work."

Chapter 43

"Do you know what I can't understand?" Ris said to Ben. "It's how you and Theo, both such nice, considerate, *good* men, haven't been able to find equally nice, considerate, good women. You're not young any more. Will either of you ever settle down?"

Lucas smiled at his wife. She didn't often play the heavy mother but he knew she felt the events of the last year keenly: Fox's accident, the revelations about Theo's assault, Caro's spitefully gratuitous disclosure about terminating her pregnancy and the peculiar business of Ben's impromptu assumption of responsibility for Nathan.

"I only want for them what we have," she had said the previous day when they were discussing their sons.

He had agreed, although their forty-odd years together hadn't been completely idyllic. Joyful though their marriage was his adjustment to it after years in religious orders had not been easy. Being with someone wasn't the problem—he was used to community—but it had taken time for him to emerge from the self-containment of an introspective life to share thoughts, hopes and plans with another. Then there was the challenge of understanding the meaning of his gifts and his growing sense of mission, and always the residual guilt he had never been able to fully erase. Ris had been typically forthright in expressing her expectations and disappointments but she had always been patient and neither had ever doubted that they were intended to be together.

He glanced at Ben, downing a late breakfast on the deck of their cottage at Counter Point after arriving the previous night from Vancouver where he had been dealing with some legal matters. Disquiet had incised new lines on Ben's face and clouded his eyes. Lucas shared Ris's concerns about their sons. Ben didn't love wisely—first there was the fiery Argentinian he had chased halfway around the world, then cold, calculating Caro, and now Beth, a fugitive. And Theo? He feared his younger son was not capable of loving at all.

"Now Ris, Beth is not out of the picture yet," he said.

"Yes, but her situation is beyond complicated. With that husband and his dubious connections, a life with her may involve trials we can't even begin to imagine."

"There is no more husband," Ben said.

Ris's eyebrows rose. "He's granted her a divorce?"

"No, he's dead."

Lucas and Ris both exclaimed. "How do you know this?" Lucas said.

"After not hearing from her for so long I hired a private investigator to find them. He was able to track them to Redmond in Washington State where Beth's husband had purchased a convenience store. He was killed in late June by a car bomb outside their home. I guess whoever was after them found them as easily as my PI did."

Ris leaned forward. "And Beth?"

"She's missing." Ben pushed away his plate and wiped his mouth.

"So she escaped?" Lucas said.

"I can only hope so. The alternative doesn't bear thinking about."

"If she escaped why hasn't she been in touch in all this time?" Ris said.

Ben sighed. "Exactly."

Ris raised her hand to her mouth and leaned back in her chair. "Oh my."

"What do you plan to do?" Lucas said.

"I don't know, Dad. Any thoughts?"

"Continue to search for her, I guess. Expand the scope to other places she is likely to go."

"The PI searched for all the Beth Wallaces in the U.S. and none of the ones he found were her. The thing is, there's a lot I don't know about Beth so I'm not sure I can offer anything else for him to go on. I could tell him to look in California where Beth grew up but it would be like looking for a needle in a haystack."

Lucas sat back and studied the long sweep of ocean stretching out before them, gunmetal gray from the scrim of cloud stretched across the sky and speckled with white chips of foam. As often happened in late August a low front had dipped down from Alaska, bringing with it the first taste of autumn.

"Then you should begin to consider the possibility that she will never return," he said quietly.

"I already have. The legal issues associated with keeping Nathan are mindboggling." He grimaced. "The one time I really should have thought like a lawyer, I didn't; in the rush to pick him up I forgot to get a guardianship letter from her."

The following week Ben had just arrived at work and sat down at his desk when his phone rang. He hadn't slept well and wasn't in the mood to talk to anyone.

"Can you get that, Cindy?" he called.

She didn't answer. He hoped it was because she wasn't there and not some kind of statement about how answering the phone fell outside her scope of duties. Sighing heavily, he picked up the receiver and grunted a greeting.

"Ben?"

Breathless with surprise he could not immediately answer.

"Ben? Are you there?"

"Oh, yes, my God, Beth, yes," he choked out.

"It's so good to hear your voice."

"I, ah … oh, Beth, where have you been?"

"It's a long story. Ben, I'm coming to Taos. I'll be arriving by bus late this afternoon."

"I'll come and get you."

"You don't have to, I can find my way."

"Don't be silly. I'll be there."

He texted the news to his family, fumbling with the keys. Time crawled—he had never known a day to pass so slowly yet somehow he managed to arrive a few minutes late at the depot. People were milling around collecting their luggage and greeting family and friends, but Beth was not among them. *Was this the right bus? Had she changed her plans?* His shoulders sagged. *Had something happened to prevent her from coming?* He looked one way then another, and as he did his eyes connected with those of what looked like a young man dressed in an army jacket with shaggy hair the color of corn. Ben scowled when the young man held his gaze and smiled shyly, then recognition dawned.

"Beth!" he said, striding towards her. They embraced briefly, Beth quivering like a bird in his arms. He touched her shorn head lightly. A hard line of dark roots edged the yellow. "Your beautiful hair," he said.

"It will grow back." Her face was pale and her eyes ringed with fatigue. "Can we go?"

He picked up the army-issue rucksack at her side and they headed to his car.

"How is Nathan?" she said.

"Thriving."

"Did he miss me much?"

The truth was that Nathan had mentioned Beth less and less as time passed. "Of course," Ben said. "But he's in daycare during the day and there are two other boys at home so he's had plenty of distractions."

She smiled wearily. "Good."

In the car she closed her eyes and leaned back against the head rest, not speaking until they pulled up to Las Sombras. When he turned off the engine she blinked awake and sat up.

"This is my uncle Fin's house. It's where Nathan and I've been living," he said.

"Is Nathan here?"

Ben shook his head. "He's off with Theo and the boys." Inside the house he showed her to the guest room. "You'll probably want to freshen up. I'll be in the kitchen."

Half an hour later she appeared, showered and dressed in cotton pants and a T-shirt creased from her pack. He rose from the table where he had been working on his laptop.

"How about some tea or coffee? And maybe something to eat?"

"Just coffee, thanks."

While he made it she wandered around the room, looking out the windows. When it was ready she sat down at the table and accepted the drink. A vehicle drew up outside. The engine was cut and doors slammed. Beth's face lit up and she set down her cup and turned expectantly to the entrance. Fox burst in first. When he saw Beth he stopped, and Nathan, who was close on his heels, bumped into him.

The younger boy elbowed his way to the front. "Mommy!"

She bent down and opened her arms. "Nathan, sweetheart."

Instead of embracing her he punched her on the chest, in her face. Ben stepped forward, grabbed one of his arms and yanked him back.

"We never, ever hit girls!" he said.

Nathan's mouth fell open and his eyes grew round with shock.

"Now, say you're sorry and greet your mother properly."

The boy's face crumpled and he burst into tears. Theo and Niels entered and stopped.

"Is everything okay?" Theo said.

Ben glanced up. "We're having a teaching moment."

"Nathan was hitting her," Fox said.

"Come here, baby," Beth said.

"Say you're sorry first," Ben insisted, but gently.

Nathan stuttered an apology and Ben released him. The boy crawled onto Beth's lap and sobbed into her shoulder.

"I'm sure you've got a lot of catching up to do," Theo said. "Come on guys, let's go."

There was a commotion for a few moments with Beth insisting that she didn't want to disrupt their routines and Theo saying that it wasn't a problem. Ben let the exchange play itself out, not saying anything but hoping they would go. Theo won out and as he, Fox and Niels started to leave, Nathan, who had stopped crying, looked longingly after them.

"Hey, ah, why doesn't Nathan camp out with us at my place tonight?" Theo said. "I'll let Leah know."

Nathan slid out of Beth's arms. She lowered them into her lap and smiled faintly.

"We'll all be back for breakfast tomorrow," Theo said, taking the little boy's hand.

When they were gone, Ben said, "Do you mind about Nathan?"

She shrugged. "I guess it was too much to expect that we would pick up exactly where we had left off."

They sipped their coffee without speaking for a few moments.

"So what's with the disguise?" Ben said.

The Lighthouse

Beth smoothed down her ragged hair and laughed ruefully. "We were so naïve. We thought a different hairstyle, a new town would be enough to throw them off our track."

"But they found you."

She nodded. "We were heading to the store that morning. I should have been in the car when it blew but we had quarreled." She made a weary motion with her hand. "The ongoing argument: why he wouldn't grant me the divorce like he promised now that he was set up with the business."

"Why wouldn't he?"

"He said he needed me to work in the store for a while longer until the transition was done and the business well set up. Anyhow, I knew he was in a hurry and hung back to annoy him." She shook her head. "The silly little things we do."

"But it was fortunate that you did, no?"

"I guess so." Her eyes filled with tears and she dashed them away with the back of her hand. "Don't get me wrong, I wanted to be rid of him but not like that. Not like that."

She gazed out towards the darkening hills in silence. Ben left her be. After a few minutes she stirred. "I'm going to have to tell Nathan somehow."

"He hasn't asked after his father at all."

"Well, they weren't together much in the last year. What does anyone remember at that age?"

"So what did you do after the explosion?"

"Stood stunned for a couple of minutes then ran out the back door. Went to a McDonald's around the corner and sat there for a long time, listening to the sirens. And thinking. I didn't know whether they'd still come after me when they realized I hadn't been in the car. Their dispute was with my husband, not me, but who knows how those guys think? I had to assume they would so I needed to disappear in a way that I couldn't be followed."

She gave him a sheepish look.

"A woman had sat down at the table next to me. She left her bag hanging on the back of her chair while she went to get napkins or condiments or something. It was a big one with an open top and I, ah, stole her wallet and left the place. I didn't want to buy a ticket out of town under my own name."

"That's why there was no trace at all of you leaving Redmond."

She nodded. "For the record, I mailed her wallet back to her later with money to cover the charge I had made on her credit card."

"So where did you go?"

"Immediately, just to Boise. It was the first bus leaving. Then I remembered a friend of my mother's, a Blackfoot artist. I used to call her Auntie Gloria. She had studied and lived in California for several years before returning home to Montana. I went there and it's where I've been since."

Ben refilled their cups. "Why didn't you call, or write?"

She acknowledged the question with a nod. "When I arrived at Auntie Gloria's I kind of fell apart. Life on the run with my husband had been hard enough but the explosion finished me off. I wondered if I'd ever be safe again. Gloria's family closed around me, first for protection then to help me heal. I had run out of money by this time and they found me a job cooking and cleaning at a wilderness summer camp the band ran. It's hard to explain, but for a while I could barely connect two thoughts let alone try to communicate with someone. And the camp was so isolated. There was little contact with the outside world, no cell or Internet service, and time just passed."

"I had begun to think I'd never see you again."

"And there were times when I wondered whether I'd ever get back to Nathan and you. I'm sorry, Ben."

There was much he wanted to say but he needed to know her mind first. "So what do you plan to do now?" he said.

She leaned back and stared blankly out the window. After

The Lighthouse

several moments she turned to him and said, "I've lost everything. The inheritance I received from my mother bought my husband's business in Redmond. It was, I thought, a fair price to pay for my freedom."

He frowned. "But can't you sell it, recover your investment?"

She shook her head. "No, it's in his name alone. That was the deal."

"But as his wife you can make a claim on his estate."

"And draw attention to myself?"

"But if it was your inheritance…"

"My mother would understand. She'd be the first person to say that it's only money and not worth putting Nathan and me at risk. But it leaves me in a difficult position." She leaned forward. "Ben, my job at the Lighthouse—could I possibly get it back?"

Chapter 44

"They have stars in their eyes, don't you think?" Leah said.

Theo stopped scrubbing the frying pan used for the scrambled eggs that morning and glanced out the window to where Beth and Ben were loading luggage into his car for the move to his parents' guest house.

"You think?" He turned to Leah. "And how about us? Don't we have stars in our eyes?"

She slipped a box of plastic wrap into a drawer and closed it. "We're not exactly hearts and flowers types, are we?"

He thought about this comment as he wandered back to his studio after Leah had left for work. Some cornflowers blooming off the path caught his attention and he plucked a few stems. In his studio he put them in a mason jar of water, set a small canvas on an easel and quickly marked out a few lines. The painting was done by lunch. He put down his brush and stepped back. Over a graduated red glaze he had painted a scattering of blue cornflowers, their intersecting leaves forming hearts.

The painting was barely dry when he presented it to Leah the next morning. She accepted it with a questioning glance and held it out for a look. After several moments she leaned it carefully against the tiles backing the kitchen counter and turned to him.

"Thank you, Theo," she said, her eyes bright.

They were deep into a long and satisfying kiss when Niels and Fox burst into the room.

"Eew," the boys said, skidding to a stop.

Theo and Leah slowly disengaged. "What are you eewing about?" he said.

"You guys are *kissing*," Fox said, his voice dripping disgust.

"It's what men and women do," Theo said. "You know, it's not going to be long before you'll be wanting to kiss girls."

"Eew! Eew!" the boys said. Fox added a few gagging noises.

"Never mind," Theo said, laughing. "How about some breakfast?"

The house phone rang as they were finishing their cereal. Leah was closest and answered it. "Yes, this is Leah," she said. After listening for a moment she left the room to take the call.

The boys had gone to school and Theo was loading the dishwasher when she returned. She set the telephone handset into its cradle and leaned against the counter hunched into herself.

"What's up, Leah? Is something wrong?"

She looked up blankly. "That was Ken."

"Who's that?"

"My…" She swallowed. "The fellow with whom I used to live."

Theo closed the dishwasher door. "What did he want?"

"He's here in Taos. He wants to see me."

He put his hands on his hips. "What about?"

"He said he wants to talk." Leah straightened up. "I'm going to meet him for a drink after work."

He opened his mouth to forbid it, but in the short time it took for him to realize he had no right to she had put her jacket on and, with a brief goodbye, headed for the door. He called out to remind her to take the cornflower painting but she didn't hear. The vivid colors of the piece glowed against the tile, mocking him.

Chapter 45

Leah pulled down the sun visor in her car and examined herself in the mirror embedded in it. That morning she had dressed as she would have any other day to make the point—to whom she wasn't sure—that her meeting with Ken held no significance. So why was she now checking her face? She flipped up the visor with a disgusted noise and got out of the car. After leaving her the way he had Ken didn't deserve any special consideration.

She paused at the entrance to the lounge in the hotel where they had arranged to meet, waiting for her eyes to adjust to the gloom.

"Leah!"

She turned. Ken strode up to her from the lobby. They regarded each other awkwardly for a moment then he bent down and kissed her lightly on the cheek.

"It's good to see you," he said.

Really? "Hello, Ken," she said.

He motioned to the lounge. "Shall we?"

She led the way to a table in a corner and they sat down. He regarded her with his Basset hound eyes and gave her a shy one-sided smile that at one time had been as familiar as her own reflection. Something wobbled in the vicinity of her heart.

The Lighthouse

She took a deep breath. "So what brings you out here?"

"Well, you."

A server interrupted, giving her a moment to consider the meaning of his reply.

"How about a carafe of white wine?" Ken said.

Lead nodded her agreement. "How did you find me?" she said after the server had left.

Ken leaned back and crossed one leg over the other. He looked older, his face and body fuller, the dark hair that once had flopped so endearingly over his forehead trimmed and smoothed back. His clothes—a well-cut silk-blend jacket, fine wool trousers and soft leather loafers—were those of the affluent Southern gentleman he had become. *I wonder how I look to him?*

"Through your publisher. There was a review of your book in our city paper. Your name caught my eye and when I read the article I recognized the main character; you know, the guy sitting in the gazebo in the park. I remember you wondering and worrying about him whenever we passed by." He paused. "I didn't know you were a writer."

"I didn't know I was either until that book came out."

The wine arrived and was served. They each took a sip.

"Naturally, I then checked you out on the Internet." Ken studied her for a moment. "I had always thought you came from a broken family and had had a difficult childhood and that's why you left home. I found out that your father is a well-known composer and your mother was quite an important physicist. My condolences, by the way."

She nodded in acknowledgement.

"Why did you never say anything?"

"I did have a difficult childhood, anything else you assumed."

"Okay, maybe, but why didn't you ever speak of your mom and dad? They sound like wonderful people."

"They are, were, *extraordinary* people, but they weren't great

301

parents." She suddenly felt fatigued by the conversation. "Look, Ken, why have you come?"

"I'm still trying to come to terms with your leaving."

Her eyebrows shot up. "*My* leaving? But it was you who broke us up!"

He frowned. "I don't understand."

"How can you not understand? And what kind of a guy sends his mother to tell his girlfriend it's over?"

His jaw dropped. "I never did that."

"Come on, Ken. She was quite clear on the matter."

He shook his head. "Leah, I swear to God I don't know what you're talking about."

She regarded him for a moment. Was it possible? "While you were in China I came home to find her in our apartment packing up your belongings. She said two things. One was that after thinking about it you had realized that I wouldn't fit into the new life you were about to begin in Atlanta. She said it was best I leave now, when I had gotten used to your being away, and that I should respect your decision and not try to contact you. She also told me to vacate the apartment by the end of the month—which was, like, four days away—because there was a new tenant ready to move in. And to add insult to injury she offered me a wad of bills, for the *inconvenience,* she said. Needless to say I didn't take it; it was too much like payment for services rendered."

Ken's regarded her with horror. "Fuck," he said, burying his face in his hands. "*Fuck!*"

Unsure of what was happening, Leah left him be. After a couple of minutes he straightened up. His eyes were flat with despair.

"How could she?" he said.

"What do you mean?

"It was all a misunderstanding," he said, his voice dull. "When I went home before Dad and I left on the trip they sat me down and started in on how as an up-and-coming doctor in Atlanta I'd need a different kind of partner, that while you'd been okay while I was going to school I'd need someone of my own class—they actually used that word—to hold my own in the city. They said that while they didn't necessarily agree with the way things worked in Atlanta, the reality was that marrying someone who didn't fit in and wouldn't be easily accepted could well limit my opportunities."

Leah felt a chill forming on her lips, her face. "And what did you say?"

He waved his hand. "Of course I said that I didn't give a flying you-know-what about Atlanta society, but they kept at me and, well, they were my parents, and with all they'd done for me—you know, putting me through school, the place in New York and the month traveling with my dad in China and Tibet—I felt I had to at least acknowledge their point of view." His face turned a deep red. "So I said I'd consider it."

"I see," Leah said.

"Look, I didn't plan to do what they wanted, I just said that to end the badgering. But my parents must have interpreted it as agreement. When I got back Mom told me that you'd left and how obviously you had also realized that coming with me to Atlanta wasn't going to work. She said I should be happy, that you'd done me a favor." He shook his head. "I still went to New York but couldn't find you anywhere and any emails I sent you bounced back. It had happened in Tibet too, but I assumed that on the few occasions when we got access to the Internet it was a problem with the service."

"Ken, our breakup, however it happened, turned my life upside down. I had nowhere to live so when Ingrid offered me the use of her family's cabin in the north I accepted. I quit my job right away—I had intended to anyway to go to Atlanta with you. My email was tied to it."

He shook his head. "What I don't get is how you just

accepted what my mother said. Did you really think I'd blow you off like that? We were going to get married, remember? Why didn't you try to get ahold of me?"

Leah was silent for a moment. Why had she never questioned his mother's actions? "I don't know, Ken. The shock of it, maybe? I had no reason not to believe your mother and I didn't want to hold you back."

He made a helpless gesture with his hand. "How could she do such a thing?"

"Oh, Ken, your parents said it all: I was a runaway high school dropout and they wanted someone with pedigree for you."

"Pedigree! You have that in spades. If only they had known about your family."

They stared at each other for several moments, Leah awash in a kaleidoscope of emotions. *What if, what if,* circled in her mind. She tried to visualize the last three years if they had stayed together but couldn't. Would she have come back to her family then? Would she have ever found Niels?

"I've looked for you everywhere, Leah," Ken said. His eyes glistened. "I've never stopped looking for you. It tore me apart losing you like that. I'm not sure I can ever love anyone again."

She wanted to say something but didn't know what. Knowing what happened left her oddly devoid of feeling. She tried to recapture the eviscerating sense of betrayal and loss that had gripped her during those months holed up in the Adirondacks but felt only an echo of all that bitterness and pain. Maybe she had spent it all in her book. Maybe it was just a matter of time healing. As it didn't seem to have done in Ken's case.

He sat up, hope brightening his face, and gripped her hands. "But now that I've found you we can put all that behind us. Come with me. Not to Atlanta." He shook his head angrily. "Not back there—I'll never forgive my parents for this. We can go somewhere new. Anywhere you'd like. Or I could come here. But we can be together now."

She drew in a deep breath. "There's something else I've never told you. I have a child, Ken. A son."

Chapter 46

Theo had tasted misery before but not often, and never the bitter, gut-grinding emotion that rolled through him that day. So, the old boyfriend was back, the guy she had been with for over five years. Leah never did say why they had broken up. She wasn't a woman you could walk away from easily. Had *she* left the guy? Was it to come here? Was he now after her to get together again?

He gave up trying to paint and went to the stable, saddled up Onyx and set off for a long ride in the mountains. He had chosen the horse because concentration was needed to control him and it helped dampen the wretchedness somewhat. They both returned exhausted. At dinner Niels and Fox quibbled endlessly over strategy for a video game they were playing.

"Enough already," Theo said sharply.

Startled, they fell silent, finished their meal and slipped away to their room. When he checked on them later they were still in their day clothes, Niels listening to something through his headphones, Fox fiddling with Lego parts strewn on the floor.

"Hey! Pajamas and bed, both of you!" He pointed to the pieces on the floor. "And clean up that mess."

Fox glanced up at him from under a furrowed brow. "Don't know why you're so grumpy," he said.

"Yeah, sorry," Theo said after a moment. He touched his

son lightly on the head and knelt to help pick up the bricks and figures.

After, he sat down in front of the television and flipped through the channels, trying to find something of interest. Nine o'clock passed, then nine-thirty. *That's an awfully long drink.* He sat up in the armchair. *Maybe Leah went directly to her trailer. Maybe she's already home.* He pulled out his cellphone to call her but set it down without dialing. If she wasn't home it would look like he was checking up on her. He leaned back in his chair and tried to focus on the screen.

It suddenly struck him that she could stay out all night without him knowing it. "Shit!" he said. He vaulted out of his chair, went to Fin's liquor cabinet and helped himself to some whisky. *What a stupid set-up, having her live out there.* He settled back in front of the television. He'd insist she move closer, either here or his place. If she didn't bugger off with her old boyfriend.

It was close to ten-thirty when he heard the back door open. Not wanting to give her the satisfaction of knowing how anxious he was, he stayed in his seat. He heard her go to the boys' room. A few minutes later she came to him.

"How's everything?" she said, her voice reedy with fatigue.

"Oh, just fine."

"Did the boys get to bed okay?"

"Yeah, no problem."

She sank into the armchair perpendicular to his. Her face was drawn and pale. Relief made him generous.

"You okay? You look awfully tired."

She turned dark, troubled eyes to him, and nodded.

"So ... how'd it go?"

She drew a long breath before answering. "I don't think I can talk about it. Not yet, not tonight." She started to rise. "I should go home. I just wanted to check on the boys."

He leaned forward and put his hand on hers. "It's late. Why don't you stay here tonight?"

She studied him for a moment and nodded. "Yes, I think I will."

"I was about to go to bed. You can stay with me."

"Oh, Theo, I couldn't."

He rose and drew her up. "Come on. Just to sleep."

In bed he tried to hold her but after a few minutes she pulled away. She shifted around for a while before slumping into sleep. Theo lay awake longer counting her breaths, turning the appearance of her old flame over in his mind. Obviously something was still going on there. Was the guy going to come back into her life? What did that mean for them?

When sleep finally overcame him it was deep and dreamless. The slamming of the bedroom door against the wall jolted him awake.

"Get up, Dad. We're going to be late for school," Fox said, coming to the foot of the bed.

Niels crowded in behind him. "Hey," he said, stopping abruptly, "aren't you supposed to be married to do that?"

Leah stirred beside Theo. He glanced at her then at Niels scowling at them.

"In theory, yes, but it doesn't always work out that way." He made a shooing motion. "Now out, you two."

Fox turned to go but Niels continued to regard them with narrowed eyes.

"Out! And close the door."

The boys finally left, Niels mumbling as he went.

"That was awkward," Leah said.

"It's time they learned the facts of life."

Leah stretched her arms above her head. "Yes, I guess they're getting to that age. Perhaps you should have a talk with them soon."

"Why me? Maybe they'd like to get it from a female perspective."

"Unlikely. I can hardly talk man to man and they'd be more embarrassed than anything."

"I guess so, but I think I'll wait until there are a few more hormones kicking around. Can you imagine all the eewing if I talked to them now?"

"I suppose." She threw back the covers and swung her legs over the side of the bed. "Your dad must have spoken to you. How old were you then?"

Theo's jaws cracked in a yawn. "I don't know ... a bit older, I think. Old enough to have an idea of the mechanics of it anyway."

She picked up her clothes. "So he wasn't able to tell you anything you didn't know?"

He elbowed himself up and leaned against the headboard. "Dad, being Dad, focused on other stuff. One thing I remember him saying, because I only understood what it meant later, was that the best sex was about giving, not taking."

Leah buttoned her blouse and smiled at him over her shoulder. "Your father is very wise."

They rushed to feed the boys and get them ready for school. When they were finally gone Leah put on her jacket and picked up her handbag.

"Aren't you going to have breakfast?" Theo said.

"I need to go home and change for work." She lifted his cornflower painting gingerly by the edges. "When will it be dry enough for me to take? I'd hate to smudge it."

"It's dry enough now," he said. "Just lay it flat on the car seat."

Despite not knowing what had gone on between Leah and her old boyfriend, Theo found a kind of peace in the normalcy of the morning. *Maybe it's going to be all right.* That night she lingered after the boys had gone to bed rather than heading home.

"You probably want to know what happened with Ken," she said.

"Only if you want to talk about it," he said mendaciously.

She nodded. "It would probably do me some good."

But when they sat down at the kitchen table with a pot of tea she fiddled with a spoon without speaking. Theo took careful, controlled sips of his drink to contain his impatience. After several minutes she threw down the spoon and threaded her fingers together.

"I met Ken at the Columbia University bookstore not long after I had started working there. He was looking for a textbook in my section." She flipped her hand. "One thing led to another. He lived in an apartment his parents owned in New York and I moved in with him a few months later. I was with him while he completed the medicine program and then his internship. He planned to return to Atlanta after to do a residency at one of the hospitals. I was going to go with him with the idea that we would eventually get married."

Theo blinked. "Oh," he said.

"Just before we were to move Ken's father took him to a medical conference in Beijing followed by a trip overland to Tibet. As a reward for completing his studies and all that."

She told him about finding Ken's mother in their apartment and what she had said.

"The next day I packed and left but I had nowhere to go. I stayed with my friend Ingrid for a couple of nights but they were leaving for France where her husband had accepted a fellowship and had sublet their apartment. She offered me the use of her family's cabin in the Adirondacks—her brother was in the Middle East and her mother didn't go there on her own. Not having any other options I accepted, expecting to stay a short time. I started to write *Three*, and the weeks stretched to almost a year. Then of course I found out Mom had died and came here."

The Lighthouse

"So why has he come after you now?" Theo said.

Leah picked up the spoon again and turned it over in her fingers for a few moments. Putting it aside, she drew a long breath before replying. "It turns out it was all Ken's parents' doing. They disapproved of me, you see, and used his absence as an opportunity to break us up. I had left before he returned and it wasn't until now that we realized what had happened."

"How did he find you?"

She explained about him seeing the review of *Three* and tracking her down. Caught up in Leah's narrative, Theo didn't consider the implications of what had transpired at first. He had thought Ken a jerk for abandoning Leah but now it seemed that he was a decent guy and obviously still cared for her. Dread fogged his mind.

"So what does he want?"

Leah sighed heavily. "He wanted us to get together again. He was so upset with his parents that he talked about leaving Atlanta and starting somewhere new."

A pit opened in Theo's stomach. "And, ah, what did you say?"

Leah drew back and looked at him directly. "No, of course."

"But it sounds like you still have feelings for him."

Leah dropped her eyes. After studying her interlinked fingers for a minute or two she placed her hands flat on the table and leaned back in her chair.

"He was a big part of my life, my center of gravity all those years when I was alone. He gave me a home when I had none. I expect I will always have feelings for him. But time has passed, things have changed. There is someone new in his life. He says it has the potential to be serious but he's had a hard time committing because of me." She turned her dark, unreadable gaze on Theo. "I told him my life is here now, that it's time for both of us to move on."

They sat in silence. Leah had nothing more to tell him and

he couldn't think of anything to say. He could have asked her to stay with him that night, Niels' moralizing notwithstanding, or even in her own room at Las Sombras, but that chance passed, so after a few minutes she got up and left.

He sat up until midnight mulling over their conversation. Leah had been open and honest about Ken, his role in her past and their last meeting, but rather than being reassured by her decision to stay he felt aggrieved by her revelations. He knew he wasn't being fair, and he doubted he would have been as forthcoming about his own past. Leah knew about Fiona, but if she had pressed him for details would he tell her as much about her and about his other liaisons, as she had called them? Not all, and certainly not everything. One of the reasons was simple self-regard: there was a pathos to Leah and Ken's story, a nobility that was absent from his own past relationships. And while she had chosen to stay, he couldn't help but feel that it had more to do with Niels than with him.

Chapter 47

"How do you think they'll react?" Ris said.

"Hard to say," Lucas said.

"Do you still think it's the right decision?"

He regarded his wife for a moment. "It certainly hasn't been an easy one. It is, I think, the logical thing to do at this point in our lives. But it's a door closing and we don't have that many doors left, do we, my love?"

Tires grinding through gravel sounded outside followed shortly by those of a second vehicle. Doors slammed and voices sounded, growing louder as they approached the house.

"Showtime," Ris said with a half-smile.

The door opened and their sons entered.

"Really?" Ben was saying.

Theo grinned at him. "And then he tripped over his feet and fell into a juniper bush."

Ben threw his head back and laughed.

Lucas's heart lifted at this new, easy camaraderie between his sons. Something had apparently changed between them over the summer. "Glad you could make it on such short notice, boys," he said.

"Good to have you back," Theo said, sitting down at the table.

Ris poured out cups of coffee and they discussed their respective summers, Beth's return and other family news.

Ris glanced at Lucas. "Shall I?" He smiled his agreement and she began. "We need to discuss something with you."

Their sons nodded attentively.

"You may recall that we came home later than usual last fall. The reason was that Lucas suffered a heart attack."

Theo and Ben exclaimed. Theo leaned forward and looked at his father with concern. "Are you okay?"

Lucas raised his hand. "I was fortunate in that as heart attacks go it wasn't severe, and I received immediate and excellent care."

"Why didn't you say something?" Ben said.

"I made a good recovery and we didn't want to create a fuss and alarm you two."

"That's why you were home so much last winter, isn't it?" Theo said.

Lucas nodded. "I am fine now."

"Nonetheless, the episode has made us think about where we are in our lives," Ris said. "We realized that we, Lucas particularly, can't continue to work at the same pace as in the past." She paused. "The upshot is that we have decided to sell the Lighthouse. It is more than he, or I for that matter, can handle comfortably now."

Their sons absorbed the news in silence for a few moments.

"That's why you didn't go ahead with the expansion last fall," Theo said.

Ris nodded. "It didn't make sense in the circumstances."

"And why you asked me whether I'd like to take over more responsibility for your affairs," Ben added ruefully. "Why didn't you say something then? I could have done more."

"You had your own concerns and it's not really what you want to do, is it?" Lucas said.

"Are there any interested buyers yet?" Ben said.

Ris nodded. "Our agent has been active."

"Already? Who?"

"Predictably some hotel chains, but the party we favor is a foundation created by several billionaires to promote global peace and prosperity. I'm sure you have heard of them." She mentioned the name. "They want to create an educational facility offering programs for future world leaders and a place to hold summits and symposia. They are looking for somewhere special, a place with the right feel and good amenities but without the distractions of a large urban center. The Lighthouse fits their criteria perfectly."

No one spoke for a moment.

"It's kind of sad," Theo said. "All that you've created over these last years—to let it go."

Lucas sighed. "Yes, it is sad, especially since we're doing it because we can no longer manage things. But we've had a great run and it's been an extraordinary experience. And other things beckon."

"What will you do now?" Ben said.

"We intend to move permanently to Counter Point," Ris said. "Your father is happiest there." She squeezed her husband's hand and gave him an affectionate smile. "I didn't realize how much he missed the ocean. We're having some renovations done over the winter to update and expand the cottage."

"So when will this all happen?" Theo said.

"We're about to sign a memorandum of understanding with the foundation to negotiate a sale. If things go well it could conclude sometime in the spring. It's also the logical time for a transition." Ris turned to Ben. "I'm sorry if that disrupts your own plans."

Ben shook his head. "Not an issue for me. Beth and I intend to move to Vancouver at some point. But the staff…"

"Yes," Lucas said. "That part is especially difficult. Many

of them will be needed to stay on, but some inevitably will be let go."

"When will you tell them?" Ben said.

"Soon, I hope. When we've signed the MOU."

"Do you need a hand with all that?"

"Yes, and that's one reason we're speaking to you now," Ris said.

"What about the ranch?" Theo said. "What's going to happen when you leave?"

"Ah, yes. That's a related but separate concern," Ris said. "Though not a condition in their purchase of the Lighthouse, the foundation is also interested in buying the land if we are willing."

"But you've had it for ages. It's, what, over fifty years now since Granddad and his brother bought the original parcel that became the stables?" Theo said.

His mother nodded. "I know. But Lucas and I don't see our future being here. In any event, a decision on the sale of the ranch also involves Fin—he owns half of it."

"One thought we had, Theo, is that you might like to take the ranch on," Lucas said. "We would sign over the stables to you."

Theo breathed out slowly. "It's a lot to absorb all at once. I need to think about it."

Chapter 48

"How can they?" Leah said.

Her words were swallowed by the silence in the Tree of Light pavilion. Theo had passed on his parents' news at dinner the previous night. "But they can't sell the Lighthouse!" she had said then. "What about Granddad's pavilion, what about the Tree of Light?"

"Well, it's part of the deal."

"But Granddad's window! I watched him design it. It was the last thing he ever did. It's like…" She waved her hands. "Like abandoning him somehow. Why do they have to sell? Can't they just get someone else to run the place?"

"The Lighthouse turns on Dad. He's what makes it what it is. Without him it's just a hotel. Even if they found someone to replace him they'd still have to worry about it. And Dad really needs to focus on staying well now."

Her uncle's health trumped everything so she had said no more. She slept poorly that night, disturbed by the idea of someone else owning the stained-glass window. On the way to work she had stopped at the Lighthouse to see if it would offer any answers. Viewing the Tree of Light only deepened her sense of imminent loss. The window quietly played with the morning sun, oblivious to its fate.

Leah's conversation with Theo about the sale of the Lighthouse had been the first real one they'd had in days. It wasn't too difficult to draw a line between his withdrawal into himself and her telling him about Ken. Since then they had barely spoken apart from saying what was necessary to care for the boys. *Why did sex always have to spoil things?* Theo wouldn't have reacted that way before. And talk about a double standard. According to Ben, Theo's own entanglements were legion and at least one of them had been serious enough to produce Fox.

Maybe she should have taken Ken's proposal that they get back together more seriously. He was a known quantity, dependable and devoted, and ecstatic about finding her again. But it would have meant overlooking his spineless acquiescence to his parents that resulted in their breakup and, as always, there was Niels to consider.

She accepted without question that her choices and actions must serve her son's interests first, but what those interests were was not always clear. Her father now believed they would be served best elsewhere. She no longer automatically disagreed with whatever Fin proposed, recognizing that, however differently they might view matters, caring and concern underlay his decrees. A move back to Vancouver was beginning to look inevitable despite the fact that it would mean splitting Niels and Fox up. And leaving Theo behind…

She shook herself. That decision could wait. The book about her mother was congesting her mind and clouding her judgement and completing it superseded everything. When it was finished she would be able to think more clearly.

Leah rinsed a pot and set it on the dishrack. "Ethan's back," she said.

Theo raised his eyebrows. "I thought he'd returned already. Didn't he say the end of August?"

"There were some complications with Jeff so he stayed away until they were settled. Anyway, I can take my vacation now."

He picked up the pot and wiped it. "Do you want to go somewhere?"

She glanced up at him. He seemed to have returned to normal, laughing with the boys over dinner and chatting to her about family matters but the tone of this invitation was hard to read. Regardless, going away right now held little appeal. She squeezed the scrub sponge dry and opened the sink drain. "We can't leave the boys."

"Ben and Beth would come and stay if we asked."

"I don't want to bother them and, besides, I'd like to use the time to write."

"It seems to take every extra minute you've got. You never have time for anything else," he said, a grumble in his voice.

She pulled off her rubber gloves and placed them in a basket under the sink. "Writing isn't like painting. I can't toss off several pieces at a time like you do. It's a long and laborious process. And having a run of uninterrupted days to work is so rare."

He fitted the pot into a drawer. "Sorry to be so…" He made a helpless gesture. "It's just, we never seem to have any time together."

She regarded him for a moment. "Theo … right now all I want to do is finish the book about my mother. I actually was going to ask if you could stay on here at the hacienda for the next little while. I know it's my turn, but I'd really appreciate having the quiet time to write."

He shook out the tea towel and folded it. "I suppose."

"Thanks." She leaned forward and brushed her lips against his. "I should go; I can still get a couple of hours' work done tonight."

Fin flew in a few days later after being away for several weeks. Dinner was a noisy affair with Niels and Fox bringing him up to date on their news. After, Fin insisted that Niels work through a new étude for cello he had written. Apart from a quick mention they did not discuss the Lighthouse sale that evening, but Leah raised the matter as they lingered over breakfast the next morning.

"The place is theirs to sell, Leah," Fin said. "And probably time they did."

"But the Tree of Light—it's your father's last creation…"

Fin held up his palm. "I know that, and letting it go bothered me too. Here's what I'm thinking." He told them that the university had approached him earlier in the year about creating a memorial of some kind to Alex. "So when Ris and Lucas told me of their plans to sell, I thought why not recreate the Tree of Light in a structure at the university as a monument to both Alex and Dad? The university will provide the land and we'll donate the building. It'll be similar to the pavilion at the Lighthouse: a place for quiet and reflection and where small events can be held."

Tears sprang to Leah's eyes. She rose and embraced her father. "Thank you *so* much, Dad."

Fin patted her awkwardly on the back. "Hey, hey, it's okay," he said.

That night Leah didn't show up for dinner. It happened from time to time and Theo thought nothing of it. When the boys had gone to their room he asked Fin about selling the ranch.

"Ah," Fin said, leaning back in his chair. "I don't know. I've enjoyed having it as a place to come to and these last couple of years…" He shook his head. "It would have been much harder adjusting to Alex being gone if we had stayed in Vancouver. But in the future? I've got new commissions for a choral work and a film score and Ebes—remember him? He wants me to collaborate on a recording project. All of this is taking me elsewhere and it's just easier to come and go from Vancouver, especially once Ris and Lucas give up the plane."

"Mom and Dad are giving up the plane?"

"No reason for them to keep it once they're gone, is there?"

Theo frowned. "No, I guess not."

Leah came to breakfast the next morning, but Angie tangled Theo up in a conversation about buying winter tires and she left before they could speak alone. She was absent from dinner that night too. The next day she didn't appear at all.

"What's up with Leah?" Theo said to Fin at dinner. "Did you guys have, ah, a disagreement or something?"

"No, why do you ask?"

"She's not answering her phone. Maybe someone should check on her, make sure she's okay."

"I talked to her after school about the meeting with my teacher on Friday," Niels said. "She said she wasn't coming for dinner."

Fin shrugged. "Sounds like she's fine. I think she's working on something."

Theo got the boys ready for bed and returned to his studio. He turned on some music and settled down with a book. Shortly after ten o'clock someone knocked on his door. He rose, alarmed—few people came to his house, especially at night. He opened the door to find Leah huddled on the other side.

"Christ, Leah, why are you knocking? Scared the hell out of me." He drew her inside and closed the door. She gave him a stricken look and burst into tears.

"What's wrong? Are the boys okay?"

"No. I mean no, it's not the boys," she said between sobs.

"What is it then?"

She shook her head, overcome. He led her to the sofa and pulled her down onto his lap. She collapsed against him in a storm of weeping. He left her to cry it out, and when her tears finally subsided he tugged a handkerchief from his pocket and offered it to her. She pressed it hard against her eyes, then blew her nose.

"Oh!" she said, "I've soaked the front of your shirt."

"Don't worry about it. What's this all about?"

She shifted off his lap, leaving her legs draped over his knees. "I finished the book about my mother," she said and blew her nose again.

"You're all done?"

She crumpled the hankie and stuffed it into her pocket. "The first draft, yes."

"Wow! But why are you upset?"

She studied him with red-rimmed melancholy eyes for several moments. "Because it's done."

"I'd have thought that's something to celebrate, not cry about."

Leah sniffed and swallowed hard. "Writing about who she was and what she did, I got to know her in ways I never had before. Mom was a puzzle, a paradox. An astonishing intellect with a profound understanding of some aspects of reality, yet ignorant of many simple day-to-day things. It was as if she was from some other dimension, trying to make her way in a strange land.

"I understand now why she was so detached when I was growing up—she wouldn't have known what to do with a child. I expect she loved me in the abstract, but the gulf between our minds was too great. As I grew older, especially in the time when Dad was gone, we had started to connect. When I left I never thought that I wouldn't ever see her again. I would give anything to know her, to speak to her now, as an adult."

Her eyes filled with tears again and she drew the hankie out with trembling fingers and wiped them away.

"While I worked on the book she was alive to me. I had the sense of her existing somewhere, not close, but still there. This evening, when I had written the last sentence of the last paragraph, when I had inserted the final period, it was like she died again and I was struck, forcibly, by how absolutely, definitively, irrevocably she is gone."

There was a ferocity to their lovemaking that night, as though Leah was trying to burst out of her skin. After, she fell exhausted into a deep sleep. Before turning out the light, Theo lay for a few minutes watching her chest rise and fall, her eyes dart beneath her lids in pursuit of a dream, and wondered at the complexity of her. When he woke the following morning, her side of the bed was empty and cold but the smell of coffee wafted into the room. She was tucked into the corner of the sofa, cradling a cup in her hands and gazing out at the lightening sky.

He greeted her with an upside-down kiss, filled a cup with coffee and sat down beside her. She had not reined her hair into its usual ponytail and it tumbled over her shoulders in disarray. He liked her best unbridled like this. "How're you doing?" he said.

"Better, thanks." She gave him a fleeting smile. "I feel embarrassed about last night though."

He sipped his coffee. "Which part, exactly?"

She dropped her eyes and her cheeks reddened. After a moment she glanced up at him. "About coming over here and crying all over you."

"Leah, you never have to feel embarrassed about anything with me."

She tugged at the hem of her T-shirt and gave a slight nod. "Still, I don't like to lose control so completely."

Her face was veiled by her hair, and after a minute of charged silence Theo drew a strand back with his finger and tucked it behind her ear.

"Does finishing the book mean we can talk about getting married?" he said.

She gave him an amused sideways glance. "Did I say that?"

"Come on, Leah. Where else can we go from here?"

She thought for a moment. "We can carry on just as we're doing. Why marriage?"

"Among other reasons, it's about setting an example."

"For the boys, you mean?"

"Yeah."

"I'm hardly the person to look to as far as setting an example goes."

"I haven't offered the best example either to this point, which is why we should do it properly now."

Leah shifted and set her empty cup on the coffee table. "There's a tradition, you know, of temporary marriages in Shia Islam culture. It's done through a contract that specifies financial arrangements, duration and other terms."

"And why would we want a temporary marriage?"

"Well, since we'd be doing this primarily for the boys we could arrange to be married until they leave home."

He started to say that it wasn't only for the boys but decided not to complicate things. "And then what? Their home dissolves behind them? And what about us?"

"We would decide whether we wanted to continue to be together. Who knows, we might have tired of each other by then."

Theo studied her, wondering if she was serious. She smiled faintly but her eyes gave nothing away. She had, he was finding, a way of keeping him slightly off balance. "Apart from the fact that we're not Shia Muslims, I think it's a lousy idea." He paused. "Come on, seriously, why do you have a problem with our getting married?"

"You mean apart from our being related?"

"Kind of late to be worried about that, don't you think? In any case, it's not illegal."

"Yes, I know that. It's just…" She grimaced. "It's so … definitive."

"You were ready to get married to Ken. Why won't you do it with me?"

Leah's face went still and she looked away. Theo knew what he had said was unconscionable but it was out and couldn't be taken back. The silence stretched on.

"Look, I didn't mean that," he finally said.

She turned back to him. "No, you're quite right, and if I were to marry anyone it would be you."

"Is that a yes?"

She smiled faintly. "I guess it is. But there's a problem: Dad wants Niels to move back to Vancouver. He's given me until the end of the school year next June to think about it."

"*Think* about it? Sounds like he's already decided."

"What he probably means is for me to get used to the idea. It's his way of being accommodating."

"And what *do* you think about it?"

She lifted a shoulder in a helpless shrug. "I'm not sure. The idea of living in a city again doesn't thrill me and the thought of moving back into Dad's house and having to live there with him is even less appealing. The thing is, I have to consider what's best for Niels."

"He might have his own point of view on the matter. He definitely showed some spirit last summer."

Leah studied him speculatively for several moments. "Would you and Fox come with us?"

"I'm not crazy about living in a city either," he said slowly. "But yeah, I'd consider it. This thing is, I think my parents want me to stay here and take care of the ranch after they sell the Lighthouse. They've offered me the stables business."

"Oh."

They regarded each other in silence for a few moments. Theo figured his parents' expectations of him taking over the ranch were entirely reasonable, a chance for him to do his bit and pay them back for all the support they had given him. It was probably their way of telling him to grow up and be responsible. The financial incentive certainly wasn't anything to sneeze at. The responsibility wouldn't be much greater than what he had now so he could continue to paint, and the income from the stables would set him up very nicely. But it looked like it would mean being separated from Leah and Niels, as well as the rest of the family. There'd be no more Sunday dinners, and without his parents' jet they wouldn't be able to travel back and forth easily or often. *No, I won't stay,* he thought. But how to tell his mom and dad?

"This is going to be an interesting knot to untangle," he said. "I need to talk to my parents, and it may be best if I do it alone."

Chapter 49

Lucas glanced up at the tap on his door. "Ah, Theo," he said, taking off his reading glasses. "Why don't you get your mother. She should be in her office."

"You wanted to speak to us about something?" Ris said when they had returned and sat down.

"I have some news: Leah and I have decided to get married."

Lucas drew back in his chair. Would this son of theirs never cease to surprise them? "This is news indeed," he said.

"I don't understand," Ris said. "I've never sensed that there was anything ... well, romantic between the two of you."

"We think it would be a good thing to do, given our circumstances, and especially for Fox and Niels."

"I see, I guess," Ris said. "But is that enough of a reason to get married? And then there's the age difference between you two."

"Nine years, but that's hardly uncommon, and with all she's been through Leah's pretty mature for her age."

"It's perhaps not the number of years so much but that you are at different points in your life," Lucas said.

"What do you mean?"

"Leah is just beginning to find herself, as a person and in her life's work," he said carefully.

"And I'm a has-been?"

Lucas winced. "No, of course not. But you have grown into your character while Leah is unlikely to remain who she is right now."

"Maybe not, but I can't see her changing in any fundamental way."

"I expect you are right."

"Dad, you're the one who said I should have someone in my life."

"Yes, of course. It's just, well, I didn't expect it would be Leah."

"Have you told Fin?" Ris said.

"No, not yet, I wanted to talk to you first." Theo started to rise. "But maybe I should give you some time to get used to the idea," he said, his tone testy.

Lucas made a calming gesture. "Don't go, son. Let's discuss this."

Theo eased back into his chair. "Something obviously bothers you about the idea."

"Well, I'm sure you realize that it's an unusual enough situation to cause difficulties in some spheres," Lucas said. "There are places, for example, where your marriage will not be legal, and that you could even be persecuted for it."

"A handful, yes, but even there it's marriage between full first cousins that isn't allowed, which we're not."

"No doubt you have researched the matter. Regardless, perceptions held by your friends, and in the community, may be uncomfortable for you."

Theo shrugged. "To the extent that anyone will know our connection, they may be. We'll just have to deal with it."

Ris had followed their exchange with troubled eyes and a hand pressed against her mouth. She dropped it to her lap. "The other aspect of being related is that your life together will never be entirely your own, that any problems will reverberate through the family. If your marriage were to end, for example, it would be extremely difficult all around."

"I'm not going into this with the intention of breaking up."

"Still, it happens."

Theo drew a deep breath. "I think what you're saying is that you don't think I'm capable of making this kind of a commitment."

"No, it's not that…"

But it was, Lucas acknowledged. He struggled to order his thoughts. His first reaction to the news had been concern for Leah—that marriage, any marriage, would dull her brilliance and draw her off her intended life path. And if she was to marry, was Theo with his peripatetic love life the best choice of husband for her? He drew his hand over his face, puzzled and dismayed at such disloyalty to his own son.

After an uneasy silence Theo continued. "There's more."

Now what? Lucas thought. "Yes?" he said.

"It's about the ranch. It was awfully good of you to offer me the stables and the opportunity to take care of the ranch and everything, but, you see, Fin's shifting back to Vancouver and he's pretty well forcing Leah to go back with him because of Niels, and of course I have to go with her, so for that reason I'm sorry but I can't do it," Theo said, the words tumbling over each other.

Lucas relaxed. "That's perfectly understandable."

Theo blinked. "You're not upset? I thought you were counting on me to stay here and look after the ranch so you wouldn't have to sell it."

"The decision to sell it or not isn't contingent on your staying here. We can keep the same crew we have now to manage things. We just wanted to provide you and Fox with a solid foundation if you were to stay," Ris said.

"Trust me, I fully appreciate what it would mean financially and the uncertainty facing us when we get back to Vancouver, but nothing's ever straightforward, is it?" Theo rose. "I should go now, I need to talk to Fin."

When he returned to Las Sombras he tackled Fin in his studio. "Leah and I plan to get married," he said without preamble.

Fin's eyebrows shot up and he looked hard at Theo for several uncomfortable moments. "Not that surprising, I guess," he finally said.

Theo exhaled the breath he had been holding. "We figure it's the best thing for the boys."

"Yes, of course. So you'll be coming back to Vancouver with us?"

"If I need to, yeah."

"Good, it'll make it a lot easier for Niels if Fox comes along." He studied Theo in silence. "Have you told Ris and Lucas?"

Theo nodded. "They're getting used to the idea."

"Don't imagine they saw it coming either." He raised an admonitory finger. "Fair warning, though: If you don't treat Leah well you're going to have to answer to me."

Theo squared his shoulders. "Likewise."

Fin laughed and made a shooing motion. "Get out of here," he said.

Theo and Leah announced their plan to Niels and Fox together.

"Glad someone's pleased," Theo said as the boys hooted and jumped about.

Leah glanced at him. "Did you really think it would be straightforward?"

Fin came into the room, growling about the ruckus. "Is that all?" he said crossly when they explained, and returned like a bear routed from hibernation to his den.

Chapter 50

"Sometime before Christmas, we figure," Theo said. The family was discussing a date for his and Leah's wedding at dinner the following Sunday.

Ben wondered at their relationship. There was nothing in how they acted, in the way they were together, to suggest they were lovers. No special glances, no cooing, no little touches. They moved around each other with a quiet, easy familiarity, like they had been together forever.

Not like he and Beth. He was so full of the joy of having her and Nathan in his life that he wanted to devour her. She had come back to work at the Lighthouse, positioning herself delicately beside him and Cindy. Her return proved timely, freeing him to concentrate on the sale of the resort. They had moved in together as well although she had resisted at first, afraid of what would happen if her husband's killers ever found her. "All the more reason," he had said. The Lighthouse sale couldn't come quickly enough now. As soon as it was concluded he would whisk them all off to safety in Canada, and they would marry as soon as his divorce from Caro came through.

"What kind of a wedding do you have in mind?" Ris said.

"Nothing complicated, Aunt Ris," Leah said. "A ceremony in front of the Tree of Light then a small dinner."

Ris leaned forward. "Leah, dear, you should call me by my name now. Or Mom, if you like."

Leah bit her lip. "Yes, of course."

"Now, who do you plan to invite?"

Theo and Leah exchanged glances. "Just the family," he said.

His mother raised her eyebrows. "That's all?"

"I guess maybe the guys at the stable and a few people from town if I asked." He looked at Leah. "How about you?"

"Ethan, I suppose. And Ingrid. But that's about it."

Ris sat up and leaned forward. "It is no small moment when one's child gets married. Especially you, Theo. There are times we wondered if we'd ever see the day." She glanced at Ben. "And I am not going to be denied a proper celebration this time. Don't you agree, Lucas?"

His father raised his hand and smiled faintly. "I think I'll sit this discussion out."

"But don't you think some of your family would like to be present?"

He shrugged.

"And we have many close friends who would be hurt to be excluded. How about you, Fin?"

"Yes, there are a few people I'd invite," he said.

Theo shifted in his chair. "We, ah, can't really afford a big affair."

"Your father and I will pay for it, of course."

Fin raised a hand. "I thought that honor fell to the father of the bride."

Theo and Leah both exclaimed in protest.

"Oh, you two!" Ris said. "Stop acting like you are paupers. We are a family here. We can do a dinner and dance at the Lighthouse after the ceremony. You can invite all your friends, Theo. We may be able to fly some of them out, and they could stay at the resort." She turned to her husband. "It would be our last splash before leaving. A chance to say goodbye to our friends."

"As long as Theo and Leah don't feel we are appropriating their occasion."

Theo looked at Leah. "What do you think?"

She looked around the table in alarm. "I have neither the wherewithal nor the inclination to organize such an affair."

"The Lighthouse event staff would put it together," Ris said. "You only have to tell them what you want. You know—a menu and flowers and some kind of a theme for the decorations. They would give you a list of questions."

Leah shook her head.

"Maybe I can help," Beth said. "I've been through it all and know the Lighthouse people. I could be an intermediary."

Ben shot her a melting glance. Neither she nor Leah were gushing women and he had been happy to see a warmth slowly growing between them.

"I'd appreciate that." Leah glanced at Theo. "If this is what we want to do."

He shrugged. "I don't see why not. It would be nice if Mick and Wes could come."

Leah drew in a breath. "I hope I won't be obliged to wear some white extravaganza."

Ris reached out and rested her hand on Leah's. "My tailor will design and make whatever kind of gown you like." She drew back and smiled. "Good, that's settled then. Now let's check with the Lighthouse and find a date that works."

"Would you have a few minutes before you go?" Lucas said to Theo as they rose from the table.

"Yeah, sure," Theo said warily. He glanced at Leah. "Can you and the boys catch a ride back with Fin?"

"Yes, of course."

Lucas led the way to his study and eased himself into the armchair. Theo sat down stiffly on the sofa.

"Son, I'm not happy with how our conversation went last week," he said.

Not happy was an understatement. "I cannot believe how clumsily I handled that," Lucas had moaned to Ris after Theo had delivered the bombshell about his and Leah's plans to marry. "And with our son, too. It's perhaps just as well I'm retiring."

"You did catch us by surprise," he continued. "We really had no idea there was anything between you and Leah." He ventured a smile. "How did you manage that?"

"It's been in my mind for quite a while but Leah wanted to finish the book about Alex first."

"Umm." Lucas cleared his throat. "On reflection, I've realized that you two have had a lot of time to get to know each other, and that your histories may have given you a special understanding. I couldn't hope for a better partner for you. Leah is a very special young woman."

"I know that."

"Being married to her may be challenging at times."

Theo smiled faintly. "I've gotten a taste of that, too."

"I also wanted to say that your mother and I are very happy you'll be moving back to Canada with us. Have you thought about where you will live?"

Theo shifted in his chair. "That's something I'd wanted to discuss with you and Mom. Fin's place is certainly large enough and it's not unlike our current arrangement, but Leah and I each need a space to work and, well, it would be nice to have a place of our own. And we'd really prefer not to live in the city. Apart from the noise, congestion and cost, it's not somewhere I'd choose to raise Fox." His mouth twisted in a wry smile. "I know full well how an impressionable kid can be corrupted by cynical urban influences. And I think Fox is especially vulnerable. I'm afraid he got the worst of us: Fiona's instability, my recklessness."

"Ah, yes, he does have his moments, doesn't he?" Lucas paused. "Why not come live at Counter Point?"

"Actually, that's what I had in mind but I wasn't sure, well, given the circumstances whether you and Mom would want us around."

"Of course we'd like to have you around. The Big House is empty and we were awfully lonely last summer out there all by ourselves."

The line of Theo's shoulders relaxed. "Thanks, that's a relief. I'm sure we can find a teacher for Niels in Victoria—there's got to be someone suitable at the university. And Leah and I should be able to find jobs."

Lucas studied his son for a moment. "Why do you need to find a job?"

"I'll no longer have the income from the stables and I doubt I can support a family completely through painting. Irony is that I'll be leaving just as my work's starting to get some traction here. I don't have much of a presence or many connections on the West Coast, and I don't expect much demand for Southwest landscapes out there. So I'll need to find a job that pays."

"What kind of work do you have in mind?"

"Well, that's the thing. My experience is pretty patchy: vineyard worker, ranch hand, itinerant artist. Maybe I can make something out of my oversight of the stables." He shook his head. "Kind of shocking how I've gotten to this age without acquiring some serious skills."

Lucas made an impatient gesture. "I have nothing against honest labor, but really Theo, you've been given a singular talent and if we can do anything for you it would be to give you the freedom to honor it."

"Dad, I can't have you support us. I mean, we intend to pay you rent and everything."

Lucas regarded his son fondly for a moment. "You know, your mother and I tried to raise you and Ben without a sense of entitlement and it looks like we've succeeded."

Theo smiled crookedly. "You mean apart from the fancy schools and private jet and college slush fund."

Lucas laughed. "Yes, of course. But still, you've both made your own way. The family wealth is there nonetheless and we try to use it for good. It's also a responsibility you—and Ben and Leah—will bear some day."

"I'm not looking forward to that day and I don't want the responsibility. Ben would be much better at it." Theo shook his head. "You know, the time when I was traveling around with Mick and Wes—it was ideal. We worked just enough to pay for what we needed to live and that wasn't much: food, a few clothes, some wheels, a place to sleep. The problem with money is that you never have just the right amount; it's either too little or too much and it always complicates everything."

Lucas nodded. "I completely understand. One of the hardest adjustments I had to make marrying your mother was to go from living in institutional poverty to this," he said, gesturing around him. "When I met Ris there was nothing about her to suggest that she came from wealth. She was a carpenter—she worked hard, lived in drafty tents, bathed in cold water, used the outdoor privies like the rest of us, ate the same monotonous, sometimes wormy food we did. Knowing wouldn't have stopped me from falling in love with her, but I'm not sure I would have done anything about it. But here I am. I certainly can't complain about the life I've led. Having money has made it possible for me to follow my heart: to write, to build a mission, to create the Lighthouse. I'd like you to be able to do the same."

Theo shook his head. "I wouldn't feel good not supporting myself and Leah probably feels even more strongly about it than me. I'll find something."

Chapter 51

Leah watched Theo silently push his food around his plate. Fin had house guests and their animated debate over the merits of a rock star conductor didn't offer much opportunity to join in.

"Is everything okay?" she said.

He looked up. "I received an official-looking communication from Australia in the mail today. It's the first I've heard from Fiona since I sent her that letter last winter. I'd completely forgotten about her threatening legal action if I wouldn't let Fox go to her. Looks like she's making good on it now."

"Ah. What exactly does it say?"

"I haven't opened it. Thought I'd give myself some time to prepare."

"Wouldn't it be better to know the worst?"

"I suppose."

"Why don't we look at it after dinner?"

Fin and his friends eventually shifted to his studio, leaving them to clean up. When that was done and the boys were put to bed Theo set a half-size manila envelope addressed to him on the table. The name Gregson and Kimble with an address in Sydney, Australia was pre-printed in the upper left-hand corner. Leah took a paring knife from the wooden block on the counter and handed it to him.

"Do you want me to stab it in the heart or something?" he said, accepting the implement.

She smiled. "Were it that simple."

He hefted the knife for a moment then ran it under the flap. A small envelope addressed to Fox and a single sheet of paper were inside. He glanced at her and unfolded the sheet of paper.

"What the…?" he said.

"What is it?"

He held up his hand and quickly skimmed through the letter. When he was done he dropped the sheet of paper on the table and laughed.

"What?" Leah said.

"It's from Matt, Fiona's husband."

"May I read it?"

He motioned towards the sheet of paper. "Yeah, sure."

She picked it up gingerly. The letterhead read *Gregson and Kimble, Marine Architects*. Matt began by thanking Theo for the thoughtful letter he had sent Fiona earlier in the year. He went on to say that she had suffered—and was slowly recovering from—a severe bout of postpartum depression. Part of her therapy involved reconnecting with her son. After much discussion they had concluded that the approach Theo had proposed made sense. The enclosed letter to Fox was Fiona's first step. The letter ended by saying that they didn't anticipate being in the U.S. in the near future and hoped that Theo would bring Fox out for a visit soon.

"Why, this is wonderful," she said, handing the letter back to Theo. "I know a bit about postpartum depression. Poor woman."

"She's bipolar, probably made it worse." Theo picked up the smaller envelope addressed to Fox. "I wonder if I should read this first. Who knows what she's said?"

"Now, that could be problematic. It would establish a tricky precedent. What would you do if you disagreed with something she had written, black it out with a pen? And when would you stop checking her correspondence? You can control access to Fox, but not the tenor and substance of her relationship with him. It will evolve in its own way."

"I suppose so. But I'll read it after he does."

"If he agrees."

"Whose side are you on?"

"It's not a matter of sides, it's a matter of fairness and trust." She thought for a minute. "And if I had to pick sides in this case, it would be Fox's."

"I can see we're going to have some interesting times ahead." Theo slipped both letters back into the manila envelope and glanced at her. "Hey, maybe we can go to Australia for our honeymoon."

She raised her eyebrows. "A honeymoon with two children in tow visiting your ex-whatever? I think you're a bit unclear on the concept."

Chapter 52

"There are going to be a few sore heads tomorrow," Ben said to Theo, nodding in the direction of Mick who had just emptied half of a bottle of wine into one of Fin's large crystal glasses.

"Yeah, well, I don't think they usually drink booze this good," Theo said.

It was the eve of Theo and Leah's marriage and Fin had shaken some cases of choice vintages loose from his cellar for the post-rehearsal dinner at Las Sombras. The rehearsal had been short as there were no attendants and Leah had declared that she would wait with Theo for the ceremony to begin rather than being delivered down the aisle like a chattel to a new owner. As the evening wore on sofas were pushed aside in the living room and people bopped around to lively rhythms. Shortly before eleven o'clock Lucas and Ris took Niels and Fox, protesting, back to their house to sleep. Beth accompanied them with Nathan. An hour later Ben checked his watch. *Time to wind things down.* There was a lot to do tomorrow. He walked through the revelers, looking for either Fin or Theo. Neither was around. He was about to check the kitchen when he caught sight of Leah in the hall near the front entrance.

"Leah!" He waved and headed in her direction.

She turned and started towards him. The front door opened,

Mick entered from the hall and followed close behind Leah. He caught up to her just before she reached Ben and flung his arm around her shoulder. Leah gave him a tight smile and slipped out from under his embrace. Ben stepped forward, ready to intervene.

Mick put his hands up. The acrid odor of weed wafted off his clothes. "Yeah, I should know better than to mess with Theo's women. Have to say I was fucking amazed to hear he was tying the knot." He screwed up his face and spoke in falsetto. "'Why get stuck with just one woman when there's so many on offer,' he used to say. And he'd have pretty much anyone he wanted, he just had to give them a look. Wes and I'd get the leftovers."

Leah's face froze.

"That's enough," Ben said quietly. He took Mick's arm, led him to the heart of the party and handed him over to Wes. When he turned to go back to Leah she was gone.

Theo appeared a few minutes later with more wood for the fire. Ben intercepted him. "Probably time to let it burn out," he said. "People should be on their way soon."

Theo set the carrier holding the logs down on the hearth. "Yeah, you're probably right." He looked around. "Where's Leah?"

"I think she's left." Ben considered telling his brother about what Mick had said but decided nothing would be gained by it.

"Oh? Well, I guess it's pretty late, isn't it?" Theo dusted log debris off his hands. "Why don't I call for the hotel shuttle to come and pick the folks up."

By the time the shuttle arrived, the driver yawning into his hand, Ben and Theo had found everyone their coats and steered them out the door. When they were gone Theo put his hands on his hips and surveyed the living room.

"Okay, let's get this cleaned up."

"I thought Angie was coming tomorrow," Ben said.

"Yeah, but I don't think Fin will want to wake up to this mess. Let's just get rid of the stuff lying around."

They collected bottles and plates and soiled napkins, put the leftover food away and pushed the furniture back into position.

"How about you, Ben? Want to crash here?" Theo said when they were done.

"No, Beth will worry if I don't get back."

They talked about arrangements for the next day and agreed on a time when Ben would collect Theo to take him to the ceremony.

It was almost two o'clock when Ben finally slid into bed and curled around Beth, responding softly to her sleepy murmurs. Despite his fatigue, Mick's rancid comments pricked his mind and he lay awake for some time. He told Beth about the incident over coffee the next morning.

"Oh, dear," she said. "Not something I'd like to hear the night before my wedding. Hopefully Leah didn't give it any credence."

"Maybe I should have said something to Theo."

"Well, you didn't, and there's no point in worrying about it now." She rose and picked up her cup. "Anyhow, I'm meeting her at a salon in town shortly to get our hair done. I'll let you know if she says anything."

"Where's Leah?" Ris said to Beth when she arrived for lunch. "I thought she was coming back with you. A package has arrived for her."

Beth glanced at Ben who was setting out the food. "She wasn't at the salon. She, ah, left a message this morning canceling her appointment."

"Really?" Ris shook her head. "She can be such a stubborn little thing. I wouldn't put it past her to show up with her hair in a ponytail."

"I'm sure it doesn't mean anything," Ben said quietly to Beth when they sat down in a corner with their plates of food.

"There's more," Beth said. "I didn't want to say anything to your mother but I've called and texted Leah several times and neither connected or received a reply."

"Why don't we drive over to her place when we're done eating?"

When Ben and Beth pulled up to Leah's trailer Linc poked his head out from underneath and bared his teeth.

"He's really a harmless old thing, but why don't you stay here while I check?" Ben said.

There was no response when he knocked on the door and the interior was dark and empty when he looked through the window. "She's not there and her car is gone," he said, getting back into their vehicle.

"Maybe she's at Fin's, or with Theo," Beth said.

"Of course!" Ben called both places but they came up negative.

"I thought she was at Mom and Dad's," Theo said.

"Oh, well, maybe she is. We're not there," Ben said and quickly ended the call.

"The Lighthouse!" Beth said. "They have a suite there for a couple of days."

Ben called the hotel reception and asked someone to check the suite. It was not yet occupied.

"Try calling her again," Ben said.

The call went to voicemail. Ben and Beth looked at each other.

"Ethan!" Ben said. They called but he hadn't seen Leah either.

"Where could she possibly be?" Beth said.

"I can't think of anywhere else to check, and regardless she should have her phone with her."

Beth gazed out the car window for a moment before turning

back to Ben. "I don't know Leah well yet, but it's possible that guy's comments last night really affected her. It would be difficult for any woman to hear something like that and she may have taken it especially hard."

"If so, you'd think she'd just have it out with Theo."

"Well, she doesn't seem to have done that."

"What would *you* do in the circumstances?"

"I'd certainly be asking myself if the man I was about to marry was who I thought he was." She made a face. "A question I would have done well to ask myself before my own wedding."

Ben began to speak, hesitated, then continued. "If you had heard something like this would you go as far as to question whether you should marry him?"

Beth blinked slowly. "Perhaps."

They sat in silence for several minutes. Ben glanced at his watch. "We should head back. I have to pick Theo up in just over an hour and I need to change first."

They checked in at his parents' house before going to the guest cottage.

"She has to be somewhere," Ris said when they mentioned not being able to find Leah. "Do you think there's a problem?"

"It's just, well, one of Theo's friends made some awful comments about him to Leah…" Ben said.

His mother frowned. "Like what?"

"About his past, you know, with women, and implying he wouldn't be serious about marriage."

"Leah should know better than to pay any attention to that."

"You would think, but where the heck is she? Her absence and silence seem quite deliberate."

His mother regarded him intently for a few moments then sighed. "Nothing we can do, is there, but let things play themselves out. I wonder if I should alert Fin."

They went to the guest cottage to dress, calling Leah every few minutes to no avail.

"Will you say anything to Theo about this?" Beth said.

"I have to, don't you think?" He shrugged on his topcoat. "What a mess."

"Hey!" Theo said, swinging open the door to Ben's knock. His eyes shone and his face was alight with joy. "Time to walk the plank, huh?"

Ben nodded absently. In his tuxedo and with a white silk scarf draped around his neck Theo looked more like he was about to walk the red carpet. As they headed to Ben's car he wondered how to break the news of Leah's absence to his brother. When they reached the vehicle, he stopped.

"Listen, Theo, there's something you should know."

Theo placed his hand on the door handle. "What? Some last-minute advice?" he said, smiling.

"No, it's about Leah. She seems to have completely disappeared."

Theo's smile faded. "What?"

"Get in," Ben said. "I'll explain on the way."

In the car Theo stopped Ben from turning on the ignition. "What's going on, Ben?"

"Leah isn't anywhere you'd expect her to be and she isn't answering her phone. No one has seen her or spoken to her all day." He went through all the places they had checked.

Theo's eyes widened in alarm. "Has something happened to her?"

Funny, they hadn't considered that possibility, Ben thought. "I don't know, maybe." He paused. "There was an incident last night and I'm thinking that's what's behind her absence."

"What incident?"

As Ben recounted what Mick had said, Theo leaned back against the seat and groaned.

"And then, when Beth said that Leah had canceled her hair appointment and we couldn't find her anywhere, we just assumed…"

"That bastard! I'll kill him."

"Did you really say that?"

Theo winced. "Oh, probably. There was a time when I was pretty clueless."

"But maybe that's not what this is all about."

Theo slowly shook his head. "I have a feeling it is. May have been a tipping point."

Ben looked at him curiously. "A tipping point?"

Theo rested his elbow on the ledge of the door's window and stared out at the mountains without speaking. The light had drained from his eyes and his face was pale. They sat in silence for a couple of minutes then Theo sighed heavily and turned to his brother.

"Leah's never been all that crazy about getting married. She figured we could just continue on as we've been to this point. I kind of bullied her into it. Because of the boys, I said."

"Ah."

"And there's this guy she'd lived with for several years before she came here. They had split up…" He made a dismissive gesture. "It's a long story. Anyway, he came to see her last summer, and although she told him she'd moved on I think she still has feelings for him."

"Oh."

"He's a doctor, could give her a much better life than I can. Probably more her speed too." He glanced at Ben. "She's really smart, you know. I mean, super smart. Like her parents."

"As I recall from school you weren't exactly stupid," Ben said mildly. "Although I've wondered sometimes, with all the stuff you gotten up to."

"And now this crap with Mick." Theo grimaced and rubbed his forehead. "Christ! What must she have thought?"

The Lighthouse

Ben shifted in his seat. "So, you think her disappearing is a way of backing out of the wedding?"

Theo lifted a hand and let it fall in his lap. "What else can I think? She's done it before to get out of a difficult situation."

Ben raised his eyebrows. "I wouldn't think Leah would handle it like this, but then you know her better than I." He glanced at his watch. "I guess there's only one way to find out, isn't there?"

He started the car and eased it down the narrow driveway. They drove in silence to the Lighthouse. When they arrived and he had parked and turned off the ignition, Theo made no move to get out.

"We should go," Ben said. "We need to be there before people start arriving."

Theo looked at him, the flawless lines of his face drawn in despair. "I don't know what I'll do if she's gone, Ben."

Ben nodded. "Yeah, I know. Come on, let's go."

They left the car and walked into the Lighthouse, through the lobby and down the long corridor leading to the Tree of Life pavilion. People smiled and offered greetings as they passed and Ben acknowledged them with a fixed smile. At the door, Theo paused. "I guess I'll just wait in here," he said bleakly.

"I can stay with you if you like."

Theo nodded and pressed on the handle of the heavy door. As the two panels swung open, Leah rose to meet them.

Chapter 53

"Ah, why don't I leave you two alone?" Ben said, backing out of the room.

When the door had closed behind his brother, Theo walked slowly towards Leah, breathless with relief. The late afternoon sun blazed through the Tree of Light, scattering petals of color on her like a benediction. She was wearing what he assumed was her wedding dress. Ris had shaken her head at Leah's choice of design and he could see that it wasn't what many women would have wanted, but the elongated lines, pale shantung silk and stylized Mandarin-style jacket suited her vaguely oriental looks perfectly. The jacket, he remembered irrelevantly, would come off for the dinner and dance.

"Hey," he said.

"Hey."

"You look really nice."

"So do you."

"Maybe we should do this more often—get all dressed up, I mean."

She had drawn her hair back into a complicated knot and pinned a few sprigs of cornflowers into it. He reached out and touched the flowers lightly. "Where were you able to find cornflowers at this time of year?"

"It wasn't easy."

He took her arm. "Look, why don't we sit down for a minute?" When they had he said, "You had us all worried, you know."

"Worried? Why?"

"No one could find you and you weren't answering your phone. We thought you had disappeared. Where were you?"

"I needed some time to myself. I went for a long walk. I didn't take my phone."

"You didn't go walking in the mountains again, did you? You know you shouldn't go there alone."

"No, I went to the river."

"So why did you need time to yourself, today of all days? Not having second thoughts, are you?" He tried to say it lightly.

She didn't answer right away as though considering his question. "Dad spoke to me late last night," she said. "One of the things he told me was that, as a wedding gift, he is transferring guardianship of Niels from himself to me. But I think you already know that."

Theo nodded.

"Why didn't you say anything?"

"Fin swore me to secrecy; he wanted it to be a surprise."

"Dad also told me about the education trust Grandad and Nana had created for me."

"Yeah, they set trusts up for Ben and me too." His mouth twisted in a brief smile. "It financed my misspent youth."

"Well, I didn't know about it, or if I did I had forgotten. And of course I've never had occasion to draw on it. I didn't want to accept it but Dad said it's mine legally and I should consider it Grandad and Nana's wedding present. It's grown to be rather a lot of money now, so we won't have to worry about how we're going to manage when we move back to Canada."

"But it's intended for your education, Leah. You should use it that way."

She smiled faintly. "Oh, I think marriage will be quite an education."

She lifted her face and regarded the Tree of Light for a long moment. "The other thing he gave me was a letter. Grandad had written it before he ... died, with the request that I receive it when I turned twenty-five, or when I married if that happened before. What with the turmoil after Grandad and Nana's deaths and my being away for so long, Dad had forgotten about it until he found it while clearing out a safety deposit box last summer."

Her eyes filled. She drew a linen handkerchief from a hidden pocket and touched it lightly to them. "Did you know they committed suicide?"

Theo nodded. "Yes."

"I never knew! I was away at school when it happened, and of course they had stipulated no service or memorial of any kind. It was your father who came for me and he gave me the news very gently. I don't recall him saying how they died but I was so upset that it didn't register if he had. Even later I never questioned the fact that they had died together. I knew Nana was very sick but they were so close, so much a part of one another, it made perfect sense to me that they would go at the same time. I feel incredibly stupid about it."

She turned anguished eyes to him. "And we've never talked about what they did amongst us, have we? Why don't we talk about it?"

Theo could still recall the poignant message his grandfather had left. It had said that Sara had little time left to live, that her illness had robbed her of comfort and the basic joys of life, that all she could look forward to in her remaining days was a mind-destroying drug-induced stupor to control the pain. That all she wished for now was a gentle, dignified end. It had asked for their family's understanding of their action and expressed their deep and abiding love and profound regret for the grief they would cause.

"Probably because it's still too painful for our parents," he said.

Leah's face was a study in sorrow. "Grandad and Nana's deaths stunned me; it took me many difficult years to arrive at a point of peace over losing them. The letter made me realize—for the first time, to my shame—how this must have affected Dad. I mean, losing both parents like that. What he did after is still not easy to forgive but I understand better now what had driven him to it."

"What did Grandad say in his letter to you?"

"I didn't read it right away; I was overwhelmed by the very fact of it, coming as it did out of the blue. When I woke this morning after a very restive night I wanted space and quiet to deal with it. So I took it to a spot on the river I especially like and read it there."

She looked again at the window, her eyes filled with unshed tears.

"Grandad said that because I was so young when it happened he was afraid I may not have understood their actions and would feel they had abandoned me. He wanted to speak to me now, as an adult, to explain their decision to end their lives with the hope that I would understand and forgive them. He said I had brought a great deal of joy to their later years and that they regretted very much not being able to share the special moments in my life."

She dabbed at her eyes with the hankie.

"I wonder what they would have made of all the awfulness that followed; I can't help but think that things would have been different if they'd still been around."

"Leah, I'm so sorry. Why didn't you tell me about it? I could have been with you. I thought…" Theo shifted in his seat. "Ben told me about what Mick said last night."

Leah fussed with the hankie in her lap. "It wasn't very pleasant."

"Yeah. I thought maybe you'd changed your mind and gone away because of it." He lifted her chin gently to make her face him. "Leah, I want you to know that I'd never do anything to hurt you. Not intentionally, anyway."

She gave him a faint, watery smile. "Oh Theo, I expect that over time we'll hurt each other both intentionally and unintentionally. The question is whether we'll be able to get through it when it happens. In his letter Grandad said that the reason he was choosing to die with Nana was that..." She swallowed hard. "He said that he couldn't bear to wake to a day without her. They had a great love." She studied him pensively. "How about us, Theo? What do we have? We've never spoken of love, have we?"

"No... I guess we haven't." He fell silent for several moments. "It's such a funny word, *love*. They say the Inuit have many names for snow but in English, the vast language that it is, the word love is used to cover so many bases that it's almost meaningless."

Leah gave him an amused glance. "It's one of what someone once called suitcase words—you know, ones that carry many meanings."

"Yeah, maybe, but for me it's still a cheap word." He unbuttoned his jacket and let it fall open. "Look, lightning didn't strike when I first met you or anything like that. I wasn't looking for anyone then. I didn't want to confuse things with Fox by bringing a woman into the picture. There wasn't anyone I'd have considered anyway; I sometimes wondered whether there'd ever be. Then you just slipped into our lives and it was comfortable and fun and, well, *right*. It took me a while to realize that maybe there was more to the relationship that had formed between us. Part of it was, of course, our being related and my not thinking of you initially in those terms. But what I feel for you has built up, kind of brick by brick, since then and I don't see this wedding as a final statement on the matter." His eyes crinkled in a smile. "If nothing else I'd marry you just to see what you're going to say next."

He paused. "But how about you? Do you love me, or whatever, enough for"—he indicated the room with a sweep of his hand—"this? Or am I maybe just a consolation prize?"

She raised her eyebrows. "You mean for Ken?"

He nodded, his heart thudding like a fist on a doomed drum.

She waved her hand dismissively. "Their inexcusable methods notwithstanding, Ken's parents were right: l wouldn't have fitted into his life in Atlanta. And besides that, well, you're different from him."

"In a good way, I hope. Despite everything?"

"Yes. But I've tried very hard not to fall in love with you, Theo."

He drew back. "Why?"

"Because being in love makes one so needy and vulnerable."

"And did you succeed?"

She studied him for a moment with her fathomless eyes. "Not really," she said with a crooked smile.

The massive door creaked open and Ben stuck his head through. "Pretty well everyone's here now. Are you guys ready?"

Theo stood up and held out his hand. "So, Leah, are you ready?"

She rose and slipped her hand into his. "As ready as I'll ever be."

Acknowledgements

I am grateful for the comments Marlyn Horsdal and the late Phyllis Smallman provided on early drafts of this work. They helped to set me in the right direction.

Dr. Marc Puts and my sister Livia Jackson provided valuable information regarding medical situations in the book. Any errors in representing them are entirely mine.

Special thanks to Simon Ogden for his sensitive editing of The Lighthouse, to Sydney Barnes for the cover design, and to the rest of the Tellwell team for their assistance in its publication.

CPSIA information can be obtained
at www.ICGtesting.com
Printed in the USA
LVHW012217110220
646635LV00001B/4